Berewic

Ʒbbanford

Tuidi

Lindisfarena

R. Till

Bebbanburg

N O R T H U M B R I A

R. Aln

Alnwic

R. Cocueda

Cocuedesae

R. Wenspic

Morðpæð

R. Reade

ɪdeburna

The Wall

R. Tine

Corebricg

R. Wiur

Ediscum

llocht

Wilfaresdun

Burh Street

Ingetlingum

Catrice

D E I R A

R. Sualuae

R. Usa

Eoferwic

NORTH SEA

Cnobheresburg

PICTLAND

DAL RIATA

BERNICIA

DEIRA

HIBERNIA

ELMET

GWYNEDD

MERCIA

EAST ANGELN

WEST SAXONS

CANTWARE

FRANKIA

Legend

○   Settlements

Ħ   Fortresses

✝   Holy sites

——   Roman roads

FOR
LORD
AND
LAND

BY MATTHEW HARFFY

The Bernicia Chronicles

The Serpent Sword
The Cross and the Curse
Blood and Blade
Killer of Kings
Warrior of Woden
Storm of Steel
Fortress of Fury
For Lord and Land
Kin of Cain (short story)

A Time for Swords series

A Time for Swords
A Night of Flames

Novels

Wolf of Wessex

FOR LORD AND LAND

THE BERNICIA CHRONICLES: VIII

MATTHEW HARFFY

HEAD
of ZEUS

An Aries Book

First published in 2021 by Aries, an imprint of Head of Zeus

9 7 5 3 1 2 4 6 8

A CIP catalogue record for this book is available from the British Library.

ISBN (HB): 9781801102223
ISBN (XTPB): 9781801102230
ISBN (E): 9781801102254

Typeset by Siliconchips Services Ltd UK

Printed and bound in Great Britain by
CPI Group (UK) Ltd, Croydon CR0 4YY

MIX
Paper from
responsible sources
FSC® C020471

Head of Zeus Ltd
First Floor East
5–8 Hardwick Street
London EC1R 4RG

WWW.HEADOFZEUS.COM

For Lord and Land
is for Geoff Jones

NORTHERN ALBION

Cair Chaladain

Sea of Giudan

Din Eidyn

D
Á
L

B
E
R
N
I
C

Magilros

R
I
A
T
A

Gillis

R
H
E
G
E
D

Caer Luel

Dacor

Du

MAN

Leofman's Steading

H
I
B
E
R
N
I
A
N

S
E
A

We

0   25 miles

0   50 km

Place Names

Place names in Dark Ages Britain vary according to time, language, dialect and the scribe who was writing. I have not followed a strict convention when choosing what spelling to use for a given place. In most cases, I have chosen the name I believe to be the closest to that used in the early seventh century, but like the scribes of all those centuries ago, I have taken artistic licence at times, and merely selected the one I liked most.

Addelam	Deal, Kent
Aln	River Aln
Alnwic	Alnwick, Northumberland
Æscendene	Ashington, Northumberland
Afen	River Avon
Albion	Great Britain
Baetica	Southern region of the Iberian peninsula, loosely corresponding to modern-day Andalusia
Bebbanburg	Bamburgh
Beodericsworth	Bury St Edmunds
Berewic	Berwick-upon-Tweed

Bernicia	Northern kingdom of Northumbria, running approximately from the Tyne to the Firth of Forth
Bristelmestune	Brighton
Caer Luel	Carlisle
Cabilonen	Chalon-sur-Saône
Cair Chaladain	Kirkcaldy, Fife
Cantware	Kent
Cantwareburh	Canterbury
Carrec Dún	Carrock Fell, Cumbria
Catrice	Catterick
Cnobheresburg	Caister Castle, Norfolk
Cocueda	River Coquet
Cocuedesae	Coquet Island
Corebricg	Corbridge
Dál Riata	Gaelic overkingdom, roughly encompassing modern-day Argyll and Bute and Lochaber in Scotland and also County Antrim in Northern Ireland
Dacor	Dacre, Cumbria
Deira	Southern kingdom of Northumbria, running approximately from the Humber to the Tyne
Din Eidyn	Edinburgh
Dommoc	Dunwich, Suffolk
Dor	Dore, Yorkshire
Dorcic	Dorchester on Thames
Dun	River Don
Dun Mallocht	Dunmallet Hill, Cumbria
Dyvene	River Devon
Ediscum	Escomb, County Durham
Elmet	Native Briton kingdom, approximately equal to the West Riding of Yorkshire

Engelmynster	Fictional location in Deira
Eoferwic	York
Frankia	France
Gefrin	Yeavering
Gernemwa	Great Yarmouth, Norfolk
Gillisland	Gilsland, Northumberland
Gipeswic	Ipswich
Gwynedd	Gwynedd, North Wales
Hastingas	Hastings
Hefenfelth	Heavenfield
Hereteu	Hartlepool
Hibernia	Ireland
Hii	Iona
Hithe	Hythe, Kent
Hrunaham	Runham, Great Yarmouth
Ingetlingum	Gilling, Yorkshire
Inhrypum	Ripon, North Yorkshire
Irthin	River Irthing, Cumbria
Ligcr	Loire River
Liminge	Lyminge, Kent
Lindesege	Lindsey
Loidis	Leeds
Maerse	Mersey
Magilros	Melrose, Scottish Borders
Mercia	Kingdom centred on the valley of the River Trent and its tributaries, in the modern-day English Midlands
Morðpæð	Morpeth, Northumberland
Muile	Mull
Neustria	Frankish kingdom in the north of present-day France, encompassing the land approximately between the Loire and the Silva Carbonaria

Northumbria	Modern-day Yorkshire, Northumberland and south-east Scotland
Norwic	Norwich, Norfolk
Lindisfarena	Lindisfarne
Lundenwic	Settlement to the west of modern-day London
Pocel's Hall	Pocklington
Rēade	River Rede
Rendlæsham	Rendlesham, Suffolk
Rheged	Kingdom approximately encompassing modern-day Cumbria in England, and Dumfries and Galloway in Scotland. Annexed by Bernicia in the early seventh century
Rodomo	Rouen, France
Sandwic	Sandwich, Kent
Scheth	River Sheaf (border of Mercia and Deira)
Sea of Giudan	Firth of Forth
Secoana	River Seine
Seoles	Selsey, Sussex
Snodengaham	Nottingham
Soluente	Solent
Stanfordham	Stamfordham, Northumberland
Sualuae	River Swale
Tatecastre	Tadcaster
Tenet Waraden	Tenterden, Kent
Temes	River Thames
Tine	River Tyne
Til	River Till, Northumberland
Tuidi	River Tweed
Ubbanford	Norham, Northumberland
Wenspic	River Wansbeck

Wihtwara	Wight (Isle of)
Wilfaresdun	Wilfar's Hill (Diddersley Hill, North Yorkshire)
Wiur	River Wear
Wudeburna	West Woodburn, Northumberland

Anno Domini Nostri Iesu Christi
IN THE YEAR OF OUR LORD JESUS CHRIST
651

Prologue

The riders didn't look dangerous to Leofman at first. He was alerted to their presence by his son, Eadwig. The boy had the keen eyes of the young and saw the four men on horseback the moment they crested the rise and started their descent into the cleft in the earth that led to the cave. Leofman noticed Eadwig staring up the slope, a look of concentration wrinkling his forehead, and he turned to follow his son's gaze. He lowered the heavy pick he had been swinging, and took the opportunity to wipe sweat from his brow. The hollow in the earth where they worked was in shadow now, as the sun lowered in the west, but the sky behind the riders was bright. The day had been long and hot, and Leofman had hoped to accomplish more, but he had promised they would be back to the house before dusk.

"Pick up the tools and place them in the cart," Leofman said.

"But, Father," whined Eadwig, "you said you would show me inside the cave today."

"I know I did, son," Leofman replied, his tone distracted as he shielded his eyes from the bright sky to watch the men urge their horses carefully along the rocky path down the side of the ravine. "But we'll have to do that tomorrow. I promised your mother I would have you home before sundown. Now, help

Swiga clear up." He glanced at Swiga, who nodded, and without pause the tall man carried his shovel over to the cart and flung it onto the back with a clatter.

It had taken a lot longer to remove the rocks than he had anticipated and he had begun to wonder at the sense in this course of action. Still, Scyldsung had shown him how the samples of rock had yielded the dull, soft metal, and the priest had told him that if there was a lot of the stuff, it would prove much more valuable than grazing sheep and planting barley on the poor soil of the windswept slopes of Leofman's land.

If he truly could sell the lead for silver as Scyldsung had said, perhaps he could buy some thralls to work the mine. It was obvious that the scale of the task would be too much for Eadwig, Swiga and him alone. He took in the size of the cave's entrance, thinking of the crumbling, overgrown ruins of the stone building at the top of the rise, abandoned no doubt at the same time as the mine. Not for the first time, Leofman wondered how many men had worked the place before it had been forgotten.

Eadwig and Swiga were busy clearing up now, retrieving the shovels and picks, and putting them in the cart. Leofman had berated himself for being overcautious in taking the implements home with them each night. After all, the rusted and broken remnants of past miners' tools had still been strewn about the cave when he had stumbled upon the place. Surely no thief would find the tools in their absence. But seeing the men riding down towards them served to reinforce his decision. Tools could be stolen, and he was not a wealthy man.

A shaft of summer sunlight briefly glinted from the lead horseman's gear. Leofman squinted to make out more details and his stomach tightened as he saw the men carried swords. Standing there in his sweat-drenched kirtle, Leofman felt suddenly exposed.

"Who are they?" asked Eadwig, his high-pitched child's voice piercing the echoing sounds of the horses' hooves in the gully.

"I don't know," said Leofman in a quiet voice, but as they drew closer, he recognised the fat man who rode at the front of the small column. "Swiga," Leofman said, keeping his tone even, "get Eadwig onto the cart. We're leaving."

Swiga didn't wait to be told twice. He scooped tiny Eadwig up and placed him beside the tools in the bed of the cart. The shaggy brown mare that was tied to the vehicle whinnied in nervous greeting to the approaching horses.

Forcing himself to appear relaxed, Leofman stepped forward to meet the riders, interposing himself between them and the cart. They were in the shadows at the foot of the gully now and he could make them out clearly. They had the hard faces of warriors. Swords and seaxes hung from their belts. None of them smiled as he raised his hand in welcome.

"Bumoth," Leofman said, "what brings you to my lands?"

The lead rider pulled gently at his reins and his sturdy horse halted. The poor beast looked tired, thought Leofman. Bumoth was a massive man, with a round gut and great slabs of muscle over his broad chest. His beard was close-cropped with a clearly defined line beneath it where his neck was shaved. Leofman wondered at the man's vanity to tend to his beard with such precision, as it only served to accentuate his bloated, toad-like jowls.

Bumoth made no effort to reply or to dismount. Leofman's disquiet intensified.

"What do you want?" he asked, an edge of frustration entering his tone.

"It is not what *I* want," replied Bumoth, offering a thin, almost sad smile. "It is what *Sidrac* wants you should be concerned with."

"These are not Sidrac's lands."

Bumoth rubbed his fat, bristled chin.

"No, they're not," he said, looking about the shadowed ravine, taking in the dark cave-mouth and the pile of broken rock before it. His eyes finally rested on the cart. Eadwig, wide-eyed and inquisitive, was peering over the edge at the riders. "Not yet."

Before Leofman could respond, the fat man snapped his fingers.

"Aescferth. Egbalth. Don't hurt the boy."

Two of the riders slid from their steeds. It seemed to Leofman that the temperature in the shadowed cleft in the earth had suddenly dropped. He shivered.

"What is the meaning of this?" Leofman was angry at himself to hear a tinge of fear in his voice.

He wished he had kept hold of the pick he had been using to split the rocks, but Swiga had retrieved it and put it in the cart. Leofman's hand dropped to his seax. The knife would have to suffice. He tugged the blade from its scabbard where it hung at the rear of his belt and moved to stand before the two men. It had been years since he had last fought anyone. He might be old, but he had stood in shieldwalls and was no coward. And yet, even as he moved, raising himself up to his full, considerable height and drawing his seax, he was uncertain of what would happen next. This was no shieldwall. He had no shield, no iron-knit shirt, and only a short-bladed seax with which to defend himself. Long gone were the days when he had stood strong surrounded by shield-brothers. Still, he was not alone. Swiga was certainly no fighter. Leofman knew the lad was loyal. He might be mute, but he was as strong as an ox.

Bumoth did not reply to Leofman's question. He looked on with a strange expression some way between a smile and a frown. The look of a man who is asked to answer a riddle to which he already knows the answer.

The two riders who had dismounted moved quickly, passing Leofman before he could intercept them. A third man in a blue warrior coat jumped down nimbly from his mount, and with a fluid motion pulled his sword from its decorated scabbard. The blade gleamed dully in the afternoon shadows. Leofman saw gold and garnets gleaming on its pommel. This was a fine sword and the man swung it with effortless speed that spoke of great skill as he stepped towards Leofman. This was no ruffian, who might be deterred by Leofman's bulk and the seax in his hand. The man's eyes were cold and unflinching; the eyes of a killer.

Leofman's mind spun. He did not understand what was happening. Panic rose within him and he forced it down with an effort. All that mattered was keeping his son safe. There was nothing else.

"Eadwig, run!" Leofman shouted, taking a few steps backwards, to draw the blue-coated swordsman towards him and away from the cart. "Swiga, don't let them near Eadwig."

He flicked a glance over to his right and for a moment his heart swelled to see his son leap from the cart and sprint away. Eadwig rushed towards the yawning cave-mouth, but there was no escape that way. The mine was not deep and the entrance was still clogged with rubble. And Sidrac's men blocked the path that led out of the ravine. With a pang of fear, Leofman realised there was nowhere for the boy to go.

Swiga, silent, but ever faithful, pulled a pick from the cart and stepped forward bravely to meet the two men. The nearest of them, a stocky young man with a sharp nose and a long moustache, dragged his sword from its tooled red leather scabbard and sprang forward in one smooth motion. He appeared very sure of himself, clearly not expecting Leofman's wide-shouldered mute bondsman to cause him any problems. But Swiga was no fool. Despite not speaking, he was quick of wits and much faster than one would expect from his bulk. Side-stepping the swordsman's swinging attack, Swiga allowed the blade to cut harmlessly through the cooling air of the afternoon. His attacker staggered, momentarily off balance. A heartbeat later, he collapsed to the dusty earth as Swiga's pick crushed his skull with a sickening crunch.

Leofman gasped. The violence had come so suddenly that his mind struggled to take it in. Blood, obscenely bright, coated the dusty pick-head. For the briefest of moments it seemed that everybody held their breath.

Nobody moved.

Then Eadwig screamed. And, as if the shrill sound of the boy's distress had awoken them, Sidrac's remaining men began to move at the same time.

Bumoth shouted something, but Leofman barely heard. His mind was filled with what he had witnessed and the bloodletting that now unfolded before him like a nightmare.

He screamed a warning at Swiga, but there was nothing he could do and Leofman watched in dismay as the second attacker's sword pierced the mute's chest. Swiga grunted, still trying to bring his heavy pick to bear on his opponent, but the bearded warrior grinned as he twisted his blade in Swiga's body. Blood gushed as he wrenched the steel free of his chest. The pick tumbled from Swiga's hand and he sagged down to his knees.

Leofman reeled, but Eadwig's cry of alarm brought him to his senses. Spinning back to face the sword-wielding warrior, Leofman raised his seax. His hand trembled.

"Ready for me now?" asked the man with a grin. It seemed he had waited for Leofman to face him when he could have cut him down while he was distracted by his bondsman's death.

Leofman did not reply. He could not drag his gaze from the warrior's cold eyes. His blood pounded, and beyond its rushing pulse his ears were filled with the sounds of his son being snatched up. Eadwig beat his tiny fists uselessly against his captor. The boy's cries soon grew muffled and Leofman wanted to look to see what the bastard had done to him.

"Don't hurt him," he said, cursing himself for the pleading tone of his voice. As a young man he had fed the raven and the wolf with Mercian and Waelisc foe-men, and now he was reduced to an old man, begging for pity. He spat. These men would show no mercy. If he was to die here, he would not go easily. They would regret crossing Leofman, son of Hutha. "Don't hurt my son," he repeated, lifting his seax and readying himself to make them pay dearly for what they had done.

"Don't worry," the swordsman said, stepping in quickly and batting aside the seax blade with a clang, "we won't."

PART ONE

SHADOWS FROM THE PAST

Chapter 1

"It appears we are in time," shouted Beobrand, raising his voice over the rush of the waves and the slap of the sail as it filled with the quickening wind blowing from the north-east. He shivered, despite the exhilaration from the speed of the ship and the relief at seeing no signs of battle on the beach before them. The wind coming off the slate-grey North Sea carried with it the bite of far-off winter.

Clutching the hemp stay tightly in his mutilated left hand, Beobrand turned to where Ferenbald leaned expertly against the steerboard. The skipper, his mane of hair and long unruly beard billowing about his face, grinned. He barked an order and a couple of the crewmen rushed to do his bidding, tightening cables and heaving on ropes to pull the sail about to better catch the wind and send the sleek ship skimming the waves towards the smudge of pale sand and the low-lying land behind it. There was a cluster of buildings there, and movement, but it was yet too far away for Beobrand to make out any detail.

"You should never have doubted me," said Ferenbald, his voice clear and filled with the joy of sailing. "I told you that *Saeslaga* would carry us to East Angeln before Penda could traipse his host across the fens from Mercia."

"I do not doubt your sea-skill, master Ferenbald," Beobrand

replied with a smile, allowing himself to relax for the first time since they had left Ubbanford. "But even you cannot control the elements."

Beobrand shuddered again and this time it was not just from the chill in the stiffening breeze. He recalled all too well the roaring waves of previous voyages.

Saeslaga topped a wave, splashing into the sea on the other side as it sped towards the coast. The spray on his tongue reminded Beobrand of swallowing mouthfuls of freezing brine when Ferenbald's previous ship, *Brimblæd*, had capsized and the freezing deep had almost claimed him. He spat to clear his throat of the salty taste, the flavour like blood. His mood soured and his memories grew dark.

A slender warrior stepped up to the prow of the ship to stand close beside Beobrand. He moved with cat-like grace, seemingly oblivious of the shifting and rolling of the deck. He glanced at Beobrand, his angular face creased in a frown. Perhaps he too was thinking of the past, thought Beobrand. He had been with them when Ferenbald's *Brimblæd* had borne them across the Narrow Sea to Frankia. And the slim gesith had also been witness to the slaughter on the storm-smashed strand after *Brimblæd* had broken apart. Their gazes met and yet neither of them made mention of those distant events. It had been years since then and, as Bassus, the huge warrior he had left back at Ubbanford, always said, it was better not to dwell on the past. In Beobrand's experience, the threads of his wyrd were so tangled that his present and future were filled with worries enough.

Beobrand turned his attention to the rapidly approaching coastline once more, squinting into the lowering sun. He was able to pick out more details now.

"Is that a ship, Attor?" he asked, pointing with his whole, right hand at the dark shapes on the beach. The sun was bright and low in the western sky. The figures on the sand were starkly lit, their shadows dark and long before them.

The slim warrior peered into the west. *Saeslaga* sliced through another wave, sending a tremor through her strakes. The dazzling sunlight glittered on the fretted foam thrown up from the prow, turning the spray into gems.

"There are two ships, lord," Attor said. "And many men. Monks, by the look of them."

Beobrand trusted Attor's eyes. Despite the warrior being older than him, his eyes were as sharp as they had ever been.

"No warriors?" said a new voice.

Beobrand turned. A young man, not much more than a boy really, stood there. He wore a fine kirtle with embroidered hems and a garnet-encrusted brooch fastened his bright blue cloak. The boy's eyes gleamed. Beobrand could not help but smile at the boy's eagerness. He had already taken up his shield and spear. As the ship pitched over another wave the young warrior lost his footing and would have fallen if Attor had not reached out a steadying hand.

"No, Cuthbert," said Beobrand with a grin. He remembered when once he too had been so eager for battle. "It seems we have arrived before the Mercians. There will be no fighting today."

The boy frowned.

"Do not look so sad, boy," growled Attor, pushing Cuthbert upright. "Only a fool seeks battle when none is needed."

Cuthbert's face darkened. Beobrand and Attor both laughed at his pouting expression. Beobrand could not bring himself to be angry at the boy.

"We were all young once," he said, slapping Cuthbert on the shoulder. "But Attor is right. Do not rush to find a fight."

"It will find you soon enough with Beobrand as your lord, believe me," said Fraomar, stepping forward to join them. He grinned and Beobrand returned his smile, hiding the pang of hurt he felt at the young warrior's words. Was there a rebuke there? Beobrand searched Fraomar's eyes, but saw no duplicity, no hint of guile. He knew better than to suspect Fraomar of a jibe. The man was honest and as straight as a spear haft. But Beobrand noticed the new wrinkles that lined Fraomar's face, and how one of his eyes drooped slightly, as if he could not decide whether to frown. The young man's hair had a premature sprinkling of frost too, and Beobrand could not forget that it was his poor judgement that had led to Fraomar's injury. A blow to the head that had almost cost him his life. He knew the man bore him no ill-will, but Beobrand could not avoid a feeling of guilt whenever he saw what his actions had cost Fraomar.

Like all of his gesithas, Fraomar's allegiance could not be questioned. Beobrand scanned the faces of the rest of the men who had travelled south with him. There was Dreogan, his soot-tattooed face marred with a long puckered scar, another reminder of the price for being oath-sworn to Beobrand. Beircheart, his handsome bearded face sombre, was helping tall Gram wriggle into his iron-knit byrnie. Despite Beobrand's assurance there would be no fighting, it seemed his comitatus, his closest hearth-warriors, were not so sure. Beobrand grunted, unsurprised. They had walked this path with him for a long time.

In the belly of the ship, the warriors were all readying themselves for battle. Huge Eadgard had already donned his byrnie and now hefted his massive axe. He muttered something to his brother, Grindan, and the smaller man chuckled.

Willow-slim Garr placed a small, open-faced helm on his head and snatched up his long-bladed spear. Finally, Beobrand watched as Ulf brushed back his straggly straw-coloured hair and secured it with a strip of leather at the nape of his neck. His was not a face prone to laughter, and the lines there spoke of hardship and pain rather than mirth. For a fleeting moment, Beobrand recalled finding the man's son slaughtered by Mercian raiders. He had considered leaving Ulf behind at Ubbanford. He needed doughty men there to defend his lands and his people. But when Ulf had heard they were heading south, that they might have to fight Mercians, Beobrand had realised he could not keep him away from another opportunity to exact vengeance on the people who had caused him such misery. Those responsible for the death of Ulf's son were all long dead, slain by Beobrand and his men in a great blood offering to Woden, but Beobrand knew that there was a void within Ulf that no amount of killing could fill.

Beobrand sighed. All of these men had suffered because of his actions, his decisions. They had killed for him and, when he had broken his oath to King Oswiu, they had stood by him. They were good men and they deserved better than he as their hlaford. He could feel his thoughts clouding with the self-doubt that often threatened to engulf him in the quiet of long nights. But now was not the time for worries and questioning. He had accepted the oaths of these men and he knew they would all sacrifice their very lives if he asked them to. He must lead them as best he could. He had their oaths and their trust, it was his duty to earn both each day.

A shout snapped him back to the present and he was glad of it.

"One of the ships has put to sea," Ferenbald yelled. "What would you have me do?"

Beobrand swung back to survey the surf and the shoreline. They were much closer now and he could see the monks thronging there. They were carrying objects down from the minster buildings and passing them along a chain of men who had waded out into the shallow water. There they loaded the chests and bales into the ship that was canted over as its keel rested on the sand beneath the water's surface.

Nearer to them, limned in the ruddy glow of the sun, came the other ship. It was low in the water, rowed by a rank of long oars. As he watched, the sail was unfurled and the ship tacked south, following the coastline away from the minster and *Saeslaga* with its cargo of armed Bernicians.

"They are running for it," said Ferenbald.

Beobrand looked from the beach and the monks labouring around the stationary ship to the seaborne vessel. Its sail luffed once as it lost the wind and then its crew adjusted the rigging and it filled, gravid with the cold breeze.

"Can you catch her?" Beobrand asked.

Ferenbald laughed.

"I am Ferenbald, son of Hrothgar, and this is *Saeslaga*. We have made the run from Rodomo to Hastingas in under a day."

Beobrand glanced back at the hirsute sailor. In spite of the concerns of moments before, he could not suppress a grin at the man's boasting.

"You should have no trouble bringing us close to her then," he yelled.

Ferenbald must have anticipated the order, for he leant on the steerboard and snapped out a command. Instantly, *Saeslaga* veered to larboard, and after a moment of readjustment as the waves caught her amidships, causing young Cuthbert to stumble again, the fine ship that had once belonged to the pirates who stole Beobrand's daughter away from Hithe, righted herself and sped off on a course that would see her intercept the fleeing ship.

"Who do you think they are?" asked Cuthbert, his voice high and full of excitement.

"I am not sure," replied Beobrand, peering into the distance. The wind pulled his cloak about his face and he shrugged it away. "What can you see? You have young eyes."

Pleased to be given a task, Cuthbert relinquished his grip on his weapons and, climbing onto the wale, he clasped hold of the bowline and leaned out precariously over the rushing water.

"Careful, boy," said Beobrand, suddenly fearful that in his eagerness Cuthbert would fall to his doom. As far as he knew the lad could not swim, so a tumble into the sea would spell his death as surely as a sword blade to the throat. He thought again of all the injuries and death that had befallen his black-shielded warriors over the years. They all understood that life as a gesithas was fraught, that nothing was certain and a man's wyrd could never be foreseen. But Beobrand could not bear the thought of this youth dying. Beobrand recalled when Cuthbert's grandmother had brought him to his hall at Ubbanford and begged the thegn to take the boy into his household.

"He is not a bad boy, lord," she said, "but he is rash. He has too much wildness about him. He is never still. Always running, wrestling and fighting. He needs a firm hand. Ever since his father died, he has lacked discipline."

Bassus and the rest of Beobrand's men had been surprised when he accepted the boy into his retinue. They knew Beobrand as a dour, sullen man, prone to drink too much. Quick to anger and slow to laugh. He did not have time for children and frequently seemed aloof and distant.

But the boy's father had been slain in battle against Oswine at Wudeburna, and Beobrand could not help feeling in some way responsible for the events that had led to the war between Bernicia and Deira. Besides, he had seen something in Cuthbert's open gaze and enthusiasm that had called to him. A few days after he had taken the boy in, Rowena, Bassus' woman, had broached the subject. The two old friends had been drinking mead late into the night in the relative quiet of Ubba's old hall, where Bassus lived with Ubba's widow. The rest of the warriors, with their raucous laughter, riddling and boasting, were in the new hall on the hill. It was pleasant to sit peacefully with Bassus and Rowena. Beobrand didn't feel the need to be the lord of Ubbanford here. Here he could merely drink and eat, rather than presiding over the antics in the hall.

"I know why you accepted Cuthbert," Rowena had said, as she refilled their horns with the good mead that Odelyna brewed. Bassus' brow furrowed and he shot the woman a glare. "Oh, don't you mind me," she said, shooing away his concerns. "Beobrand is no fool. He must see why he took the boy in so readily."

"The boy's father is gone," Beobrand said, his words slurring slightly. "He needs discipline and it is a good thing to train young men in the ways of war."

"Yes, yes," she replied, shaking her head and filling her own wooden cup. "But there is more here, is there not?"

"What do you mean?" asked Beobrand, wary at being confronted with something he had chosen not to think of too closely. Rowena always made him uneasy. She was as direct and fearless in conversation as he was in a shieldwall and, like his sword, her words often found their mark.

"You know what I mean," she replied, meeting his gaze.

"I like the lad," he said. "It is true. Even though at times he is as difficult to control as a wild cat." Just that day Cuthbert had got himself into a fight with Eldred, Elmer's oldest son, over a race. Cuthbert was exceedingly competitive and when he believed Eldred to have cheated by using a shortcut, he had knocked him to the ground and beaten him almost senseless. It had taken Beircheart and Gram to drag Cuthbert off the bleeding young man. Beobrand shook his head and took another sip of the mead. Could it be that he recognised himself in Cuthbert? The single-mindedness, the sudden flares of violent anger? "Maybe I see some of myself in the boy," he said, his voice barely more than a whisper.

Rowena smiled and shook her head again.

"Perhaps," she said, "but I think it is more than that."

"What, woman? Speak clearly. I have never enjoyed riddles."

Rowena sighed.

"You wish for a son."

Her words had stunned him to silence for a heartbeat. Then his cheeks had grown hot.

"I have a son," he said. But even as he said the words, he sensed the truth in what the grey-haired lady of Ubba's Hall had said. It was true that he had a son, Octa, but the boy had spent many years in the household of King Oswiu. Now he was a warrior in the atheling Alhfrith's comitatus. He was closer to the king and his son than he was to Beobrand. He barely saw the boy anymore, especially as he had been avoiding Bebbanburg ever since the fight with Heremod at Wulfstan's hall in Deira.

The last time they had crossed paths had been at Wudeburna. Oswine of Deira had finally allowed himself to be goaded by countless border raids into amassing a host and marching on Bernicia. Oswiu had called on his most trusted thegns and met him at Wudeburna. There had been terrible slaughter. The waters of the river there had been so thick with the blood of the fallen that the men wondered whether its name, Rēade, had been some kind of omen. Beobrand and his Black Shields had stood in the centre of the shieldwall, but he had seen Octa, beneath Alhfrith's lion standard. Octa had grown into a tall, strong warrior, just like his father and his uncle namesake. Beobrand's heart had swollen with pride when the Bernicians had been victorious and Oswiu had named Octa personally for his valour in the battle. The king had presented him with a finely wrought sword he had taken from a fallen Deiran thegn, and the Bernician fyrd-men had cheered him. Beobrand had sought Octa out that night to congratulate him, but it became quickly clear that his son could barely stand to converse with his father. After a few stilted words from Beobrand and grunts from Octa, they had parted company and they had not seen each other since. Beobrand remembered all too clearly the stab of almost physical pain he felt as he looked into the strong young face that was so similar to both Beobrand's beloved brother and the lad's mother, Sunniva. Sunniva and Octa were the two people Beobrand had most loved on middle earth and all that remained of them were ashes, bones and memories. To gaze into eyes so like theirs was an exquisite agony. It was not even the disdain in his son's eyes that hurt him, it was the lack of love.

"You have a daughter too," said Rowena, with a sad frown.

"And yet I feel you seek in Cuthbert something else that you cannot find in Octa or Ardith."

"What do you think I seek?" Beobrand snapped, feeling his anger kindle into life.

Bassus reached out his one hand and placed it on Beobrand's shoulder.

"Calm now, lord," he said, his voice deep and rumbling in the shadowy gloom of the flame-licked hall. "Rowena means no harm."

Beobrand sighed and stared into the flames of the hearth fire, as if he would find the truth there.

"Mayhap you are right," he said at last. "The gods know I am not close to Octa. And Ardith..." His voice trailed off as he thought of the pretty young woman he had not known existed until a few years before. She was married now, to Brinin, who was a passable smith, and they seemed happy enough. And yet, Ardith was ever distant from Beobrand. She was thankful for everything he had done for her, but he was certain that whenever she looked at him she was reminded of her past, of the trauma of being taken by raiders and transported to Frankia, and of the horror and fear and blood that had followed. And perhaps she thought too of the years before he had known she was his; years when she suffered at the hands of an abusive father. "Ardith is not close to me," he concluded.

He had thought much on what they had talked about that night. He did not like to admit that Rowena might be right, but he could not deny that he enjoyed spending time with Cuthbert. The boy was thoughtful and intelligent, in spite of the streak of anger that ran through him like a vein of quartz through flint. And he was strong and quick to learn. He had the makings of a good warrior.

Saeslaga juddered as she ploughed through a foam-crested wave, sending a shower of spray over Beobrand. Cuthbert clung on to the stay and let out a whoop of excitement.

"Careful," growled Beobrand, but the youth did not appear to hear him.

"It doesn't look as though there are any warriors aboard," he said.

Beobrand glanced at Attor, who confirmed what Cuthbert said with a nod. Letting out a long breath, Beobrand began to relax. Perhaps they would be able to see the day out without any bloodshed. He touched the Thunor's hammer amulet at his neck and offered up silent thanks that their careening voyage south had seen them beat Penda to Cnobheresburg.

Ferenbald altered their course and *Saeslaga* shifted slightly in the water. The sailors on the other ship hurried to adjust the sail and the oars rose and fell with increased urgency, but after a few heartbeats Beobrand could clearly see that neither the vessel, a broad-bellied wallowing trader, or the crew on the ship fleeing the minster, were a match for Ferenbald, his men and *Saeslaga*. In moments, Ferenbald had brought them within a spear's throw of the other ship. Garr stepped forward, raising a light throwing spear menacingly. Few men could make that throw in the strong wind and from the pitching deck of a ship at full sail, but if anyone could, it would be Garr, who was the best spear-man Beobrand had ever seen. Beobrand held up his hand to halt the tall gesith. All along the beam of the ship they pursued, he could see pale faces beneath tonsured pates. It was as Cuthbert had said. These were no warriors.

Taking a deep breath, Beobrand bellowed across the waves.

"We mean you no harm!" he shouted. "We have come from Bernicia."

He paused, but there was no reply, no change to the sail. The oars still rose and fell quickly, clumsily pulling the ship away from the beach.

"I am Beobrand of Ubbanford, Thegn of Bernicia," he yelled, using the huge battle-voice that could cut through the clamour and screams of the shieldwall. "We are not your enemy." When again there was no response, he filled his lungs once more. "I come from Bebbanburg in the name of my lord Oswiu, King of Bernicia," he lied.

Oswiu did not know that he had travelled south. There had been no time to tell him, even if Beobrand had wanted to speak with the king. When Ferenbald had brought the tidings of Penda's imminent attack on Cnobheresburg in East Angeln, Beobrand had known he had to act. He would not ordinarily have been moved to action by the plight of the East Angelfolc. He cared little for Anna, their king. And while Beobrand had many reasons to despise Penda of Mercia, whom Ferenbald had told him was marching into the south-east, Beobrand would not have travelled there to confront him. They had stood on the opposite sides of shieldwalls many times before and Beobrand had the scars and nightmare memories to prove it. One day he hoped to put an end to the vicious killer of kings, but Beobrand was not fool enough to believe his warband had the strength to tackle the warlord of Mercia's host alone. Penda's end would come in a great battle of warhosts led by kings, not in a skirmish.

And yet, when Ferenbald mentioned that he had heard from a trader in Eoferwic that Penda meant to punish Anna, king of the East Angelfolc, for harbouring King Cenwalh of Wessex, Beobrand had grown suddenly cold, despite the roaring fire and the great press of men in his great hall. The hall on the hill at Ubbanford was filled with light, warmth, laughter and good cheer as it always was when Ferenbald visited. The skipper of the *Saeslaga* often travelled north from Cantware to trade. When he did, he made sure to sail up the broad Tuidi to visit his old friends in Ubbanford. He usually stayed for a few days while they talked of the news in Albion, Frankia and even far-off Hibernia. But this time, they had set out at first light the morning after his arrival. And where usually Ferenbald would leave laden with bales of wool, casks of strong mead and barrels of smoked salmon, instead of such goods, Beobrand and several of his comitatus were aboard the ship.

Beobrand would not travel south to confront Penda or to aid King Anna. But he would put to sea and risk everything to help a friend. For he knew that one of his oldest friends was at the minster of Cnobheresburg.

Chapter 2

Beobrand sighed with relief as the heavy ship they pursued let the wind slip from its sail. The urgent pace of the rowing slowed and the broad-bellied merchant ship began to wallow and rock on the surf. He knew that Ferenbald would have easily overhauled the other vessel, but it was good that his words had done enough to cause her skipper to slow and allow them to close without the need for a lengthy chase.

Ferenbald shouted a couple of commands and his men rushed to obey. Their course adjusted so that *Saeslaga* would slide alongside the other ship at a safe distance where they could converse, but would not be at risk of crashing together.

"Is Coenred of Lindisfarena aboard your ship?" shouted Beobrand as they slipped closer.

When there was no reply, he raised his voice to a bellow, allowing an edge of anger to creep into his tone.

"I seek Coenred, brother of the brethren of Lindisfarena! Is he aboard your ship?"

He spat the words across the expanse of surf between them, the anger he so often fought to control lending them a hard, dangerous quality. It was not difficult to loosen the leash on the ire within him. Beobrand gripped the rope that supported the mast so tightly that his knuckles showed white. It was quite another thing to calm his fury if it broke free. He could not count the times he had saved Coenred's life over the years. But the monk was a stalwart friend and had in turn saved Beobrand and often risked much for him. When Ferenbald told him of the imminent attack on the minster of Cnobheresburg, Beobrand had immediately recalled the news he had heard from old Aart a fortnight before. The peddler, knowing they were friends, had told Beobrand how Coenred had accompanied a young novice called Wilfrid south to Cantware. After leaving the young man in the court of King Eorcenberht, Coenred had headed to Cnobheresburg, where he planned to study under the holy brother Fursa, known throughout the land for his Christian piety.

"Do we stop at Bebbanburg?" Ferenbald had asked as they had set sail from the mist-shrouded shingle on the river Tuidi in the shadow of the tall hill and the great hall atop it.

Beobrand shook his head. For a moment his mind had been filled with the vision of Eanflæd, the scent of her golden hair, the softness of her flesh pressed against his, the taste of her lips... He had seldom visited Bebbanburg these past years. It was better that way. He did his duty when called upon by the king who had his oath, but he could not bear to spend time in the presence of the man. Or his queen. There were too many questions Beobrand could not answer.

And too many temptations.

When he saw Eanflæd, he was filled with a terrible longing; the call of a desire he knew they could never answer. When she looked upon him he saw his own passion reflected there, but there was fear in her eyes too. Fear of what would occur if they should ever succumb to their mutual attraction. He longed to see her, but he was not such a fool that he believed the glances that passed between them would go unnoticed for long. To be near the queen placed her in danger, so he stayed away.

The only good to come of this was that by avoiding Eanflæd, he also evaded Oswiu.

"Do you not need to seek leave from the king?" Ferenbald had asked as he had effortlessly guided the sleek ship out into the deepest part of the river. His crew expertly pulled on the oars as one, rowing *Saeslaga* almost silently into the dawn haze; the only sounds the quiet fish-splash of the oar blades and the creaking of the tholes.

"Oswiu is a good Christ follower," Beobrand said, making the words sound like an accusation. "His God loves to forgive. So I would rather seek forgiveness from him than permission." He stared along the wide watery path of the Tuidi as it led them towards Berewic and the North Sea. "Besides, the weather is favourable and there is no time to waste. We cannot dally at Bebbanburg."

And so they had hurried south. The weather had held and the winds had been friendly and in only two days they had reached their goal. All the while Beobrand's nerves had been stretched almost to breaking. He pictured what would happen to the monastery and the monks there should Penda, the savage pagan king of Mercia, reach Cnobheresburg before them. He had witnessed what befell innocents in the face of warriors allowed to give free rein to their basest desires. The screams and visions of murder and violation frequently disturbed his sleep. He tried not to imagine Coenred caught at the monastery between Penda's warriors and the sea. But like scratching at an itching scab, his mind kept on returning to scenes of violence and death. The relief he had felt at seeing the monks readying the ships to sail had been welcome after the nerve-fraying voyage. All he wanted now was to be sure his friend was safe.

"Do not make me ask you again," Beobrand shouted across the waves. "If you do not answer, I will be forced to think the worst and we will board." Ferenbald had turned *Saeslaga* now, so Beobrand stepped down from the prow and called out from the belly of the ship.

Either Beobrand's threat or the mention of the king of Bernicia was enough to coax a response from the laden ship. One of the pale-faced men stepped up to the wale. His hair was flame-red and his pallid eyes were wide with shock and fear.

"Lord Beobrand," he said. "I am Foillan, abbot of the brethren here." The abbot's voice carried the lilt of the Hibernian tongue. It reminded Beobrand of old Aidan, Bishop of Lindisfarena.

"I thought Fursa ruled here," said Beobrand.

Foillan shook his head.

"Fursa is my brother. He has gone ahead of us to pave the way in Neustria across the Narrow Sea."

"So you are fleeing to Frankia? You know of Penda's attack?"

Foillan made the sign of the Christ rood in the air over his chest.

"We were warned by our good and most humble king, Anna." He glanced back at the minster buildings, the beach and the distant figures still loading the other ship on the shore. "But we must not tarry here. By the grace of God we have been spared and now we must carry the holy relics and artefacts away to safety. I thank you for coming to our aid. I have heard many tales of your exploits." He hesitated, perhaps searching for the right words. "I now see you are a good man, Beobrand of Ubbanford. Christ will reward you in heaven."

Beobrand hawked and spat into the sea. He was not a good man and cared nought for what this pasty priest had heard about him.

"Do not speak to me of the Christ," he shouted. Foillan crossed himself again. Beobrand noticed several of the other monks did the same. Beside him, Attor too made the symbol of the four points of the cross over his chest. Beobrand ignored them all. "I have not come to your aid. I come to help my friend, Coenred. Is he here?"

Foillan's cheeks flushed and he did not answer. Beobrand wished they had boarded the ship. Then he could shake the holy man by the throat. He glowered at the Hibernian, sensing that his hesitation could only mean one thing.

"He is not on your ship, is he?" he asked, his tone as sharp as a blade.

Tight-lipped, Foillan shook his head.

"The blessed brother Coenred is at the beach, helping to load the other ship." Beobrand looked back to where the other ship still rested on the shore. There were many monks there. He wondered if they would all fit aboard a single ship. As if he could hear Beobrand's doubts, Foillan continued. "With the Good Lord's providence they will all be able to float away to sanctuary soon enough. The Almighty is wise and all powerful and will surely give Anna the strength to hold Penda's forces at bay for long enough for the remainder of the brethren to escape."

"King Anna is here?" asked Beobrand.

"Oh, yes. He sent a messenger with word that we were to take all of value and flee. He has led his warband to our defence and they now stand before Penda, close by on the road to Norwic."

"How far are they?"

"If you hurried, you could march there before nightfall. It is very near, which is why we cannot delay any longer. Master," Foillan said, turning to a dark-skinned, weathered-looking man with a bandy-legged gait, "take us to sea with all speed. To safety. To Frankia."

The skipper began shouting orders and though the ship was still sluggish from being so laden, the crew knew what they were about. Soon the merchant vessel's sail was full of wind again and the ceapscip was pulling away.

Beobrand cursed silently. By the gods, Anna, King of the East Angelfolc, ally of Oswiu and friend of Bernicia, was fighting against Penda barely out of sight of the minster buildings.

"You want me to follow them?" shouted Ferenbald from the

stern. "Or perhaps bring us alongside so that you can board her?" He grinned, seemingly pleased at the idea of attacking the slower ship.

Beobrand shook his head.

"Take us in to the beach. Coenred is there."

Without a word of reply, Ferenbald snapped his orders. *Saeslaga* quickly swung away from the lumbering trader and tacked against the wind, back towards the land.

"Cuthbert," Beobrand said, "fetch my byrnie, helm and shield."

The boy's eyes were wide and his cheeks ruddy from the excitement as he jumped down from the bow and hurried to obey his lord. Moments later he returned, staggering under the bulk of the iron-knit shirt, the black-painted shield and, atop it all, Beobrand's great helm, with its boar-carved cheek-guards.

With practised ease, Beobrand wriggled into his byrnie and quickly tightened his sword belt about his waist to take some of the armour's familiar weight from his shoulders. Placing the helm on his head, he looked back at his men. They were grim-faced and sombre now, ready for what they must do. Only Cuthbert was smiling, though Beobrand noticed that the colour had drained from his face as his excitement changed to the uncertainty of growing anticipation.

"Get your shield," murmured Beobrand. Cuthbert started, then rushed to retrieve his newly painted linden board and the bright-bladed spear that, like its owner, was untested in combat.

"You think there will be a fight, lord?" Cuthbert asked breathlessly.

Beobrand sighed and scanned the mass of black-shielded warriors in the belly of the ship. They had all been ready for battle for some time. Were they merely cautious or had they travelled with him for so long that they had foreseen how this day would end? He knew not, but there were no finer warriors in all of Albion. As ever, the sight of them filled him with pride.

The ship cut through the waves, flinging spray into the faces of the men as they all turned towards the approaching sand.

"Come, my gesithas!" bellowed Beobrand, pulling Nægling from its scabbard so that the fine patterned blade caught the lowering sun. "It seems there is killing to be done today after all!"

Chapter 3

Cuthbert's lungs burnt and his legs were leaden as he struggled to keep up with the warriors who ran along the dusty track. They had left the sea and the cluster of minster buildings behind them some time ago. The land was flat, with only very shallow rises. On each side of the path grew lush cow parsley, feathery water dropworts and wild carrots. Alders and willows rose in clumps from beside the meres, streams and ponds that dotted the landscape. When he glanced over his shoulder, Cuthbert could see the glint of the Whale Road in the distance, but no sign of Cnobheresburg now. The minster had been lost to view as the land dipped down to the shore.

"Not too much further now," called the monk who led them. His name was Coenred, Beobrand's friend that had seen the lord of Ubbanford rush south to rescue him from danger. Cuthbert wondered at the past the two men shared. He hoped that one day he would find such a friendship, someone he could count on to come to his aid no matter the consequences.

Like all the others, Coenred's face was flushed from the exertion of running, but Cuthbert cursed inwardly that he had fallen to the rear of the group. He was the youngest there and it shamed him to see Beobrand and his gesithas, encumbered by their battle gear, still able to keep up a faster pace than he.

Coenred, head shaved to the crown and with long hair flowing down his neck in the way of the Christ monks, met Cuthbert's gaze and smiled, encouraging him. Cuthbert gritted his teeth and pushed himself to greater speed. He grew level with the bulky, tattooed Dreogan and huge axe-wielding Eadgard, who both lumbered along the path. Grinning to himself, Cuthbert grunted, and with another effort, he passed them both. He would not be last.

Moments later, Coenred halted and held up a hand to his mouth, indicating for them to be quiet. They halted in a cloud of dust. The air was hot and the men panted like hounds after a hunt. Sweat streaked their faces. The sun was low in the sky. They had not tarried for long at the beach. *Saeslaga* had ground to a halt on the sand close to the ship being loaded by the monks. When Beobrand and his gesithas had leapt into the shallow water and splashed ashore, the brethren had scattered, perhaps believing them to be Penda's warriors. But Beobrand was taller than most men, and with his byrnie and great helm he was an imposing figure. Coenred had quickly recognised his old friend and rushed down to greet him. They had embraced, the monk speaking in an excited rush. What was Beobrand doing with Ferenbald? How had they come to be here? Had they been sent by Oswiu?

Beobrand had cut him off.

"All your questions can wait. We have come to take you to safety, but we learnt from Foillan there," he nodded in the direction of the ship receding into the south, "that King Anna is fighting Penda nearby."

"Penda is south, I think," replied Coenred. "At the great ditch."

Beobrand frowned. On the voyage south Cuthbert had heard the men whisper of the battle at the great ditch; how the earth had been soaked in so much blood it had turned to a quagmire. It had been a terrible battle and a dreadful defeat. When Cuthbert had asked Beobrand to tell him of his exploits there, the lord had grown surly and snapped that he did not wish to talk of things best left forgotten. It seemed he did not like to be reminded of the battle, even by his old friend Coenred, for he stiffened, shook his head and sighed.

"So who is Anna facing?"

"I do not know," replied Coenred. "The king was here with his hearth-men when word came that a warband of Mercians was approaching. He ordered Foillan to pack up all of the treasures of the minster and to flee on the boats. He would hold the Mercians at Hrunaham."

The dour-faced warriors nodded their approval on hearing these words. Cuthbert had been in their presence long enough to know that what they admired most was bravery and honour. A king who would place himself between an enemy and his people was gōd cyning indeed. Beobrand clearly agreed.

"We cannot flee without first seeing how the king fares," he said. "The East Angelfolc are allies of Bernicia and I would not have it be known that I had been able to aid their king and instead headed to sea like a scared monk."

The monks had tried to explain the different tracks and turnings the warriors would need to follow to reach King Anna and his warband, but with the sun dipping in the west, Beobrand had shaken his head.

"We need someone to guide us. It will be dark soon and if we are to reach the king before nightfall, we cannot risk becoming lost."

And so it was that they found themselves running after Coenred along the narrow paths and causeways that led through this watery land. Coenred had been at Cnobheresburg for nearly two months and liked to walk the paths of the surrounding area, so he knew the place well enough. Besides, none of the other monks seemed inclined to volunteer. They were visibly pleased when it was the Bernician who offered to lead the warriors. It was not far at all and, as they slowed where Coenred had halted near a dense stand of alder, Cuthbert half-expected to still hear the wash of the waves on the sand and the cries of the monks as they loaded the ship.

But it was not the monks and the surf they heard. Instead, over the rustle of the wind through the trees and the wittering of sparrows and finches, came the unmistakable crash of weapons against shields and of men shouting in anger and pain. The sounds were clear, but the fighting must still be some way off, for the noise was reedy and distant.

There was a bend in the path ahead, and the land beyond was obscured behind the alder wood.

Beobrand ran his fingers through his thick fair hair. Like all of the men, he had removed his helm for the run and his pale blue eyes seemed to burn from his sweat-streaked, flushed face. He glanced at the setting sun, perhaps calculating how much light there was left in the day.

"Attor. Cuthbert," he said in a low voice. "I need your sharp eyes. Make your way through those trees and tell me what you see. I would know the numbers of friends and foe-men. And the disposition of their forces."

Cuthbert felt as though his chest might burst, such was the feeling of pride that filled him.

"You can count on me, lord," he said. A thought came to him as he pictured what they were about to do. "But should we not take Coenred with us?"

"Why?" Beobrand snapped, clearly impatient. A distant roar of a charge drifted to them. This was followed by the sound of two walls of shields and men crashing together like waves hitting a cliff.

"He knows King Anna and his men. If things are confused, he will be able to tell us who is friend and who is enemy."

Beobrand did not hesitate. He gave a terse nod.

"Good thinking," he said. "Coenred, are you willing to go with them for a closer look?"

The monk looked surprised, but nodded. He gave a twisted smile. Cuthbert noticed that his face was pale now, the colour gone from his cheeks.

"I have come this far, have I not?" said Coenred.

The rest of the warriors scooped water from a stream that trickled beside the path while Attor led the way to the alders and slipped into the cool shadow beneath their foliage. Cuthbert wished that he had taken a moment to slake his thirst, but Attor was already hidden from view, with Coenred close behind, so Cuthbert hurried after them. The monk looked frightened to Cuthbert. Coenred's eyes were wide and his face pallid. Cuthbert could barely breathe, such was his own excitement and fear as they stepped into the tree-gloom. Fleetingly, he wondered whether he looked as scared as Coenred.

It took him a moment for his eyes to grow accustomed to the shadows. Attor was moving stealthily away from them, picking his way between the boles of the trees, as silent as a wraith. Cuthbert rushed to keep up, snapping twigs and trampling through ferns. Brambles and briars snagged at his kirtle and leg wraps. Attor spun around and glared at him. When Cuthbert reached him, the warrior gripped his shoulder painfully and hissed into his ear.

"You will walk with care, young Cuthbert, or I will slit your throat. Then you would be silent!"

Cuthbert felt his anger bubble up within him. What was the point of being silent when a battle raged on the other side of this small stretch of woodland? But a glance at the wicked-looking seaxes that hung from Attor's belt and the fierceness of his glower made Cuthbert bite back his retort.

Cautiously, they moved on. The sounds of battle were muffled by the trees and plants that tangled the ground beneath the shade of the canopy, but they were getting closer.

Without warning, Attor pulled them both down into a crouch and then indicated that they should continue on all fours. A man shrieked with a high-pitched wail that no man should make.

Cuthbert shuddered. Somewhere out there in the warm light of the setting sun, another man was sobbing, crying for his mother. Cuthbert's gorge rose and he swallowed back the bile that burnt his throat. This was madness. He was but a boy, not a warrior. How had he been such a fool as to think he could stand shoulder to shoulder with Beobrand's famed Black Shields? He looked over to where Coenred crawled ahead with Attor. The monk's face was set, his jaw tight, but even he seemed to look less afraid now, more resolute than Cuthbert felt.

Cuthbert spat the foul taste from his mouth into the leaf mould. The stink of loam, the green rich stench of the life and death of the forest, filled his nostrils. Taking a trembling breath, he pressed on to where Attor and Coenred had halted. They had lowered themselves into the undergrowth and slithered forward a little way further. Cuthbert joined them and his heart quailed at what he saw through the parted fronds of the ferns.

They overlooked the path where it came out after curving around the woodland. Perhaps a hundred paces away, the track turned to the right. It was built up there to form a narrow earthen causeway raised from the broad expanse of water on either side. It was there that Anna had chosen to make his stand against the attackers. Cuthbert could immediately see the virtues of the location. It was narrow and an approaching force could not flank the defenders. A small number of warriors could hold a larger force at bay for some time. And this is what King Anna had done.

But at a great cost.

There were corpses strewn across the elevated pathway, with bodies tumbled into the reed-clogged waters and lying broken and blood-soaked on the slope.

It was clear from their vantage point who the defenders were. They stood beneath a banner topped with what looked like a golden crown and draped with a blue standard. They were outnumbered by the enemy warband. But they had acquitted themselves well. There were many dead and injured on the other side, lying at the side of the path or sprawled down the banks of the mere. The waters lapped red, whether from the reflection of the setting sun or the blood of the fallen, Cuthbert could not tell. He could make out where the defensive line had been forced back along the causeway, leaving a scattering of death behind them.

As he watched, the Mercian shieldwall, which must have still numbered some fifty or sixty men, roared and rushed towards the defenders. The East Angelfolc bravely stood their ground, taking the full force of the charge on their shields. Spears found flesh and men reeled back, crying out in pain and dismay. One dark-bearded Mercian took a vicious slash to his forehead and blood sheeted down his face, blinding him. He flailed about him, probing blindly with his spear towards the enemy shieldwall, before one of Anna's men hammered a sword blade onto the top of his head. The man's helmet was cleaved in two. Splinters of bone and gobbets of brains mingled with the blood that drenched the bearded man's face, as he fell back to be trampled by his own shield-brothers as the Mercians shoved the East Angelfolc back, step by step.

Cuthbert breathed through his mouth in an effort not to succumb to the roiling sensation that twisted at his stomach, but a moment later, his body convulsed and hot vomit gushed onto the earth before him.

Cuthbert spat and wiped his sleeve against his mouth. The pool of puke gave off a vile odour that, coupled with the vision of slaughter before them, threatened to make him vomit again. Attor placed a hand on his back. Cuthbert looked at him sharply, expecting an angry rebuke, but Attor seemed to feel no ill-will towards him.

Coenred was as pale as new curds and Cuthbert wondered whether the monk might be sick too.

"Come," Attor whispered. "We've seen enough." Attor's face was hard and sombre.

He began sliding backwards, retracing their movements. Coenred followed.

Cuthbert, holding his breath so as not to breathe in the stink of his vomit, took one last lingering look at the scene before him. He scrutinised the men fighting on the causeway. He swept his gaze across the path, the shimmering of breeze-rippled water, the swaying rushes and reeds and the smattering of drooping willows that jutted from the flooded land to the west of where the observers lay.

Then, glad to be moving away from the steaming pool and the slaughter, he slipped back through the leaf litter and joined the others.

When they were well within the shadows of the trees, they stood and Attor led them back to where Beobrand and the others waited. They did not move with stealth now. There was no chance that the men on the causeway would hear them. Moments later, they crashed out of the undergrowth. Beobrand and Fraomar both started and turned to face them with their swords drawn. Cuthbert noted that all the warriors had placed their helms on their heads and none of them had sat to rest. They were taut and tense, ready for battle.

Recognising them, Beobrand sheathed his sword.

"Tell me," he said.

"They've been fighting for some time," Attor said. "There are perhaps three score Mercian whoresons. The East Angelfolc are being pushed back, but they have not given Penda's men an easy time of it."

"King Anna yet stands?"

"His banner is still held firm," replied Attor. "But the Angelfolc are outnumbered at least twofold, maybe threefold. They cannot withstand much more of this."

"If we go to their aid, do you think we will alter the outcome?"

Attor thought for a few heartbeats and then sighed. He shook his head.

"The Mercians would see us coming. We would be fresh to the fight, and would kill some, I am sure. We are the Black Shields after all." He shrugged and offered a mirthless smile at his boastful words. "But we are but eleven men." He shrugged again. "Perhaps we would give the monks a bit more time to finish loading their ships, though by now they might already have put to sea. But in the end..." He looked pointedly at Coenred. He didn't need to say the words. They had come to rescue the monk. If they were to all die here, Coenred would likely be killed as well.

Beobrand stood silent, unsure how to proceed. No doubt weighing up his obligations to his friend, to his men, and to an ally king from this realm far from their home.

At last he made his decision.

"It sounds hopeless," he said, his voice hollow. "I do not like to turn away from brave men, but there is nothing to be gained from us sacrificing ourselves." The men looked sombre. None of them spoke in support of Beobrand's words or against them. This was his decision to make, not theirs. They would follow where he led, but they did not need to be pleased about it.

With a long sigh, Beobrand turned to face east again. His shadow stretched stark and long before him. The sun was touching the tree tops in the west and the sky was aflame with its red light.

"Come, my gesithas," Beobrand said, his voice lacking its usual force. "Let us take Coenred back to the ship. To safety and the sea. This is not our land. Let us head homeward."

Some of the warriors frowned, glancing sidelong at one another, clearly unhappy with their lord's command. But not one of them spoke and they began to traipse after him back along the dusty track. They walked like men defeated, despite not having traded a single blow with the enemy.

"Wait," cried Cuthbert. He had not known he was going to speak, and his voice cracked in his throat.

Beobrand turned to face him, a scowl on his features beneath his great helm.

"Cuthbert, what is it?"

Cuthbert's mouth was dry and sour. He coughed and spat to clear it of the foul acid taste, a bitter reminder of his weakness. His mind had been spinning as they hurried back through the trees. He pictured the two lines of warriors fighting on the raised path. In his mind's eye he saw how the path turned first to the south around the alders and then to the west, where it became the causeway with the meres to either side. He conjured in his thoughts all that he had witnessed: the warriors, the path, the water, the plants and trees. And suddenly, with a brilliant explosion of light in his mind to rival that of the sun, he saw the way.

"We could yet beat the Mercians, lord," he said, and he was surprised at the strength of his own voice. He swallowed at the lump in his throat. "But it will be dangerous and we would have to hurry."

Beobrand stared at him, his blue eyes burning in the setting sunlight.

"You have a plan?"

"I do."

Beobrand grinned, his teeth showing like a wolf that had scented its prey.

Chapter 4

Beobrand shuddered. The water that lapped about his chest was chill, especially so after the warm air of the afternoon and the breathless sprint from the minster. All about him, his men waded through the dark water, holding their weapons above their heads in an effort to keep the metal free of iron-rot.

Before slipping into the water on the far side of the path, they had briefly contemplated removing their byrnies. The iron-knit shirts would need to be cleaned thoroughly after such a dunking and none of the men relished the idea of the hard work that would be necessary.

"If you are able to gripe about cleaning your byrnie this night," Beobrand had said, "then you will be alive. Hard labour is not a bad price to pay for life."

The men had grumbled, but there was no denying the sense of their lord's words. And despite their complaints, they had seemed pleased when he had ordered Coenred to hide beneath the trees and then told the rest of them they would follow Cuthbert's plan. It was fraught with danger. Beobrand fretted that he was leading them to their doom, as they slid into the cold water and trudged through the deep mud behind the thick reeds, in the shadows of the towering willows. But the truth was that he was as pleased as his gesithas that they were making their

way towards the battle on the causeway and not away from it.
He had seen the disappointment on their faces at the decision he
had made to return to the beach, to *Saeslaga* and to safety.
He had a duty to his men. He had no wish to lead them to an
almost certain death, and yet, was that not the way of the man
they had sworn their oaths to? The Beobrand of Ubbanford who
never backed down from danger, who would run through fire to
fight his enemies and defend his own?

He shivered again. Perhaps he was growing old. Or his spirit
had been broken along with his oath on that fell afternoon at
Ediscum, when Heremod and his warriors had been slain.

The sounds of battle grew louder now as they squelched
past the line of willows that had kept them hidden from the
causeway. Now would come the most dangerous moment,
the time when they would be exposed to the men on the raised
path and yet still gripped by the cold water and thick, clinging
mud that seemed to hold them back, clutching their ankles
with invisible hands intent on pulling them to their doom in
the marsh.

He waited for the others to reach him. The last rays of sun lit
his face, warming it, despite the chill that enveloped him from
the neck down. His arms ached from holding Nægling in its
ornate scabbard above his head. He rested its weight on his helm
and surveyed the men.

Fraomar reached him first. He was covered in muck, his hair
plastered dark to his face. Shortly after they had started along
the line of trees, he had slipped beneath the waters, disappearing
into the gloom, and it was only Garr's quick reflexes that had
saved him. The tall spear-man had plucked him from beneath
the murky water. Fraomar had spluttered and coughed, spitting
out foul water and cursing. He swore he had felt the claws of
a creature take hold of his leg and drag him under towards its
watery lair. Attor made the sign of the cross, as did some of the
other men. Beobrand touched the Thunor's hammer at his neck.

All of the men spat or uttered prayers against the evil that lurked in the marsh. Lesser men would have turned back, but these were the Black Shields, and they would not turn away from danger, seen or unseen. They had pressed on, all the while hearing the fighting raging on the causeway to their left behind the willows. The sun was setting and there was no time to waste.

"We must hurry now," whispered Beobrand. "Cuthbert's plan has got us this far." The boy's face was smeared with mud, but he smiled back, clearly glad of his lord's praise. Above his broad grin, his eyes were wide and frightened. He was clearly terrified of what he had set in motion. Beobrand was proud of the boy's courage, for a man who is not scared is not brave. "From here on they will be able to see us. The instant we head towards the path, we go as fast as we can. No shouting, unless they see us. The gods might smile on us yet. If we can get there without being seen, we form the shieldwall and attack the Mercians from the rear."

"And if they see us?" asked Grindan, his expression grave.

"Then we hurry and kill the bastards!" Beobrand forced himself to grin. What the men needed now was for their hlaford to smile in the face of death, to show no fear. His actions had the power to lift the spirits of his men, and it was spirit above all that would see them triumph. "There is no time to waste. The sun is almost down and we can end this and save our allies before dusk." He swept them all with his stern gaze. "If we make haste. Ready?"

All of his men nodded in reply. They were bedraggled and muddy, their pale skin and bright eyes showing from beneath begrimed helms. They unslung their shields and drew their weapons. With a sigh of regret, Beobrand slung his baldric over his shoulder and allowed Nægling's fine scabbard to splash into the foul-smelling marsh water. There was no way to keep it clean and dry now. He dragged the pattern-bladed sword free and the lowering sun set its blade afire. He wriggled his left arm into the leather straps he used on the rear of his shield to hold it firm and make up for the weak grip of his half-hand. With a final nod to his gesithas, he splashed past the twisted bole of the last willow tree and made his way as quickly as he could through the chest-deep water towards the causeway and the shieldwalls that struggled there.

Nobody noticed them for a time and they made good progress. The water, catching the light of the afternoon sun, felt warmer here and, as he sloshed forward, it grew increasingly shallow. In a matter of half a dozen paces it was at his waist and the going was much easier. Swinging his legs in great strides he powered through the ever-shallower water. He could hear his men hurrying behind him, splashing and grunting with the effort of trying to run through the mud and murk of the mere. The water lapped about his thighs now and he was moving faster with every step. Ahead of him and to his left, he could see the rear of the Mercian shieldwall, writhing like a great beast. The setting sun glinted on the byrnies and blades of the warriors there. Beobrand offered up a silent prayer of thanks to Thunor and Woden. Cuthbert's plan had worked. They had circled around through the marsh unseen and now they would fall on the Mercians from behind. The effect would be devastating.

That was the moment when a Mercian saw them.

A shout of alarm rose not from Beobrand's left where the men battled on the causeway, but to his right, further along the path. A man stood there, his head bandaged with a blood-stained rag. He was shouting and pointing at the approaching Bernicians as they splashed their way laboriously through the mire towards the path. As Beobrand watched, others joined him. Each of them was injured in some way. One hobbled forward, using a spear as a crutch. Another held a sword in his left hand, his right hanging awkwardly at his side, the sleeve of his kirtle dark with blood. In moments, there were about a dozen of the wounded warriors. They must have been left there, behind their lines, unable to stand in the shieldwall any longer due to their wounds. They might not have sufficient strength for the shieldwall, but seeing the new threat coming from the north, they were brave enough to move to block them.

Beobrand surged forwards as quickly as he was able, cursing as the mud clung to him and the sodden kirtle beneath his iron-knit shirt weighed him down. A quick glance to his left showed him that the main Mercian force, fully engaged in their fight with King Anna's warband, had not heard the warning from their injured comrades. Perhaps Cuthbert's plan would yet work, thought Beobrand grimly. But they could not leave armed foe-men behind them. There was no honour in slaying wounded men, but such was the way of war.

The injured Mercians had formed a ragged shieldwall along the side of the path and they still called out to their shield-brothers for help. Gone was the time for stealth. Beobrand let out a great roar and sprang from the cold water, splashing mud and muck about him like some marsh monster of legend.

"Death! Death!" he bellowed, releasing the tethered beast of his battle-ire to do its work.

The man before him was the Mercian with the bandaged head. He thrust a spear at Beobrand. Catching the point on his linden board without thinking, Beobrand sprang up the slope to tear out the man's throat with Nægling in a spray of crimson. The Mercian fell back and Beobrand was amongst them, like a wolf among lambs. These were warriors, brave and true, but they were all lessened by their injuries and were no match for Beobrand. He lay about him with Nægling, feeling the blade bite deep into flesh, sinew and bone.

All the while his voice rose over the clamour, tearing at his throat with its ferocious fury.

"Death! Death!"

In a few heartbeats his comitatus were with him. Grindan severed a Mercian's arm at the shoulder. Fraomar, dark with mud like a fiend from the deep, hacked down a pleading man. There would be no quarter here, no mercy. Eadgard's axe hewed into a tall Mercian's chest, sundering the links of his byrnie and splintering his ribs. The dying man tumbled to the dust of the path, wailing like a woman in childbirth.

All about Beobrand his gesithas were slaughtering the injured Mercians. They could not stand against the deadly prowess of the Black Shields. And yet one of his warband was not truly a Black Shield. Not yet.

Beobrand felt a terrible chill wash over him, colder than the water of the marsh, as he saw Cuthbert, kirtle hanging lank against his youthful slim frame. The boy had found himself alone at the furthest point away from the battle on the causeway. He faced a tall brute of a warrior. It was the man with the ruined arm, who now held his sword in his left hand. He had no shield and was wielding his blade in his weaker hand. Any of Beobrand's hearth-warriors would have taken him in an eye-blink. But Cuthbert was little more than a child. Beobrand's heart twisted as he saw the young man aim a thrust with his spear at the Mercian. Faster than he had any right to be for such a burly man, the injured warrior dodged the attack and smashed his sword into the ash haft of the spear. The wood splintered and Cuthbert lost his grip on the weapon. The warrior kicked the spear away, leaving Cuthbert unarmed.

Nobody else had noticed Cuthbert's plight. They were all intent on their own battles, the bloodletting that came so naturally to them. With a cry of anger and despair, Beobrand sped towards Cuthbert and his assailant. The boy caught a vicious sword blow on his shield, then stepped back quickly, out of reach of the stronger man. Good, the boy had remembered something of his training. Beobrand had to pull up short to avoid colliding with Ulf, who was locked in combat with a blond brute swinging a hefty axe. Almost without conscious thought, Beobrand sliced his sword blade into the Mercian's neck. The axeman crumpled and Ulf flashed his teeth in thanks to his lord.

Beobrand looked up and his breath caught in his throat.

"Cuthbert!" he bellowed and sprang onward through the melee.

The boy was sprawled on the earth and for a sickening heartbeat Beobrand was sure the Mercian had slain him. But then he saw Cuthbert raise his shield to deflect a downward thrust from the one-armed assailant. With a savage grin, the warrior kicked the board aside, pinning it beneath his foot. He raised his sword for the killing blow. Cuthbert's eyes were wide with terror. Beobrand knew in that instant that he would not reach the boy in time to save him.

The Mercian's sword began its downward arc at the same moment that Beobrand flung Nægling. It was a wild throw, borne of desperation. But despite being too far from the Mercian to slay him in hand to hand combat, only a dozen paces separated them, and at such a distance, it was hard for Beobrand to miss. He watched as Nægling spun flashing through the warm afternoon air. Cuthbert closed his eyes in preparation for the death strike that would pierce his chest.

The Mercian's blade never found its target. Beobrand's sword struck the side of the man's head with enough force to fling him from his feet. The blade hit point first, burying itself deep in the man's skull. He was dead before he hit the earth alongside Cuthbert. His sword tumbled harmlessly into the dust beside the young Bernician.

The slaughter of the injured was almost over as Beobrand skidded to a halt beside Cuthbert and the dead swordsman. Beobrand placed his foot against the Mercian's head and, stooping to grasp Nægling's grip, he tugged it free of the man's skull. Glancing back at the causeway, he saw some of the Mercians at the rear of the shieldwall peering back at what was happening behind them.

"Shieldwall!" he shouted, and his gesithas began to fall into place around him with slick, practised ease.

Beobrand kicked the Mercian's sword towards Cuthbert who was still sprawled, pale and shaking in the dust.

"Take it," Beobrand said. "It is your sword now."

Cuthbert grasped the hilt and pushed himself up, trembling and unsteady.

Attor, his two vicious seaxes dripping with blood, moved to stand beside Fraomar, who had taken his place to Beobrand's right. To his left, Dreogan was shuffling into position. Cuthbert swayed, and then collapsed.

"Come on, lad," said Dreogan. "There'll be time to rest later."

It was then that Beobrand noticed the bloom of blood on the boy's breeches. The wool was already dark with the mud from the mere, so the blood had not been immediately evident. Now the sunlight picked out vividly the slick red sheen on Cuthbert's left leg. The boy's face was as pallid as lamb's wool.

Beobrand grimaced at the sight. Had he been too late after all? He had brought the boy here, but this was no place for a child. This was a realm of killers, of butchers of men.

"Beobrand!" Attor spoke his name, his tone sharp. "No time now to mourn the fallen. Those Mercian bastards know we're here. If we are to have any chance of victory, we must attack now."

Beobrand pulled his gaze away from Cuthbert's inert form. Attor was right. Some of the Mercians were turning to face them. The longer they were given to regroup and plan to defend against this fresh threat, the slimmer the chance Beobrand and his Black Shields would have. Cuthbert's plan had brought them this far. Now to see it all the way through.

"My brave gesithas," Beobrand shouted. "Now is the time these Mercians learn what it is to face Bernicians!" He glanced to either side to check that all of his men were in place. The ground between them and the Mercian line was strewn with the corpses of the injured men they had just slain. It would make the footing treacherous, but he could see no better way to break the enemy line.

"Boar-snout!" he bellowed and, knowing his men would execute the manoeuvre with precision, he sprinted forward at the tip of the wedge that would drive into the Mercian shieldwall.

Chapter 5

"Stop staring at me like that," Cynan said. "I know what you are thinking." He kicked Mierawin, his bay mare, into an easy gallop that he knew Ingwald would not be able to match on his stocky, short-legged gelding. The man was not much of a rider and could never rival Cynan on horseback.

"Lord! Wait for me," Ingwald shouted over the drum of the horses' hooves and the rush of the wind through the trees that loomed at either side of the path. In many places, the oaks and beech trees arched their boughs over the trail, forming a living tunnel. Cynan usually loved riding between his hall, Stagga, and Ubbanford along this tree-lined path that he knew as well as he knew his own palm. But today his mind was swirling with concerns and worries. If only Beobrand had taken him south with him. That was where he should have been and, not for the first time, he cursed his hlaford for leaving without him. Instead Cynan had received word from Bassus after Beobrand had already left with Ferenbald aboard the ship they had taken from the pirates on the coast of the Narrow Sea. Cynan did not begrudge them the sea voyage. He remembered the fear of drowning in the cold, unforgiving depths. He was much more at home on the back of a horse.

Cynan nudged Mierawin with his knees, turning her slightly

in anticipation of the beech branch that he knew jutted out into the path around the next bend.

"Careful of the branch coming up," he shouted over his shoulder. Ingwald was urging his mount into a reckless run and Cynan did not want the man to be hurt. All he wanted was a moment of peace. A moment to collect his thoughts and not have to contend with his hearth-warrior's knowing glances. He had been happy to ride with only Ingwald for company. There should be no danger on the oft-travelled track between Stagga and Ubbanford, and Ingwald was usually a good companion. He did not speak too much, only offering his opinion when asked. But today, his silence seemed to carry a host of unspoken questions. His sidelong glances were pregnant with accusations. Cynan wished he had ridden alone.

Gods, why had Eadgyth said such a thing?

The beech bough whipped past on his right and Cynan allowed Mierawin to slow her pace slightly. It felt good to let the mare have her head, but he would never forgive himself if she came up lame as a result of his madcap dash through the shadowy forest. The trees overhung the path here and it was as dark as dusk, easy for his mount to miss her footing.

He pulled gently on the reins, slowing Mierawin to a comfortable canter.

The trees passed more slowly now, but he barely noticed. All he could think of was what had occurred that morning. Life had been good. Everything was as it should be. Apart from the annoyance at Beobrand leaving him behind, all was well. In fact, Bassus had said it was an honour to be asked to watch over Ubbanford in the lord's absence. After all, someone needed to protect the folk and there would be other chances to add to his hoard of battle-fame. Yes, Bassus was right. After a day of sullenly stalking about Stagga, Cynan had finally come to terms with the situation. He would keep the warriors occupied, training them for when Oswine of Deira chose to march again. His mind was at ease once more and he had told Eadgyth as much just the night before as they sipped their mead in the fire-lit shadows of the hall.

She had known he was happy with his lot again, and so it had come as a shock when she had voiced her question without warning. What madness had possessed her to ask such a thing of him?

Mierawin carried him on along the forest path, but he was barely conscious of the movement of her cantering. He witnessed absently the light lancing through the canopy of leaves, lowered his head without thinking to avoid low hanging boughs, but his mind was elsewhere.

Was it truly such a foolish notion? She was a comely woman and he liked her well enough. But to even consider her request filled him with a dreadful sense of betrayal. She was Acennan's widow!

If they wed, nobody could consider it a hasty marriage. It had been nine long years since Acennan's death. So much had changed since then. The last time he had seen Acennan alive Cynan had been a headstrong young gesith, an erstwhile thrall with nothing more to his name than that which Beobrand and Acennan had given him. Now he was the master of the hall at Stagga; hlaford to a warband of his own. He could scarcely believe it when Ingwald and the others had remained with him after the battle at the gates of Bebbanburg. More warriors had come too, bringing their shields and their oaths when they had heard that Cynan the Waelisc Black Shield now resided in the great hall of Stagga.

It did not sit well with Cynan that he should reside in the very hall that his friend and mentor had built for his bride. The Waelisc warrior had loved Acennan like a brother, and felt nothing but affection for his widow Eadgyth and their children, Athulf and Aelfwyn. He had allowed them all to remain in the hall, merely adding a small partitioned area at the rear where he could have some privacy. He might be the man Beobrand had placed in charge of the land to the north of the Tuidi, but he was no lord and certainly did not feel worthy of Acennan's hall. But over the last three years he had grown to think of Stagga as home. His friendship with Eadgyth was easy-going. She would often sit late with him talking about all manner of things. He found her company relaxing and she had a way of helping him to unravel problems. His head was not good at dealing with the complexities of running the household. Eadgyth seemed happy enough to continue to administer the provisioning of food and drink, and to weigh the grain and produce given to the lord of Stagga by the ceorls who resided in the shelter of his protection. With Eadgyth's meticulous planning, the inhabitants of the hall never wanted for anything. She was in control of the affairs of the hall, and Cynan was content.

And now that Athulf was of age, Cynan had begun to train the boy in the ways of shield, spear and sword. He enjoyed spending time with Acennan's son. The boy had his father's stocky strength and natural ability with a weapon. He reminded Cynan of Acennan in many ways and it seemed natural to him that he should pass on the knowledge to the boy that Acennan had imparted to him all those years before. Had it perhaps seemed to Eadgyth that Cynan was fulfilling the role of father? Mayhap she believed he might as well fulfil that of husband too.

Cynan could hear the clumsy gait of Ingwald's gelding approaching, so he slowed Mierawin to a trot and waited for him to catch up.

"You managed to avoid that branch then," said Cynan with a sidelong glance at Ingwald, who slowed his cantering horse to a trot beside him.

"Aye," said Ingwald. "Thanks for the warning." He grinned sheepishly. "I had forgotten." Ingwald was several years older than Cynan, with a bald head and skin as dark as a nut. He was slim and did not look like he would amount to much in a fight. But he had been with Cynan since they had first met at Hefenfelth over three years before and Cynan knew that despite the man's slender form, he was deceptively strong, and he could not have asked for a more loyal and brave warrior to ride at his side. Cynan smiled to himself.

"What?" Ingwald asked.

"I was just thinking that you are a good man to ride the trail with."

Ingwald returned his smile, evidently moved by the words.

"Thank you, lord," he said.

"As long as I don't need to get anywhere quickly, that is."

Ingwald chuckled.

"Well, I cannot deny that I will never be the rider you are. But I get there in the end."

"Yes, that you do."

They rode on in silence for a while. They would be at the Tuidi soon. Cynan hoped that Bassus would give him good counsel. For whatever way he looked at things, he could not see a path out of this. He did not wish to cause offence to Eadgyth and yet he could not imagine making her his wife.

"So, she finally asked you then?" said Ingwald, breaking the silence.

Cynan looked at him sharply.

"What do you mean 'finally'?"

Ingwald laughed.

A magpie burst from the branches of a hazel. It swooped down, angrily flapping across the path in a streak of black and white to where a handful of starlings and sparrows were pecking at the earth that had been exposed by the recent uprooting of an elm tree. The smaller birds took flight and vanished into the undergrowth a heartbeat before the magpie reached them. Mierawin sidestepped and tossed her mane. Ingwald's gelding shook its head and snorted, halting in its tracks. The older man was almost unseated by the sudden stop, but he managed to stay on the horse's back. Patting the animal's neck, he nudged it onward once more.

"Well?" said Cynan when Ingwald had caught up with him again.

"You really had no idea?" Ingwald asked, his tone incredulous. Cynan turned to him.

"No," he said, thinking of the branch at the bend in the path. "A friend would have warned me."

His face flushed as he recalled the conversation that morning. He had come back from an early morning training session with the men. Eadgyth had welcomed him to the hall with his favourite meal of rye bread, salted curds and a light ale. The morning was warm and bright, and the weapons practice had gone well. It felt good to work the men hard, to build up a sweat and to feel his muscles ache from exertion. The exercise had made him forget for a time his concern for what Beobrand might be facing in the south. He had made his peace with being left behind, but he did not trust anyone to protect Beobrand as well as he would. It was his place to be at his lord's side.

But if not there, what better place than sitting in the doorway of the great hall of Stagga, looking out at the cluster of thatched houses with the forest beyond the stream, its small timber bridge hazed in the morning light?

He sipped the ale and smiled at Eadgyth in appreciation. Licking his lips, he dipped the fresh bread into the thick curds and took a bite.

"You are a goddess among women," he said, talking around the mouthful of food. "This is fit for a king."

She looked at him coyly then, a flicker of a smile playing on her lips. Her hair had a lustre from brushing and he noted that she wore her best dress of green linen and the necklace of amber and glass beads he had given her as a gift. Her cheeks were flushed and her blue eyes caught the sunlight with a glimmer.

"Or fit for a husband," she said, raising an eyebrow.

He chewed on another piece of bread and curds, enjoying the taste, rolling it around on his tongue. Realising what she had said, he shot her a glance. She was staring at him, a strange expression on her face. But they had been friends for many years and he knew her well enough to see the serious meaning behind her words. He swallowed with difficulty, washing the wad of food down with a gulp of ale.

He shook his head at his own blindness. How could he have missed the signs that must surely have been there for him to see?

The forest was thinning out now and there was light ahead where the path led down to the ford across the wide waters of the Tuidi.

"This friend thought you had eyes in your head," said Ingwald. "Why would I warn you of something I thought you could see perfectly clearly?"

"Well, I could not see it," snapped Cynan, angry and embarrassed. "Was it so clear to you?"

"Not just to me," said Ingwald.

"What do you mean?"

"Everyone knows."

Cynan flushed.

"Everyone?" he asked. Could it be true? Was he such a fool?

Ingwald sighed.

"When is the last time you had a woman?"

"What sort of question is that?"

Ingwald shrugged.

"It is a question, like any other."

Cynan pondered, biting his lower lip. He did not like where this was headed.

"There was that servant at Bebbanburg," he said at last. Cynan was a handsome man, and he had influence now. There was never a shortage of women willing to spread their legs for him.

"And before that?"

"Domhnulla at Ubbanford." She was a thrall, but she had come to him and he never forced himself on her. She seemed to enjoy his company for she often came to his blankets when he slept in Beobrand's hall.

"When did you last have a woman at Stagga?"

Cynan contemplated this, feeling his cheeks redden.

"It doesn't seem right."

"Not with Eadgyth there?"

"I suppose..."

Ingwald grunted.

"Does she not run the household for you?"

Cynan said nothing.

"And do you not find her pleasing company?"

Cynan frowned.

They rode out from beneath the shadows of the trees. Ingwald glanced at him.

"You dote on her children as if they were your own." The afternoon sun was warm on their faces. Cynan's cheeks were already hot.

"So if Eadgyth is in all ways like your wife, why not give her a morgengifu and make her so?"

"She is not in all ways like my wife," replied Cynan, his voice small.

"Ah," said Ingwald. "I see."

"No," said Cynan, spurring forward towards the ford, "you do not see." He was suddenly filled with a simmering impotent rage. "She is my friend's widow and I have offended her." He spurred Mierawin down the shingle beach and splashed into the cold water of the river. "And that is the last thing I wished to do."

On the other side of the ford, nestling in a bend of the Tuidi, were the familiar houses of Ubbanford. The hill to the east dominated the scene. It was topped with trees and Cynan could see the hall there, overlooking the settlement and the smaller, older hall that was surrounded by the huts, barns and animal pens of the inhabitants.

Ingwald's gelding entered the ford behind Cynan at a trot, sending up a great spray of water that seemed to hang in the bright sunshine like shards of silver or shattered glass. Cynan, feet and leg wraps soaked through, urged Mierawin out of the river and up the shingle and sand on the south bank. An instant later, Ingwald joined him. His face was sombre. Cynan felt sorry for him. Eadgyth's comments were not Ingwald's doing. He was about to say as much when a shout cut through the peaceful afternoon like a sword blade. Angry screams rang out from the settlement. A woman's furious shrieking. Other voices raised in shared outrage.

Despite the warmth of the day, Cynan felt suddenly cold. He had been left in charge of these people. It was his duty to protect them and keep them safe in their hlaford's absence. His worries about offending Eadgyth, of whether he should wed her or not, were as nothing when compared to the safety of the folk of Ubbanford. These were Beobrand's people and they had accepted him, Cynan, the young Waelisc thrall who became a warrior, into their midst as one of their own. A deep booming voice was added to the mayhem that emanated from Ubba's Hall in the settlement.

"That's Bassus!" Cynan said.

Their conversation now forgotten, both riders heeled their mounts into a gallop and hurtled up the path towards the buildings and the shouts of anger.

Moments later Cynan reached the area of open ground before the old hall. A throng of people were gathered there. Bassus towered over everyone. Using his bulk and considerable strength, he shoved back some of those crowding around him. One of those he pushed fell back, sprawling onto the earth. Cynan recognised Maida, Elmer's wife. With a shock, Cynan realised that many of those screaming at Bassus were women. The sun glinted on iron and Cynan was shocked to see that more than one of the women had vicious-looking knives in their hands.

"That's my wife," yelled Elmer and surged forward, seemingly ready to fight Bassus over his treatment of Maida.

"Enough!" bellowed Cynan.

At once, everybody turned to face him. He had not dismounted and so looked down on them. He recognised the faces of usually calm women contorted with fury. Ingwald reined in beside him. He placed his hand on the hilt of his sword, but did not dismount or draw his weapon. He seemed unsure of what he was seeing or what he should do. Cynan knew how he felt.

"Elmer," he snapped. "Help your good wife up." With a face like thunder, the wide-shouldered warrior went to his wife's side and pulled her to her feet. Cynan shifted his attention to Bassus.

"What is the meaning of this, Bassus?"

The giant let out a long breath.

"I am trying to prevent a hanging."

Cynan saw then that the massive warrior was shielding a small figure beneath the muscled slab of his one arm. He had lost the left one before Cynan had met him. When he was a young man, with both arms, he had been King Edwin's champion. He must have been formidable indeed. Now, as a one-armed old man with greying hair, he was still a powerful presence and not easily ignored.

"What crime has been committed?"

"Murder!" shrieked the grey-haired woman closest to Bassus. Her face was a mask of hatred and rage.

"Lady Rowena," he said, unsettled to see the old woman so riled, "what murder has been done? Who has been killed and who is the accused?" He hoped that he could calm this situation. Beobrand could stand in judgement at a trial. Cynan wanted no part of that. His life was too complicated already without having to preside over a murder trial.

"She is not accused," spat Rowena. "The Mercian bitch is guilty. Of that there is no doubt."

A cold sliver of concern pricked at the nape of Cynan's neck. Something in Rowena's words... The person held by Bassus was a woman, he saw that now. And she was strangely familiar to him. The fair hair, the angle of the head, the slender form of her neck, all tugged at Cynan's memory.

"How can you be so sure this woman is guilty?" he asked.

"Because we saw her drive the knife in."

Cynan reeled.

"And who has she killed?" he asked. His voice was hollow and sounded far off to his own ears. He was certain now what Rowena was going to say, but how could it be? It made no sense.

"She slew Reaghan without a thought. When that poor lass had shown her nothing but kindness."

Cynan peered down at the frail-looking woman whom Bassus gripped against his great barrel of a chest. She turned to stare up at him and his breath caught in his throat. He had never thought to see her again.

"Sulis?" he said. He had been sure she would have been dead years ago. "What are you doing here?"

She stared at him and the memories flooded back. Her pain and suffering, and her dark, rage-filled desire for escape and vengeance. The last time he had seen her she had been walking into the west with nothing to her name but her hatred and the madness that had gripped her.

"I came looking for you, Cynan," she said.

Chapter 6

Beobrand slipped his arm out of his shield's straps and let the linden board fall with a clatter onto the dusty ground. Reaching down to one of the dead Mercians, he wiped Nægling's blade on the man's kirtle until it was free of most of the gore. He sheathed the sword, thinking that he would have to get Cuthbert to clean it properly later.

At the thought of the boy, his heart sank. There had been no time to check on him, but Beobrand had seen the quantity of blood that soaked the boy's breeches. He had seen enough of battle and its injuries to know when a man had lost too much lifeblood to survive.

He sighed. Untying the leather thong that held his helm in place, he removed it and wiped sweat from his face with his free left hand. His fingers came away smeared with blood. For a heartbeat he wondered if he had taken a cut to the head, before realising that the blood was from his foes. There had been great slaughter on the causeway. The Mercians had been numerous and valiant, but they had been shocked at the abrupt change to their circumstances. When the Black Shields had hit the rear of their line with the wedge-shaped formation they had practised countless times, the Mercians had buckled. The men of the East Angelfolc, on seeing Beobrand and his gesithas coming to their aid, had been filled with renewed energy. They had rallied around their king's banner and fought with the ferocity of cornered boars. The battle had raged on for some time as the sun sank behind the western horizon, but in that first moment when the boar-snout had collided with the Mercian force, Beobrand had known that victory was theirs. He knew well that it was morale and the hearts of the men in a shieldwall that win or lose a battle, and the tide of the fight shifted in that instant.

A Mercian near him groaned and pushed himself up onto his knees. The man was pale, his hair and beard dark with blood from a huge gash on his head. As he turned to look at Beobrand with a vacant stare, a lengthy flap of his scalp flopped over his left eye. He pushed it back onto his head again, as if it were simply an errant lock of hair. The warrior had the look of one who does not know where he is or how he got there; like a child awoken from walking in their sleep.

"Attor," called Beobrand. The slender warrior, face, arms and chest slick with the blood of his enemies, turned to do his lord's bidding. Beobrand nodded towards the wounded Mercian. "See that a couple of them live. I would question them."

Attor trotted over to the Mercian, who was now trying to stand. The Bernician punched him hard in the face and then fell on him, tugging at the warrior's belt in order to bind him with it. The Mercian flailed about him, moaning pitiably. Attor punched him again.

"Dreogan, help him," Beobrand said to the bald, grim-faced warrior. The blood spatter from the fighting and the spray of drying mud from splashing through the marsh made his tattooed face even more monstrous than usual. Beobrand turned away, not waiting to see what Dreogan would do. His men would obey him without hesitation.

He became aware of a dull ache in his right wrist. Looking down, he noticed that the steel strips strapped to his forearm were dented and scratched. He dimly recalled stopping a Mercian axe on his arm. He shook his head, thankful for the metal protection. He would have to get Brinin to hammer the damage out once they returned to Ubbanford. He placed his helm atop his shield, clenching and unclenching his fist. By Woden, that hurt. But there seemed to be no long-lasting harm. Now that the fighting was over, other aches and hurts from the combat began to make themselves known. The ribs on his left side ached, and his head throbbed. Both reminders of past battles. He rubbed his hands over his face again and saw that they were trembling as they always did after battle.

"Beobrand?" called a deep voice he did not recognise.

Dropping his arms to his side, he balled his hands into fists in an effort to stop the trembling. He was unsure why it troubled him after all these years, but he still thought of the shaking as a sign of weakness. He grimaced as his bruised forearm pressed against the tight metal guard.

"Is that you?"

That voice again. There was something familiar in the tone, but he could not place it.

Turning, he saw a stocky man striding towards him past the scattered corpses of the battle. The last rays of the setting sun fell hot and red on the man's face. He still wore a helm with a nose guard, so Beobrand could not immediately make out the warrior's features. And then it came to him.

"Offa!" He strode towards the older man and took his forearm in the warrior grip. He had not seen Offa since the calamity at the great ditch, but he was glad it was this thegn in charge here. He was a good man. Offa clutched Beobrand's arm tightly as befitted a warrior of renown. Beobrand gritted his teeth against the pain, forcing himself not to wince.

"I do not know why or how you came to be here today," said the burly thegn with a broad grin. He looked about them at the dead. "But if you had not arrived when you did, I fear the worst."

"He is the answer to our prayers, Offa," said a new voice.

Offa turned to the newcomer. He was tall and slim, with broad shoulders and a narrow waist. His face was handsome and angular, his hair long and held back from his eyes with a silver circlet. He wore a byrnie of polished rings, his breeches were dyed linen of dark red. Around his neck was a finely crafted torc of gold.

"Lord," said Offa. "You are wounded and must rest." Rounding on a shorter man, Offa snapped, "I told you to tend to the king, Guthlaf."

The short warrior looked exhausted.

"Sorry," Guthlaf mumbled.

"Do not pick on Guthlaf," said the king. "Introduce me to the man who has saved us. Did I hear you correctly? Is this the great Beobrand Half-hand?"

Beobrand's first instinct was to hide his left hand behind his body, but he forced his hand to relax, revealing the missing fingers. He did not like to be reminded of how he had lost the digits, but after all these years he was resigned to be known for that mutilation by men the length and breadth of Albion.

Offa sighed and nodded.

"It is, lord king," he said. "Beobrand, this is King Anna, son of Eni, lord of all the East Angelfolc."

The king smiled. His face was very pale, his eyes glowing with a febrile light in the ruddy glow of the western sky.

"It is a great pleasure to meet you, Beobrand. I have heard much of your exploits and I see they were not exaggerated."

The king reached out his hand and stepped forward. Beobrand offered his hand, tensing his jaw against the pain he knew would come. But the king did not grip his forearm as he had expected. To Beobrand's dismay, Anna's eyes rolled back in his sockets and he collapsed. Without thinking, Beobrand leapt forward and caught the king as he fell, then lowered him gently to the ground.

Guthlaf dropped by his side. He took the king's wrist in his hand, then pulled back the fine byrnie to reveal a dark stain of blood on the crimson of his breeches. Peeling back the sodden linen, he uncovered a long cut that welled with bright blood against the pallid skin.

"Well?" snapped Offa, the strain clear in his tone.

"He lives," replied Guthlaf. "The wound does not appear that bad."

Beobrand said nothing. It was true that the cut did not seem deep, but he had seen men die from mere scratches that had become elf-shot.

"This time," snapped Offa, "see that you stop the bleeding. And keep him still when he wakes. You do not want our lord's death on your hands." Guthlaf looked as though he might puke at the prospect, but Offa did not wait for a response. Stepping away from the prostrate form of the king, he began barking orders to his men to gather up what they could.

Beobrand admired the man's control. The men needed a leader, someone to give them commands so that they would not succumb to the fear of their uncertain future.

"I owe you my thanks," Beobrand said.

"Me?" Offa looked confused. "Why?"

All around them the men were hurrying about the gathering gloom to strip valuables from the dead. Beobrand watched as Attor and Dreogan heaved the injured Mercian to his feet. His hands were bound behind his back and they half-dragged the man towards where Beobrand stood with Offa.

"You led my men to safety after the rout at the ditch," Beobrand said. "When Ecgric and Sigeberht fell..." he faltered. The shame of fleeing from the battle was still a bitter memory. He pushed it aside. It was long ago now and it did not do to dwell on the past. "If not for you, Offa," he went on, "they might well have died there along with so many others."

Offa's face clouded, perhaps remembering the faces of men he had not seen since the slaughter at the great ditch near Beodericsworth.

"You owe me nothing, Beobrand," he said, his tone gruff. "But if you ever did, you have repaid me today. Things would not have gone well for us here, I fear."

"Perhaps I have something else I can give you as a sign of my gratitude."

"What is that?" asked Offa.

Beobrand turned to Attor and Dreogan, beckoning them forward. They pulled the Mercian along with them, his scalp still flapping obscenely over his blood-drenched face.

"I thought you might like to question this one."

Offa frowned as he looked at the Mercian, but he nodded his thanks.

"I would know the whereabouts of your pagan king, Mercian," he snarled. The injured man recoiled from Offa's ire, but Dreogan and Attor held him firmly. "Where is Penda?"

"I... I don't know," stammered the Mercian.

"Tell me all that you do know," said Offa, his face in shadow as the last of the light bled from the sky.

Before Beobrand could hear the man's answer, a raised voice called his name.

Coenred!

He scanned the gloaming.

"Beobrand!" came the call again. Coenred was at the west end of the causeway, where the wounded Mercians had made their futile stand. Beobrand sprinted towards the monk, past the fallen and the stooped warriors looting the corpses. As he grew closer he could make out Coenred kneeling in the dust beside a crumpled figure.

"I told you to wait for us back at the alders," said Beobrand, his voice harsh.

"And yet I did not wait," replied Coenred. "I heard the fighting was over. It seems you had forgotten me." Beobrand was about to reply, when Coenred cut him off. "No matter. We need to get this boy back to the monastery, if he is to have any hope of living."

Beobrand reeled. For a heartbeat his head swam, as if with too much mead.

"Cuthbert's alive?"

Coenred looked up at him from where he knelt. He nodded.

"I am a skilled healer, Beobrand, and the Almighty in His wisdom often answers my prayers, but I cannot raise men from the dead."

"I thought no man could survive such a wound," muttered Beobrand, aghast that he had left the boy for dead.

"Well, Cuthbert is no man," replied Coenred, an edge of anger creeping into his tone. Beobrand frowned, but said nothing. "He is a boy," finished the monk. "And he has the strength of youth. Now, I have bound the wound as best I can. It has staunched the bleeding, but I need to clean the cut or it will take on the wound-rot. There is no time to be wasted, if we wish to rescue him."

Beobrand looked down at the inert form. Gods, he hoped the boy would live. He should never have brought him south.

"Help me lift him," he said.

Coenred hesitated.

"Be careful not to open his wound."

Beobrand grunted, but saw no reason to reply. Bending down, he got hold of Cuthbert's arm and, with Coenred's aid, lifted him and stood upright. By Woden, the boy was light. Holding Cuthbert in his arms reminded him of carrying his son's sleeping form to bed. The last time he had done that had been years before. Octa had been much younger and lighter than Cuthbert, but the recollection of his son's relaxed slumbering body was suddenly fresh, Beobrand's senses full of the shadows of memory.

"Pick up that sword," Beobrand said, nodding at the fallen Mercian's blade that lay in the dirt near Cuthbert.

Coenred curled his lip in disdain.

"If the boy lives," said Beobrand, "he will want that blade. It is his now. And, as you said, we have no time to waste."

Coenred gave him a sidelong look that was heavy with

judgement, but the monk held his tongue and retrieved the weapon.

Beobrand strode back along the causeway. A drawn-out wail of pain drifted to them, but Beobrand could not make out any details from this distance. There was a compact group of figures surrounding the wounded Mercian, but what they were doing was obscured by their bodies and the gathering darkness. Another howling cry rent the dusk air. Coenred made the sign of the Christ cross over his chest. No more sounds came from the group and when Beobrand and Coenred arrived, the throng of warriors was dispersing, the excitement over.

Beobrand glanced at the ground between Attor and Dreogan. The Mercian was sprawled in a growing pool of dark blood pumping from a deep cut to his throat. The man's eyes had been put out. Attor stooped to wipe his seax blades on the dead man's clothes. Coenred made a small sound in the back of his throat at the sight of the tortured Mercian and turned away.

"It seems the whoreson's memory just needed some coaxing," said Offa, his tone brittle and hard. "Penda is on the march with his full host. This small warband was sent ahead to try to pin King Anna here at the coast."

"How long?"

Offa shrugged.

"A day. Perhaps two. But who can say the Mercian told the truth?"

"And the fyrd of the East Angelfolc?"

"Amassed to the south to hold Penda's host at bay." Offa let out a long breath. In that moment, his face shrouded in shadows, he looked old and exhausted. "I fear the fyrd will once again prove no match for Penda and his wolves."

"We cannot hope to stand here against Penda," Beobrand said. "Not with so few men and the king wounded." Cuthbert moaned quietly in his arms, but did not awaken. They could not remain here. "I have a ship at the minster. We will take Anna north to Bernicia. He will be safe there in the court of King Oswiu."

Offa scowled and rubbed at his beard.

"Nobody will be safe when Penda finds the king of Bernicia is giving refuge to the object of his anger."

Beobrand hawked and spat to clear the sour taste from his mouth. His arms were beginning to ache from Cuthbert's unconscious weight.

"I don't think Penda could wish more harm on Bernicia than he already does. Penda is filled with so much hatred for the sons of Æthelfrith. And Oswiu has been his sworn enemy for years." Beobrand thought of the flames at Bebbanburg and how Penda had come close to defeating the Bernician stronghold. He saw in his mind's eye, Oswald's dismembered corpse at Maserfelth. No, the enmity between Oswiu and Penda was absolute. "I doubt this will change anything," he said, his tone sombre.

"Still," said Offa, looking down at his unconscious king, "Penda will not take kindly to the king of East Angeln escaping with his life to live in comfort in the north."

Beobrand peered at the fallen form of Anna. Guthlaf was cradling the king's head. Anna's skin was as pale as moonlight in the encroaching dusk. Beobrand leaned in close to Offa so that none of the gathered men would overhear.

"He has to live first," he whispered. "What chance has he here?"

For a heartbeat, Offa was silent. Beobrand wondered if he was going to rebuke him for doubting his king's survival, but a moment later, the gruff thegn nodded and turned to face the warriors of East Angeln.

"Collect the king's standard, and the banner of our enemies. Take no more than you can carry. We return to the minster." In a lower voice, he said to Beobrand, "Very well, my friend. Let us take my king to the safety of Bebbanburg."

Chapter 7

Cynan drained the mead from his drinking horn. Domhnulla, the pretty Pictish thrall he had often bedded in the past, quickly stepped forward and refilled the vessel. Cynan made no acknowledgement of the young woman and did not notice the scowl that passed across her features. He rubbed his hands over his face, feeling the rough stubble of his unshaven cheeks. Letting out a long sigh, he stared into the fire that burnt in the centre of the hall. The day had been warm, but there was a chill in the evening air and so a fire had been lit on the hearthstone.

"Careful, lad," said Bassus in a low whisper.

Cynan turned to him, wondering what the huge man was warning him of. He had enough concerns already. His mind swirled with worries. When he had left Stagga that morning he had been uneasy about the conversation with Eadgyth. Had he upset her? Should he marry her? Was marriage even what she wanted, or had he misinterpreted her meaning?

Now those things seemed trivial. Sulis had returned, and the instant he saw her again, everything had changed. He had dared not even admit it to himself, but he had never truly let her out of his mind. He would often find himself dreaming of what might have been if he had turned away from his duty all those years before and wandered into the west with her. Would they have been happy? Would they have had children?

"Careful?" he asked Bassus absently, his mind still focused on Sulis and the past.

Bassus chuckled.

"By Tiw's cock," he said, "you are a foolish one." Cynan frowned, unsure what Bassus was talking about. This only made the one-armed giant's smile widen. "She may be a thrall, but she is still a woman. They are strange cattle, women. But even a fool knows they do not like to be spurned. I'd keep a close eye on your manhood when you sleep tonight."

What was he speaking about? Sulis was still Beobrand's thrall, he supposed, but it seemed strange to refer to her as such. She had told them much about her life since then, how she was a respectable goodwife now, married to a freeman in the west of Bernicia, in the mountains of the old kingdom of Rheged. And he had not spurned Sulis, he had helped her. If not for him, the women of Ubbanford would have slain her more quickly than wringing the neck of a hen for the pot. The womenfolk had been incensed and saw no reason for a trial. And the worst thing was that Cynan knew Beobrand would agree with them. The fact that Cynan had convinced the women that they must wait for their hlaford's return had merely delayed Sulis' death. For when Beobrand returned to find Reaghan's killer locked in one of Ubbanford's barns, he would not tarry long in taking her life as payment for the death of his woman. The thought of this roiled in Cynan's head.

Bassus clicked his fingers in front of Cynan's face.

"Wake up, boy," he said. "Don't look so confounded." He lowered his tone and nodded towards Domhnulla who was now serving some of the other men from the pitcher she carried. "I am speaking of Domhnulla, not that murderous vixen, Sulis."

"Oh," replied Cynan stupidly.

"Last time you were here you took her to your bed, and

judging from the squeals we all heard that night and the grin on her face the next morning, the wee thing had a good time. Now you act as though you've never seen her before." He shook his head and Cynan noticed that most of his hair was now the grey of old ashes. When had Bassus grown old? "I'd say you have enough trouble with women at the moment," Bassus went on, "without angering the thralls too."

Cynan offered him a thin smile. The coupling with Domhnulla had been pleasurable and vigorous, it was true, but she did not occupy his mind in the same way as Eadgyth and Sulis. He sighed and took another sip of the mead. He sat at the high table in Beobrand's absence. To his left sat Bassus and beyond him, Udela, Ardith's mother, was eating quietly. She had offered him the Waes Hael cup and ordered food to be prepared, but as ever, she was subdued when Beobrand was away. Cynan did not understand their relationship. For a time he had believed they were lovers, but then he had begun to question that assumption. For the most part the two of them were friendly enough, and Beobrand was happy to allow Udela to run his household, but there was no passion that Cynan could see. Much like Eadgyth and himself, he pondered ruefully. He pushed the thought away, preferring to think about Beobrand's problems, rather than his own.

Cynan knew that many of Beobrand's oath-sworn men suspected their lord's attraction to Oswiu's queen, Eanflæd. Cynan was sure of it. And worse still, he thought the feelings were mutual. He had seen how the queen looked at Beobrand when she believed nobody was paying attention. Cynan never spoke of it, choosing to change the subject whenever it came up amongst the gesithas. Nothing could ever come of such a doomed love. To even think of such a thing was madness. Such a union could spawn nothing but pain.

And what of his feelings for Sulis? Wasn't that also madness? Years before, he had stood before Beobrand, preventing him from killing her. That had been before they had known that

Sulis' knife had slain Reaghan. Beobrand had never mentioned that dark day to him, but Cynan knew that because of his actions, Sulis yet lived. Ever since that moment, there had been a coolness, a shadow, over his friendship with Beobrand. Now he had intervened on her behalf once more, but to what end? There was no doubt that she was guilty of Reaghan's death. Beobrand would slit Sulis' throat for what she had done; for what she had taken from him.

Cynan was not often fearful. He was brave and would stand in the centre of any shieldwall, no matter the odds against them. But the thought of seeing Sulis killed filled him with dread. His stomach twisted to imagine Beobrand's wrath when he saw her in Ubbanford.

Picking up his small eating knife, Cynan began scratching at his fingernails, cleaning the dirt from under them. Eanflæd, Eadgyth, Reaghan, Udela, Sulis. How had the women in their lives tangled the threads of their wyrds so? He could still not truly believe that Sulis had walked back into his life after all this time, bringing with her a storm of doubts and yearnings he had long since pushed deep into the darkest recesses of his being, far from the light of his thoughts.

Without truly seeing, his eyes followed Domhnulla's progress as she poured mead for the men at the long benches along the length of the hall. These were the gesithas who remained in Ubbanford. Some of their women were there too, though Rowena was conspicuously absent. She had been furious with Cynan's intervention earlier in the afternoon, and Bassus had looked harried and dejected when he arrived at the new hall without Rowena at his side.

Cynan noticed that Tatwine, Ardith's boy, was sitting with the warriors. Gods, how the years passed. Tatwine had grown suddenly these last few months. Soon he would be old enough to carry spear and shield. He wondered what Udela would think of that.

Domhnulla glanced in Cynan's direction and, heeding what

Bassus had said, he flashed her a broad smile that he did not feel. The grin seemed to do the trick though, for she met his gaze and smiled before lowering her eyelids and heading away down the hall in search of more drink.

"That's better, lad," said Bassus, smiling as he took a swig of his ale. "Perhaps when next you seek to plough that furrow, she'll be ripe for you."

"What are you two whispering about?" asked Ardith, leaning past her mother.

Bassus blushed.

"Nothing to concern you, little one," he said.

"You know I don't like it when you call me that," she replied. "I am a child no longer." She placed her hand over the swell of her belly and Bassus flushed again. The young woman was flaxen-haired with piercing blue eyes which she had now fixed on her father's old one-armed steward. There was no doubting that she was Beobrand's daughter. That gaze could make the strongest man quail.

"You are quite right, Ardith," said Bassus, regaining his composure. "But you must forgive me. You are young, and to me most men, and all women, young and old, are little." He grinned.

She raised her cup to him in acknowledgement. She was usually quiet, but this evening she was more loquacious than normal. Perhaps it was the drink, or the joy of being with child, but Cynan thought it was something else.

"You truly think my father will kill that poor woman?" she asked. Her eyes glimmered, like chips of ice in the firelight.

Bassus took another draught of ale and frowned.

"I think if Cynan here hadn't helped me to ward off Rowena and the other ladies, Sulis would already be dead."

Ardith bit her lip.

"It does not seem right," she said at last. Cynan noticed how Udela watched her daughter, her eyes glowing with love and pride.

"It is the law," replied Bassus, his face clouding. "Sulis was a thrall and she fled. And when she did, she stabbed Reaghan. There is no doubt that she is a murderer."

"But Cynan said that such terrible things had been done to her…" She glanced at Cynan, as if she wanted him to say something in her defence, or perhaps in defence of Sulis. He said nothing. He had already said enough about Sulis.

"What had happened to her does not change what she did. She killed Reaghan. And the truth of it is that Reaghan had shown her nothing but kindness." To Cynan's surprise, Bassus' eyes welled with tears. The big man cuffed at his face and blinked repeatedly. He coughed, then, reaching for his ale, he drained his horn and waved Domhnulla over for mead.

"But for the women to want to kill her without a trial," Ardith said, shaking her head. "That is wrong."

Bassus nodded his thanks to Domhnulla and took a mouthful of the strong mead.

"You speak true," he said. "There is a right way to go about things, no matter what you think and even if the ends are the same."

"But the lady Rowena does not agree with you?"

Bassus chuckled quietly.

"There is much that the lady Rowena and I do not agree on. She is as strong-willed as she is beautiful, and I would have it no other way." He looked wistfully into his drinking horn before taking another sip.

"But to want to kill the woman," said Ardith, "after what she told us… and in her condition."

Bassus sighed. When Cynan and Ingwald had managed to push the folk of Ubbanford back from Sulis, he had been shocked to see the curve of her stomach beneath her dress. Like Ardith, Sulis carried a babe within her and it was this that had both intrigued Ardith and also allowed Cynan to convince the angry women that to seek Sulis' immediate death was wrong.

"If you slay this woman as you wish," he had said, "then you will not only be taking her life in payment for the murder she committed, but you will be making murderers of yourselves in the eyes of the law and before God."

After that, the people had backed away, grumbling and resentful. All but Rowena that was, who had still shrieked that Sulis should die without delay. Bassus had led her away and Cynan and Ingwald had secured Sulis in one of Beobrand's barns. Ingwald remained there guarding the door. Cynan had not trusted Rowena not to return with a knife.

"It is not so simple," Bassus said in reply to Ardith. His broad bearded face, strong and lined from laughter over his long life, looked worn, tired and sad. "Rowena…" he started, but his voice cracked. He took a sip of mead and continued. "When Reaghan died, Rowena took it very hard. There was a time when she loathed Reaghan, but that was long ago and all the bad blood between them had been forgotten before Sulis came. When Reaghan was killed, it was as though Rowena had lost one of her own kin. Edlyn was already married and had left for Morðpæð, so Reaghan became like a daughter to Rowena. That year we lost so much. So many were killed. At Maserfelth. Here…" Bassus stared into the flames of the fire for a time, as if trying to see into the past, or perhaps to sear away the memories of all those who had gone to the afterlife. "To lose loved ones is not something that can easily be forgotten," he said. "Or forgiven."

"You are right, of course," said Ardith. Bassus nodded in mute acknowledgement and drank deeply. "Which is surely why this Sulis woman should be judged in accordance with the hurt that had been done to her." Ardith's cheeks were flushed and her eyes burnt with a cold fire that Cynan recognised as dangerous when seen in Beobrand's gaze. "Is it not true that she had been abused most cruelly by the man Rowena's daughter called husband?" asked Ardith, her tone sharp and accusing. "That he killed her son before her eyes?"

Bassus slammed down his drinking horn, spilling the contents onto the linen cloth that Udela insisted be placed on the high table.

"Enough, child," he roared. "You do not know what you speak of."

"I am not a child," Ardith replied, her voice clipped and cold.

Bassus was breathless with his anger, as if he fought hard to hold it in check, like a roped horse that bucked and pulled at the halter.

"Then do not speak like one," he replied, calming his voice with difficulty. "Things are rarely simple."

"You think I do not know this?" she asked, and her words held in them the dark memories of her past. Cynan had been there in Rodomo when they had rescued Ardith. He had some inkling of the horrors she had endured. No child should have to face the monsters Ardith had encountered.

Bassus let out a long sigh. He too knew of her past.

"I know you are no stranger to woe, Ardith," he said. "But these matters concern things that happened before you came to Ubbanford. You cannot understand them as we do. We were here, and you were not."

Ardith scowled and Cynan thought she meant to continue her argument with Bassus. He looked about the hall and realised that a hush had fallen over all those gathered there. Everybody was staring at the high table, watching the clash of opinions that had unravelled the peace of the meal. Udela placed her hand on her daughter's arm and Ardith, perhaps thinking for the first time that she might have overstepped herself, closed her mouth. Blinking, she scanned the faces of those who watched her in the light of the hearth fire and the flicker of the rush lights. She blushed a darker shade of red in the ruddy flame-glow.

"I am sorry, Bassus," she said. "I meant no offence."

Bassus drew in a great breath. Shaking his head, he said, "You could never offend me, little one."

Cynan thought he detected a slight stiffening in Ardith at the use of Bassus' term of endearment, but she merely smiled a tight smile and looked down at where her hands rested in her lap.

Bassus gulped down a mouthful of mead. The sounds of conversation in the hall picked up again as people realised the conflict was over.

"So, tell me of the difficult decision you have to make," Bassus said.

For a heartbeat, Cynan was unsure what he meant.

"You said something about Eadgyth earlier," Bassus prompted. "Is it what I think it is?"

"Probably," Cynan replied. His face grew hot and he supposed he blushed as red as Ardith. He again felt like a fool for not anticipating Eadgyth's proposal. He had come here for Bassus' counsel, so now he recounted the morning's conversation with Acennan's widow.

Bassus whistled quietly.

"And instead of giving her an answer, you fled here?" He emptied his horn of mead and signalled to Domhnulla for yet another refill. Cynan knew from experience that it would take many more hornfuls before Bassus began to slur his words. He had never known any man able to consume more drink than the one-time champion of Northumbria. Bassus thanked the Pictish thrall and waited until she had moved away before continuing. "You really are a fool when it comes to women," he said. "You anger your bed-thrall here and offend the lady of your hall back at Stagga."

Cynan sighed. He did not need to be reminded of his stupidity. He was thankful that Bassus chose not to mention Sulis amongst the women who caused him to be foolish. The gods knew he had not ceased thinking about the Mercian woman since he had laid eyes on her that afternoon.

On seeing his morose expression, Bassus rested his horn on the table and slapped Cynan on the back. The strength of the blow caused Cynan to reel in his chair. The man may be old, but he was strong! Cynan was pleased that Bassus was not his enemy.

"Do not mope so," Bassus said. "Your problems can be solved simply."

"Indeed?" Cynan could not see how.

"Of course!" Bassus laughed. "You tup Domhnulla tonight, then you travel back to Stagga on the morrow with a clear head and tell Eadgyth you would be honoured if she would call you her husband. She is a good woman. Handsome too. You would be a fool not to marry her."

Cynan snorted.

"As simple as that?" he said.

Bassus lowered his voice to a growling rumble of barely suppressed laughter.

"As simple as ploughing two furrows when you only have one ox," he said, clapping Cynan on the back again.

Cynan smiled, but his mind was in turmoil. If only it were so simple.

"Sounds easy enough," he said, pushing himself up from his carved chair. "I suppose I just need to be careful not to ever have the two furrows in the same field."

Bassus guffawed at this. Cynan stood.

"Where are you going?" Bassus asked.

"I need a piss, and then I am going to take some food and drink to Ingwald." He sniffed, hesitating for a heartbeat. "And to the prisoner. A woman with child needs to eat."

Bassus frowned at the reminder of Reaghan's killer.

"Be careful, Cynan," he said, watching him go.

Cynan glanced back at the giant, trying to see the true meaning behind the words. He settled on the one that was easiest to respond to.

"I think Ingwald and I can control one pregnant woman," he said, and strode along the length of the hall, past the watchful gazes of those seated at the benches, and into the cool darkness outside.

Chapter 8

The trip back to the minster was a blur to Cuthbert. He was dimly aware of being carried, his head lolling against a man's broad shoulder. He opened his eyes, but they would not focus and he could make no sense of what was around him. It was dark and he shivered against a sudden chill in the air.

Cold. So cold.

He trembled like a linden leaf in a storm. Could nobody place a cloak around him? Was there not a fire where he could warm himself?

Cuthbert tried to ask these questions to the man who carried him, but the words clogged in his throat and he could not make himself understood.

Voices. Whispers in the gloom. All about him like bats flitting in the night.

But what did they say? He could not discern the words. After a time he wondered if he heard people speaking at all.

There were rattles and grunts, the panting of tired men. The crunching trudge of boots in the dust.

Cuthbert drifted into a half-sleep.

What had happened? His memories were a tangle of briars, snagging and scratching within his mind. He could not piece together the events that had led to this moment. There were flashes of a sunset, glimmering blindingly on a polished blade. The leering grin of a stranger.

A stabbing pain.

Cuthbert moaned as the man who carried him stumbled. The jolt sent a searing agony lancing into his knee. Why did it hurt so? He wanted to look down, but his head felt too large and cumbersome for him to control its movement. He let it flop back against the unyielding iron links of the byrnie that encased a heavily muscled shoulder.

After what might have been an age or a few heartbeats, a swarm of voices murmured around him. Cuthbert yet shivered, but he sensed that he was being wrapped in woollen blankets against the cold that assailed him.

The world grew hushed and he was gently rocked as his mother had done when he was just an infant and not a spear-bearing warrior, one of Beobrand's feared and famed Black Shields.

Deep down he knew he was not a child any longer and his mother was long gone. And yet she was there with him and he was glad that she had come to cradle him in his pain and confusion. He wasn't as cold now and the gentle motion of his mother's arms carried him into a deep slumber.

When he awoke, the first thing he saw was a man's face. It was the face of a young man, with kindly, sad eyes. The face was encircled in an aura of glowing golden light.

Cuthbert, warm and comfortable now, was still being rocked slowly, soothingly.

"Mother?" he said, trying to rise. He wanted to see her. It had been so long since he had last rested on her lap like this. As he moved, a sharp shock of pain speared into his left knee and he cried out.

"Hush, Cuthbert," said the golden man. "Let me see your wound."

The glowing halo made the man's features dark, in shadow. Without waiting for a reply from Cuthbert, he bent down, pulled back the blankets that covered the young man's legs and delicately peeled back a stained bandage that was wrapped about his knee. Removing the bandage, the man lowered his face to the wound and sniffed.

The cold air against his skin made Cuthbert shiver, but it revived him somewhat. He attempted to bend his leg, but the sharp pain made him wince.

"Do not move," said the glowing man. He discarded the soiled bandage and turned to someone behind him that Cuthbert could not see. "Pass me the clean cloth." There was a muffled response. "Yes," he replied, "the poultice too."

Cuthbert lay back as the man administered to his wounded knee. First he wiped it clean with a hot wet cloth. Cuthbert cried out. The skin was swollen and tender and each touch was like a knife digging into his flesh. Next, a warm, sweet-smelling poultice was applied. This was soothing, and Cuthbert sighed. He could feel his mind drifting again as the pain subsided and the golden man wrapped a clean bandage around his leg.

"Are you an angel?" croaked Cuthbert. He had heard the priests speak of such beings. They were said to be beautiful and kind, God's messengers on middle earth. Perhaps God had sent an angel to cure him of his injury.

The man smiled. Supporting Cuthbert's head, he offered him a cup to drink from. He drank. It was cool water and he could feel it refreshing him as it trickled down his parched throat.

"No, Cuthbert," said the man. "I am no angel."

In that instant, the light of the sun reflected from the surface of the water in the cup onto the man's face. It was Coenred, Beobrand's friend, the monk. The bright sunlight had shone through Coenred's long hair, turning it into a brilliant golden crown.

"Rest now," said Coenred. He replaced the blanket over Cuthbert and moved away, leaving him to stare up at the bright blue of the sky. Smudges of white clouds scudded there. A gull flitted across his vision and Cuthbert finally realised where he was. He could hear the rush of the water beneath the hull, the creak of the ship's timbers as the billowing sail that rose high on its mast pulled the vessel across the waves.

He could recall nothing of how they had reached the ship and knew not where they were heading, but for the moment, he was content that he was safe. The pain in his knee was replaced with the warming ache of the poultice and, despite what Coenred had said, Cuthbert could not be free of the thought that the Christ had watched over him, sending an angel to ensure he was safe from harm and to bring him back from the brink of death.

The rolling motion of the ship, the groaning of the flexing strakes, the murmur of the men, the distant shrieks of the gulls in the sky and the nebulous memory of his mother's touch, soothed him back into a sleep where he dreamt of men with golden crowns and great feathered wings like those of giant sea birds.

Chapter 9

Cynan peered into the darkness inside the barn. He had carried a small oil lamp with him, but it would take him some time to strike a spark to create a flame. He contemplated taking the prisoner outside. The night was dry and there was light enough from the moon and stars. He could hear Ingwald settling himself against the wall of the barn to eat the food Cynan had brought for him from the hall on the hill. He would have no secrets from Ingwald, he knew. Whatever he talked about tonight he would not hide the truth from his gesith, and yet somehow, it felt right that he should meet with Sulis away from view, in the gloom. Perhaps, he pondered, he shouldn't even light the lamp, leaving them both in darkness. But even as the idea rose like a silent fish breaking the surface on the pool of his thoughts, so he rejected it. He had to see her face, stare into her eyes. It had been years and he needed to be able to ascertain the truth of her words as she spoke. And, he wondered, mayhap uncover the truth of his feelings for her.

He could just make out the shadow of her amongst the barrels and sacks at the far corner of the building. Moving with cautious slowness, as if afraid he might spook a wild animal, he stooped and placed the items he carried on the hard earth floor. The shadow at the rear of the barn shifted and Cynan felt his heartbeat quicken. He was as nervous as if he were entering the lair of a wolf rather than a storage hut occupied by a defenceless woman. And yet, had Sulis not killed before? Was she not dangerous? He recalled her sullen silence as he had carried her northward towards Ubbanford, and her cunning at stealing his seax, which she had used to cut into her wrists, attempting to end the pain that had engulfed her. He had saved her life then, bandaging her and taking her to the monk, Coenred, who had tended to her wounds. The body had healed, but her soul had remained damaged. Later, Sulis had gone on to kill Reaghan. Without him, Sulis would have died, so was he responsible for Reaghan's death? He thought that perhaps he was. At least in part. The thought of it had often made him furious, wishing for an outcome that could never be. But now he felt a different emotion, the same feeling that had come over him when Beobrand had confronted Sulis by the Wall: a deep desire to keep this damaged woman free from harm. He had saved her then and he could not bring himself to regret it, despite the hurt she had caused.

He dropped his hand to his belt, checking that his blade was safely in its sheath. He still wore the same seax there, the weapon Sulis had used to cut herself. The blade had been a gift from Beobrand when Cynan was a thrall. The seax carried many memories and he treasured it. It reminded him of who he had been, of how he had met Acennan and Beobrand, and of what he had become. A thrall was not permitted to bear arms, and yet Cynan was now a freeman, with land, wealth, men and weapons. He did not think he would recognise the boy he had been when he had been beaten and tormented by Halga and Wybert all those years before.

"I am going to light the lamp," he whispered in a soothing tone, as if talking to a child, or a nervous animal. The last time he had seen her, she had seemed to be little more than a savage creature, intent on vengeance; searching for any way to dispel her anguish and pain.

By the thin light puddling on the earth through the open door he set about his task. His hands trembled and he was not sure whether from fear or anticipation at seeing her face again. Or maybe there was some other cause for his uncertainty. To speak to Sulis, he would need to confront his own actions and feelings. Although Eadgyth's proposal had unnerved him, his history with Sulis was a vastly more knotted tangle of memories and emotions he had long since chosen not to attempt unravelling.

It took him several tries before he got a spark to take in the tinder. With each strike of the stone and iron, he was tempted to glance towards the woman who looked on silently, to catch a glimpse of her face in the spark-flash of light. But he forced himself to focus on the task in hand. Eventually, a small ember began to glow in the dried fungus tinder and he blew gently on it, coaxing it into life. He fed the tiny coal a few wood shavings he had taken from a pouch. The smell of smoke grew strong and a moment later the light of a small flame flared brightly within the confines of the barn. Cynan quickly lifted the burning tinder to ignite the lamp's wick. The flame lengthened, wavering in the light breeze from the open door. Quietly, he reached outside and pulled the rough planks of the door, closing out the night and enclosing him here, inside with Sulis.

He suppressed a shiver.

At last, he allowed himself to look at her. Her eyes glowed from the shadows, reinforcing the impression of some wild forest creature. The flame light flickered, making the shadows dance. Her features seemed first contorted into a scowl and then a heartbeat later twisted into a grimace. The small flame settled now that the door was shut. The shifting shadows stilled, as the guttering of the flame subsided and the light became more constant. Gone was the wild animal hiding in the dark. Sulis was just as he remembered her, her high cheekbones sharp in the shadowed darkness. Perhaps there were more wrinkles about her eyes, as if from laughter. He did not think he had ever seen Sulis smile, let alone laugh. Perhaps she had truly found happiness in the intervening years. She certainly was not laughing now. She appeared sombre and exhausted in the gloom. Cynan peered at her for a long while and was pleased that he could detect none of the madness and rage that had gripped her all those years before.

"I brought you food," he said. His voice rasped and he was again shocked by the depth of feeling this woman conjured within him. He swallowed against the dryness of his mouth and offered her the platter of bread and meat. She did not move. He took a step towards her, and with a sigh she rose and took the proffered food. "I have ale too," he said, lifting the cup. Without a word, she accepted it and returned to her position at the far end of the barn. She sat atop a sack of grain, with her back against a barrel.

"Thank you," she said, her voice barely more than a whisper. She set aside the food and drink. "But I am not hungry. I must speak with you."

"I am here to speak, but you must eat and drink." He stared into her eyes, feeling himself becoming lost in their depths. "And not just for yourself."

She sniffed.

"There is no time. I must tell you of why I came here. I need your help." Her words came quickly now. Cynan held up a hand to silence her.

"I will hear your tale when you have eaten."

She eyed him, perhaps weighing his resolve. Seeing no give in him, she sighed and fell to eating. He watched her in silence, settling himself down on the ground with a pile of sacks behind him. She ate quickly, taking great mouthfuls and washing down the food with gulps of ale.

When she had finished, she set aside the plate and cup.

"Thank you," she said again.

He marvelled at the change in her since he had seen her last. She gave thanks and asked for help where before she would have snarled at him, spurning any offer of aid.

"For someone who was not hungry, you managed to eat that quickly enough."

She offered him a sad smile, then stood, letting out a small grunt with the effort of rising. The bulge of her belly was clear as she straightened. Grimacing, she placed a hand on the small of her back. He stood too, suddenly concerned.

"Are you well?"

"I am healthy enough," she replied. "But it seems my story will have to wait a few moments longer."

Cynan stepped away from her, suddenly wary, remembering the vicious, broken creature she had been. His hand rested on the hilt of his seax.

"Do not fear, brave Cynan," she said, with the ghost of a sardonic smile on her lips. "I mean you no harm."

He felt foolish. What harm could this small pregnant woman do him?

"You seemed unable to wait to speak a moment ago, and now you do not wish to talk?"

She snorted.

"Some things cannot wait. When this babe chooses to be born, it will come."

Cynan was alarmed.

"The child is coming now?"

"No," she replied, shaking her head. "That will be some months yet, God willing, but carrying a babe inside causes some things to become more urgent than normal." Gazing at him expectantly, she rubbed a hand on her lower abdomen. He was confused, unsure what she was getting at. "Especially after eating and drinking," she went on, speaking slowly and pointedly, as if to a slow child.

Still he did not reply, merely shaking his head in confusion.

"I need to piss, Cynan," she said at last, her voice tinged with frustration.

Cynan's face grew hot and he was glad of the dark within the barn to hide his embarrassment. He hesitated. Could this be some trick to escape? She had come to Ubbanford voluntarily and seemed desperate to speak with him. Surely she would not flee. And if she did, would he care? He contemplated the idea. He would not chase after her. He had no wish to see her face justice. He turned to the door, to hide the confusion he felt. Pushing it open, he said, "We're coming out."

Sulis disappeared into the darkness and Cynan stood outside the barn, Ingwald beside him.

"You think she'll come back?" Ingwald asked after a while.

Cynan sighed. Staring into the night, there was no sign of her now. The only sound was the hushed rustle of the breeze in the trees down near the Tuidi.

"I don't know," he replied at last.

"Do you want her to?" Ingwald said, voicing the question that played in Cynan's mind.

Before he had a chance to answer, Sulis returned. Without a word, she slipped inside the barn once more and, with a sidelong glance at Ingwald, Cynan followed her.

He pulled the door closed behind them, and they positioned themselves as before, with the warming light of the oil lamp glowing between them. They stared at each other over the flame.

"Well?" Cynan said, breaking the awkward silence. "You could not wait to tell me what brings you here and yet now you sit as if mute."

"I am sorry," she said, her voice small in the darkness.

"It is not I who needs your apology," he said, his tone suddenly harsh.

She nodded slowly.

"If he was here, I would tell him I am sorry for what I did."

"If Beobrand were here, you would be dead already," replied

Cynan. As he said the words, he heard the truth in them. Beobrand was perhaps less impetuous than he had been, but he was not a forgiving man and his anger was legendary.

"Perhaps you would have stayed his hand," she said, her eyes searching his, "as you did once before."

"I saved you then. I am not sure I could do so again."

"Not sure you could, or that you would?"

"Who can say?" He could sense himself growing angry. "But now is not the time for such questions. Now is the moment for you to tell me why you came here."

"You heard some of it before."

It was true. While the women had bayed for her blood like hounds scenting a hind, she had given them a garbled account of her plight and why she had come. But it made little sense and there were as many gaps in her story as a blanket that had been discarded and gnawed by field mice.

"You told us enough to stop the women taking the blood-price for what you did," he said, his tone flat and hard, like ice. He would not allow this woman to distract him. "I would hear all of it now. The whole tale."

Her eyes glimmered as if with tears and she suddenly seemed tiny. He had the urge to take her in his arms, to comfort her. Gods, was he bewitched? He clenched his fists and placed them in his lap. He stared at her.

"Well?" he said.

She held his gaze in the lamplight for a time, before nodding.

"I am not the woman you knew all those years ago." Her voice was very quiet. Cynan leaned forward, straining to hear her. "I am truly sorry for what I did. I was..." She hesitated, biting her lip. "I was drowning in sorrow and anger. What they had done to me..." Her voice caught in her throat and she let out a trembling sigh. "I did not know that Reaghan had died. I just wanted to escape." Cynan thought of Beobrand's grief and felt his own anger blossom, hot and furious in his chest.

"But she did die," he spat. "You killed her."

Sulis' eyes brimmed and she blinked back tears.

"I cannot change what happened. I have prayed many times that I will be forgiven by God." She leaned forward, reaching out a hand as if to clutch his, but he was too far from her and she let it fall back. She tugged and pulled at her skirts, worrying at the wool. "I would pay the weregild," she whispered, "if I could. I know nothing I do can bring her back, but I would see the blood-price paid."

"You say you have a husband now," Cynan said, remembering what she had said that afternoon. He ignored the prickle of jealousy he felt. "I doubt that he is a wealthy man, if you are travelling alone, and in your state too." He narrowed his eyes. "Or have you run away again? Is your husband looking for you?"

"No." Her voice was firm, resolute. "I love him." Again Cynan felt the scratch of envy. "My husband, Leofman, is not wealthy, but he is a good man. I do not flee from him."

"If you are not running, how came you to Ubbanford. And why do you seek me?"

"I need help. I did not know where else to turn."

"Your husband should be the first man you turn to. You say he is a good man."

"He is. And he is brave. But Leofman cannot stand up to those who would steal from us."

"Steal what from you? You said your husband was not wealthy."

"He is not," she hesitated. "But he might be soon. And yet there is no time for that. I need your help now. They have taken something from us more valuable than all the silver in middle earth."

Cynan frowned.

"Explain yourself."

And she did. It took her a long while to lay it all out. When she finished, Cynan's head was spinning. Could she truly have changed so much? This woman seemed sincere and loyal to the husband she had met after fleeing from Beobrand all that time ago. He understood why she had come to him now. It was his battle-skill she wished for. And, as she was keen to point out, he was an honourable man, who had saved her life on two occasions. Was she playing on his emotions? Did she know the power she still held over him? She clearly loved this Leofman, but if what she said was true, the poor man was badly injured and in no position to defend them or their lands. Or to retrieve what had been stolen from them.

Cynan looked at her in the dim light of the lamp. He felt the stirrings of something deep within him, a feeling he welcomed beyond the anxiety caused by Eadgyth or even the roiling maelstrom of emotions awoken by Sulis. Biting his lip, he thought of the things he could do, that which he should do and, slowly, he began to comprehend what he would do.

He opened his mouth to tell Sulis what he had decided, when a rapping at the door of the barn made them both start. The intimate spell that had been cast between them in the gloom was shattered. A heartbeat later, the door rasped against the uneven ground as it was pulled open.

Chapter 10

Beobrand staggered, catching hold of the taut mainstay as *Saeslaga* canted to the side. The journey northward had been much slower than when they had hurried towards East Angeln. Not only was Ferenbald's sleek ship heavily laden with the additional weight of King Anna and his hearth-warriors, and what they had taken from the minster, but the wind still blew from the north, forcing them to tack along the coast.

"It would have been quicker to walk," grumbled Offa, who stood at the wale beside Beobrand.

A wave shattered over the side of the ship, dousing them both in cold spray. Wiping the water from his face, Beobrand pushed his long, fair hair out of his eyes.

At times on the voyage he had fixed his attention on a point on the coastline, a tall tree or a memorably shaped hill, or the pale sand of a cove. He would watch these landmarks as the ship tacked over and again, and it was always disheartening to see how little they had advanced after what seemed an age. And yet Ferenbald just laughed when the warriors complained of the slow progress.

"We'll get there when we get there," he said with a grin. To see the skipper at the steerboard, so confident and assured, always lifted Beobrand's spirits, despite their lack of speed.

"We'll get there when we get there," Beobrand said now to Offa. The older man groaned. How many times had they heard Ferenbald speak those words in the last two days? A dozen? Two dozen?

"By Christ's teeth," said Offa, "if I never hear those words again, it will be too soon."

Beobrand squinted into the distance. At least it had not rained and the days had been clear. Some of the men had been stricken with the sickness that came from the tossing motion of sailing, but in truth, despite being a slow journey, it had not been a bad one. Beobrand had certainly endured much harsher conditions.

"Attor," Beobrand said, pointing northward to a shadow rising out of the grey sea, "is that one of the Farena islands?"

Attor shielded his eyes.

"No," he said, and Beobrand's heart sank. The Farena islands were just to the south of Bebbanburg and would mean they were almost at their destination. "I think that is Cocuedesae, the island at the mouth of the Cocueda."

Beobrand pictured the island's location with respect to Bebbanburg. It nestled close to the mainland, about a day's ride south from the fortress. He nodded.

"Not too far now," he said to Offa.

"Good," replied the grizzled thegn. "I have had quite enough of sailing. I am grateful to you, but truly, I know not how much longer I can abide this rolling and rocking. It will do us all good to be on dry land, I think." Offa looked over Beobrand's shoulder. Following Offa's gaze, Beobrand saw Coenred approaching from the stern of the ship where a small awning had been raised just before the steerboard. The wind tugged at the monk's long hair and pulled his habit about him, flapping the wool around his thin legs like banners. Coenred looked pale and tired, thought Beobrand. The monk did not enjoy sea travel any more than Offa, and he had been busy ever since they had pushed off from the beach at Cnobheresburg.

"How do the patients fare?" asked Beobrand. He stooped down and retrieved a skin of wine they had brought with them from the minster. The second ship that had carried the brethren away had been dangerously low in the water when they had set off, and Abbot Foillan had been forced to leave behind many barrels and sacks of provisions. Beobrand had ordered all of them lifted into *Saeslaga*. He had promised that whatever they did not consume on the voyage, Ferenbald could keep and dispose of as he saw fit. There were jars of honey, skins of wine, sacks of barley flour and even some earthenware flasks of wine and oil that had come all the way from distant Frankia. The stores would fetch a good price in Lundenwic or across the Narrow Sea. This probably explained why Ferenbald's mood was as buoyant as his ship.

Beobrand tossed the wineskin to Coenred, who nodded his thanks and took a deep draught. It was good Frankish wine, filled with the taste of the warm sun of the south, of fruits ripened under cloudless blue skies. Coenred took a second long pull on the skin, before wiping his mouth with the back of his hand and pushing the stopper back. He returned the skin with some reluctance.

Beobrand grinned.

"What?" said Coenred, raising an eyebrow.

"I was just thinking of how Aidan frowns on the brethren of Lindisfarena partaking of mead or wine."

Coenred sighed.

"Well, I am thirsty," he said, which made Beobrand laugh.

"And you have earned a drink."

"Yes," replied Coenred, with a twisted smile of his own, "I believe I have." He stretched out his slender hand again and Beobrand gave him the skin once more. Coenred unstopped it and raised it to his lips. "Besides," he said, his eyes twinkling in the afternoon sunshine, "the abbot is far away."

When he had finished drinking, Beobrand took back the

skin. He weighed it in his hand. It was considerably lighter than moments before.

"It is a good thing we will be at Bebbanburg soon," he said. "Ferenbald would have no profit from this trip if it went on much longer. Now, the patients?"

The colour had returned to the monk's cheeks and his fatigue seemed to slough from him like snow from a steep roof when the spring thaw comes. Beobrand always marvelled at the resilience of the monk. Coenred looked weak and often frightened in the face of danger, but Beobrand knew of none braver and no truer friend.

"The king is much improved," he said, as much to Offa as to Beobrand. "He should make a full recovery with rest, good food, and," he winked at Offa, "good wine."

"This is welcome news indeed," said Offa, slapping the monk on the back.

Beobrand knew that the older thegn, and the other gruff warriors from East Angeln, had fretted over their lord's health. He thought back to the night after the battle at the causeway. They had trudged eastward into the darkness, following Coenred, who'd led them along paths they would have surely missed in the gloom. Four of Offa's warriors had carried Anna atop his shield and Beobrand had allowed Eadgard to take Cuthbert in his huge arms. There was little talk amongst the men as they walked. The East Angelfolc had fought long and hard and lost many. Now their king was borne aloft on his shield and they were fleeing from an implacable warlord who had swept through their land and slain their kings in recent memory.

In spite of the victory at the causeway and the triumph of giving the brethren of the minster long enough to flee, this must have felt to Anna's proud hearth-warriors like a defeat.

Beobrand had been glad to be leaving Cnobheresburg. But the elation he had felt at finding Coenred well had fled. And the excitement of battle had dissipated as soon as the last enemy had fallen, leaving behind the all too familiar trembling hands, sour mouth and aching limbs.

That feeling of despondency had remained with them as they travelled north. The king of the East Angelfolc was sorely wounded and the men left behind their kin and country to be trampled and abused at the hands of Penda and his Mercian wolves. The sound of laughter was rare aboard *Saeslaga* as they tacked against the relentless wind that seemed to want to hold them away, as if the gods themselves were pushing them back to confront what they had left behind.

"There is no sign of wound-rot?" Beobrand asked. "No fever?"

"No," Coenred said. "The king is feeling much better. The good Lord has answered my prayers and I am sure Anna will return to full health soon."

"Go," Beobrand said to Offa. "Tell your men the good news." Offa needed no encouragement. His joy at these good tidings was evident on his face. He hurried into the belly of the ship, where the East Angelfolc were huddled together. Beobrand watched them while Offa told them of their king's health. The usually dour men nodded and smiled.

"It is a good thing you have done there," Beobrand said to Coenred.

"It is God who has healed the king," he replied. "Anna is a good follower of the Christ and it is God who has made him well. I am merely the instrument of the Almighty's healing."

"Well, it is good for the king that you were there to act as your God's instrument." Beobrand glanced back at the stretched leather that served as an awning over the men Coenred was treating for their injuries. He was scared to enquire after the other patient, but he took in a deep breath of the cool salty air. Gripping the stay tightly, he prepared himself for the worst.

"And Cuthbert?" he asked. "How does the boy do?"

Coenred puffed out his cheeks before letting out a long sigh.

"He is recovering well," he said.

"He will keep the leg?" asked Beobrand. Dark thoughts of the boy needing to have the leg removed had plagued his dreams.

"Cuthbert will keep his leg," replied Coenred. "He might limp a bit. The blow to his knee was quite severe. But other than a hitch in his step, God willing, he should make a full recovery." The monk fell silent and stared out at the grey swell of the sea. "He believes I am an angel," he said at last.

"An angel?"

"A messenger from God," said Coenred, his cheeks flushing. "I have tried to tell him I am no such thing, that I am just a monk whom God has seen fit to use as his means to heal the sick and infirm here on middle earth, but Cuthbert will have none of it." Coenred looked genuinely embarrassed by the boy's insistence that he was some otherworldly creature. "He keeps asking to see my wings."

Beobrand could not hold back his laughter, and several of the crew and King Anna's hearth-warriors looked at him as his guffaws rang out over the rush of the waves and the creaking of the ship's timbers.

Relief at hearing of the boy's recovery warmed him like the wine, but as his laughter subsided, his face clouded.

"The boy is not moon-touched, is he?" asked Beobrand. "Did he damage his head in the fight?" He had seen men take blows to the head and never be the same again. He glanced at Fraomar, his feelings tinged with the ever-present guilt at the warrior's wound.

"I do not think so," replied Coenred.

"And yet he believes you to be an angel." Beobrand could not keep his smirk from his face.

"Well, yes, but his mind is sound," said Coenred. "And I do not think Cuthbert is mad to think such things."

Confused now, Beobrand turned to face his friend.

"Are you saying that you are in fact an angel?"

"Of course not," said Coenred, flushing at the suggestion. "But there are more things under heaven than we can understand. Perhaps an angel came to him in his need while I tended to his wound."

"But you did not see this magical creature?" asked Beobrand, touching the Thunor's hammer amulet at his neck to ward off any magic that might be abroad on the ship.

Coenred was silent for a time. He looked up at the sail as it strained and billowed. It was dark against the red glow of the last light of the day.

"Do you see the wind?" he asked. "And yet, it is strong enough to blow this ship across the waves. Perhaps, as close to death as he was, Cuthbert could see the spirits and angels that are all around us."

Beobrand spat over the side of the ship into the foaming surf and touched the hammer amulet again.

"Perhaps," he said, his voice uncertain.

"Well, angel or no angel," said Coenred, apparently happy to move the conversation on, "Cuthbert was wavering at the doors of death for a time and now he is much better. I think this is something we can both be thankful for."

And indeed Beobrand was thankful. The thought that he had led the boy to his doom in East Angeln had preyed on his mind and disturbed his dreams. To know that Cuthbert would live lifted the oppressive weight of responsibility from his shoulders.

Beobrand was still smiling when the land to the west grew dark. The mood on the ship had improved vastly and the sight of the crag of Bebbanburg, topped with the great timber fortress and its palisades and watch towers, lifted their spirits yet higher.

"With any luck," shouted Ferenbald, "we will be dining in the great hall of King Oswiu this night." He grinned as his expert crew did his bidding to catch what wind they could to take them towards the beach beneath the walls of Bebbanburg. "And I am the luckiest man you will ever know!" The men roared with delight at Ferenbald's bravado and Beobrand joined in their celebratory cheers.

Men often referred to him as being lucky, and Beobrand loathed the term. His life had been just as full of loss and sorrow as luck and success. And what defined luck? Did wyrd determine whether a man would obtain fame and glory, or did a man's own mettle forge his path? He glanced back at Ferenbald, grinning and shouting from the helm. Beobrand knew not the answers, but he had sailed with Ferenbald enough to know that if anyone deserved the title of lucky, it was *Saeslaga*'s skipper. He was also skilled and brave, and never turned away from a challenge. Perhaps that was why he succeeded where others would fail.

Beobrand gazed up at the shadowed shape of the fortress of Bebbanburg. He had been avoiding the place for too long. He did not relish the thought of climbing the steps to where he was bound to face Oswiu and Eanflæd, but he had no choice now. And, as Ferenbald steered *Saeslaga* skillfully into the shadows beneath Bebbanburg's looming walls, even the thought of having to confront Oswiu's wrath and Eanflæd's studious indifference could do nothing to dampen his good humour.

True to his word, Ferenbald's luck held. The wind shifted into the east, allowing *Saeslaga* to skim over the waves of the incoming tide, riding high up the sand of the beach between other ships and boats dotting the strand. Above them, the sky was the colour of hot bronze and the walls of the fortress were dark. Sparks of light began to flicker there as torches were lit. They would be climbing up to Bebbanburg in the dark.

As he jumped from the ship and his feet splashed into the surf, feeling the give of the soft sand beneath, Beobrand had a sudden sense of having lived this moment before. He glanced up at the imposing sight of the seat of the kings of Bernicia, remembering a day far in the past when a much younger man had arrived on this very beach.

Ferenbald shouted at his crew to stop their dallying and set to heaving the ship higher up the sand. The sound of his voice, so like his father Hrothgar, served to further transport Beobrand into the past. He had been little more than a boy, the same age as Cuthbert, when he had first seen Bebbanburg. That boy had been filled with pain and the anticipation of seeing his brother, Octa. He sighed. His anguish had soon increased and he had never seen Octa again.

"Beo," Coenred called to him and he turned. "Help me with Cuthbert."

The boy was leaning against the monk, his skin pallid and his eyes bright. But he was upright, and seeing him thus made Beobrand smile. He shook his head, moving back to the side of the ship to help the young gesith climb down. Had he really been as young as Cuthbert when he had come to Bernicia? It seemed a lifetime ago. Where had the years gone? He would be a grandfather soon. By the gods, how that news had made Bassus laugh.

"Call *me* old now, will you?" he had said, slapping Beobrand hard on the back with his one powerful hand.

Beobrand was still unsure of his own feelings on the matter. He was happy for Ardith and Brinin, and yet the idea awoke a sadness within him. All he had ever wanted was peace and a family to call his own. But however he tried, he could not cling on to love. Sunniva and Reaghan were both ash. He could never have Eanflæd. His son was a stranger to him, and Ardith was distant, another stranger who shared his blood.

Wading into the cold water, he reached up to where Coenred and Cuthbert waited. He lifted Cuthbert down easily, again marvelling at how light he was. Still, the boy was alive and recovering. Coenred swung his legs over the wale and dropped down with a splash.

The monk took in a deep breath.

"It is good to breathe the air of Bernicia once more," he said.

Beobrand nodded, forcing himself to push aside his maudlin

thoughts. He had travelled south to rescue Coenred. He had been successful, and returned with so much more; a king no less.

He glanced over to where Offa was coordinating the East Angelfolc. They lifted their king down. They were attempting to convince him to sit atop his shield, so that they might carry him, but he waved them away.

"I am your king," he said, "and I will lead you. I do not mean to be borne into the fortress of Bebbanburg like an invalid."

The men grumbled, but Offa barked orders and they fell into line behind King Anna.

Beobrand called out to Eadgard. The giant axeman trotted through the shallow surf.

"Think you can carry Cuthbert up there?" He indicated with his head in the direction of the brooding buildings high above them.

"This one weighs no more than a lamb," Eadgard replied. "I could carry him all the way to Ubbanford if you want."

"I will walk," said Cuthbert. "I am your gesith, not an invalid." Beobrand grunted at hearing the king's words echoed by the boy.

"That you are, Cuthbert," he said, smiling to take the sting from what he was about to say. "You are my man, and I command you to allow Eadgard to bear you up to the fortress. When you are well again, you will walk, and fight, but for now, you will do my bidding."

Cuthbert frowned.

"The sooner you recover," said Beobrand, "the sooner you will be of use to me once more. The gods alone know how long until we will be called upon to fight again. I will need all my gesithas then."

At the talk of battle, Cuthbert seemed to grow even paler, but he nodded. With Coenred's help, he clambered onto Eadgard's back and they set off towards the steps that led up to the fortress.

Beobrand hurried over to where the men of East Angeln were

gathered around their king. Anna was leaning on Offa's shoulder. His jaw was set, his face the colour of milk.

"Lord king," said Beobrand, "it gives me great joy to see you on your feet."

"Praise be to the Lord and to your friend the monk there. Without his skills, I fear I would have been carried thence to Bebbanburg," he gestured at the shield his men had prepared for the purpose, "for the dead cannot protest." Offa and several of the East Angelfolc made the sign of the rood over their chests. Some spat into the sand. They did not like this talk of their king's death.

"Well, I am glad that you will not need to be carried," said Beobrand. He looked up to where Eadgard, with Cuthbert on his back like a great sack, was beginning to mount the stairs that were hewn into the rock. Grindan, Eadgard's brother, was with them. "But it will be dark soon and the steps can be treacherous," he fixed Offa in his gaze, his meaning clear. "Take care not to slip. And allow me to lead you."

Offa and King Anna nodded and they all set off, leaving Ferenbald and his crew to secure *Saeslaga* above the tide-line.

It was full dark when they arrived, dishevelled and tired from the climb, at the door to the fortress. Word of the royal visitor must have reached the inhabitants of Bebbanburg, for the gates were open, when usually they would have been closed to the night. The courtyard beyond was lit with bright torches and several braziers and it thronged with people. Beobrand's heart clenched as he surveyed the faces of the folk gathered there to welcome the king of East Angeln.

Eanflæd stood beside her husband. Her eyes glittered like jewels in the flame light, and Beobrand found himself drinking in the sight of her. Her radiance was brighter than any of the torches or fires. Her skin glowed. Her lips shone, so temptingly. He remembered the taste of them. The queen wore an elegant dress of blue linen, edged with cream-coloured silk. The fabric clung to her form. He would never forget the sensation of her slender curves pressed against him. His chest tightened, as it always did when he saw her. By Woden, he should have headed directly back to Ubbanford. But that was not possible. He had brought the king of the East Angelfolc to Bernicia and it was his duty to see him safely within the walls of Bebbanburg.

Forcing himself to look away from Eanflæd with difficulty, Beobrand swallowed against the dryness in his throat to see Oswiu staring directly at him. The king had aged these last months. Grey streaked his beard and the hair at his temples. Oswiu narrowed his eyes, but Beobrand could not read his expression.

Beobrand became aware of an awkward stillness. Everyone was looking at him expectantly. Taking a deep breath, he squared his shoulders and drew himself up to his full height. He towered over all those gathered there apart from Eadgard, who had moved to one side with Cuthbert and Grindan, clearly anxious to be out of the gaze of the king and queen and their retinue.

"My lord king," Beobrand said, "I have the great joy of introducing you to the rightful king of the folk of East Angeln." He turned to where Offa, red-faced and sweating despite the cool breeze from the sea, held his king upright. Anna, sheened with sweat, trembled beside the thegn. Beobrand was sure that if Offa were to release his hold on him, the king would collapse. By the gods, the man's stubbornness might well cause his death, he thought.

"Anna, son of Eni," said Beobrand, "king of all the people of the East Angelfolc, this is Oswiu, son of Æthelfrith, lord king of Bernicia."

"You are well come to Bebbanburg," said Oswiu.

"I thank you, lord king," said Anna, his voice wavering

and quiet and nothing like his usual forceful, confident tone. Beobrand caught Offa's eye and the older man gave a slight shake of his head. "You are most gracious to allow me to stay here," Anna went on. "I seem to have lost my own kingdom." His voice cracked and his legs gave way beneath him. Offa struggled to hold him and Oswiu leapt forward. He stumbled and grimaced as if in pain, though Beobrand could see no cause. There was a moment of confusion as Anna's hearth-warriors jostled for the right to support their king.

"Stand back," growled Offa, leaving just one burly warrior on the other side of Anna. Between the two of them, the king would not fall. But his head lolled and he appeared to have swooned.

Oswiu was shocked by what he saw.

"The king is wounded!" he shouted. "Why is he walking and not carried?" He looked accusingly first at Offa, who merely shook his head, and then, increasingly angry, at Beobrand.

"The king refused to be borne by his men," Beobrand said. "He insisted he would meet you not as an invalid, but as a fellow king."

Oswiu frowned. Beobrand noted that he was leaning slightly to the side, favouring his left foot.

"Well, he has done that now," Oswiu said. "I pray to God his pride, and the weakness of those who should offer him counsel, have not been his undoing." The East Angelfolc grumbled, but Oswiu ignored them. This was his fortress and his land. He cared nought for the feelings of warriors of a sick king who had lost his kingdom. "Brytnere," he snapped, "see to it that King Anna and his people are given lodging. And have Utta attend the king."

Coenred stepped forward from where he had stood in the shadows near Cuthbert.

"I will tend to the king's wounds, if it pleases you, lord," he said. His voice was steady in the face of Oswiu's anger. Beobrand felt a glow of pride for his friend. He had changed much in the years since they had first met. The Coenred who stood before Oswiu now was far from the scared boy Beobrand had encountered at Engelmynster. Oswiu glowered at Coenred before waving him away. "Very well. I know you are skilled in the arts of healing. Ensure that King Anna recovers."

"I will tend to him to the best of my abilities," said Coenred, his tone sombre. "If God wills it, he will get well."

Oswiu fixed him with a hard stare.

"Then pray that it is God's will," he snarled.

After Brytnere, Bebbanburg's steward, had led the men of East Angeln away, Oswiu rounded on Beobrand.

"You fool," he spat, his voice a sibilant hiss. "What have you done?"

Beobrand could feel the eyes upon him of all those gathered at the gates. His gesithas squirmed. Over Oswiu's shoulder, Beobrand caught a glimpse of Eanflæd's beauty. He swallowed and looked away from her. He could not afford the distraction. Looking down, he met Oswiu's glower with his ice-cold stare.

"Lord, I have brought to your hall an ally king," he said, keeping his tone even.

"You dared to openly battle in my name in another kingdom?" The king was furious.

Beobrand did not alter his tone or expression. He knew how easily he could infuriate the king and some part of him revelled in it. Perhaps, he thought, he had not grown so much in the years since first he had come here as a boy after all.

"I fought in my name, lord," he said. "And in the name of God," he added, knowing that Oswiu could not dispute the righteousness of saving the Christ-following king.

For a long moment, Oswiu did not reply. He bunched his hands into fists and Beobrand wondered whether the king meant to strike him.

At last Oswiu shook his head.

"You care nothing for God. This was for your own ends." He

peered at Beobrand, as if he could see his thoughts. "Why did you go to East Angeln?" he asked.

Beobrand contemplated lying or saying something that would antagonise Oswiu. But he pushed aside the idea as that of a fool. Was he baiting the king because he was jealous of him? What did he hope to gain from this? He swallowed the bitterness that flooded his mouth whenever he saw Eanflæd and Oswiu together. This was a deadly game he played.

"I heard of Penda's attack. I knew that Coenred was there. He is my friend. I owe him my life."

"And your life is mine," replied the king, whispering the words past his clenched jaw.

Beobrand nodded. Oswiu had his oath, it was true.

"I could not leave Coenred to be slain," he went on. "When we arrived, we found King Anna battling against a band of Mercians. It seemed like the right thing to bring them north. I thought you would wish to have an ally king here with you."

"You had no authority," hissed Oswiu. He drew in a deep breath, calming himself with difficulty. He stared at Beobrand, perhaps thinking about the pieces on the tafl board of the kingdoms of Albion that the thegn of Bebbanburg had moved. "By bringing Anna here," Oswiu said at last, "you will have diverted Penda's ire at the shaming of his sister in our direction. We have no need of further enemies. We have our fair share."

"Penda is already our enemy," said Beobrand, looking about him.

It was dark now, and the soot on the walls could not be seen. Although much of the palisade had been rebuilt, there were still sections that bore the scars of the fire Penda had lit at the gates in an attempt to raze the fortress. When the sun shone on Bebbanburg, the reminder of Penda's enmity was clear.

"By Christ's bones, man, do you think I do not know that? But we have a battle to fight now, without having to contend with Penda too."

Oswiu's words jarred and Beobrand thought for a heartbeat.

"Oswine has moved against you?"

"Yes," replied Oswiu, his face stern. "It would seem he has finally found the bravery to meet us once more in the field." Beobrand thought of the constant Bernician harrying of the borderlands with Deira, the steadings burnt, the crops trampled, cattle driven north. The ceorls and freemen murdered all in the name of a war that Oswine of Deira never wanted. Beobrand said nothing.

Oswiu shifted his weight, wincing as if in pain. Again, Beobrand noted how the king limped when he moved. He wondered at it, but could not bring himself to enquire as to Oswiu's health.

"Wulfstan has amassed a host and marched towards the Wall," the king went on. "Alhfrith and Ethelwin have ridden to meet him at Corebricg, but I want you there too. After all, it is your own failure to follow my commands that has led us here." Beobrand tensed, but did not react to the king's goading. Oswiu too, it seemed, enjoyed riling Beobrand. "This will give you a chance to finish what you should have done years ago," Oswiu said, a cruel glint in his eye. He knew that Wulfstan was Beobrand's friend and no doubt had his suspicions about what had occurred at Ediscum. "A chance to avenge Heremod and Fordraed's thegns." Beobrand held Oswiu's gaze without blinking. Whatever Oswiu might suspect, none of Fordraed's men yet lived, and the dead did not talk.

"Of course, lord," Beobrand replied. "I will do my duty, as ever. But you do not ride with us?"

Oswiu tensed.

"It would seem the good Lord has seen fit to test me in many ways," he said. "Alas, I cannot walk, let alone fight."

"What ails you, lord?"

Oswiu waved the question away.

"It is just my foot. It troubles me from time to time. It will heal soon enough, as it has before, but until it does, I would be of no use in the shieldwall."

"I am sorry, lord," Beobrand said. "Your presence will be missed when we stand against the Deiran host."

Beobrand wondered at the king's illness. It would be a loss indeed not to have him in the shieldwall when battle commenced. Oswiu was a brave warrior and a strong leader. Morale would suffer.

"The Almighty will restore my health, but your king had need of you two days ago when my son and warmaster rode forth." Oswiu scowled at Beobrand. He could see the pain hidden in the king's pinched glare and his simmering anger. "You should have been with them, Beobrand," he went on. "I sent word to Ubbanford. Imagine my surprise when I heard that one of my thegns, the great Beobrand, and his Black Shields were not in Bernicia at all, not where their king thought them to be, but far to the south on an errand I knew nothing of."

"I left Cynan at Ubbanford, lord," replied Beobrand, "with most of my men. Cynan is a good man."

"So you say." Oswiu frowned. "Well, you know my thoughts on the matter. That Waelisc man of yours is not one to be trusted."

Beobrand felt his ire kindling within him.

"But lord, Cynan has ever been true to me and to you. He has proven his worth many times in battle. He is as loyal as any man I know. I would trust him with my life."

"Well, perhaps with your *life*," replied Oswiu, with a sardonic smile, "but I do not think you should trust him to protect your lands."

"I do not understand your meaning, lord," replied Beobrand. He could make no sense of Oswiu's words, but a sliver of disquiet traced down his spine.

"You are lucky that you have honest Bernician men like Elmer to lead your gesithas when you are away. But I think your trust of that Waelisc upstart is misplaced."

Beobrand's unease grew.

"Lord? Has something happened to Cynan?"

"Happened to him?" Oswiu shook his head. "I would not know. But he was not where he should have been. And neither were you. My messenger returned to tell me that your Black Shields, led by Elmer, had answered my call, but that you were chasing monks in East Angeln."

"And Cynan?"

Oswiu shrugged.

"That treacherous Waelisc cur has ridden into the west. Back to his people I dare say."

Chapter 11

Cynan nudged Mierawin into a trot. He dared not urge the mare to further speed for fear that one of the horses might become injured in the darkness. The moon was bright and there were few clouds to hide its light, so when the ground was open, they could see their path well enough. But there were many dips and swells, fords over burbling streams, and gnarled trees and bracken grew thick beside the track the riders followed. The moon shadows were impenetrable and could easily hide a rut, a sharp stone, a twisted root or even a badger's sett. If one of their mounts should break a leg or pull up lame, this quest would be over before it began. He did not like to ride at night, but he'd had no choice.

When Bassus discovered what Cynan had done, he would be furious. He might attempt to follow them. Cynan hoped that Ardith would prove persuasive enough to waylay any pursuit. Gods knew she had been convincing earlier when she had come to the barn where Sulis was being held.

Scanning the ground ahead for any obstacle that might hurt the horses, Cynan shook his head in the darkness. By the gods, how had it come to this? Not so long before he had been talking to Sulis in the quiet gloom of the storage hut, and now he was leading a small group into the west to face an unknown foe. And for what? He glanced behind him at his companions, their faces pale smudges in the dark. He could make them out well enough by their size and how they rode. Sulis was in the middle of them. Was he a fool to jeopardise all he had for this woman? Probably. But that was a risk he had chosen to take. Now he also had two others to worry about. Beobrand had warned him that to lead men was difficult. Cynan had not truly understood his lord then. But now he knew the weight of responsibility and he wondered if he would ever be content to lead others into danger. Truth be told, he hoped he would never cease to be concerned for the men and women who put their lives in his hands, for what sort of man would he be then?

He waited for the first rider to catch up and then kicked Mierawin on again, falling into step beside Ingwald astride his dumpy gelding.

"How far will we go tonight?" asked Ingwald, keeping his voice quiet so that only Cynan would hear him.

"Far enough."

They rode on in silence.

"We could still go back," the older man said. Cynan could barely make out his words over the horses' hooves and the jangle of the harness.

"I am not turning around," he said. "I told you as much already. But you are free to return. And take Brinin with you. You would be doing me a service."

"My place is at your side, lord." Cynan could hear the smile in his words at the use of the title. "And it would be no service to you if I were to leave you to face an enemy alone."

"But what enemy?" Cynan asked, not expecting an answer. He thought back to what Sulis had told him. He was resigned to aid her, he had known it as soon as he had entered the dark barn and seen her face in the lamp light. He could never turn away from helping her.

"You say they took her boy?"

Cynan nodded in the dark.

"Yes. And they killed a bondsman too. And beat her man till he was almost dead."

"All for silver?"

"No, for lead, which it seems can buy a man silver." Sulis had recounted how her husband had found a cave on their land. And in that cave he had found old tools, long abandoned. But the rusted picks and spades had shown him that men had been there, though gods knew when, for he had never heard of any man digging into the earth there and he had lived in those parts all his life, as had his father and his father's father.

They rode on for a way, cresting a hill and gazing down onto an open moorland. There was no sign of campfires in the dark. Good, if they did not light a fire, they would be invisible to any pursuers, at least until dawn.

"So tell me," said Ingwald, "how does a man take lead from the ground?"

"I do not know." Cynan swerved Mierawin to avoid a dark pool of shadow beneath a spreading ash tree. "We can ask Sulis' husband when we get there. She said that he spoke to a holy man who found some ancient parchments with all manner of knowledge. The priest, it seems, was able to discover the secret of how to bring forth the lead from the stone."

"And why does she think her son was taken? And her husband attacked?"

"I don't know why," said a woman's voice in the darkness. Both men shifted in their saddles, surprised to see that Sulis had caught up with them. She rode the small pony she had ridden into Ubbanford the afternoon before. "They were both at the cave when it happened," she continued. Cynan had heard her account of events before, but he listened intently and said nothing. It was good that Ingwald should hear it for himself. Cynan pulled gently on Mierawin's reins, slowing the animal almost imperceptibly so that Brinin, the final rider, would be able to close the gap and hear Sulis' tale in her own words. If they were to risk everything for this woman whom they did not know, they should hear what she had to say.

"They were meant to have returned before sundown, but dusk came and there was no sign of them." Sulis' voice held the sharp edge of despair as she recalled that night. "I wanted to ride out then, in the darkness, but Alfwold would not let me."

"Alfwold?" asked Ingwald.

"My husband's bondsman. He tends the sheep in the high pasture and helps about the place. Alfwold made me wait until morning. I did not sleep that night. I knew something terrible had happened. I was sure they were both dead." She shivered. "We rode out into the hills before dawn and when I saw Leofman lying there beside our cart and no sound or sign of Eadwig…" Sulis' voice trailed off and for a time they rode in silence as she composed her thoughts. Cynan turned to see Brinin riding close now. After a long while, Sulis continued. "I thought the worst at first," she said, her voice jagged from the memory. "Leofman was so pale. But then he groaned. They had hurt him so badly," her words caught in her throat, turning to a sob. She sniffed and none of the men looked at her in the darkness. "But my husband had put up a fight. He told us he had injured one of the men who had attacked him. Cut his arm with his seax."

"He knew who they were?" Brinin asked.

"Yes," she said, and her voice was hollow. "He said they were Sidrac's men."

"Sidrac?" said Brinin.

"He is the son of Tohrwulf, the local ealdorman."

"I know ealdorman Tohrwulf," said Cynan. "He was at Caer Luel after Maserfelth. He must be very old now."

"He is," she hissed. "Old and drunk. His sons rule his lands now, as if their father were already dead."

"Perhaps," replied Cynan. "But he is yet a lord of Bernicia and he must follow the king's laws. As must his sons. We will see this wrong put right. This Sidrac will pay the weregild for what he has done."

She did not reply but he thought he saw her shaking her head in the darkness.

"And what of my Eadwig?"

"Sidrac will return your son to you."

"But why did they take the boy?" asked Ingwald. "And why attack your husband?"

"I do not know the answer to these things," she replied, her tone bitter. "Why do men ever do the things they do? I struggled to get sense out of Leofman when we found him, but he said it was something to do with the land. The land and the lead. There are riches to be made from the metal and Sidrac is a greedy man, everyone knows it. But why he took Eadwig, I do not know."

She fell silent and they rode on into the night. Cynan scoured the dark land for a suitable place for them to make camp.

"It was madness to ride all this way," he said into the darkness, "alone and with child."

"Perhaps," Sulis replied. "Madness or desperation. Who knows? I have changed, Cynan. I have been happy these last years, where I never thought I would find contentment again. But I am still the same woman you knew. I am no man's to be threatened or commanded." Her voice took on a hard, sharp quality which made him think of splintering ice. "If I could, I would ride in search of the men who did this thing," she said. "I would kill them myself. But alas, I was born into the body of a woman and I have not the strength or the skill for such things."

Cynan could think of few stronger than this small woman who rode beside him in the night.

"But I do?"

"Yes, Cynan," she replied. "You do."

He wondered at the nature of things. It was true that men were stronger and wielded the power over life and death of the people of middle earth, and yet, was it not the women who truly commanded them? Sulis had asked for his aid and now three warriors rode into the west at her bidding. And was it not another young woman who had convinced them to this course of action?

He recalled the door of the barn grating as it was pulled open. The lamp light had splashed onto Ardith's face. She had her father's direct, icy gaze and she had stared at them both for a time before entering and demanding to know Sulis' story.

On hearing of the woman's plight, Ardith had stood, smoothing her dress over her swelling belly.

"I will speak with my father and make him understand," she said with a certainty that reminded Cynan of Beobrand.

"You think I should go with her?" Cynan asked, his tone incredulous. He had thought she might try to dissuade him.

Ardith nodded.

"Beobrand will understand," she said. Cynan thought that unlikely. "When I was in need of aid," she went on, holding her gaze on Sulis, "he came for me." She turned to look at Cynan, her eyes gleaming by the flame of the small lamp. "Would he want a man of his to turn his back on a woman in distress?"

"You don't understand," Cynan said. "She was his thrall." He glanced over at where Sulis sat in the corner. "She is the murderer of his woman."

Ardith's eyes had narrowed.

"Those are obstacles that can be surmounted."

Cynan had been confused.

"You are a wealthy man," Ardith said.

After that the plan had quickly fallen into place. It made sense, but Cynan knew Beobrand well enough to know he would be furious at having been duped. And the women of Ubbanford would be resentful of him and Ardith. Cynan had told her as much.

"I will deal with Rowena and the others," Ardith said. "And with my father. I will agree with him the weregild for Reaghan's death and the price he paid for Sulis, and vouch that you will pay him the silver on your return."

Thinking about the conversation now, Cynan wondered at the reception he would get if he returned. He doubted Beobrand would forgive him easily. Perhaps this was madness after all. If it had been foolish for Sulis to ride eastward, how much more foolish was it of him to ride towards danger, leaving behind an angry lord and a depleted hoard of silver?

But Ardith's words had pierced his guard easily enough. The truth was that he had already made his decision when Beobrand's daughter had arrived, and her suggestion had provided him with an elegant solution and an unexpected ally.

"Very well," he'd said. "Agree the blood-price and the cost of Sulis' freedom with your father." He had turned his attention to Sulis then, who had been sitting in silence as they talked. "I will go with you to Rheged."

"I cannot thank you enough," she'd said. "If I am able in the future, I will repay you."

He shook his head.

"The silver is not important." Angering his lord was though, but he did not speak the words. "I am but one man," he said. "I am not certain what I will be able to achieve."

"You will not be only one man," said a voice from the shadows beside the door. It was Brinin, Ardith's husband, the smith. His face caught the dim light, showing the dark scar that traced his cheek. "I will go with you," he said.

Ardith had paled and pulled the young smith outside into the darkness. There had followed a whispered argument between the couple. Cynan snorted to remember it now. Brinin was a brave man, of that there was no doubt, and it seemed that in spite of her strong will and cold glare, Ardith did not always get her way. After the heated exchange, in which Ardith reminded Brinin that she was carrying his child, their firstborn, and that he should not seek to place himself in danger, Brinin had finally said, "So, it is all very well for you to send Cynan away to risk his life, but if I feel I should join him, I should not go? This woman is with child too. Would you want a stranger to turn his back on you, if you needed help?"

Ardith had glowered at him then. Tears streaked her face when at last she nodded and embraced her husband.

Ingwald had not bothered to say he would be going with Cynan too. He was his oath-sworn man. No words were needed.

Once the decision had been taken, they had gathered up their things quickly and quietly in the darkness. Most of the people of Ubbanford were yet in the great hall on the hill and nobody stumbled upon them as they prepared to leave. They had mounted up and ridden out before the moon was at its zenith. The only person watching them go had been Ardith. She had not cried any more, but clung for a long time to Brinin, whispering urgently into his ear words that he alone could hear.

Cynan surveyed the dark horizon ahead. He thought he remembered a stream flowing from a stand of alder that would serve well as a campsite and would shelter them from view. They trotted down a steep slope and laboured up an even sharper incline. There was no conversation now. They were all tired and Cynan wondered what the others were thinking. Were they silently berating themselves for following him on this fool's errand? Questions swarmed his mind like angry bees. But he did not voice them. The night was wrapped about them like a shroud and his concerns would keep until the morning.

They pressed on, but the alder wood he was expecting must have been further than he had remembered, for there was no sign of the trees for a long time. Perhaps he had been mistaken and there was no such copse. They needed to rest soon. Sulis' head was nodding and Cynan thought he had heard Ingwald snoring in his saddle. They could not continue for much longer like this. He had begun to think they would need to make camp somewhere else, when finally he saw the moonlight picking out the swaying branches of the alders. As they grew close, he heard the rustle of the wind through the boughs and the calming burble of the water that flowed from the hills along a dark gully.

They made their way under the shelter of the trees. Here, nobody would see them from afar. With any luck, they could sleep without being disturbed before setting out once more into the south-west. Sulis slid from her pony with a moan. Holding her lower back, she staggered into the bushes. When she returned, the men had already removed the horses' saddles and were brushing down the animals with handfuls of dried grass. Cynan was adamant that they must do this, no matter how tired they might be.

"We have a long way to travel on horseback," he said.

Ingwald did not comment. He was used to his hlaford's insistence on care of their mounts. Brinin groaned. Perhaps he was already regretting his decision to go against Ardith, Cynan pondered.

"If you treat your horse well, it will serve you well when needed," Cynan said. "When you are done with that, Brinin, take them to the stream to drink."

"What should I do?" asked Sulis. Her face was pale in the gloom, her eyes dark. Her voice bore the weight of all that had happened to her in the last few days. She was exhausted.

"Here," Cynan said, passing her a blanket. "You need to rest now, so that we can ride on in the morning. We'll keep watch."

She hesitated, then shook out the blanket, and, wrapping it around her, lay down in the tall, thick grasses that grew close to the trees.

"Get some sleep," whispered Cynan to Ingwald. "I will take the first watch."

Ingwald yawned.

"Wake me when you can no longer keep your eyes open."

He did not wait for a reply, but stretched out in the lee of the twisted trunk of an alder. He pulled his cloak about him, shifted his position, and started to snore. Brinin came back with the horses. Cynan took the reins from him and whispered that he should rest.

He tethered the horses beneath the trees and settled himself with his back to a broad bole. From this position he could watch the path they had followed. He listened to the night. The wind's murmured whispers through the leaves of the trees; an owl's hoot, far away to the south; the trickle of water over the pebbles in the stream bed. After a long time, a movement in the dark drew his attention. His hand dropped to the hilt of his seax, but a moment later he smiled. It was a fox. The animal crept close to their camp, sniffing the air. Cynan stood and the fox halted its stealthy approach, staring at him. A heartbeat later, it turned and with a bounding, unhurried run that sent its tail bobbing behind it, it vanished.

All the while, Cynan's head teemed with thoughts and questions, but he could come up with no answers. When his eyelids were drooping and he had caught himself on the verge of sleep more than once, he roused Ingwald silently and lay down in the warm place he had left in the crushed lush grass.

It felt to him as though he had only just closed his eyes when he was being roused by a hand shaking him. He jolted awake, looking about him, confused and groggy from sleep. The land was suffused with the wolf-pelt grey of dawn.

"Lord," hissed the voice of the man who had awoken him. It was Brinin. Cynan glanced about them. The horses were hulking shadows beneath the alders. Ingwald and Sulis were both asleep. The long blades of grass were wet with dew.

"What is it?" Cynan whispered.

The scar that ran along Brinin's face was dark and grim in the dawn light. He was pointing into the east where the sun was lightening the sky.

"Someone is coming."

Chapter 12

Beobrand and his Black Shields rode southward on borrowed steeds. Offa and six of King Anna's hearth-warriors travelled with them. Oswiu's men had rescued the king and he now resided behind the protection of the walls of Bebbanburg, so Offa and the others were Anna's gesture of goodwill to his Bernician ally. The message was clear: as East Angeln's enemies were Bernicia's, so Bernicia's foes would be fought by the East Angelfolc.

They had left at first light and Beobrand could almost feel Oswiu's glare boring into his back as he'd watched them ride away from the palisade. Despite playing down his ailment, there was no denying that the king was in too much pain to travel, let alone fight. His frustration at his inability to lead the Bernician warhost against Oswine and the Deirans had made Oswiu even more foul-tempered than usual.

As they had saddled the horses in the dawn, Grindan had voiced aloud what perhaps others were thinking.

"It seems passing strange to me that after all this time seeking war with Oswine, Oswiu should now be unable to fight," he said, tightening the cinch beneath a chestnut stallion's belly. Eadgard nodded. He never refuted what his brother said.

"Remember Maserfelth?" he rumbled. "No sign of Oswiu there, either."

"He was happy enough to be at Din Eidyn," said Ulf, leading the stocky dun mare he had been given out into the shadowed courtyard.

"And Cair Chaladain," said Attor, swinging himself up lithely onto his mount's back. "God knows he was not shy to wet his blade then."

He raised an eyebrow, his crude double meaning clear.

Offa and Anna's men readied their horses in silence, but they were listening intently.

"Enough!" snapped Beobrand. "Oswiu is our king and he is no craven." His men looked at him strangely, but had said no more, instead busying themselves with preparing their gear and horses.

As they cantered south, Beobrand thought about the incident. It was true that the king had not brought the promised reinforcements to Maserfelth and many good men had died there, including Oswiu's older brother and king at the time, Oswald. And at Cair Chaladain, Oswiu had revelled in the wanton abuse of the Pictish women after the battle had been won. Spoils of war, he said. The warriors' due. Beobrand disdained him for that. And yet he had seen Oswiu fight at the centre of many shieldwalls. He had stood alone with him in the dark against assassins who had been sent to kill Beobrand, but had only succeeded in slaying Fordraed and starting the war with Deira. No, the king was no coward. But was that why he had spoken out in his defence?

The truth of it was that seeing Eanflæd standing at Oswiu's side, his arm about her waist as she led him limping back to the hall where they sat together at the high table, Beobrand had been filled with a dreadful burning jealousy. This was why he stayed away from Bebbanburg. And yet that was not all. He loathed seeing the king and queen together, for not only did it make him envious of their bond, their intimacy; the shared affection of husband and wife. He was also overcome with a cutting sense of guilt. She was not his woman and yet he yearned for her, and he knew that seeing him caused her pain too.

His men suspected his secret, he was sure. He trusted them to keep it. And yet he could not abide them speaking out against their king when it was he who had done wrong, not Oswiu. His gesithas' loyalty heartened him, but made him acutely aware of his own shortcomings.

The men sensed his dark mood and did not attempt to coax him into conversation as they rode towards the Wall.

At midday, they rested at Alnwic, a small collection of buildings where Deira Stræt crossed the River Aln. After fording the river, they had dismounted and eaten some of the provisions Oswiu's steward, Brytnere, had given them.

Beobrand sat beside the river, chewing on a hunk of rye bread. He found a piece of grit in the bread and spat it out into the water. A shadow fell over him and he looked up. It was Attor.

"Don't worry about the lad," he said.

Beobrand sighed.

"Which one?" he asked.

The slender warrior grinned and lowered himself down beside Beobrand.

"Cuthbert," he said. "He's a good boy."

Beobrand nodded.

"Yes, he is. And eager too!" Cuthbert had been furious when Beobrand had told him he could not ride with them.

"Aye. He takes his duty to his oath more seriously than most, that's for certain." Beobrand frowned, flicking a glance at where Offa sat with his men. Attor held up his hands in apology as he saw Beobrand's expression and realised how he might construe his words to be referring to Beobrand's own oath that had been shattered on a warm afternoon in Ediscum in a welter of blood. "I just meant that Cuthbert is an earnest boy, that is all. Still," he went on, meeting Beobrand's cold gaze, "the young find being earnest so much easier than the old."

Beobrand chuckled without mirth.

"Are we old then?"

"Well, you are to be a grandfather soon, lord," Attor smiled. "But you have a few years in you yet, I think. I have passed forty summers and I tell you, I feel those years now. When I awake on a cold morning, I can feel all the aches from injuries in battles that took place so long ago I can barely remember them."

"Your body remembers though."

"Aye, the body remembers."

Fleetingly, Beobrand recalled the taste of Eanflæd's mouth, the touch of her nipple hardening under his palm. He rubbed a hand over his face. Yes, the body always remembers.

"What do you think has happened to Cynan?" he asked, pushing aside thoughts of Eanflæd. He had left the Waelisc warrior in charge at Ubbanford and Stagga, and he could make no sense of the tidings that he had not been there to answer the king's call.

"I have no idea, but we will find out soon enough." He took a long swig from his water skin, then offered it to Beobrand, who shook his head.

"I cannot fathom it," he said.

"Well, one thing that my years have taught me is that there is no point in fretting over that of which we have no control. Elmer will tell us when we reach Corebricg."

They rode on and Beobrand was thankful to Attor. He felt less burdened with worries after their talk, even though they travelled towards war. But war was a beast he understood well. It was savage and deadly, a vicious writhing mass of steel and blood, and yet the emotions it conjured were simple. When the shieldwalls clashed, he would allow the killer within him to be unleashed and he would, for a time, have no concerns apart from the glee of bloodletting, the joy of overpowering his enemies and leading his men to victory.

This was what made him a formidable warrior and why he was useful to Oswiu. He had accepted this, and despite the nightmares filled with the screams and agonised faces of those he had slain, he had long since admitted to himself the dark reality that he enjoyed the simplicity of the shieldwall's storm of steel. And yet, if he took pleasure in killing, what kind of man did that make him? Of that, he was uncertain, and when the nights were long and his slaughter-filled dreams kept sleep from him, he did not much care for the man he had become.

The day was warm, bright and long, and when they reached Morðpæð there was still plenty of light in the sky, so they pressed on, leaving behind Fordraed's grand hall without halting. Beobrand glanced at Beircheart as they trotted past the path that led to the hall. The bearded gesith gave no indication of his feelings. Fordraed's widow, Edlyn, resided in the hall at Morðpæð and Beircheart had often visited her there. Beobrand knew the warrior wanted nothing more than to be wed to Rowena's daughter, but the past made shackles for them all, it seemed. Beircheart was held back by something, perhaps guilt at how Edlyn's husband had died, though Beobrand knew well enough that Beircheart had nothing to do with Fordraed's demise. Or maybe it was a feeling of inadequacy that Edlyn's mother had perpetuated. Rowena had never wanted her daughter to wed one whom she deemed to be beneath her station. Beobrand vowed that when they returned to Ubbanford, he would speak with Rowena and confront the matter. He had watched on for too long as Beircheart and Edlyn longed for each other. Gods, thought Beobrand, if he could not have the object of his desire, he would do all in his power so that his loyal gesith might do so.

They halted for the night at the hall of one Dunna, a thin man with wispy hair and a threadbare, sweat-stained kirtle. An older man than Beobrand by at least ten years, Dunna was nervous, and never seemed comfortable. His wife, Geatfleda, was younger than Ardith. She was a true beauty, with smooth skin and expressive dark eyes. The men stared at their hostess, and Beobrand, like the rest of them, wondered at the match between the ageing thegn and this vision of youth.

"This Dunna must be a truly wealthy man," whispered Offa, after Geatfleda had offered them the Waes Hael cup. She moved along the line of wide-eyed warriors, each of whom accepted the vessel with obvious pleasure. "Though he does not look it."

Beobrand watched the young woman and the men's reaction to her. These warriors, brave in the face of screaming enemies brandishing blades and seeking their death, were transformed to little more than blushing, abashed boys in the presence of such beauty. Beobrand watched as the slender Geatfleda glided on to Eadgard, who towered over her. He nodded at whatever words of welcome she uttered and stooped to pluck the proffered cup from her delicate hands. What must it be like to possess such power and yet remain so powerless?

Before Beobrand could reply to Offa, Dunna came to sit on his gift-stool at the centre of the high table.

"Lovely, is she not?" Dunna asked.

"Indeed she is," replied Offa. "We were just saying you are a man of true wealth."

Dunna had laughed at that and clapped his hands for the food to be served. Despite the poor quality of his clothes and the plainness of the building that had none of the carvings and ornaments of the great halls of the land, the fare that was brought out by a couple of women was rich and plentiful. As the evening progressed, Beobrand relaxed, surprised at the lavish food and drink on Dunna's table. There was a thick hare stew, griddled trout and sweet pastries adorned with bright summer fruits.

Offa spoke with Dunna, keeping him occupied. Beobrand was content to drink in peace, watching the interaction between their host and his wife. Geatfleda was attentive and smiled whenever the lord of the hall spoke. She appeared to truly love the man, despite his age and dishevelled aspect. Again Beobrand marvelled at the power of women and how the bonds of love and affection can never be truly understood.

At first light, they rode on, refreshed and sated. Dunna and Geatfleda came out of their hall to wave them on their way and Beobrand noted that all of the riders turned in their saddles to wave back.

Clouds had gathered in the north over night, but the day remained dry and they made good progress along the wide road left by the men of Roma. It was late morning when they reached the great Wall.

"By Christ's teeth," said Offa, gazing up at the crumbling gatehouse that rose above the wall. "I had heard tell of the Wall, but I had never thought to see it. And I did not believe what I had been told." He whistled low, gazing at the high stone wall that followed the land into the distance to east and west.

"It is humbling, is it not?" said Beobrand. As always when he saw the Wall, he was unable to understand how such an edifice had been built. It was constructed of great slabs of grey stone, with gates and towers at intervals along its seemingly endless length.

Beobrand led them through the gap in the Wall where timber gates would once have blocked their way. Their horses' hooves clattered on the cobbles, echoing around them as they passed. Offa and the men from the south craned their necks to look at the Wall and the buildings, their mouths agape.

"Was this built by giants as the scops say?" asked Offa. "I had thought it the fancy of song-spinners, but now that I see it with my own eyes, I can believe it."

"Coenred tells me it was the men of Roma, far to the south, who built the Wall and this road we ride upon. They ruled these lands long ago."

Offa nodded.

"In my heart I know this to be true, and yet I see here the work of a giant's hands, not those of men."

They paused briefly to the south of the Wall. The East Angelfolc stood by their mounts, chewing their food and staring at the undulating line of the stone structure as it stretched off into the hazed distance, dividing the land. Behind the Wall, in the north, the sky grew darker as the clouds rolled southward towards them.

The clouds chased them south as they pressed on towards Corebricg. The sky behind them was black and ominous and the riders' mood soured as the day's light dimmed. A cold wind picked up, pushing them on.

They passed the ruins of more Roman buildings, all broken red tiles and cracked bricks, before clattering over the remains of a great bridge across the Tine. The same cunning that had erected the Wall held aloft the huge blocks of stone that arched over the water below. Only one of the arches had collapsed and was now bridged with stout planks of timber.

"Will it hold?" asked Offa, his eyes wide at the drop to the stone-strewn river.

Beobrand had passed over the bridge many times before and always felt the thrill of peril at crossing so high above the wide water.

"It will hold," he said, before dismounting and leading his horse over the timber portion of the bridge.

They crossed without incident and cantered south. There was the scent of smoke in the air and they could all sense they were close to their destination; to where warhosts would meet. The first splatters of cold rain were beating at their backs when they spotted the tents and standards of the Bernician host.

Beobrand reined in his mount and stared down at the gathered fyrd. Smoke from many cook fires hung over the jumbled mass of shelters and men.

The force was arrayed to the west of the road. A good place for a battle, thought Beobrand. The land sloped towards the south, meaning an enemy coming from Deira would need to meet them at a disadvantage. And the western flank of the Bernicians was protected by a dense wood.

Further off to the south, blurred by distance and the rain that had begun to fall more heavily, Beobrand could make out the dark sprawl of another host.

This place was close to where Oswald had led them to victory against Cadwallon all those years ago. Beobrand recalled the storm then, the crash of thunder and flash of lightning as they had met the Waelisc in battle in the darkest part of that storm-rent night. Beobrand peered into the distance, squinting as the rain fell harder, but he could not make out any of the banners and standards of the far-off Deirans or even the closer Bernicians.

"Who do you see?" he asked Attor, who had ridden up next to him.

Attor raised a hand to shield his eyes.

"Ethelwin's black raven banner," he said, "and Wynhelm's red wyrm. And Alhfrith's blue stallion too. There are others, but I cannot make them out at this distance. Those three are easy enough to see though."

Beobrand gave him a questioning glance.

"They are on the move," explained Attor.

"On the move?"

"Yes, lord. See?" He pointed. "They are riding southward, towards the Deirans. No more than a dozen or so riders."

A movement closer to them drew their attention. Six riders cantered up the slope from the Bernician camp. Offa and the rest of the men drew in around Beobrand. They sat astride their mounts as the wind and rain buffeted them.

As the riders reached them, Beobrand was pleased to see that he recognised the leader, a thickset man with a red-veined face and long thinning hair that was pulled back and held at the nape of his neck by a leather thong.

"Well met, Reodstan," Beobrand said. He liked the man. He was a good fighter, loyal and strong.

Reodstan lowered his head in recognition.

"Lord Beobrand," he replied, taking in the riders around him with a warrior's eye. "You are well come to this place. Though I wish you had not brought this rain with you." Reodstan had fought against Cadwallon too, and Beobrand wondered what dark memories he had from that night.

"I see Ethelwin and Alhfrith Atheling are on the move."

Reodstan glanced over his shoulder.

"Aye," he said. "Oswine sent a messenger. They ride to parley, though what for, I know not. Oswiu wants this fight and Ethelwin will give it to him."

"Well, I will tell you what they say," said Beobrand, grinning at the man.

"Lord?"

"We did not ride all this way to miss the fun. Attor, Offa," Beobrand snapped. "With me. We ride to parley. The rest of you, follow Reodstan here down to the camp. And Fraomar, find Elmer."

"Beobrand," Reodstan called out, "do not do anything rash."

But Beobrand ignored him. Spurring his mount forward, he rode past Reodstan and the others, urging his horse into a gallop. He looked back over his shoulder as the wind pulled his cloak to stream out behind him. Offa and Attor were close behind.

The rain scythed down from the dark clouds, bitter and cold on his face. But despite the chill omen of the black sky, he grinned, for he could smell battle on the breeze now, as surely as he could detect the smoke from the fires and the tangy odour of sweat from his horse. And as they galloped down the hill, throwing up great clods of earth from their horses' hooves, Beobrand's concerns and worries washed away from him.

War was coming and he rode to meet it.

Chapter 13

Sulis' back hurt. With every jolt of her pony's gait, she felt as though she had been stabbed in the kidneys. She gritted her teeth against the pain and continued riding in silence. She would not slow them down. The longer they took, the more chance that something terrible would have happened during her absence. Her mind was filled with horrific thoughts of death. In her dreams the night before, as she lay exhausted beneath the trees, she had relived the sight of Leofman's broken body, the anguish in his eyes that he had allowed Eadwig to be taken.

She would never forget the moment Alfwold and she had found her husband. Leofman had clung to her, digging his fingers into her arm so hard that he had left bruises on her pale skin.

She had not been able to tear her gaze away from Swiga's mottled, fly-blown corpse. Her mind was a maelstrom of terror that her son might be lying amongst the rocks, his tiny body blood-stained, his skin as pallid and lifeless as the stone.

"I promised to protect you both!" Leofman said, his words desperate. "I should have stopped them." He'd sobbed then, and she had held him in her arms, cradling his head as she had cradled Eadwig when he fell on the ice last winter and sprained his wrist.

She had once, long ago, held Osgar that way too, comforting

him, consoling him when he cried. His father had said she made him soft, but a boy needed his mother's love. And Osgar had not been soft. He had defied that fat Bernician bastard, Fordraed, and his men. They had beaten her and she had not spoken. When they had threatened Osgar, he had squared his shoulders and refused to speak. That was when they had started hitting the boy. He was so small, so weak. But never a coward, never soft. He had not spoken. It was she who had been soft. But what mother would not have spoken out to save her child from pain and torment?

The pony stumbled as they forded a shallow river. The sudden movement sent a lancing agony into her back. The ache radiated into her distended belly, but she was glad of it. Pain of the body she could cope with. It was the suffering of her soul and the black memories that filled her head with the beating bat wings of dread that she could not abide.

She recalled Osgar's eyes as the huge warrior with plaited beard had sawed his seax into the boy's throat. She could picture vividly the colour of the blood as it fountained and how her son's eyes had filled with horror and fear. She had been meant to protect him. She had given herself to those brutes to keep Osgar alive, and for what? To watch his lifeblood pour from him in moments? She had screamed until her throat was raw and she could not breathe, but the rough warriors had pulled her away and thrown her, trussed and bound over the back of a horse. She had wanted to run to Osgar, to hold her dying son to her breast and whisper to him that everything would be well. She was his mother and it was her role to comfort him, even in that final moment when he departed middle earth and what was left of her life was shattered completely. The warriors had denied her even that, and she had been carried away, leaving behind her dead son all alone in the mud beside their home as the flames burst from the thatch, sending billowing clouds of smoke as black as despair towards the heavens.

She had been lost then for a long time. Some part of her had died and she did not believe she would ever find it again. And then one day she had met Leofman.

At the mouth of the mine, she had seen the same agony in her husband's eyes as she had felt all those years before. He was Eadwig's father and it was his role to protect the boy. He had failed and was distraught.

"You did all you could," she'd whispered to him, stroking his hair whilst looking down in shock at his battered and bleeding body. "You are but one man and there were many of them. And yet you still wounded one, you say."

He grimaced.

"Aye, I cut him badly. But you are right." He'd tried to push himself up, grunting with the pain. "I am just one old man."

"I did not say you were old."

Leofman grimaced.

"Maybe not. But it is the truth of it. If I were still a young man, they would not have beaten me so easily."

"Hush, husband. You cannot blame yourself."

It was in that moment she had decided to ride to Ubbanford. They needed a younger man to confront those who had done this, a warrior who would not be afraid to stand up to swordsmen and spear-men. She had a deep hatred for the warriors of Bernicia. They had stolen her beautiful boy from her, violated her, enslaved her and broken her spirit. And yet there was one gesith in the north she sometimes thought of. He was not one of them, not one of the Angelfolc, but a Waelisc. He had saved her. In spite of her twisted fury and loathing, he had rescued her, first from her own devastating pain and then from Beobrand's raging hatred and need for vengeance.

"Do you need to halt?"

She started at the voice. She had been clutching the reins tightly, staring at the path ahead, so wrapped in the hurts of her body and her mind that she had not noticed Cynan swing his horse around and ride back to her. She looked up at him now. He was more handsome than she had remembered, broader of shoulder, harder of face. And where he had once seemed uncertain of himself in her presence, he now exuded the power that comes from leading men into battle. As soon as she had seen him in Ubbanford, gazing down at her from the saddle of his bay mare, she had known she had not been mistaken to leave Leofman in Alfwold's care. If there was any man who could help them, it was Cynan.

She shook her head, lowering her gaze. Her back screamed at her and her full bladder ached. By Woden and all the gods, how she wished she did not have the weak body of a woman. She might not have the strength of these men, but she would not slow them down. They were still at least two days from the farm she shared with Leofman, Eadwig and Alfwold.

"I am well," she mumbled. "We should ride on."

Cynan expertly guided his mare close to Sulis' pony. With a lithe movement, he grabbed the reins, tugging them from her grasp. Again she cursed her own weakness.

"Nonsense," he said. "You are exhausted and need to rest."

She grabbed for the reins, but he held them tightly.

"We stopped not long ago," she said, her voice cracking.

He pulled her pony to a halt and stared into her eyes.

"Would you have us ride to save your son, only for him to find he has lost his mother on the journey?"

The rider who was bringing up the rear reached them.

"Is there problem?" he asked, his accent strange and musical.

"Sulis needs to rest a while, Halinard," replied Cynan. "Ride on to the others and tell them to make for those birch trees. I will ride with Sulis."

Halinard nodded. Touching his heels to his horse's flanks, he cantered after Brinin and Ingwald who rode together some way further along the trail they followed over the hilly land of Bernicia.

Halinard was a Frank and she liked him instinctively more than she liked most men. He had caused some commotion when he had ridden out of the rising dawn that morning. For a time, Cynan had squinted into the glare of the sun, trying to make out who pursued them. Brinin and Ingwald had readied their shields and swords, but Cynan had shaken his head.

"Whoever chases us has surely ridden through the night and must have come from Ubbanford, so they are a friend." He had peered into the east, shading his eyes with his hand. "They may not be friendly at the moment, but we will not fight them, whoever it is. This is my doing and I will not allow either of you to be blamed." A moment later, he had turned to them with a shrug. "I don't know why he rides after us, but it is the Frank."

"Halinard?" asked Brinin.

"You know any other Franks?"

Halinard The Frank turned out to be a man of few words, but after he had dismounted, he shared some of the bread and cheese he carried in his saddle bags while the men probed him with questions until they understood how he came to be following them.

It seemed his daughter, Joveta, had found Ardith crying. They were friends and Ardith soon told Joveta what they had decided and how Brinin had ridden into the west with Sulis, Cynan and Ingwald. Joveta had gone to Halinard's wife, Gisela, with the news. The women all agreed that to aid Sulis was the right thing to do, but there was no consoling Ardith over the loss of her beloved Brinin. On hearing this, Brinin had scowled and walked over to the horses, where he listened to the rest of the story with his back to the group.

"Ardith is afeared that something happen to Brinin," Halinard said at last in his lilting voice. "Joveta and her mother said it would be better if I ride with you. Safer if more of us."

"What did you think?" asked Ingwald.

Halinard looked at Cynan's man as if he were simple.

"It matters nothing what I think," he said. "Gisela had made her mind already."

The men all nodded knowingly. Halinard, a large man with broad shoulders, smiled ruefully. This Gisela was clearly a woman not to be trifled with. Sulis thought she would like to have met her.

They had reached the birch now, and Halinard, Ingwald and Brinin had dismounted to rest. A stiffening breeze shook the branches above them and Sulis shivered. To the north, the sky was bruised and sombre. There would be rain soon, she thought. Her back throbbed and she hesitated, unsure how she would be able to climb down from her pony. An instant later, Cynan was at her side. He lifted her down easily. She nodded her thanks and walked painfully under the cover of the trees where she could relieve herself without being seen by the menfolk. Gods, it felt as though she needed to piss all the time. She did not recall it being so when she had carried Osgar or Eadwig. Nor had her back pained her so then. But she was older now, she supposed, her body weaker than it had been. Adjusting her dress, she made her way back through the bracken to where the men waited with the horses.

Halinard said something and the others laughed. Sulis tensed, suddenly feeling very alone. She wished she had a woman friend like Ardith or Gisela, someone to speak to of all the things that men did not seem to care about or understand. It had been many years since she had spent any real time with women. With Fordraed's raid on her home, Sulis had not only lost Osgar and her husband in the ensuing battle between Penda and Oswald at Maserfelth, she had also lost her friends. Some had been slain, others had been taken with her to Ubbanford.

Cynan looked up when she returned.

"Water?" he said, offering her a skin.

She drank sparingly, not wishing to need another stop so soon. She handed the skin back.

"We should ride on," she said. "There is still a long way to go."

"You are sure?"

"My son is in danger," she replied, her voice harsh, despite the kindness he had shown her. "I cannot bear to tarry here not knowing what has befallen him."

Cynan stared at her. Making up his mind, he nodded.

"Come then," he offered his hand. "Let me help you mount."

She hesitated. She was not oblivious to the way he looked at her. Perhaps once, she might have entertained the thought of being with this handsome Waelisc warrior. But she was Leofman's now. Her back still ached and she was unsure she would be able to climb into the saddle without help, so she took his hand and allowed him to propel her up onto the pony. Her back screamed out as she settled onto the saddle, but she offered Cynan a tight smile of gratitude.

The others swung up onto their mounts and in moments they were riding once more.

"Better?" asked Cynan, concern for her on his face.

She nodded. She did feel better than before, and yet her back still throbbed. But she would not hold them back.

They rode in silence for a time. Cynan seemed worried for her and deliberately hung back, keeping close. The wind picked up, rustling the long grasses in swaying waves across the moors and meadows. The brooding clouds in the north were riding the wind, bringing cold and rain. They would have a wet night of it.

"What happened to the other women? Aefentid and Willa, and the others?" Sulis asked, breaking the calm that had descended between them.

Cynan had to think before answering.

"Of course," he said, "they came north with you, didn't they?" The mention of the women that had come to Ubbanford as thralls made him awkward. A reminder of her own past and his part in it.

She nodded, but said nothing. The memories of that journey

and the weeks after it were as dark as the clouds roiling in the northern sky.

"Aefentid is still with us at Stagga," Cynan said. "She married a farmer. They have two children. A boy and a girl."

"She is free now?"

"Yes. Beobrand gave her and Willa to Eadgyth, the lady of the hall, and it must be four years ago now that she freed both of them."

These tidings made Sulis' head spin. Aefentid and Willa had been good women; her friends. She was overcome with a wave of happiness that they had found contentment and a new life. But a darker emotion tinged her thoughts, colouring them like a drop of blood spilt into a bowl of water. She was envious. Could she have remained there? What would her life have been like if she had stayed and not thrown her world into disarray again with her spite and hatred? But what good did such thoughts do? If she had not left Ubbanford, she would not have met Leofman, and Eadwig would not have been born. For those things alone, she could never regret what she had done.

"What of the others?" she asked.

Cynan rode in silence, staring off at the hills that loomed in the distance. Beyond them were the mountains and lakes of the land she now called home.

"The winter after you came was a bad one," he said at last. "It snowed for weeks and everyone got sick. Eacnung never saw the spring." He sighed. "She is buried at Ubbanford."

Sulis tried to conjure up the face of the girl in her mind, but beyond a shock of dark brown hair, she could not recall Eacnung's features. They had never been close, but to hear of her death saddened Sulis. She remembered that winter and its endless snows. She had been close to death herself, from hunger and cold, when Leofman had found her. It was madness to look back at what might have been. Maybe if she had stayed in Ubbanford, she would have succumbed to the same illness as Eacnung.

"Edrys is still serving Rowena, and seems happy enough."

"For a thrall?" Sulis said bitterly.

She thought of the shrill shrieks of the old woman as she screamed for her death, and wondered how content Edrys could truly be.

"Rowena treats her more as one of her kin than as a slave. She does not beat her, even when other mistresses would. Bassus has told me she was not so soft before I knew her. Age, or perhaps Bassus, has softened her."

Sulis looked at him askance. Rowena did not seem soft to her, but who truly knew anyone? And people change. She thought of Leofman, his strong arms lifting her from the nest she had made in the snow. The place where she had thought she would welcome death.

"It is interesting," she said. "The influence others can have on a person." She glanced at Cynan. Men had taken so much from her, but it was also men who had given her contentment, a son. Life. "What of Ellenweorc?"

"She is now part of Edlyn's household."

Sulis frowned, trying to place the name. She had heard it before, she was sure.

"Rowena's daughter," offered Cynan.

And then it came to Sulis, and she stiffened in the saddle, the ache in her back forgotten.

"She is Fordraed's woman?" The memory of the toad-faced thegn made her shiver.

"She was his wife, yes." Cynan kept his features expressionless.

"Was?"

"Fordraed is dead."

"Good," she said.

Cynan snorted and she thought she saw him nod.

They rode on. Far to the south, the hillside was dotted with sheep. High above them circled a buzzard, languidly riding the freshening breeze, its broad wings flapping slowly every now and then to keep aloft. Cynan scanned the horizon for threats, but found none.

"So," he said, "tell me how it is that you came to be married to a man of Rheged."

Sulis sighed. The last time she had told any part of this tale was to Eadwig. By Christ's blood, she hoped her son was safe. Whenever she lowered her guard, her fears for him threatened to smother her in their black wings. With difficulty, she pushed away her worries and turned her mind back to the time when Leofman had found her.

"It was that winter after I left when he saved me."

"Saved you?"

"Yes. Without him I would have perished. Lord forgive me, but I would have been glad of death then. I had wandered along the path of the Wall into the west for weeks. I had no destination in mind. I just walked. I begged for food where I could." She hesitated. She shook her head. Saddened to remember what she had done and who she had become. But that seemed so long ago now. "Begged or stole. I was more animal than woman that winter, I think. My mind had left me when…" Her voice faltered. She could not bring herself to talk of what had happened to her at Fordraed's hands, did not want to put into words how Osgar had died alone in the mud.

Cynan said nothing. She wondered what he thought of the woman she had been when he had stopped Beobrand from striking her down.

"I did things…" she said, her voice trailing off as she thought back to those chill, dark days, and the deeds she had done. She shivered. "I did what I needed to do to survive. Though truly, I don't know why I bothered. I longed for the release of death." She had never spoken so openly about those painful days with anyone, not even Leofman, but Cynan had been there at the beginning of her descent and somehow, the knowledge they shared unburdened her.

"Perhaps the body does not wish for death, even when the mind thinks it does," he said.

"Perhaps. Or mayhap it was my wyrd to survive. The Lord alone knows there were enough times when I should have died."

"Well," he said, "I am glad you did not."

She glanced at him, and the honest concern on his face made her turn away.

"I would have died in the snow, if not for Leofman." She allowed her pony to follow the horses in front. It plodded along, but with each step the pain in her lower back stabbed at her. Grimacing, she pulled her cloak about her as the wind picked up, bringing with it cold from the north and the smell of rain. She shuddered to remember that freezing day years before. Cynan was watching her, waiting for her to complete her tale. She took a deep breath and ploughed on, pushing aside the memories like great drifts of snow, to uncover the truth beneath.

"He would have been within his rights to beat me," she said, her voice not much more than a whisper now. Cynan's eyes narrowed. He was full of questions she could see, but he waited for her to go on in her own time. "I had wandered as far as the mountains of Rheged. How the snows glistened when the sun shone on those short days, but the nights... So cold. I'd followed a trail of smoke down into a valley. I was out of my mind with hunger and when I saw the barn, I did not hesitate." She looked back at who she had been then. A wild, unkempt stray. She would have done anything for food. Had done terrible things. And she had been filled with such rage. She hated the men who had taken her life from her and loathed their women for allowing them to do it. Shame washed over her at the memory of stabbing Reaghan. That was a sin that would stay with her always. "Stealing had become natural to me," she went on, "so I sneaked into the barn and took whatever I could. When I heard someone coming from the house, I fled out into the mountains. It was snowing hard and night came on quickly. Despite the food I had stolen, I was sick and so cold. I lay down in a ditch, and allowed the snow to fall around me. I had made a decision then to allow death to claim me." She took in a deep breath. "Something had reached me, piercing through my hatred and fury. That was no way to live. Better to be gone than to go on in such pain and torment."

To speak so honestly of the events that led to her first meeting with Leofman frightened and thrilled her in equal measure.

"I think I was nearer to death than life when Leofman came. It was his barn I had stolen from and he had chased after me, tracking me through the snow. It had been easy enough to follow my path. But he did not seek to punish me." She shook her head, marvelling, as she always did, at her husband's kindness. "No. He told me later that he was sure I would die. But he had been to the chapel at Dacor the day before and listened to the priest there speaking of the Christ and how he is a good shepherd to his flock. Leofman did not see a thief who had taken what was his, he saw one of Christ's flock in need of help." She cuffed away the tears that welled in her eyes. "For the first time in many months, I was not judged for what I had done. And there, close to death as I was, I was too ill to judge myself."

Cynan did not speak for some time. The sky grew darker and rain began to splatter around them. His horse shook its head and he patted its neck absently. Brinin, Ingwald and Halinard rode ahead of them, out of earshot. Every so often they glanced back to check on their progress.

"So Leofman is a follower of the Christ?"

"He is. He's a good man. His faith saved me."

"You follow Christ too?"

She nodded. It was unusual for her to speak of these things. Her days were spent with Leofman, Alfwold and Eadwig on the farm. Occasionally, they would head into Dacor to attend mass and to listen to the priest's sermons, but she did not often put

voice to her understanding of God's teaching or to her own faith
in the one true God.

"Do you?" she asked.

Cynan shifted uncomfortably in his saddle, apparently more
disturbed to be speaking of such things than she was.

"I am just a warrior," he said. "The old gods or the new, make
no difference to me. It seems that the followers of all gods are
killed as easily. Sickness, famine and war strike down the Christ
followers as often as those who make sacrifice to Woden."

"But it is Christ who allows forgiveness," she said, her voice
taking on the warmth of fervour. "God is good and His son died
to save us all from our sins. Leofman nursed me to health the
way he would a lamb that had strayed into the snow. But more
than that, he helped me to see that God forgave me." She let out
a ragged breath. "And that I could forgive myself."

Clearly uncomfortable with the conversation, Cynan changed
the subject.

"How much land is Leofman's?"

"It is a sizeable area," she said. "Several hides. It is bordered
by mountains to the north and a huge lake to the south."

"King Oswald gave him his lands?"

"Yes, after a great battle. Hefenfelth. The king ordered his
host to pray under a great cross, like the rood on which Jesu was
slain. Leofman found his faith beneath that cross. He fought
in the centre of the shieldwall and the king noted his bravery.
Leofman sometimes talks of the great feast and gift-giving at
Bebbanburg that followed. But he never speaks of that night-
time battle at Hefenfelth."

"He must have been a formidable warrior to have caught the
king's attention," said Cynan.

She knew that Beobrand also gained the king's favour after the
same battle. He had been gifted and raised up to the rank of thegn.
Sulis had seen him fight. She shuddered to recall his ferocity in
combat, the impassive glower as he had killed his enemies before

the Wall. The gruff command to slay those who had surrendered. Beobrand was nothing like her Leofman and she could scarcely believe that her husband had stood beside, and faced, such killers in battle. She had asked him what he had done to deserve the gift of land, but he had never told her. He would just shake his head and say, "Oswald was gōd cyning."

"Leofman is a strong man, but truly, I cannot think of him as a warrior. He tends to his crops and sheep. He brings life to the land. He is no killer."

"And yet he was gifted land by the king for his service."

"Yes. There is some good grazing pasture for sheep on the slopes, but not much land for planting crops. Too rocky and steep for a plough." She smiled despite the pain in her back. "He says he thinks that's why Oswald gifted it to him. No use for a real lord, but good enough for a ceorl like him."

"Until he found the lead in the cave."

She furrowed her forehead.

"Yes. Until he found the lead."

They did not speak for some time. They had ridden down a slope and were heading up a rise now towards the sheep that were scattered about the hillside. The buzzard had gone from the sky. A dozen or more crows flapped above the riders, cawing in their angry voices.

"If the land is not so good," said Cynan, "and with powerful men against you, perhaps the best course would be to leave."

"It is our land," she said. "Why should we leave? Besides," she said, and her voice took on a hard, brittle edge, "Sidrac has taken Eadwig."

Cynan's face was as hard as stone in the storm-dark of the afternoon.

"I will help you get your son back," he said. The rain began to fall in earnest now, the noise of it threatening to drown out their words. "I will make the men who hurt your husband pay. In silver or in blood. But some battles are best avoided. This

Sidrac and his father are powerful men. You cannot hope to stand against them for long."

"My husband was given the land by the king. It is written in the land grants, signed by the holy hand of Oswald himself. Leofman gave me part of that land as my morgengifu." She remembered his smiling face as he told her how he had paid the monks at Caer Luel to write up a new deed with her name on the land that stretched between the old broken ash tree and the brook in the west. It was some of the richest pasture land and it would provide her with enough to live off should she need it. "The land is ours," she said, shouting now over the growl of the rain.

Cynan sighed.

"I have land. Your family could return with me to Stagga. It wouldn't be much, but it would be enough for the three of you. It is fertile land and I could always use a good, strong man such as your Leofman."

She looked at him sharply. His hair was plastered to his head and rain ran down his face.

"And what would your woman think of that? Giving away your land to one such as me, a woman who was a thrall. A murderer."

"I have no woman," he said, with a strange look. "I have not taken a wife."

His tone and impenetrable expression intrigued her. There was a story there, she thought.

But before she could form the words to unravel that quandary, Cynan pushed his hair out of his eyes and said, "I am going to speak to that shepherd." He nodded towards the horizon where she could make out a figure stooped against the cold wind and the rain that now fell in seething sheets from the leaden sky. Cynan touched his heels to his mare's flanks and cantered away, leaving her staring after him.

Chapter 14

The rain swirled about Beobrand as he pushed his borrowed mount into a gallop down the slope towards the small group of riders beneath the swaying standards and banners of Bernicia. A quick glance back showed him that Offa and Attor were not far behind him. In moments the three of them would reach their destination. Beobrand breathed deeply of the chill, damp air, allowing the rushing wind and sheeting rain to dampen his battle lust. He could feel his desire for the release of combat straining at its bonds within him. Perhaps soon would be the moment to unshackle that beast, but now was the time for cooler heads. Maybe there was yet a way to avoid adding the blood of countless dead to the rain that soaked the earth.

At his approach, the men in the party looked around. Some turned their mounts, dragging swords from scabbards, shifting their positions to protect the atheling and their other leaders from the threat of attack that came galloping towards them through the downpour. Beobrand reined in before one of the more eager warriors could attempt to skewer him on a spear. His horse sent up a shower of mud and water as its hooves scrabbled for purchase on the wet turf. Beobrand scanned the faces of the men. He recognised most of them, but one made him pause.

"Octa," he said. "Waes hael."

"Father," his son replied with a nod of his head, but no other sign of recognition or warmth.

Beobrand met his son's cold gaze for a few heartbeats, wondering at the young man who sat astride the horse before him. Octa wore a fine iron-knit shirt. Atop his head was a simple but well-made helm. His cloak was held in place by a brooch that glimmered with gold and garnets in spite of the louring clouds and rain that had dimmed the light of the sun. In his hand he carried a gold-hilted ring sword with patterned blade. This was a warrior of worth and renown. He was as tall as his father, broad of shoulder with the same ice-chip eyes. And yet Beobrand fancied he could see Sunniva in his son's face. The thought twisted at his heart. He had lost the boy's mother the day Octa was born. In the years since, he had lost his son too.

Offa and Attor drew in their steeds beside Beobrand. Another rider pushed his way through the jostling ranks to face them.

"Lord Beobrand," he said. "Good of you to join us on this fine day." The rain dripped from his great helm, trickling from the nose guard like an icicle in the spring thaw. The bristles of the boar crest on the crown of the helm were flattened and lank.

"I would not miss it for anything, Lord Ethelwin," replied Beobrand.

Ethelwin looked beyond Beobrand and the riders that flanked him, peering into the rain-smudged distance. He was a thickset man with a solid, corded neck and strong shoulders. Beneath his helm, Beobrand could just make out the scar that he had picked up in some long-forgotten campaign. Behind the helm's protection, Ethelwin's nose was twisted and broad where it had been broken.

"The king did not ride with you?"

"Alas, no. His foot pains him terribly." Beobrand thought that the excuse did not perhaps sound worthy of a king, so he added, "He can barely walk."

Ethelwin nodded grimly.

"It shall pass soon enough," he said. "He has been afflicted by this ailment before. Aidan told him it was a result of all that Frankish wine he likes so much, but I know not of any man who could dissuade Oswiu from drinking what he pleases."

"He is stubborn indeed," said Beobrand. "Few men can prevail on him when he sets his course."

Ethelwin stared at him appraisingly, as if weighing his words for some hidden meaning.

"Talking of setting a course," he said at last. "I heard you had sailed south. A pleasant trip, I hope."

Beobrand chuckled at the man's light tone.

"Pleasing enough, if you find pleasure in wading through fens and facing superior numbers in a shieldwall."

Ethelwin grinned, showing the gaps where several of his teeth had been dislodged in brawls and combat.

"Such sounds like a warrior's dream. But how came you to be fighting so far south?"

"It is a long story that can keep for later. But the fight ended in victory and me bringing to Bebbanburg King Anna of the East Angelfolc. This here is his man, Offa. He is a true friend. Brave and steadfast. We stood together years ago at the battle of the great ditch."

Ethelwin whistled and nodded a welcome to Offa.

"You are a fighter then, Offa. If you have the praise of Beobrand here."

"I fight when I need to," replied Offa. He wiped a hand over his face, clearing it for a moment of the rain that pelted down on them. "And I am thankful for Beobrand's appearance in the south. If not for him…" His voice trailed off as he thought of what might have been. He coughed to clear his throat. "His Black Shields rescued us and our king."

"Perhaps I am in time to save another king this day," said Beobrand, kicking his horse forward. "You ride to parley?"

Ethelwin frowned, but after a moment's hesitation, swung his horse around to follow Beobrand to the head of the band of warriors. Offa and Attor joined the group who rode behind, beneath the banners and standards that hung lank and dripping from their crossbeams.

At the front of the small column Beobrand found another face he recognised. He rode up close to Wynhelm and held out his hand to the old thegn. Wynhelm leaned over in his saddle and grasped Beobrand's forearm in the warrior grip. His grip was firm and strong, despite the increasing amount of silver in his hair.

"It is good to see you, Beobrand," he said.

They kicked their horses into a trot. In the distance Beobrand could make out the shadowed shapes of horsemen waiting beneath standards of their own. They were yet too far away for him to make out details, but there seemed to be a similar number of them as the Bernicians. A dozen or so.

"It has been too long," replied Beobrand. "And you are getting old."

Wynhelm laughed.

"And you are as brash as ever, I see. Do not forget, we ride to parley, not to fight."

Beobrand offered him a smile.

"I will not forget. I too am growing older, Wynhelm."

"And wiser?"

Beobrand puffed out his cheeks.

"I doubt it, but perhaps less rash than I once was."

"Do you admit then that the mighty Beobrand is slowing down with age? Next you will be telling me you have seen the light of the Lord and that you watch angels flying in the heavens."

Beobrand started at the mention of angels. He thought of Cuthbert and the boy's vision. Unbidden, he glanced up at the dark sky above, but the only thing he saw were the brooding clouds. Rain spattered into his eyes and he wiped them with the back of his hand. Wynhelm laughed again, thinking he was making jest.

"No. No Christ for me, and no angels," said Beobrand. "But believe it or not, I am to be a grandfather this summer." He touched the Thunor's hammer amulet at his neck and spat into the mud to ward off any evil that might come from speaking of Ardith's child before it was born. "If the gods will it."

"Have you heard that, Octa?" shouted a young man who rode beside Wynhelm on a tall white horse. It was Alhfrith, the atheling, heir to Oswiu's throne. There was much of his father in him, and little of it endeared the atheling to Beobrand. He was a valiant warrior, of that there was no doubt. But he was young and filled with the certainty of his position. His tone made Beobrand clutch his reins tightly. He was tempted to tumble Alhfrith from his horse. Alhfrith turned in his saddle to look back at where Beobrand's son rode. "You are to be an uncle. Your sister is carrying that smith's brat."

"She is not my sister," replied Octa, and Beobrand sighed. He had not been close to Octa for many years. The boy had spent too long in Oswiu's household and Beobrand had done little to bridge the gap he had felt growing between them. But ever since he had returned from the voyage to Cantware and Frankia, bearing Ardith and Udela with him, Octa had grown ever more belligerent towards him, especially whenever there was a mention that he was not Beobrand's only child. For a time, Beobrand had hoped his children would grow to love each other. To have the bond with a sibling was something he had known and lost. He craved it for his son, but now he was certain Octa and Ardith would never be more than distant kin. They shared blood, but that did not make them friends.

"It seems you have much to tell us, Beobrand," said Wynhelm.

"But not now," snapped Ethelwin. They were close to the waiting Deirans now and Ethelwin addressed the Bernician party before they were near enough to be overheard. "Keep your mouths shut and let me do the talking." He looked pointedly at Beobrand, who ignored him. Wynhelm caught Beobrand's eye and held out a steadying hand. He patted the air before him gently. His meaning was clear. Be calm. Do nothing foolish.

In response Beobrand kicked his horse forward into a gallop ahead of the others.

"Wait, you fool," shouted Alhfrith, but Beobrand did not slow down.

A few heartbeats later he was reining in his mount before the gathered Deirans. He could hear the rest of the Bernicians urging their horses forward to join him, but he did not turn to see their progress.

"You always like to make an entrance, don't you, Lord Beobrand," said one of the thegns in the centre of the Deiran ranks. He was a handsome, dark-bearded man. His helm was plain, his byrnie dull from the grease that had been rubbed on it to protect from the damp. The sword that hung at his side had an elaborate hilt, garnet encrusted and gleaming, but the brooch that pinned his cloak was a simple ring and pin of bronze. He smiled at Beobrand.

"I find it the best way not to be forgotten or overlooked, Wulfstan," replied Beobrand with a grin.

Wulfstan chuckled and touched his heels to his horse. Beobrand stood his ground and awaited the Deiran thegn's approach. When he reached him, Wulfstan leaned across his horse's neck and clasped Beobrand's arm in the greeting of equals. Around them, Ethelwin, Wynhelm, Alhfrith and the other Bernicians were clattering to a halt.

"Watch yourself," hissed Wulfstan for Beobrand's ears alone. "Odda has Oswine's ear. He is desperate for war."

Beobrand gave him a slight nod to show he had understood his words. But there could be no further talking without being overheard, so Wulfstan spun his horse around.

"Alhfrith Atheling," he said with a nod. "Lord Ethelwin."

And with that, Wulfstan walked his horse back to his own people.

Before he had turned his mount around once more to face the Bernicians, another thegn nudged his horse a step forward. Beobrand recognised him as Odda. His face was unblemished and handsome. His chin was shaved, but a wispy moustache adorned his upper lip. Odda's byrnie shimmered, his arms were decorated with several warrior rings, and his cloak was pinned with a gold and garnet brooch of lavish and cunning design. Where the rest of the Deirans bore no shields, or carried them strapped to their backs, this young thegn held his brightly painted shield with its red star on a black field as if he were proud to display it. Or perhaps, Beobrand thought, he felt in need of protection.

"Do you come to offer your surrender?" Odda barked. "Does Oswiu renounce his claim to the throne of Deira?"

Alhfrith spurred his white horse forward, tugging angrily at the reins after a couple of paces to halt the animal.

"We come to do no such thing, Odda, son of Orc," he snapped. His horse stamped and snorted, the beast's breath billowing around its head in the cool afternoon air. "We come to defend what is ours by right of blood and marriage. Deira is ours."

"Yours, is it?"

It was King Oswine who spoke now, his voice calm and soothing. The king of Deira wore no helm, but his chestnut-colour wet hair was held out of his eyes by a circlet of gold. Beneath the fine white cloak around his shoulders, he was bedecked in a burnished shirt of iron rings. Oswine was tall and elegant, with an earnest mien and deep, intelligent dark eyes. Beobrand had always liked the man. He reminded him of Oswald. Oswine now stared at Alhfrith. The atheling held his gaze for a long moment, before looking away.

"Deira is my father's by right," he said, his voice less forceful under the king's glare.

"We have come to talk," said Ethelwin, his tone placatory. "There is no need for further bloodshed."

"It is a little late for that, Lord Ethelwin," said Oswine, shifting his attention to the warmaster of Bernicia. "The time for talk has passed."

Beobrand took a deep breath.

"No, lord king," he said. "It is never too late to parley for peace. We can form the shieldwalls and drench the earth in the slaughter-sweat of good men, both Deiran and Bernician, but to what end?" He met the king's gaze. Out of the edge of his vision he saw Wulfstan nodding. "Let us talk."

"On what authority do you speak for Bernicia?" asked Oswine.

Beobrand sighed.

"With the authority of one who has seen too much senseless killing for one lifetime. The gods know I have sent my share of enemies to the afterlife. I do not wish to slay more of those I think of as friends. Allies."

"This is a trick, lord," said Odda, and Oswine flicked a glance his way.

"A trick?"

"It must be, lord king. A ruse. For when has Beobrand ever wished for peace?"

"I think there is sense in what Lord Beobrand says," Wulfstan said. "I have known him for many years and he is no fool." He looked pointedly at Odda as he uttered these last words.

Odda scowled.

"Fool, am I?" he snarled.

Wulfstan smiled and shrugged.

"If the helm fits the head."

Odda's cheeks flushed. Beobrand snorted.

"Laugh at me, would you?" Odda said, turning to face Beobrand.

Beobrand held him in his stern glare.

"Battle is no laughing matter."

Another Deiran rode forward, urging his stocky mount to shove past the tightly packed horses and riders. He was a thickset man, with a long dark beard and jutting eyebrows. His hair was streaked with silver and his nose was scarred from a past battle. Beobrand recognised the man as Brunwine, who men called "The Blessed" after his seemingly miraculous ability to triumph in combat. Brunwine was the champion of Deira. Feared in combat, he was as respected as he was loud when at the mead benches; famed as much for his booming voice as for his prowess in battle. Now, he raised his famous voice so that nobody could ignore it. Like thunder it rolled over them all.

"Lord Beobrand is right," he roared. "There is little to laugh about in war. And there is certainly no mirth in seeing your countrymen slain. Which is why we are here, is it not?" These last words were almost shouted.

"Nobody is laughing," said Beobrand, keeping his voice low and even. "I do not wish to fight you, Brunwine."

The huge champion let out a roar of laughter.

"I am sure you do not! You would rather talk, it seems."

"I would spare bloodshed, if we are able."

Brunwine's face was set in a furious scowl now, all trace of humour gone.

"Perhaps you should have told that to your bastard of a king before he sent his men to raid Deiran lands."

Alhfrith growled at the insult to his father.

"Enough!" snapped Oswine, in the tone of a father tired with his children's arguing. The men fell silent. Oswine chewed his lip, looking from his thegns to Beobrand, Ethelwin and Alhfrith.

"Is Oswiu here?" he asked. "Perhaps it would be prudent to talk."

"My father is not with us," snapped Alhfrith. "But I speak with his voice."

"Hush, Alhfrith," Beobrand murmured, though he doubted his words would have any effect on the headstrong atheling.

"I will not be silenced by you or any other thegn," Alhfrith hissed.

Beobrand sighed.

Oswine narrowed his eyes.

"Where is your father, boy?" Oswine asked.

"I am no child," said Alhfrith, his voice as hard and cold as iron. Beobrand turned in his saddle and found Octa staring at him with undisguised contempt. He had seen both Alhfrith and Octa fight; had watched them batter their enemies into submission and death. The atheling was right, he was no child. And yet, he was that most dangerous of things: a man, with a warrior's strength and battle-skill, with the fleet mind and quick temper of a boy.

"My father is at Bebbanburg," Alhfrith continued, when Oswine said nothing. "He is ill, but I am here in his stead." He drew himself up in the saddle and squared his shoulders.

Oswine was silent. Odda leaned in close and whispered into his king's ear. Beobrand cursed inwardly.

"If you speak with Oswiu King's words, young Alhfrith Atheling," Oswine said, "what does Oswiu say?"

Alhfrith puffed out his chest and Beobrand knew then that any chance of averting battle had been lost.

"He says that you are an invading warhost and we have a God-given right and duty to defend our land and our people. You must disperse and return immediately to Deira, or face the might of Bernicia, shieldwall to shieldwall."

"What you deem invasion, I call retribution," said Oswine, all softness gone now from his tone. "Too long have I borne the insults of your raids into my lands. Too many of my people have been slain. There is only one way that we will return to Deira without spilling Bernician blood."

"And what is that?" asked Ethelwin. Ever the pragmatist, the warmaster was keen to seek a peaceful outcome.

"That your king pays in silver and gold for the lives of those Deirans who have been killed at his people's hands. Pay the blood-price, and we will return home. He can renounce his claim to the throne another time. For now, I cannot return empty-handed. I must give my men plunder. They demand payment for their ceorls slain; for the steadings burnt and the cattle stolen away by Bernician raiders. What say you, Ethelwin warmaster?"

"Bernicia will never pay!" said Alhfrith, his voice as harsh as a crow's croak. The rain pelted the land and thunder rumbled in the distance, like the sound of a memory from the battle between Oswald and Cadwallon that had been fought here all those years before. Water trickled down Beobrand's spine, but he would not allow himself to shiver.

Oswine stared at the atheling for several heartbeats.

"Then prepare your men," he said at last. "For tomorrow at dawn, we shall meet them in the field."

Brunwine shook his head.

"Too late for words, it seems," he said in his echoing voice.

Without waiting for a response, the king and his champion swung their horses around to the south and began their way back through the driving rain towards the miasma of smoke that hung over the Deiran battle host.

Odda glowered at Beobrand.

"I will look for you tomorrow."

"It will not be hard to find me. Just look for the heap of Deiran dead."

Odda squared his shoulders, perhaps searching for a cutting reply. But after a couple of heartbeats, he turned his horse around and followed Oswine. As soon as they were certain their king was a safe distance from the Bernicians, the rest of the Deiran thegns and ealdormen rode away. The last warrior to leave was Wulfstan. Before he did so, he met Beobrand's gaze and gave a small shake of his head.

Beobrand sighed and pulled his mare's head around to begin the wet ride back to the Bernician camp.

Alhfrith's voice, loud and stark, boomed out for all to hear.

"On the morrow we will send those cowardly Deirans back south with their tails between their legs."

"I wish there were some women in the camp," said Octa. "I would like to put my own tail to use between a nice bed-thrall's legs. Battle always gets my blood up."

Alhfrith and the other warriors of his comitatus laughed.

"When we return to Bebbanburg with the news of our victory, there will be many willing women who will be as wet as this day for the returning heroes."

"But warmer, I hope," shouted one of the young warriors.

The men laughed again.

Beobrand said nothing. Alhfrith was certainly no child, but he was no king either. As he listened to the young men bragging and boasting about their upcoming exploits, he was suddenly glad that Cuthbert was not there with them. The lad was so eager for battle, so filled with the desire for glory. Beobrand looked at Octa. Were all young men so? Surely he had been no different. Some would say he was still rash and prone to leap into combat when calm should prevail. But this fight against fellow Northumbrians? Not for the first time, he thought of the futility of this war between Oswiu and Oswine and wondered at where it would end.

He knew that when the sun rose, he would do his duty and stand against the Deirans. His oath was to Oswiu and so he would fight. And when the blades sang and the men screamed in the clash of the shieldwalls, he would be lost to the fury of battle. But when the battle was over and the dead lay scattered across the land to feed the foxes, wolves and ravens, then, he thought, they would all regret not seeking a peaceful outcome.

After a time, none of the others would engage the atheling in conversation or meet his gaze. The band of riders fell silent and they rode north with their heads dipped against the rain.

Chapter 15

Cynan pulled his sodden cloak about his shoulders and lowered his head, allowing Mierawin to walk where she would. She could follow the path well enough now. They had ridden for a long while across windswept moors where the rain had lashed at them. The wind whipped down from the slopes of the mountains to the north, slapping the rain into their faces like stones from a sling. It had rained incessantly for the last day and night, and for a long while there had been no trail to follow. But Sulis had led the way well enough, and at midday they had reached a muddy track that ran alongside a birch wood.

"Soon we will be on my husband's land," she said.

None of the men had replied, but Cynan had noted Ingwald checking his weapons, sliding his sword out of its scabbard to see that it would not stick if it was needed. Halinard's hand dropped to the hefty seax that hung at his belt. For a time they all rode straighter in their saddles, more alert and ready for danger. But soon the constant soaking from the rain, the hiss of the downpour and the wind whispering through the trees, had them once again slumped in their saddles. Cynan shivered. The gods knew what the others were thinking, but his thoughts were dominated by warm halls, roaring hearth fires, good mead and greasy mutton. He could have been back in Stagga, sipping mead with Eadgyth in the comfortable hall. With a pang of guilt he thought of Acennan's widow. He had left her with her question unanswered. He'd fled to Ubbanford and then embarked on this wild errand. He saw her eyes, beautiful and full of intelligence, in his memory. What he wouldn't give to see her now. He longed for her counsel and her friendship. Did he desire more than that? The idea unnerved him. It did not sit well within his thoughts, but there was no denying that his mind returned to Eadgyth whenever it could. Still, it was uncomfortable. No matter how he approached the notion of Eadgyth and marriage, like a boot with a pebble inside, he could not find a way for the idea to fit correctly in his mind.

He wiped away the water that slicked his face. Perhaps he would not have had an easy time of it if he'd returned to Stagga, but it would certainly have been drier and warmer than riding through this chill rain in Rheged.

"How much further?" he asked, wishing to change the subject of his thoughts as much as anything.

"Since we passed the thorn bush on the hill," Sulis said, pointing back the way they had come, "we have been on our land. There is not far to go now."

Cynan raised himself up in his saddle and shielded his eyes against the rain. Some way off, the steep scarp of a mountain rose to be veiled by low-lying cloud. Closer to the riders, the path meandered down into a valley that was dotted with copses and small woods. A few pale sheep were scattered along the hillside.

It was a peaceful-looking place, much as Sulis had described it. Remote and hilly. A great gift from King Oswald to a trusty warrior no doubt. Some good grazing, some forests for wood and mast. Enough to provide for a few families, but nothing that would make a man rich.

Cynan reined in and flicked his gaze back over the valley

below. Something had pulled at his senses. Sulis pulled her pony to a halt beside him.

"What is it?" she asked.

By way of answer, he held his hand up for silence.

Halinard, Ingwald and Brinin rode up.

"What have you seen?" asked Ingwald, peering in the direction that Cynan was looking.

"Listen," Cynan said. "I heard something on the wind."

"What?" asked Brinin.

Cynan hissed for silence and for several heartbeats they all sat astride their mounts without speaking. Mierawin snorted and shook her great head. Without thinking, Cynan patted her thick mane. Perhaps he had imagined it after all. He was about to kick the mare into motion once more when he heard it again. A thin sound, reedy with distance, almost drowned by the rain and the wind. But it had been piercing enough to make out.

He looked at the others and saw on their faces that they had heard it too.

"Was that a scream?" asked Brinin.

"Could it have been a bird?" asked Ingwald.

"No," shouted Sulis, her voice rending the quiet that had fallen around them as they strained to hear. "It was a scream."

Cynan looked at her. She was pale, her wet skin as white as a gull's wing. She was pointing down into the valley. For a time he could see nothing to explain her reaction. Then, with a start, he saw movement. There were men down there. And horses. As he watched he saw the dull gleam of steel. A moment later, the piteous thin scream reached them again. Whatever was happening, someone was being hurt and Cynan felt his anger flare like a beacon within him.

"This is your land?" he snapped at Sulis.

"It is."

"And the only people here are Leofman and your bondsman?"

She nodded.

"Alfwold, yes."

Cynan watched the movement on the path below for a heartbeat and made his decision.

"Brinin," he barked, "stay with Sulis. Protect her. Watch what happens. If things go badly for us, flee. Keep her safe."

Brinin opened his mouth as if to respond, then closed it and just nodded.

Cynan pulled his sword from its tooled leather scabbard. He drew in a great breath of the cold moist air.

"Halinard, Ingwald," he said. "With me."

He dug his heels into Mierawin's flanks, and the mare shot off at a gallop down the hill. Ingwald and Halinard rode with him. He did not know what they were riding towards. But he had heard the screams and, as they sped down the path, he thought he could see a lone figure being tormented by several mounted men. Whatever the man had done to deserve such abuse, Cynan did not know. Nor did he truly care. He had been wrestling with his worries and concerns ever since leaving Ubbanford like a thief in the dark of the night. He could feel those worries falling away from him as he galloped towards the clump of men beside the towering tree on the track. It felt good to be done with his turmoil of concerns for a while. There was no time for such things now. He kicked Mierawin on to renewed haste. The man closest to him turned, his mouth a dark circle of surprise. In his hand he held a sword, its blade cold and grey in the rain-slick afternoon light. No, the time for thoughts was done. Now was the time for action, and Cynan felt the thrill of it thrumming in his blood.

They had ridden across Albion expecting trouble. It seemed at last, they had found it.

Chapter 16

"**D**eath! Death!" Beobrand yelled in his battle-voice, rallying his men. Beside him, his black-shielded gesithas held firm, stepping forward slowly as their foe-men fell back or were slain by the implacable onslaught. As inexorable as wyrd, the shieldwall advanced. It was slower going now, the earth churned to a mire of mud, spilt guts and blood. The world was filled with the screams of the dying, the roars of rage of the killers and the soon-to-be killed, the cataclysmic crash of shields on shields and the smithy clang of metal on metal.

The first attack had come shortly after dawn, just as Oswine had said. Beobrand had worried that the Deirans might attack at night, and had told Ethelwin to double the watches on the pickets around the camp. The warmaster, recalling Beobrand's warning at Bebbanburg that had prevented the fortress falling to a stealthy night-time sortie, had nodded and ordered more guards to be posted and for the fyrd to be alert and ready for action. None of the men had slept well, but there had been no night attack. Oswine was a good follower of Christ and would not lie, not even to defeat an enemy. Such honesty would surely be his downfall, Beobrand had thought, as the Deiran shieldwall had formed in the drizzle-damp dawn.

In that initial clash in the watery grey light, with the rain still falling from a slate-hued sky, the ranks of both forces had been thinned of the inexperienced and the unlucky. Like chaff separated from the wheat by the thresher's flail, that unfortunate crop of warriors had fallen. After a gruelling time of bloodletting, each side had grown tired and, as if by mutual agreement, the two shieldwalls had fallen back several paces. Men had bound wounds and taken the opportunity to take a gulp of water before the next furious assault. Some had dashed out to drag back injured comrades who were too weak to walk or crawl behind their lines. Others were left between the shieldwalls; a blood-soaked harvest of the scything blades of these grim-faced reapers, these trained and hardened warriors. These killers of men.

The second coming together of the warhosts was different from the outset. Each enemy that remained had been tempered in battle and would not break easily. Every step was hard-earned and each encounter between individual warriors was drawn out and filled with peril. Along the Bernician line several men fell, but the shieldwall stood strong, and the gaps were plugged quickly. And still, Beobrand and his Black Shields advanced. No Deiran lord's warband could withstand the brunt of the Black Shields' assault. The combination of strength, well-drilled coordination and bravery made them almost unstoppable. When coupled with their battle-fame and the reputation of their half-handed leader, they seemed invincible.

Beobrand caught an axe blow on the rim of his shield. With a twist of his wrist, the Deiran's attack was deflected away from Beobrand's face and, too slow to recover his balance, Nægling tore out the man's throat. As the warrior collapsed to his knees, hands clutching uselessly to stem the flow of blood from the gash in his neck, Beobrand hammered his sword blade into the crown of the man's helm. It rang like one of the church bells he had heard tolling for the Christ's prayers at Eoferwic, and the Deiran went limp and sprawled to the earth, unmoving.

Dead or dying was all the same to Beobrand, just as long as he was no longer a threat. Quickly, Beobrand looked at Nægling's blade. It was patterned like the skin of a snake, or rippling water, and it was smeared with the blood of many foes. With relief he saw the metal was not bent and its edge still held. It was a risk to batter the blade against a helm, but now was not the time to be protective of his sword's edge. Now was the killing time, and he would ensure that any foe who fell before him was no longer able to wield a weapon. He would not risk an injured man's knife stabbing up from under the shieldwall. He had lost his lord, Scand, that way and he would never make that mistake himself.

To his right, Attor, shield in hand for once and one of his wicked seaxes in the other, grinned with savage glee.

"Come to die, you piss-guzzling, goat-swiving, sons of pox-riddled whores!"

As Beobrand watched, Attor pushed an opponent back and, dropping low, hacked his seax into the Deiran's shin. The man had no armour there and he screamed pitifully. He tried to stand, but staggered, unsteady and disoriented by the pain. Grindan, who fought on Attor's right, drove his sword into the wounded man's belly. Beyond Grindan was his brother, Eadgard. His huge axe slashed up and down, flicking rain and blood from its heavy head as it splintered shields, sundered helms and snapped sword blades. The Deirans were falling back in the face of such ferocious opposition and Beobrand dragged his attention back to the enemies who stood directly in front of him.

Dreogan was on his left, and as they stepped forward, adding pressure on the Deiran ranks, the tattooed warrior pointed with his dripping sword further along the line, towards the left where Ethelwin had placed Alhfrith and his comitatus. Octa was there, and Beobrand's breath caught in his throat as he glanced in the direction of Dreogan's bloody sword tip. The line had lost its shape and was bending. All was chaos, a surging mass of fighting and dying. Where was Alhfrith's blue stallion banner? Had the atheling and his warband been overrun?

"The young ones are showing us how it's done," grumbled Dreogan.

All at once, the picture fell into place and Beobrand made sense of what he saw. The atheling's stallion standard had not fallen. The Deirans had not overwhelmed Oswiu's son. Alhfrith had pushed his warband like a wedge into the Deiran ranks! There was his banner, surrounded by Deirans as the atheling and his hearth-warriors fought with bold abandon. Beobrand thought he caught a glimpse of Octa, towering over the enemy warriors, but then he was lost to view in the jostle and shove of the heaving warhost that surrounded them.

"By Tiw's cock," shouted Beobrand, "what is that fool doing?"

Dreogan grunted as a stocky Deiran clattered into his shield. Beobrand, still with no enemy of his own close enough to strike, swung Nægling, cleaving into the man's neck. Dreogan's opponent bellowed like a bull and turned with an almost comical expression of fury towards Beobrand. Dreogan leaned over his shield and pulled his sword viciously across the man's exposed throat. He crumpled to the quagmire beneath their feet, clawing at his throat and gurgling on his own lifeblood.

"Maybe not such a fool," said Dreogan, pointing again with his sword. Beobrand looked at where he indicated and saw Oswine's golden cross and lions standard.

Looking back at Alhfrith's position, Beobrand nodded.

"He is going to try and take Oswine," he said, shocked at the audacity of it. He may be foolhardy, he thought, but he was brave.

"That's the sort of thing you would do, lord," yelled Fraomar from further down the line.

By Woden, it was. Perhaps he was getting old after all. A few years earlier he would not have hesitated to undertake such a daring attack. He shook his head and blinked the rain, sweat and blood from his eyes. He was dismayed at his own hesitation. And Octa was with Alhfrith. He could not let them be surrounded and overcome.

"Come, my brave gesithas," he shouted in his loudest voice. "The atheling needs us. See there? The cross and lions of Oswine King?" He pointed with Nægling's patterned blade at the Deiran king's banner. "We will meet Alhfrith there and, if the gods will it, we shall take our lord king's enemy and put an end to this war."

The Black Shields roared their appreciation of their lord's words.

"With me then!" he yelled. "Let us race the atheling and his young warband to the king's banner. And men." They paused expectantly. "Let us be the first ones to our destination."

With a roar, they redoubled their efforts, surging forward and cutting deeply into the Deiran shieldwall.

Chapter 17

Cynan surveyed the scene as he galloped towards the small group of men clustered on the muddy path in the shadow of the towering oak. There were six of them standing beneath the massive tree. Their horses looked up from where they had been cropping at the grass beside the path. One of them whinnied an anxious greeting to the approaching horses. Mierawin did not respond. Her ears were flattened against her head and her thrumming hooves ate up the remaining distance to the tree in a few heartbeats.

It was only when they were within a spear-throw of the men on the path that Cynan saw the object of their attention and surely the man they had heard screaming from far off on the ridge of the hill. He was not a young man, with a bald pate and wisps of grey hair at his temples. But his body had a wiry strength and his arms and face bore the weathered tan of one who spends all of his life outdoors. He had been stripped of his kirtle and was lashed to the broad bole of the oak. A rope was looped about his throat, while others bound his arms and body, holding him tight against the rough bark of the tree's trunk. He strained at his bonds, his chest, arms and stomach all corded muscles, hard and angular as he grunted with effort and pain.

The pallid skin of his chest and stomach was streaked with blood from several deep cuts.

Cynan pulled on Mierawin's reins. Throwing his right leg over her neck, he slid from her back before she had stopped moving. Without pause, he tugged his black shield from where it was tied to the saddle. Ingwald and Halinard, not such accomplished riders, were reining in and dismounting some paces away. Cynan slapped Mierawin's rump, sending the mare cantering out of harm's way.

The men on the path had all turned to face the threat of these three strangers who had galloped out of the rain. They abandoned the man hanging from the tree to his moans and grunts as he struggled in vain to free himself.

"Who in the name of Woden and all his children are you?" said a thickset man with a close-cropped beard that accentuated the roll of fat beneath his chin. His tone was part angry and part amused, as if the sight of the three riders was some kind of jest that only he understood.

Cynan was in no mood for jesting.

"Who I am is not important," he snapped.

"What is important then?" asked the man, with a half-smile playing on his lips.

"That you are not welcome on this land. Climb onto your horses now and ride away."

The man looked about him at the five other men. They clearly had not come expecting a fight, but Cynan noted that they moved like warriors, spreading out across the path. They stared at Cynan coldly as Ingwald and Halinard joined him with their swords drawn and black shields in hand. The man in the tree moaned. Cynan flicked a look at him and felt another surge of ire. The men beneath the oak had no shields. They wore warrior jackets and cloaks. They might have had byrnies underneath their coats, but it seemed unlikely as they did not seem to be ready for war and none had a helm on his head. No, it appeared to Cynan that these men, warriors all, had come to this place for much easier prey.

"And what if we decide to stay?" said the fat-jowled man.

The rain picked up in intensity, filling the world with its sibilant song. Cynan met the man's gaze. Water trickled into his eyes and he blinked it away.

"If you do not leave, we will make you. And you will look worse than him," he nodded at the man dangling from the oak, "when we are done." He held the fat man's gaze, unblinking now in spite of the rain running into his eyes.

One of the warriors stepped forward. He was tall and slender of build, in a dark red leather warrior coat. His arms were adorned with silver rings and his belt had a gold and garnet buckle and trimmings. At his side hung a sword with a golden pommel cap. His right arm was held close to his chest, hanging in a sling made from a strip of stained linen.

"You would come here and insult us, Waelisc cur?" he sneered. Cynan's lilting tone clearly marked him as one who was not of the Angelfolc, even though he now lived among them.

"I do not insult you," Cynan replied, his voice as cold as the wind that shook the boughs of the oak. "But to do so would not be difficult. For only cowards torment and torture a man. Six of you, with swords, against one poor old man. No, it would not be hard to insult men such as you." He hawked and spat. "If indeed you are men."

"Why, you whoreson!" the man growled, making to approach. The fat leader pulled him back.

"No, Hunberht, now is not the time. Not with you injured."

"I could take this one with my left hand."

Cynan laughed then, a wave of mad fury washing through him.

"Go on then," he said, dropping his shield to the mud and taking a step forward. "Just the two of us. No shields. Come on. If you are so brave, then show it."

Hunberht twisted his left hand around and awkwardly dragged his sword from its scabbard. It was a fine blade, with flowing patterns on the metal and an elaborate carved hilt. This was the sword of a warrior. A weapon fit for a king's hearth-warrior, or even a king himself. Cynan's blade was less gaudy, but it would kill well enough.

The leader stepped forward and interposed himself between them.

"Hunberht, you cannot fight thus. This is madness."

He began to push the slimmer man back towards the tree and the waiting horses.

"Just as I thought," shouted Cynan. "Craven, all of you. It is one thing to torture an unarmed ceorl, quite another to stand toe to toe with a swordsman. Go on now." He flicked his sword at them disdainfully. "Leave this land and do not return."

"I am no coward," said a man with a heavy brow and long black hair that tumbled over his muscular shoulders. In his hand, he held a sword. There was blood on the blade that must have come from the poor wretch bound to the tree. The sight of it made Cynan's lips curl back to show his teeth. "I will fight you," said the man.

"Aescferth," said the leader, his tone imploring now, "we have not come here to fight."

"Be silent, Bumoth," said the one called Aescferth. "Nobody names me a coward and lives." He strode forward, out of the shelter of the tree and into the heavy rain. "When I kill you, your two friends can ride away. But I'll take your horse and your gear." He let out a barking laugh and rolled his head around to ease the muscles of his thick neck. "I don't kill for free."

Cynan smiled.

"And if I slay you," he shouted, so that the other men would hear him over the rain and the wind, "the five of you will ride away." The leader was still restraining Hunberht who glowered at Cynan with undisguised loathing. The fat leader nodded.

"You'll never beat Aescferth," he said. Cynan did not take his eyes off the approaching warrior, who was swinging his sword in great arcs to limber up his long sword arm.

"You five will leave if I do," Cynan repeated.

"Aye, we'll leave," muttered Bumoth, his words almost lost in the wind-whisper and hiss of the rain. "You have my word."

"I imagine the word of a coward is worth little," said Cynan, stepping out to meet Aescferth.

The broad-shouldered man's eyes narrowed and Cynan knew immediately that he was going to attack. With a growl, Aescferth charged, swiping his sword through the rain. Cynan let him come towards him, at the last moment dodging out of the deadly blade's reach. Aescferth had long arms, which, coupled with formidable strength, made his attacks dangerous. But Cynan quickly saw that, whilst he had some sword-skill, Aescferth was no master. He relied on speed, reach and shock to overcome his opponents. Against a less-experienced man, one who had not stood in countless battles and skirmishes, a man who had not trained relentlessly with the famed Black Shields, such tactics would surely bear fruit. Cynan would not be so easily beaten.

Another series of slashes saw Cynan skipping away. Aescferth let out a guttural roar. Cynan laughed, easily dodging all of the warrior's wild attacks. He did not want to risk the edge of his blade by clanging his sword against the swings of this bear of a man.

"Fight me," shouted Aescferth, his anger building. Red-faced, he bellowed and rushed Cynan again. This time, his swiping blade came too close and Cynan was forced to parry the blow. Deflecting the attack as he sidestepped, Cynan allowed Aescferth to pass him by in a rush.

"You are not worthy to fight me," hissed Cynan. "You are as clumsy as a child with a stick. And as harmless."

Furious now, Aescferth spun about to renew his onslaught.

But Cynan had anticipated the man's movement and had

reversed his own, bouncing lightly on the balls of his feet. As Aescferth turned, Cynan sprang forward, for the first time using his own sword to attack. The grip tugged gently in his hand as the sword's sharp blade cut through the man's woollen warrior coat and opened his belly. Aescferth roared with anger, frustration and the pain that now swelled within him. He blundered towards Cynan, but the Waelisc warrior backed away quickly.

"Come to me, you craven whoreson," he said, beckoning to Aescferth. "Not so easy when your enemy carries a sword, is it?"

With a cry, Aescferth rushed forward, raising once more the fine sword that was streaked with the blood of the man he had been torturing. Cynan stood his ground, ready to finish this now. But he would need no more blows to secure the victory. Aescferth halted his charge and staggered to a halt. His eyes grew wide and his face crumpled as he looked down at his midriff. It seemed that Cynan's blade had cut more deeply than he had thought, for blood sheeted down Aescferth's groin and legs, and, as Cynan watched, the man's gut-ropes began to tumble from the gaping wound. Aescferth let out a pitiable moan and dropped to his knees. Relinquishing his grip on his sword, he fumbled at his innards in a useless attempt to shove them back into his body.

Cynan tasted bile in his throat as his gorge rose. He turned away from the dying man.

"Now, mount up and begone," he shouted, his voice hoarse.

He wondered if the men beneath the tree would charge at the three black-shielded warriors standing in the pelting rain on the muddy path.

"Ready, lads?" he muttered, stooping to retrieve his shield.

"Always," replied Ingwald. He was at Cynan's right in a heartbeat, Halinard at his left. Cynan was glad of their presence beside him.

After a few heartbeats of silent staring, the men in the oak's shadow began to mount up. The one called Hunberht scowled at Cynan with death in his eyes. If any of them was going to attack, it would be him, but it seemed sense prevailed, for he too at last walked to his horse and with obvious athleticism, especially for a man only able to use one arm, he swung himself into the saddle.

"Well fought, lord," Ingwald muttered.

Near to them, Aescferth was mewling like a new-born lamb.

"Don't leave me, Hunberht," he cried.

Cynan was not sure that the men would hear him, what with the clatter of their horses' hooves and noise of the rain and wind in the leaves of the oak. Cynan looked to the man who was tied there. He was staring at him with an expression of desperate hope on his face. Moments before he had been certain of death, now he had been saved.

"Don't leave me," repeated Aescferth, his voice little more than a gasping sob now.

Cynan spat into the mud.

"They are leaving you to die," he said, his words as vicious as blades. "It seems even cowards can keep their word."

Aescferth gazed up at him. He knelt where he had fallen, his arms clutched about his stomach and a large puddle of blood oozing around him. His skin was white and his lips held the blue tinge of death.

"Not long now," said Cynan savagely.

Aescferth sobbed again and fumbled in the blood-drenched mud. At last, his fingers found the hilt of his sword. He grasped it. With a rattling sigh and a shudder, he died, slumping into the muck.

The warriors beneath the tree were all mounted now. The leader, Bumoth, kicked his brown gelding towards Cynan a few paces.

"You're a dead man," he said.

"No," replied Cynan, nodding at Aescferth's corpse. "He is."

"This isn't the end of it," shouted Bumoth. "We'll be seeing you!"

"Good. I can kill the rest of you then."

"You're a dead man," Bumoth repeated, swinging his horse around. The four other riders had already touched heels to their horses and were now galloping away. Bumoth kicked his own mount to follow them, but after only a few quick steps, he reined in his gelding and turned it again.

Cynan expected some parting insult, some clever quip the fat man had thought of, but instead, Bumoth spurred his horse towards the oak. Too late, Cynan realised what he was going to do. He started to run, but he was too far away and would never reach Bumoth in time.

"No!" he shouted, but Bumoth ignored him.

The man who was tied to the tree screamed.

As Cynan watched, the fat man drew his sword and hacked its blade into the bound man's throat. Blood fountained in the grey shade of the oak. Cynan was still some way off and yet he sprinted as fast as he could, as if he hoped he might staunch the man's blood. But even as he ran, he knew with a terrible certainty that the man was as doomed as Aescferth.

Bumoth wheeled his horse around and, with a yell, he kicked it into a gallop.

When Cynan reached the oak, the man was dead. His blood covered his limp, pale body and streaked the bark. It dripped from his bare feet, pooling on the moss-covered earth between the tree's roots. Looking up at the old man, Cynan could not shake the impression that his open eyes were staring accusingly into his. *You could have saved me*, they seemed to say.

Cynan let out a ragged breath. Ingwald and Halinard came running up. Neither man spoke. They merely looked from the dead man on the tree to the retreating riders, already blurred by the rain and the distance.

"Help me cut him down," said Cynan.

Chapter 18

"Watch out!" yelled Beobrand.

Even as he shouted the warning, he threw himself forward, his scarred and splintered shield raised. He could see that Elmer would never react in time to defend against the spear thrust. The big man, who had led the remainder of the Black Shields from Ubbanford, was fully occupied with a heavily armoured warrior whose face was hidden behind the metal plates of a grimhelm. The Deiran was tall and strong and hammered blow after blow upon Elmer's shield. The ferocity of the attacks gave Elmer no time to counter. It was all he could do to deflect the strikes, his movement hampered as it was by the crush of men around him.

Beobrand grunted as the spear-point that had been aimed at Elmer rammed hard into his shield. For a moment, there was pressure on the linden board, and then the iron point scored across the hide-covered wood and skittered dangerously off the shield's surface and into his chest. Beobrand twisted, taking much of the force from the blow, but it still felt as if he had been struck in the ribs by a hammer. He breathed thanks to Woden, Thunor and all the gods that his byrnie was strong and the rings had not sundered. Almost without thought, he pushed himself forward, allowing the spear to scratch across his chest. An instant later, he wrapped his sword arm over the spear's ash haft, clamping it tight to his body. Using all his weight, he heaved on the spear. There was resistance as its owner pulled back, but Beobrand applied all his considerable bulk, leaning onto the shaft as well as tugging it. He staggered as it came away from the hands of the Deiran who had held it. Beobrand laughed, filled with the joyful lust of battle now. He swung Nægling again, letting the spear fall to the churned earth of the battlefield. It disappeared and was quickly trampled into the muck.

Beside him, Elmer, lips pulled back in a savage snarl, was still taking the brunt of the attacks from the thegn in the grimhelm. Beobrand watched for a moment. A heartbeat seemed an age to him when he was in the flow of battle. When the swords sang and the stink of slaughter caught in his throat, Beobrand could anticipate the movements of his enemies almost before they knew themselves what they would do. The steel-storm roared like an inchoate beast, terrifying and cacophonous to most, but to Beobrand it was the sword-song, and by its music he could gauge the way a battle was going as a fisherman might sense the play of a trout on a line.

Beobrand saw an opening. Without hesitation he smashed Nægling into Elmer's adversary's iron-clad chest. The hit was strong, but the byrnie was stronger still and did not give. And yet the attack served its purpose. The man's vision was impeded by the great helm he wore and so he turned involuntarily to see who had delivered the bruising blow to his side. In that instant, Elmer seized his chance. He lowered his tattered shield and sent a perfectly aimed sword slash into the tall man's neck, between his byrnie and his great helm.

Blood flowed in a glut, spraying Beobrand and Elmer. The Deiran thegn, blood pumping from the wound that would take his life, still tried to batter down Elmer's defences, forcing him once again to raise his shield to catch the shower of strikes.

Another Deiran stepped forward and Beobrand stabbed him

beneath his shield, opening the big artery that ran down the inner thigh. As the man collapsed in agony, Beobrand finished him off with a hacking chop to his neck.

Elmer's opponent, weakening quickly now, stopped swinging his sword and finally toppled onto the corpse of Beobrand's latest foe.

"Onward, my brave gesithas!" Beobrand bellowed.

They were so close now. They had fought hard for what seemed an age, moving forward step by step as the Deirans fell to the skill and tenacity of the men of Bernicia. There was no give in Beobrand's Black Shields, and soon enemies had sought to push back into their own ranks when they saw they must face the half-handed thegn of Ubbanford and his warband.

And so the mass of enemies had begun to part before them and now they were at the tight throng of Oswine's hearth-warriors. The thegn in the grimhelm had been the first, but there were more now, forming a wall of wood and steel around their king. Over to his left, Beobrand could see Octa, his face lathered in a mask of blood, sword flinging up gobbets of flesh and sprays of blood in the rain-streaked air. Alhfrith was by his side and the two young men were hacking a swathe through the Deirans. Brunwine was there too, bellowing and roaring like a great aurochs. Blood speckled his face and ran dark in his full beard. The Deiran champion was a terrifying sight, and he stood directly in the path of Octa and the atheling.

Beobrand offered up a silent prayer to Woden to watch over his son, and glanced about him.

He was unsure when or how their battle line had shifted, but Elmer was now on his left, Gram on his right. There was no sign of Offa and the other East Angelfolc and Beobrand wondered briefly where they were. He could see Fraomar, Attor, Grindan and Eadgard too, but none were in the positions in which they had begun the battle. It had been a deadly seething mass of shoving and hacking, slipping in the mud, warriors falling to be pulled back to their feet moments later or to be cut down where they lay, adding their lifeblood to the quagmire. The stench of shit and piss and the iron-sharp tang of blood filled his nose.

"Oswine is ours!" shouted Beobrand. "Let's end this now! To me!"

His gesithas began to form up around their hlaford as quickly as they could. They tightened up their shieldwall, pulling back and forming into the boar-snout, preparing for another push.

"Ready?" Beobrand yelled. "Onwards!"

They rushed forwards as fast as they were able, which was not much more than a walk. The mud was strewn with corpses, shields, helms and weapons, and the men tripped and stumbled as they moved over the uneven footing. Despite this, they still drove a wedge into the protective line around Oswine. The king's cross and lions banner, lank and bedraggled in the rain, swung limply from the pole that was raised only a spear's length behind the shieldwall.

A cheer went up from the left and the Deiran line shuddered.

"For Bernicia!" screamed Beobrand, and his men took up the chant. With a surge of effort, they heaved and he felt himself shoved forward. A warrior before him had somehow snagged his seax in his own baldric. The man looked up at Beobrand with wide eyes as he struggled to free his blade. Beobrand did not blink as he sliced Nægling's blade across the man's eyes. Blood sheeted. The man screamed, adding his horror and pain to the tumult. Blinded, he finally tugged the seax loose and swung it about him desperately. Without hesitation, Beobrand slammed Nægling once more into the man's face. Bone crunched beneath the blade and the Deiran dropped like a bull under the butcher's blade at Blotmonath.

With a savage roar, Beobrand leapt over the corpse to meet the next foe-man.

"Their king is ours!" he shouted. "For Bernicia!"

His black-shielded warriors were fighting with ferocious fury, but they faced the strongest in the Deiran warhost now – the king's comitatus – and their advance slowed as they were each confronted with formidable foes.

The warrior who loomed before Beobrand wore a polished helm with nose guard and cheek plates. The helm was crested with a great, red-dyed horse-tail plume that trailed down his back. The man's black shield was blazoned with a red star. He was young and arrogant and his face twisted into a sneer as he faced Beobrand. It was Odda, the man Wulfstan had warned him about.

"The scops will sing of this moment!" he shouted.

"They always sing of war," spat Beobrand, readying himself for the attack he knew would come.

"They will sing of your death by my hand," screamed Odda, and swung at Beobrand's head.

Beobrand raised his shield, but suspected a feint. Just as he'd thought, Odda shifted his weight and changed his sword swing in an attempt to gut Beobrand. Anticipating the move, Beobrand lowered Nægling and parried the blow. Then, as fast as thought, with a twist of his wrist he sent a thrust into Odda's groin. Odda had expected either to have struck Beobrand, or for the thegn of Ubbanford to have been on the retreat. And yet it was not only Beobrand's strength, speed and sword-skill that made him one of the deadliest adversaries in all of Albion; it was also that he never backed down. Odda's eyes widened in shock as he felt the bite of Beobrand's blade, as it buried into his inner thigh, beneath his byrnie and deep into his flesh. Beobrand recognised the expression on the young warrior's face. He had seen it many times before on the faces of those whose ghosts haunted his dreams. Odda had been so certain of his prowess. He was not the first warrior to underestimate Beobrand, and would surely not be the last.

Odda, wide-eyed and pale, swiped another attack. Beobrand took the sting from the blow on his shield, and then hacked into the man's sword arm, just above the wrist. Blood bloomed and soaked Odda's sleeve. It was not a strong blow, but enough to make Odda drop his blade. He tried to stagger back, away from the deadly warrior before him, but he was held fast by the pack of bodies behind.

"There will be no singing of your death, Odda," Beobrand said, driving Nægling into the Deiran's throat. Odda's eyes bulged in horror at the approach of his own end. Beobrand twisted Nægling, wrenching the blade free. Odda collapsed into the mud. This battle was what he had wanted. What all young, foolish warriors seek. They long for the glory, the battle-fame. The crash of the shieldwall. Too often all they find is a pathetic death, choking on their own blood as their life ebbs from them into the soil. For an instant, Beobrand felt sadness wash over him. He shook it away. Now was not the moment for remorse or sorrow.

Another ragged cheer came from the left. Beobrand raised himself up to his full height and could just make out Octa and Alhfrith reaching Oswine's banner bearer.

"Are we going to let the atheling beat us to the prize?" Beobrand shouted. The Black Shields who heard him over the chaotic thunder of battle roared in defiance. Beobrand flicked another glance at where his son fought, towering over most of the Deirans. The fighting was furious there, and his heart was gripped with fear for his son. But Beobrand could not watch for more than a heartbeat, for another warrior was stepping over Odda's corpse to meet him.

With a lurching twist in the pit of his stomach, he recognised the dark-bearded thegn.

Wulfstan.

Beobrand spat onto Odda. Of all the foe-men he might have to confront, that it should be his friend was cruel indeed. He had risked everything to save Wulfstan once. Now, in the rain-splattered seething mass of mud and death, he did not know how he could save him again. The gods must be laughing.

"I see Odda got what he deserved," shouted Wulfstan, holding his shield and blood-smeared sword in the defensive warrior pose. Either side of them, the Bernicians and Deirans clashed, trading blows and dealing death.

"Odda was a fool," said Beobrand.

"We are all fools, are we not?" replied Wulfstan, and leapt forward to attack.

Beobrand took the blow on his shield and sent a half-hearted riposte at Wulfstan that the Deiran easily parried. Beobrand thought perhaps his friend would seek to give the appearance of fighting, but would hold back, not wishing to slay one with whom he shared a friendship. But even as he thought this, so Wulfstan hammered his sword into Beobrand's black shield, attempting to turn it. The board splintered and Beobrand felt the thrum of the impact in his arm.

"Do not look so shocked, Beobrand," laughed Wulfstan. "We are enemies by order of our lords. Our oaths say we cannot be friends today."

Beobrand felt a hot stab of rage. Wulfstan would speak to him of his oath! By Woden, he had broken his oath for this man. He had sullied his word for Wulfstan, and now this?

The Deiran sent a probing thrust at Beobrand's legs. Beobrand pushed the sword blade away with the rim of his shield, but too slow. He felt the keen edge of the sword cut into the flesh above his right knee. He grunted and shook his head to clear it of thoughts of friendship and broken vows. Wulfstan was his foe now; the sworn enemy of Oswiu King. Girding himself for what must come, Beobrand watched the Deiran, focusing again, willing his anger and pain to once again transport him into that harmony of calm frenzy where he was faster than any man and no enemy could stand before him and live.

"You repaid your debt to me, Beobrand," Wulfstan said, perhaps noting the change in his opponent. "Now we meet as enemies in battle, nothing more."

Nothing more? What else was there?

With a growl of rage, Beobrand charged forward with his shield, clattering the iron boss into Wulfstan's and forcing the Deiran back. As the shorter Wulfstan staggered, Beobrand sent a slicing cut at his exposed leg, opening up a deep cut just above his right knee, mirroring the wound he had received by Wulfstan's hand.

They pulled apart. Beobrand was surprised there was space for movement, but the men about them were less closely packed than they had been until moments before. Wulfstan's eyes widened as he felt the warmth of his own blood soaking his breeches. Neither man looked away to see what had caused the shift in the battle. They had each drawn blood and were wary now.

A lull was falling over the battlefield. Beobrand often thought that shieldwalls were like living things with their own thoughts and life. For in every battle there were moments when the men would act as if with one mind, and there was no explanation for it that Beobrand could fathom. Perhaps it was wyrd, perhaps the will of the gods, or maybe just happenstance, but such a change was occurring now, and he longed to look about him to make sense of it. But whether oblivious to the change, or angered by his wound, Wulfstan would not allow him the respite. The Deiran thegn rushed forward, leaping over Odda's crumpled bloody form and swinging his sword in a great overarm arc. Beobrand caught the blow on his shield, hearing the board splinter again under the strength of the attack. In the same instant, he pivoted and sent his own scything cut at Wulfstan. The Deiran soaked up the force of it on his shield.

Shouts came from the left. Something had happened there, and Beobrand's stomach knotted at the memory of seeing Octa and Alhfrith forcing their way towards Oswine's banner. The shouts were loud and filled with dismay, but he could not make out the words as Wulfstan came at him again. Beobrand parried and riposted once more, but neither man scored a telling blow. Wulfstan was panting now, his breeches on his right side soaked and dark with blood. Beobrand's leg burnt from the cut he had received, but he knew his wound was not as deep as Wulfstan's. The Deiran was losing a lot of blood and was weakening.

"The atheling! The atheling!"

The shouts were clear now, strident with despair. Beobrand feared the worst. If Alhfrith had been slain, the Bernicians would lose heart. On such things rested the fate of shieldwalls. He had seen it countless times before. The loss of morale could prove deadlier than the most vicious attack.

Other words came from the Deiran host, intermingling with the shouts from the Bernicians in a confusion of sound like the crash of waves against the cliffs near Bebbanburg. They were but sounds with no meaning that Beobrand could detect from this distance over the tumult of the fighting that, whilst easing slightly, still raged all around him.

Wulfstan attacked again and Beobrand saw that the man was slowing. His mouth was agape and he panted. Whether from his exertion or from the pain of the cut to his leg, Beobrand could not tell. Beobrand parried and shoved him back, shield against shield.

Wulfstan, off balance and weakened as he was, stumbled. His heels caught Odda's sprawled corpse and Wulfstan tumbled over to lie on his back in the mire. Beobrand stepped quickly towards him. Wulfstan still held his sword and was certainly not defenceless, but Beobrand knew that now was the time to end this.

He hesitated as he looked down at Wulfstan's pale features. By Woden, he did not wish to kill this man. He thought of Wulfstan's wife and children back at Ediscum. He had not saved Wulfstan from Heremod's blade only to slay him now.

"Finish it," hissed Wulfstan through gritted teeth. "You owe me nothing, Beobrand. It was our wyrd to fight, it seems."

And then the words from the Deiran host rang out, as clear as the screech of a gull over the wave-rush noise of the North Sea.

"Oswine! The king is fallen!"

There was a sudden hush about the battlefield. Beobrand glanced to the left and saw that Oswine's standard had vanished. And in an instant, like water rushing from a cracked jug, so the fight fled from the Deirans. They fell back from the Bernicians, like a receding tide, leaving behind them the charnel house flotsam of battle: broken bodies and discarded weapons. The tide-line of defeat.

"Black Shields!" Beobrand bellowed in his battle-voice. "Hold!"

All along the line the Deirans were fleeing. Many Bernicians rushed to follow, but Beobrand called his men back. He did not want them chasing after the retreating Deirans. They would become dispersed about the battlefield and many small fights would break out. There was safety together.

Wulfstan still lay at his feet and Beobrand stared down at him. His knee throbbed with each beat of his heart, but as quickly as it had come, so his anger at Wulfstan evaporated. The Deiran was merely fulfilling his oath to his king. It was not he who had done anything wrong. And it was certainly not his fault to have reminded Beobrand of his past weakness.

Beobrand took a step closer and Wulfstan lifted his blade.

"You will not be needing that," said Beobrand. He jabbed Nægling into the soft earth, and reached out his hand. Wulfstan blinked up at him, the rain falling into his upturned face. He did not move. "It was our wyrd to fight," said Beobrand, "but it is not your wyrd to die this day, my friend."

Wulfstan hesitated for a heartbeat before dropping his own sword and taking Beobrand's hand, allowing the tall thegn to haul him to his feet.

"Go," hissed Beobrand.

Wulfstan stooped to retrieve his sword with a grimace of

pain and then, with a nod, he turned and hobbled after the routed Deiran warhost. Beobrand watched him and let out a ragged sigh. Reaching down, Beobrand pulled Nægling from the ground and wiped its blade clean against Odda's cloak. It took him three attempts to sheath the sword, such was the trembling of his hands.

His gesithas were closing in around him now. All about them lay the dead and the dying. Beobrand scanned the faces of his men. Fraomar seemed dazed, staring off into the south after the fleeing Deirans. Dreogan had picked up a gash to his head and his face was caked in blood. Many of the others were wounded, but as far as he could tell, all were hale enough.

"Attor," he called, not seeing the wiry warrior and fearing the worst.

Attor jogged up from where he had been pulling an arm ring from a huge brute of a warrior who had been pierced through with a spear that yet jutted from his guts like a banner pole into the rain-driven air. Attor's face was a mask of mud and blood, but his teeth showed white as he grinned.

"Lord?"

"Take Beircheart with you and find out what's happened to Alhfrith."

Attor nodded and made to go in search of the atheling. Beobrand grabbed his shoulder, holding him back.

"And Attor," he said, his mouth filled with the sour taste of loss and fear, "find my son."

Chapter 19

The rain had lost its fury as they trudged down the track to the small house Sulis shared with Leofman and their son, Eadwig. The sight of her home, with the cloud-wreathed mountains behind and smoke trickling from the thatch, should have filled her with joy, but Sulis could not stop gazing at the shape slumped over Brinin's saddle. Alfwold's blood-smeared corpse had been wrapped in a cloak and lashed to the horse with the rope that had previously held him against the rough bark of the oak to be tortured.

Alfwold was a good man. He had served Leofman and her well ever since she had arrived, and for many years before that. He had always been kind to her and Eadwig. She watched as the limp form beneath the blanket bounced with the gait of the horse. Brinin walked at the animal's head, leading it by its reins. She followed close behind on her pony.

She had wept for a time when she had seen Alfwold lying in the dirt beneath the oak. But her tears had dried now. She watched Cynan, Ingwald and Halinard riding ahead and wondered at the violence she had brought into her world. She had been far off, but had seen Cynan cut down Aescferth as easily as she would have killed a hen for the pot. At first she had been shocked, her stomach had turned and she had questioned what she had done in bringing these men here. Then she had seen Alfwold, and her heart had hardened once more. She recognised Aescferth as one of Sidrac's men. It was Sidrac, not she, who had brought death and killing to this small parcel of land deep within the mountains of Rheged.

They were all subdued and quiet when they arrived at the house. The men slid from their mounts and she noticed that Cynan placed his hand on the pommel of his sword. Their eyes darted as they looked around the land surrounding the farm.

Cynan made his way to Sulis and offered her a hand, all the while looking around warily; scanning for danger. He helped her down from the pony, peering into the distance in the direction they had come as if expecting pursuit. Her back did not pain her as much now, but she was exhausted and longed to be inside, dry and warm.

Halinard and Brinin untied Alfwold and were carrying the wrapped corpse towards the house when the door swung open.

Cynan moved away from her and drew his sword. Ingwald stepped in front of the men who bore Alfwold's body, pulling his own blade from its scabbard.

The huge shape in the doorway took a faltering step outside into the rain and her heart soared to see Leofman on his feet. He was pale and leaning on a stick, but he was alive and he offered her a weak smile.

"Sulis, my dear," he said, his voice deep and warm, "I thought I had lost you too." Frowning now, he looked at the armed men. "Who are these men? Do I need to fetch my axe?"

"They are friends," she said, rushing past Cynan and the others to embrace the giant of a man. He encircled her in one of his massive arms and she enjoyed the feeling of safety of his broad chest and firm belly pressing against her. He smelt of woodsmoke, honey and sheep's wool. And there was something else, something that soured her mood once more. Underlying his familiar scent, she detected the sharp taint of sickness.

"Cynan," she said, "this is my husband." Then, to Leofman: "We bring bad tidings." He looked from the grim-faced warriors with their swords in hand, to the wrapped body carried between two of the newcomers.

He let out a long sigh.

"I imagine we could all use a drink then," Leofman said. "You had better come on in out of the rain."

Brinin and Halinard brought Alfwold's body inside and laid it on one of the large rush mats that covered most of the hard-packed earth floor. The two men then wordlessly went outside to tend to the animals. Sulis called after them that there would be room for a couple of the beasts in the barn. The others would need to find shelter in the lee of the house.

While they saw to the horses, Sulis broke the news of Alfwold's death to Leofman. He closed his eyes for a long while. Groaning with the pains of his battered body, Leofman bent down and pulled the cloak away from his bondsman's face. She had watched Cynan close Alfwold's eyes before he was wrapped in the cloak, but they were open once again and staring sightlessly at the soot-stained thatch and beams of the roof.

"Did he die well?" Leofman asked, staring into Alfwold's dull eyes.

Sulis glanced at Cynan. Her throat was tight, she could not speak.

"As well as any man dies when set upon by six cowards," said Cynan.

Leofman wiped a hand over his face.

"If they mean for us to leave this land, they do not know Leofman, son of Hutha." He covered Alfwold's face once more and with difficulty lowered himself onto a stool by the fire. Sulis held on tightly to his hand, helping him down, steadying him. He winced. His leg pained him, that much was clear. "This is our land."

Brinin and Halinard came in from seeing to the horses. They removed their cloaks and shook them outside the door.

"Fetch our guests ale," said Leofman. "Alfwold brewed some not two days ago and his ale is always good." He fell silent and looked down at the shape under the cloak.

There were not enough stools or chairs for all of the men, so she decided to bring a wooden chest over. It was large and filled with clothes and bedding. It was too heavy for her to lift and she began to drag it. Brinin and Halinard hurried over to help. They carried it to the fire with ease. When they had all settled themselves around the hearth, she poured ale for each of them. They took the cups with nods of thanks.

"There is no point clinging to this land if to do so will see you slain," said Cynan, accepting a wooden beaker from Sulis.

"They have our son," said Leofman. "And look what they have done…" His words caught in his throat. "We are no cowards to flee from the likes of Sidrac and his ruffians. This land is my family's. Gifted to me and my heirs by Oswald King himself."

"I will bring back your son to you," said Cynan, "but to remain here is folly. You two cannot stand against this Sidrac and his gesithas. That Bumoth is a brute."

"That fat toad," Leofman spat into the embers. "When my leg is healed, I will split his skull with my axe." Sulis trembled beside her husband. She had never before heard him so angry and with a shock she realised that she believed he would indeed kill the man, if he was given the chance. This was a side of him she had never seen before. She looked at him sidelong and noticed for the first time how hard his face could appear in the flicker of the hearth flames, all angles and shadowed crevices, like chiselled rock. She wondered then at what Cynan had said about a king's gift. Surely Leofman must have done something of great renown to receive such a reward. But he never spoke of it and she had never pried, content to let him have his secrets, as she had hers. He seemed to sense her unease and patted her knee.

"I would welcome that fat whoreson's death," said Cynan, staring at Leofman over the fire. His face swam and rippled in the heat. "But even if you could kill him, there are many more of them. You are but one man. There is no shame in taking your family to safety."

"No shame?" Leofman shook his head. "Would you flee, Cynan? Tell me, you who has ridden across Albion to save my son. Would you run away if you wore my shoes?"

Cynan held Leofman's gaze for a long while and Sulis trembled once more.

"I know not what I would do," Cynan conceded at last. "But I am not you, and you are not me."

"And Eadwig is my son and Sulis my wife." Leofman pushed Sulis to stand. "Refill the man's cup, woman," he said, his tone harsh.

She blushed and did not meet Leofman's eyes as she poured more ale for Cynan, then the others, and finally Leofman. When she had finished, her husband's anger appeared to have abated somewhat and he patted the stool at his side for her to sit once more.

Ingwald whispered something to Cynan and the Waelisc man nodded.

"How far are we from Sidrac's hall?"

"In this weather," Leofman pondered, "perhaps half a day's ride."

Cynan nodded.

"If we are lucky, Bumoth has ridden for home and will stay there until this rain passes."

Leofman snorted and raised his eyebrows.

"We should not count on luck. Of late, I have not had much of it."

"No," Cynan said, nodding. "Ingwald will take first watch."

Ingwald stood, drained his cup of ale and handed the empty vessel to Sulis. Taking his cloak and sword, he opened the door and stepped out into the gathering dusk. The rain had turned into a drizzle and the evening was quiet and grey. He leaned against the wall of the hut, drawing his cloak about him and pulling the door shut.

"So, tell me, Cynan," said Leofman, his voice rumbling in the hut's warm gloom, "how is it that you know my Sulis? And how is it that you would come to her aid on the other side of Bernicia?"

"Husband, hush," said Sulis, her face hot at his implication, though she knew there was something to what he was suggesting. She had played on the feelings Cynan held for her.

"No, Sulis," said Cynan, "Leofman has the right to know the manner of man who sits at his hearth." He stared at the older man, his eyes bright and his jaw set. She was suddenly terrified of what he might say. She had buried her past for so long and now she wondered what digging it up might bring into the light. "I knew Sulis long ago," Cynan said. "She was in need of help and I did my best by her." He sighed.

"Cynan saved my life," Sulis whispered.

"And how did you repay him?" asked Leofman, his meaning clear.

She thought back to who she had been then, filled with anger and resentment; the darkness that had engulfed her.

"With spite and hate," she murmured, staring at Cynan's handsome features in the ruddy fire glow.

For a long while, Leofman said nothing. A log shifted on the embers, and sparks flew up towards the blackened beams.

"Sulis tells me you found her shortly after I last saw her," Cynan said. "She said you saved her life too."

Leofman nodded.

"And it seems I got better payment for my troubles than you ever did, lad." He let out a barking laugh and Sulis relaxed. "She has made me a fine wife, though she has not been the most obedient." He squeezed her leg affectionately. "She is headstrong, but hard working and a fine mother. She is a marvel to me." He turned to look at her. She could see nothing but love in his gaze. "Even now she has secrets I never dreamt of. And," he said, raising his cup in Cynan's direction, "powerful friends willing to risk their lives for her."

"For Sulis and for Eadwig," said Cynan.

Leofman grew sombre again.

"How do you think to bring him back to us?"

Cynan shook his head.

"I know not. Why have they taken him, do you think?"

"I have thought much on this," said Leofman. "All I can imagine is that by holding him hostage, they think to bend me to their will in some way."

"But if they want the land and the mine, why do they need you alive at all?"

"I do not know, but at the mine, after I had fought them and they'd grabbed Eadwig, I heard Bumoth telling the others not to harm the boy." He let out a long breath and took a mouthful of ale. "I don't think I could have slept these past nights otherwise."

"So, the boy is part of their plan," mused Cynan. "But what plan?"

Leofman glowered into the fire.

"I do not know."

They fell silent. Outside the wind picked up, causing the house to creak. A horse whinnied and Sulis strained to hear any other sound that would alert them of trouble. But the swarthy warrior, Ingwald, was out there protecting the door. He would warn them if an enemy approached.

Into the quiet, Halinard, the oft-silent Frank, spoke.

"You say the old king gifted you the land?"

"Yes, for me and my heirs."

Cynan suddenly looked at Sulis. Fear gripped her, though she was not certain why.

"When did Sidrac, or anyone around these parts, last see you?" Cynan asked her.

"I don't know. Why? What does that matter?"

"No," said Leofman. He shook his head, incredulous. "You think it could be so?"

Sulis was suddenly cold.

"What? What is it?" she asked.

"Think," said Leofman, nodding now as he saw the sense in what he was saying. "It has been at least four months since you visited Dacor with me. After that, you had the sickness and then we were busy moving the flock up to the higher pasture. When last you were seen hereabouts, you were not so big."

She shivered, despite the fire-glow warmth.

"Sidrac does not know I carry your second child."

Leofman nodded slowly, his face terribly serious.

"As far as they know, Eadwig is my only heir."

"If you die," said Halinard, "Eadwig is owner of the land."

Sulis placed her hands upon her distended belly, as if she could protect the infant within from the horrors of the world.

"Until my baby is born," she said, her voice barely a whisper, "Eadwig *is* your only heir."

"What are we going to do?" asked Leofman.

"First," said Cynan, squaring his shoulders, "we must take Eadwig back from Sidrac."

"And how do you propose that we do that?"

They fell silent again, each pondering the future and the quandary before them. Sulis' mind was a whirl of worries and questions. Had Bumoth and the other warriors beneath the oak seen her and recognised her? Could they have seen from that distance that she was heavy with child? Could it be that Sidrac would seek to kill her and her unborn child? Did he know that she was carrying Leofman's baby?

At last, Brinin, his young, scarred face hardened by the shadows, interrupted her thoughts. He raised himself up to sit straight on his stool and cleared his throat. They all turned to look at him and Sulis thought perhaps the young man would not speak. He met her gaze and she nodded in encouragement. Whatever he had to say, she would rather hear it than continue to drown in the whirlpool of her dark thoughts.

He swallowed and coughed to clear his throat.

"I have an idea," he said.

Chapter 20

Beobrand rubbed at the cut above his knee. It itched and he wanted nothing more than to pull down his breeches and scratch at it with abandon. But such sweet relief would have to wait. He met Oswiu's glare. He had not wished to return to Bebbanburg. Instead he had longed to rush back to Ubbanford to make sense of the news that Elmer had brought. Sulis had returned and Cynan had freed the thrall and headed off into the west with her. And he had taken Brinin and Halinard with him too! Beobrand could scarcely believe it, but Elmer was a steadfast man and not prone to fancy.

"Well, Beobrand?" repeated Oswiu, impatiently drumming his fingers on the arm of his great carved gift-stool. "Can you add anything to what Ethelwin has already told me?"

Beobrand forced himself to push aside his concerns over Cynan and that murderous bitch, Sulis. He scanned the faces of those sat at the high table. These were the ealdormen and the most trusted thegns of Bernicia. On the other side of the king was Anna, King of the East Angelfolc. On his left sat Offa, his left eye darkened by a great bruise, but otherwise hale after the battle. Offa and his men had acquitted themselves well. One of his gesithas had been badly injured, another had paid the ultimate price, earning Offa and his king, Oswiu's gratitude.

Wynhelm met Beobrand's gaze and nodded. There were few Bernicians around the king whom Beobrand considered his friends. He was glad that Wynhelm, at least, was there. And he was equally glad that the queen was not in attendance. It was the prospect of seeing Eanflæd that twisted his guts, unnerving him more than facing any foe in battle.

"No, lord king," Beobrand said. "There was much confusion at the end, but later we pieced together what we think happened. I believe it was as Lord Ethelwin described."

"And what is your understanding of what occurred?" asked Oswiu.

"As the warmaster said, it seems that first the atheling was struck a mighty blow by one of Oswine's hearth-warriors." He glanced over at Oswiu's son. To look at him you could not tell that he had been toppled like a tree only a few days earlier. "He took a great hit to his side, which cracked some ribs, and he fell."

"Thank the Lord he was spared," exclaimed Utta, the priest.

Beobrand frowned.

"I think we should thank the smith who made his byrnie," he said. Several of the gathered men laughed. Oswiu scowled. The priest glowered at Beobrand.

"His comitatus," Beobrand went on, "believing him mortally wounded, cried out in despair. But they are brave warriors all, and they did not crumble in the face of sorrow."

"And your son, Octa," said Oswiu, his tone quiet. "Was he the bravest of them all?" He reached for one of the fine, green glass goblets before him and took a sip.

"Is that wise, lord?" whispered Utta. "You have only just recovered from the gout."

"By Christ's thorny crown, man," snapped Oswiu. "I am the king and I will drink when I please!"

The priest lowered his gaze. His cheeks flushed red like an admonished child.

Beobrand sniffed. His feelings for Octa were mixed. There was pride there, and relief that he had escaped the battle unscathed, and yet there was also something else, something darker, that he did not choose to dwell upon. When he had seen him after the battle, his heart had soared to see him well. And yet Octa barely spoke a word to him as he had hurried back to Alhfrith and the atheling's retinue. Beobrand was just another old warrior to Octa now. The young man was certain his day had come and that the sun was setting on his father's time. Perhaps he was right, thought Beobrand sourly, but the dismissive attitude made him want to slap the boy.

"Many men won battle-fame that morning, lord king," Beobrand said. "Octa was but one of them." He gave a sidelong glance at his son, who had been given an honoured seat beside Alhfrith for his role in the battle. Octa gazed back impassively. For several heartbeats father and son did not break the stare. At last, Octa shrugged and picked up his cup to drink. Beobrand did not permit himself a smile, but he was glad of the small victory over his arrogant son. Had he been so full of self-belief when he was Octa's age? Probably.

"But Octa took Oswine's banner, did he not?" said Oswiu, signalling with a sweep of his hand at the staff with its crossbeam from which hung the Deiran king's standard of a golden cross and four rampant lions. The banner now leaned against one of the central carved columns of Bebbanburg's great hall.

"That he did," replied Beobrand. "And it seems that by doing so, the Deirans were routed."

"How so?" asked Oswiu, even though he had heard the story just moments before from the lips of Ethelwin.

"It appears that upon seeing the standard fall, the Deirans believed their king to have been slain."

"And what happened?" Oswiu rubbed his hands together and smiled. He clearly relished the telling of this tale and wished to hear it again.

There was little glory in it, thought Beobrand. He remembered the shouts of despair and the rushing men, fleeing through the mud. There had been slaughter then, but he had held his men back, not wishing to expose them to an unexpected rallying of the Deiran host.

"The Deirans ran," he said, his tone flat.

"Ha!" Oswiu clapped his hands in glee. "I wish I could have been there to witness my cousin's humiliation."

"Oswine King escaped the place of battle with many of his hearth-warriors," said Beobrand, keen to remind Oswiu that this had been no sweeping triumph.

"Indeed." Oswiu scowled. "It seems you missed the opportunity to end this war once and for all."

Beobrand sighed.

"I sought to have Oswine join you under the branch of truce before the first blow was struck."

"So I heard," said Oswiu, placing his goblet on the board before him. He stroked his moustache and pondered Beobrand. "Why did you do such a thing, when I had asked for war?"

"I thought you would rather obtain peace. Oswine seemed ready to speak and I believe he would have offered good terms."

"You do, do you?" said Oswiu, shaking his head. "And since when has the mighty slayer of men, Beobrand Half-hand, sought peace over war?" He raised his goblet once more to his lips and then faltered, as if a thought had just come to him. "Could it be that you had other motives for not wishing to fight?"

A chill ran through Beobrand. His knee itched. Not for the first time he wished he had headed straight for Ubbanford. But now thought he began to understand Ethelwin's insistence that he return to Bebbanburg.

"I am loyal, lord king," Beobrand said, his voice as quiet as a blade being drawn over a whetstone. "My men fought as well as any there. Your foe-men were heaped before us."

"Oh, I am sure that the doughty Beobrand and his Black

Shields killed many. But," he said, stroking his chin, "there was one you failed to kill." He sipped his wine and his eyes narrowed.

Beobrand looked at Ethelwin. The warmaster met his gaze, but gave no sign of his thoughts.

"Who did I fail to kill, lord?" Beobrand asked. He knew the answer. When there had been no mention of it after the battle, he had believed that none besides his men had witnessed what had occurred. Clearly, he had been wrong.

"Why, I hear that bastard, Wulfstan, walked away from the battlefield."

Beobrand did not blink as he met Oswiu's glare.

"He did not walk easily," he said, keeping his voice flat and free of emotion. "He was injured."

"By your blade?"

"Yes. We fought and both drew blood."

"And yet you both left the battle with your lives."

"We did."

"And how is that so?"

"We are both lucky, it would seem."

"Do not take me for a fool, Beobrand," Oswiu growled.

The hall was as still as a tomb now. Every man leaned forward to better hear the confrontation between Beobrand and the king. They could sense there would be blood.

"I would never do that, lord."

"And yet you lie to me," said the king, his voice cold now, as hard as the rock on which the fortress of Bebbanburg was built.

Beobrand's mind raced. He could think of no words that would save him from Oswiu's wrath. The king had sent him to kill Wulfstan once before and Beobrand had returned alive; the only casualties of that confrontation had been Heremod and Fordraed's gesithas. Many, including Oswiu, had doubted his version of the events at Ediscum, but none were left to refute them. Someone had clearly seen his interaction with Wulfstan in the last moments of the battle and Oswiu had had his suspicions of Beobrand's loyalty confirmed.

"I do not lie to you, lord king," replied Beobrand, his tone flat. "I fought with Wulfstan. We were both injured and he fled when the Deiran host was routed."

"And so you deny allowing my enemy, Wulfstan of Ediscum, to escape?"

Beobrand swallowed the lump in his throat. His wound itched. He longed for a drink. Gods, what a fool he had been to think he could retain his honour after he had broken his oath. Such was the wyrd of an oath-breaker. He could not stand here before Oswiu, his oath-sworn lord, and lie. That was the way of a coward. He scanned the stony faces of the men seated at the high table. Was that a thin smile on Alhfrith's lips? Beobrand frowned. Was it the atheling who had seen him raise Wulfstan up and allow him to flee? Whoever it had been, there was no avoiding the truth now. He must face his king's judgement for his actions. Beobrand drew in a deep breath of the smoke-laden air of the hall.

But before he could utter the words that would damn him, another voice spoke out.

"Lord Beobrand did not allow Wulfstan to escape." All eyes turned to the speaker. It was Ethelwin, Oswiu's warmaster. "I vouch for his word."

Beobrand had thought the man sought his downfall by bringing him here. It seemed he had been wrong about many things.

Oswiu turned to face his warmaster.

"Do you refute the word of my son, Ethelwin? Alhfrith told me that from where he had been carried by his gesithas after his injury, he witnessed Beobrand pulling Wulfstan to his feet, conversing with him and sending him on his way, when he could have easily slain him."

"From where I was positioned in the shieldwall, I had a good view of Beobrand and his Black Shields. What Alhfrith described to you did not happen."

Oswiu frowned.

"Could it not be that you are mistaken?" he asked. "After all, Ethelwin, my son's eyes are younger than yours."

There was a smattering of laughter.

"That is true," Ethelwin said, nodding. "But as you say, the atheling had been wounded and was in great pain."

"I know what I saw, old man!" Alhfrith stood, sending his chair clattering over.

Ethelwin turned to face him. Alhfrith was flushed and furious. The warmaster's calm demeanour only seemed to anger him further.

"Ah, but can you be certain?" Ethelwin asked.

"My eyes did not deceive me!"

"I have stood in many more shieldwalls than you, Alhfrith Atheling. I have killed many more men." Ethelwin met the atheling's gaze and let the weight of his words reach all who listened. "It is easy for younger, more headstrong warriors to become confused in the chaos of battle. And when one has had his ribs smashed by an enemy axe, it is hard to focus on what others are doing or saying."

"I saw Beobrand allowing Wulfstan to escape," said Alhfrith, but there was an edge of doubt in his voice now.

"I do not doubt that is what you believe to have seen, but it was not so, was it, Lord Beobrand?" Ethelwin turned his gaze to Beobrand. Beobrand swallowed against the dryness of his throat. The warmaster had saved him from Oswiu's wrath, just as Beobrand had saved Wulfstan from the slaughter at Corebricg. Beobrand had been ready to discard all pretence and to face the consequences. With each lie, he felt himself diminished; a lesser man. And yet, if he spoke the truth now, Ethelwin would suffer, alongside him. He looked over at the furious face of Alhfrith, in many ways so like his father. Beobrand squared his shoulders. No, he would give neither Oswiu, nor the atheling, the satisfaction of seeing him toppled from his position, especially if it now meant taking Ethelwin with him.

He turned back to face the king.

"It is as Ethelwin says, lord king," he said. "Your son must have been confused with pain. I am your servant and you have my oath. Your enemies are my enemies. My sword is yours, as ever it has been."

Oswiu glowered at him for a long while.

"Father," blurted out Alhfrith, "do not listen to them. These are lies."

"Silence!" snapped Oswiu. "You will not accuse Ethelwin and Beobrand of such things. This was a misunderstanding." Alhfrith clamped his mouth shut, but his face was thunderous. Octa beside him shook his head as he stared at his father, and Beobrand wondered what his son knew and what he had seen. "I am glad the matter has been resolved," continued Oswiu. "Now we can celebrate the victory without this cloud hanging over us." He fixed Beobrand with one last stare before clapping his hands. "Brytnere," he said. The steward stepped from where he had been awaiting the king's instructions.

"My lord?"

"Serve the feast," said Oswiu.

The ealdormen and thegns all began to talk at once.

Brytnere bowed his head and hurried away. Oswiu turned to speak with Utta, who sat beside him. Beobrand had been dismissed. He let out a long breath and turned to leave the hall. He would be glad to be free of the scrutiny of the king and his retinue. Beobrand was not meant for such intrigue. Sweat trickled down his spine. As he headed for the great double doors of the hall, one face was turned towards him. Beobrand felt the glare and looked back to see Alhfrith following him with his eyes. The atheling's face was rigid, his jaw's muscles bunched and working as he ground his teeth together.

"You've made an enemy there," said a voice close by. Beobrand turned to see Ethelwin. The warmaster had followed after him and now matched his step as he walked the length of the hall, leaving the hubbub of conversation behind them.

"I don't think he liked me to begin with," said Beobrand, with a thin smile. "I fear my son has soured his mind about me, though the gods alone know what wrong Octa thinks I have done him."

"The young need no reason to be angry," replied Ethelwin with a smirk.

"Still, it does not pay to anger an atheling," said Beobrand.

"Perhaps not, but I would rather make an ally of Beobrand of Ubbanford than Alhfrith, son of Oswiu. The boy still has much to learn."

They walked out into the courtyard. The door wards stood up straight upon seeing the warmaster and the lord of Ubbanford. It was dusk, and the shadows were long, filling much of the fortress with a cool gloom. After the warmth of the hall, it was cold and Beobrand wished he had not left his cloak inside. He led them away from the guards, where nobody could overhear their words.

"Why did you speak up for me?" he asked when they were far enough away. In the distance, he could hear the whisper of the high-tide's surf washing against the rocks below Bebbanburg.

"I said only what I saw," said Ethelwin.

Beobrand looked at him for a long time without speaking.

"You fought close to Wynhelm, did you not?" he asked at last.

"Aye, I did."

Beobrand frowned.

"Then you were far from where I stood with my Black Shields. You could not have seen what happened between Wulfstan and I."

Ethelwin shrugged.

"Perhaps I was mistaken," he mused, rubbing his neck.

"Battles are full of noise and chaos." He bent his neck forward, placing his hands behind his head and pulling. There was an audible crack and he grunted. "But I knew it could not be as the atheling said."

"Why? If you were too far to see what happened, how could you speak out against the atheling?"

Ethelwin raised an eyebrow.

"For if you had allowed the thegn of Ediscum to flee, that would make you a traitor. And I know that Beobrand of Ubbanford is no traitor." He stared into Beobrand's face. Above them, several gulls circled, screeching and calling. "Am I wrong?" Ethelwin asked.

Beobrand's mouth was dry and his knee itched more than ever.

"I am no traitor," he said.

Ethelwin beamed.

"Good," he said, slapping Beobrand on the back. "Then you would do well not to do anything that might make young men, confused by the tumult of battle, believe you are." He gripped Beobrand's shoulder and leaned in close. "Be careful, Beobrand. There are always people watching what men of power do."

He gave Beobrand's shoulder a squeeze and then walked off quickly back to the hall.

"Don't be too long checking on your man, Cuthbert," he called back as he went. "The feast will begin soon."

Beobrand stared after Ethelwin until he had disappeared once more into the hall. Taking a long breath of the cool air, he looked up at the birds wheeling above him in the darkening sky. By Woden, he wished he had ridden straight to Ubbanford. Here, surrounded by the stout timber walls of the fortress, he felt in more danger than in the midst of battle.

With a sigh, he went in search of his gesithas and Cuthbert, hoping that seeing them would go some way to improving his mood.

Chapter 21

Cynan twisted his head around until his neck crackled. His body was stiff, cold and wet. He peered out through the leaves of the bracken at the cluster of buildings and the large hall, outlined by the grey light of the dawn. There was still no movement, but soon the household would rise and then they would see whether the gods were with them; if their plan would work. Beside him in the dark, Leofman coughed. Cynan again questioned the wisdom of bringing the old warrior with them. The truth was that the old man had been invaluable in helping them get there, but Cynan still worried that he would hamper them when events began to unravel, as they were bound to do. No plan remained intact once the enemy was engaged. Cynan did not want to save Sulis' son only to lose her husband. Not that Leofman had left him any choice. Sulis' husband was as strong-willed as he was tall and burly, and he would not hear of being left behind.

"How many of you have been to Sidrac's hall?" he'd asked, raising an eyebrow, knowing the answer. "And who among you knows what the man looks like?"

Cynan had shaken his head.

"If you slow us down, it might put Eadwig in more danger."

Leofman pulled himself up to his full height and lifted his

great axe that looked as though it would be just as good at splitting skulls as chopping firewood.

"I am not young and my wounds still ail me," he grumbled. "But I am strong and I will not hinder you." He fixed Cynan with a glare that was hard and yet also pleading. "Eadwig is my son," he said, his voice cracking. "It is his father's place to bring him home."

Cynan had looked to Sulis then. She had shrugged.

"Do you think I can stop him when his mind is set on something like this?" she asked.

And so Cynan had reluctantly allowed Leofman to lead them up and over the pass between the towering slopes. The man did not complain despite his obvious discomfort, and as the night wore on and the darkness closed about them like a shroud, Cynan was glad of his presence. He was unsure he would have been able to find the path and there were steep escarpments along the western edge of the track that could see an incautious man and his mount tumble to their deaths.

It had rained all that long day after their arrival, and despite the pressure they all felt to ride off straight away in search of Eadwig, Cynan had commanded them to rest. They had ridden hard for days, and Leofman was still in need of healing. So they had slept fitfully in the small house, one of them outside on watch at all times.

They had gone over Brinin's idea often as the rain splattered the thatch and the wind shook the hut. They turned over the plan, approaching it from different directions, probing it for weaknesses and trying to second guess what Sidrac and his men would do. Leofman knew Sidrac's hall and the lay of the land thereabouts, and he thought it could work. It was the simplest of plans and one that reminded Cynan of his past. It was its simplicity that would hopefully give them a chance, he thought. Both he and Brinin knew it could work, as they had witnessed similar tactics succeed before. With luck they would find success again, and this dawn would see them rescue the boy and escape with their lives.

They had left as the sun was setting, painting a blood-red swathe of the western sky beneath the black clouds that spoke of more rain to come. To Cynan it looked like a sword cut had opened the clouds to let out the blood of the sun. It had rained during the night as they rode, and without Leofman to guide them, they would surely not have found Sidrac's hall. As it was, they almost rode right up to the structure before they realised where they were.

Leofman was directing them, but Cynan was riding ahead a short way, scouting for danger. It seemed unlikely that anyone would be abroad on such a night, but Cynan was cautious. The weight of responsibility was heavy on his shoulders and he would not risk these men's lives by being overly confident. The rain had stopped falling and the sky in the east was beginning to pale behind the looming peaks when he had stumbled on Sidrac's hall. A northerly wind had picked up, and as the clouds scudded southward, the moon, that had been hidden for most of that long night ride, shone a sudden silvered beam onto the straight lines of the hall. It was barely a spear's throw from Cynan. His breath had caught in his throat as he thought of the sound of Mierawin's hooves on the path. On a silent night, the clop of hooves in the darkness would rouse sleeping men from their blankets as quickly as a bucket of cold water to the face, or the smell of smoke.

He had sat still, stroking Mierawin's mane and whispering to her, willing her not to pick up the scent of horses in Sidrac's stable and nicker in welcome. The wind sighed through the trees that lined the ridge behind the shadow of the hall. A hint of woodsmoke carried on the breeze and Cynan cursed himself for not noticing it sooner. No sound came from the building. He let out a sigh of relief. It seemed he was far enough away for the sound of his passage not to reach the hall over the rustle of the tall trees in the distance.

He had spun the bay mare around and walked the horse back to intercept the others. He had wanted to gallop, but had been worried at the noise the hooves would make in the still of the night.

It appeared that nobody within the hall had been alerted to their presence. The night had remained silent as they dismounted and led the horses off the path and into a gully clogged with willows. It was muddy, but sheltered from the wind and the horses would be safe enough tethered there. A small stream ran along the floor of the gulch, and Cynan was careful to tie the horses some way beyond the line of detritus – twigs, grass and mud – caught on the boles of the trees and in low branches. The last thing they needed was to have the gully flooded by the rains and to find their horses drowned.

The dell was some distance from the hall and they had trudged through the gloom until they found what they were seeking. They smelt it long before they reached their destination. The acrid tang of old piss and shit caught in the throat. Ingwald cursed and gagged.

"Gods," he hissed, "some plan this."

"Would you rather just knock on the door and ask for Eadwig?" asked Cynan in a sharp whisper.

Ingwald spat in the gloom.

"I think I would," he whispered.

"There is a small stand of trees just north of the midden pit," Leofman said in a hushed tone. "It shouldn't smell as bad there." He grunted with the pain in his leg as they moved the last few paces. Halinard reached out a steadying hand. Cynan thought the older man might refuse the Frank's aid, but after a moment's hesitation, Leofman placed his hand on Halinard's shoulder. Gods, the man could barely walk. If it came to a fight, he would not fare well.

The eastern sky above the shadows of the mountains was now the wolf-grey of dawn. They could see the hall and the outbuildings ever more clearly as the sun coloured the sky. They dared not speak further, as if seeing the buildings somehow made them, and the chance of being heard, more of a reality. Cynan breathed through his mouth. The wind rustled the boughs of the ash trees above them. It blew past the trees and over the midden pit, away from the watching men, but the stench still reached them and stung their noses every now and then when the breeze shifted. All about them, seemingly oblivious of the stink, birds sang, welcoming the dawn with their cacophonous chorus.

The men were all silent now. They knew the plan and the time to discuss it had long since passed. Settling themselves down as comfortably as they could in the wet leaf mould and bracken, they pulled their damp cloaks about them and watched the hall.

Cynan sighed. He recalled the first time he had ever laid eyes on Beobrand and Acennan. They had been lurking near Grimbold's midden, and Cynan had been a thrall then, all skin and bone and bruises from the beatings he received at the hands of his master's son and his comitatus. Cynan's hand fell to the seax that hung at his belt. Beobrand and Acennan had given him the weapon that day in payment for his service to them. The moment he had held that forbidden blade he had begun to believe he might actually be free of Halga and his vindictive gesith, Wybert. They were both dead now, and he was a slave no longer. He snorted to think of the twists of wyrd that had led him here, still with the stink of a midden in his nostrils, all these years later.

The sun had not yet crept above the mountains, but the sky was bright and it was full day when the doors of the hall opened and several men came out. They were talking loudly, but were too far away for Cynan to hear details of their conversations. Snatches of their words reached him on the wind. A couple of them made their way over to the building that must be the stable, while another half a dozen began walking towards the midden.

"Stay hidden and silent," Cynan hissed. "There are too many of them. We wait."

None of the others replied. They all lowered themselves down even further, hoping that the thick foliage would hide them.

The men were dressed as if for a journey, with cloaks over their shoulders, and seaxes and swords sheathed at their hips. They sauntered over to the stinking pit and loosened their breeches. A couple of them sighed as they let out long streams of steaming piss.

Cynan recognised Bumoth amongst them. The fat man belched and spat as he pulled up his breeches. A thin man with a wispy moustache and straggly beard hawked and spat out a thick wad of phlegm.

"You think they'll be stupid enough to still be there?" he asked.

Bumoth shrugged.

"The lord commands and we obey," he said. "What do you think, Ludeca?" he asked a third man. Ludeca was tall and broad shouldered, and yet strangely stooped, as though his head weighed more than his neck was able to support.

Beside Cynan, Leofman tensed, and to his horror the old man began to rise. Cynan pushed him back down, wincing at the grunt of pain Leofman let out.

The men at the midden turned away. The tall one with the stoop hesitated, half-turning his head towards the stand of ash. Cynan held his breath. After a moment, Ludeca looked back to Bumoth and the others.

"Let's hope they are," he said, hurrying after his comrades. "We need to finish once and for all what you started. And, if what Fleameld says is true, the bitch needs to die too."

Leofman tried to rise again, but Cynan was ready this time and held him still with an effort. The voices of the six men became muffled with the distance and as Cynan and the others watched, the men at the stables led horses out to them. They spoke briefly, then the six men mounted and kicked their horses into a canter south.

Leofman was struggling beneath Cynan's grip.

"Stay still, you fool," hissed the Waelisc warrior into the older man's ear. He watched as the men at the stable made their way back into the hall and the doors swung shut behind them. Somewhere close to the buildings a cock crowed. Cynan finally released his hold on Leofman.

With a groan, the old man pushed himself up.

"What is it, man?" said Cynan. "We have made provision for this. Sulis is safe."

Imagining that Sidrac's men might return in search of vengeance, they knew they could not leave Sulis alone and unprotected at the farm. Leofman had told them of a small hut in the hills where he or Alfwold would sleep on occasion. It was remote and only his family knew of it, and so they had packed provisions onto her pony and sent Sulis off to stay in the bothy until they returned.

Leofman's face was twisted in horror.

"Sulis is in danger. You heard them."

The man was trembling with emotion. Cynan could sense their plan falling apart soon after the first sighting of the enemy.

"You said that nobody knew of the bothy," he said, desperately trying to allay Leofman's fears.

"I thought that was so," Leofman replied, his whisper taut with anguish. "I thought only Eadwig, Sulis and I knew about it now. But there was another." He let out a shuddering breath. "A man I believed was dead."

"Who?" asked Cynan. "Who is this man?"

"His name is Ludeca."

"The tall one with the strange neck?"

"Aye. I'd thought him dead for years."

Cynan's mind was spinning.

"We cannot chase after them now," he said. "To do so would

be to lose this chance to free Eadwig. With so many of Sidrac's men gone, we won't get another opportunity like this again."

Leofman stared at Cynan for several heartbeats. His face was pale in the shadow of the bracken and the trees. At last he nodded.

"It is worse than him knowing the place where Sulis is hiding," he said, his voice almost a sob. He rubbed a hand across his face. "I think I finally understand what Sidrac plans, and why he took Eadwig."

"How so?" asked Cynan. The cockerel crowed loudly in the distance and all of the men started. If they were not careful, they would be seen now that the sun was up. He pulled Leofman down again. "How so?" he repeated in a harsh whisper.

Leofman met his gaze with the look of one close to despair.

"Ludeca is my brother."

PART TWO

RESCUE AND RETRIBUTION

Chapter 22

"It all makes sense now," said Leofman, breathless with the shock of what he had witnessed. "Don't you see?" Cynan had pulled the big man back down to lie prostrate in the wet undergrowth. The scent of the earth and rotting leaves went some small way to cover the stink of the midden, but not enough for them to breathe freely.

Cynan nodded. With the discovery of Leofman's brother, Sidrac's plan was becoming clearer.

"If you die," he said, "Eadwig becomes the owner of your land." He glanced over at the hall. There was no further movement there, but surely soon the rest of the household would be out and about their chores. "If this Ludeca is your kin," he went on, "he can claim Eadwig on your death."

"And control of the mine," finished Brinin.

"There is more cunning in this plan than my brother ever had," said Leofman. "I cannot understand how he came to be part of it."

"You thought him dead?" asked Ingwald in a hushed tone.

"Aye." Leofman sighed and stared at the curling leaf of a fern that was bejewelled with drops of rain. His features clouded as he looked far back into a past he clearly thought he would never revisit. "I thought he'd been killed years ago…" His voice trailed off and they all grew silent once more.

Cynan's head was filled with questions. But they could wait. Now was not the time for conversation.

"How Ludeca still lives and how he became involved with Sidrac are questions for another time. Now we need to focus on the job in hand. We have been given a gift here."

"A gift?" hissed Leofman. "Those men have ridden in search of me and Sulis. They will not find me, but she is alone."

Cynan thought of Sulis, slender and elegant of limb, but with the round swell of her stomach impeding her movement, causing her to waddle. She was certainly no weakling to be fearful of men, but she was small and would be defenceless against the six warriors who had ridden south. If they found her.

"I like it no more than you," he said. "But think. Six of Sidrac's gesithas are no longer in the hall. You said he had no more than a dozen or so warriors in his household. His numbers are halved. This makes our position stronger. We must rescue Eadwig and then we will ride to Sulis' aid." He fixed Leofman in his stare. "Pray that they do not find her."

Leofman did not look convinced that the Lord would answer his prayers. The old man began muttering under his breath and Ingwald clasped his shoulder.

"Do not fear," he said. "Sulis is a strong woman."

Leofman shook his head as if he thought Ingwald was a simpleton. He opened his mouth to speak, but a sharp hiss cut him off.

"Lord," whispered Halinard, who had not taken his gaze from the hall and the outbuildings while they had been talking.

Cynan followed the Frank's pointing finger. Two men had walked out of the hall and were making their way in their direction. A couple of hounds, one long-legged and rangy, the other squat and strong, bounded before them. Cynan cursed.

Those dogs would uncover their hiding place as easily as if they had been a brace of partridges.

"Is that him?" he hissed.

There was a pause as Leofman peered at the approaching men. Cynan's blood rushed in his ears as he prepared for action. The dogs would be upon them in an eye-blink.

"Is that Sidrac?" he repeated, anxiety sharpening his tone. The taller of the two was young and walked with the easy swagger of one used to being obeyed. He matched the brief description Leofman had given them of the son of Tohrwulf. Leofman remained silent and Cynan wanted to slap the man. Why had he come with them, if not to help them at this moment? "Is it?" Cynan repeated, knowing that the time for action was upon them. The nearest hound, a scruffy-looking brown and white lurcher, raised its head from where it was sniffing something in the mud and stared right at him. With a bark, it bounded towards the trees.

"Aye, that's him," said Leofman at last.

Cynan let out his breath in a rush.

"Halinard, Ingwald, take the one in the blue kirtle. Brinin, with me." The dog was close and it slowed its run, perhaps uncertain of what it sensed beneath the trees. Its barking had become incessant now, high-pitched and piercing. Sidrac and the other man were still not as close as Cynan would have liked.

"What is it, Slætan?" called the short, stocky man in the blue kirtle. "What have you found there?" He altered his course and began walking towards where Cynan and the others were hidden. They could wait no longer.

"Ready, men?" whispered Cynan, unsure if they would hear him over the dog's barking. The second animal, a thick-chested, wire-haired mutt with a wide jaw, loped over to see what the first dog had found. Without waiting for a response from the men lurking in the foliage, Cynan sprang up and ran at Sidrac, drawing his sword as he went.

"Now!" he bellowed.

He heard the leaves and branches snapping as the others burst out of the undergrowth behind him. For a single heartbeat, both of the dogs stopped barking in shock and the two men's mouths fell open in almost comical surprise. Cynan was past the hounds and the shorter man in an instant and speeding towards Sidrac.

The lord of the hall was fast. After the moment of shock, he spun about and sprinted back towards the hall. Cynan pounded after him. Behind them, he heard crashing, shouting, growling and barking.

Sidrac was hollering as he ran.

"We are under attack," he shouted. "To arms! To arms!"

The man was quick and if he had been any further away when Cynan had set off in pursuit he might well have reached the sanctuary of his hall. But Cynan was not only a great horseman, he was also one of the fastest runners in Beobrand's warband and often won foot races against the warriors of other lords. He frequently spent his time training his body, sprinting up and down the valley and hills surrounding Ubbanford. He was glad of that as he chased after Sidrac. He was close to the hall now. As Cynan watched, the doors swung open and men piled out. He could hear the rest of his own men still a ways behind. If he did not capture Sidrac now, he would have to face half a dozen armed men alone. He reached out his left hand in desperation and felt his fingertips brush the man's woollen mantle. Snagging his fingers into the cloth, he clutched it tight and yanked Sidrac backward. Sidrac was strong. He did not fall, but tried to shake himself free, all the while screaming at his men to come to his aid. Sidrac dropped his hand to the seax that hung from his belt. Cynan pulled him back hard and placed the cold edge of his sword blade against his throat. Behind them, the dogs were still filling the morning with their raucous yapping.

"Tell your men to halt," Cynan whispered into Sidrac's ear. He could smell ale and oats on his breath. They had come to a halt now, and Cynan wrapped his left arm around Sidrac, holding him as close as a lover. Sidrac said nothing. He snarled and attempted to shake his captor off. Cynan pressed the sharp edge of his sword into the man's neck, breaking his skin. "Now," he hissed. "And stop struggling or die."

Sidrac grew still.

"You're a dead man," he said.

"So people keep telling me," replied Cynan. "And yet it is my sword at your throat, so call your men off now, or I will paint them in your lifeblood." He applied pressure on the blade and Sidrac gasped.

"Stay where you are," he said, his voice strained. There were seven men, each in different stages of readiness for a fight. Three bore shields, a couple held spears, the rest had seaxes or swords. None of them wore a byrnie, but all had the rough faces and hard eyes of killers. Cynan recognised Hunberht, his right arm still in its sling. The man scowled at Cynan. He held a sword in his left hand. A couple of the warriors with shields began to creep to Cynan's left. Cynan pressed the blade again into the soft flesh beneath Sidrac's chin. "Don't move, Hussa," Sidrac said. Both of the men halted.

Running footsteps approached from behind, but Cynan did not turn. He trusted it was Brinin.

"Good," he said to the glowering men before the hall's doors. "Do as I say and…" he glanced over his shoulder to see how his other comrades fared. Brinin, his scar dark in the morning sunlight came to halt and took up position close to Beobrand. Further away, the dogs were still barking, jumping forwards to snap at Halinard and Ingwald. The animals seemed too frightened to attack, but were dogging their steps as they made their way towards the hall. Behind them lay the crumpled form of the man who had been with Sidrac at the midden. The sun lifted above the peaks and its light gleamed from the naked blades in the warriors' hands. Both Ingwald's and Halinard's swords were smeared in blood. Cynan had meant to say that nobody needed to die, but now he altered his words. "Do as I say," he repeated, "and nobody else needs to die."

"Who are you?" snapped Sidrac, making no effort to struggle, but clearly not cowed.

"Who I am is unimportant," said Cynan.

"You killed Aescferth."

Cynan recalled the man's clumsy attacks beside the oak.

"Then you know who I am," he said. "I did not wish for bloodshed, but Aescferth had it coming."

"He was not much more than a child," said Sidrac.

"He was old enough to torture a man," said Cynan, his tone bitter and chill.

"He was too young to die."

"Any man old enough to stand against me with a sword is old enough to die."

Sidrac tried to turn to look at Cynan, but the Waelisc man reapplied pressure on his sword, to prevent him from moving and to keep him facing his men and the hall.

"What do you want?" snarled Sidrac.

"I want to talk to you," replied Cynan. "But first I want you to command one of your men to tie up those dogs. Over in the stable. I don't wish to kill those dumb beasts, but if they keep on their yapping, I think I might be tempted to."

The barking had grown progressively louder as Halinard and Ingwald approached.

"One of you," shouted Cynan to the gathered men, "drop your weapons and take those dogs to the barn there and tie them up."

"They were Cynehelm's animals," said the youngest of the men, a scrawny, tall man about the same age as Beobrand's son, Octa.

"I care nought whose dogs they were," snapped Cynan. "Take them away from here, or we'll kill them."

The young man looked to Sidrac, who gave the smallest of nods.

"Go on now, Raedmund," he said.

The boy dropped his spear to the wet earth and moved towards the animals. Their hackles were raised and they were still growling and snarling at Ingwald and Halinard. For a time it seemed that the young warrior would not be able to coax them away, but in the end, he plucked up the courage to grab the taller hound by the scruff and drag it towards the stable. He called out to the stockier dog and it reluctantly followed. The men waited in silence until the dogs quietened down and Raedmund returned.

"So," said Sidrac, his voice calm once more, "what is it you want?"

Before Cynan could answer, Leofman's booming voice said, "You know full well what we want, you bastard. Bring me my son, now."

Cynan turned to see the tall warrior limping towards them, squinting into the rising sun. In his hand he held his great axe.

"Leofman, son of Hutha," said Sidrac, "it seems you have saved us a trip to find you."

"You'll pay for what you did to my arm, you old fucker," said Hunberht, taking a step forward.

"Maybe one day," said Cynan, shaking Sidrac for emphasis and renewing the pressure on his throat. "But for now, fetch Eadwig out of the hall."

Sidrac hesitated.

"We know what you were planning, Sidrac," said Cynan. "The game is up. You will not take Leofman's land. With Leofman alive, holding his heir is no use to you."

Sidrac stiffened and Cynan prepared to react if the man tried to free himself. But he did not move, instead he spoke.

"I could use the boy to get what I wanted from Leofman here. What do you say, old man? You sign a new deed giving me the mine and I give you back your son?"

Leofman made to respond, but Cynan cut him off.

"You are in no position to barter with anybody, Sidrac. Have one of your men bring out the boy and we will exchange you for him."

"How do I know you will let me go?"

"You don't, but I am the one with the blade at your neck, so you'll have to trust me."

After a long moment, Sidrac sighed.

"Go on, Raedmund," he said. "Bring out the boy."

The young man slipped inside the hall and moments later returned with a small boy. At only seven years of age, Eadwig was tiny next to the tall youth, but he did not pull away from the hand Raedmund placed on his shoulder. He glared in defiance at Sidrac, and Cynan recognised Sulis in the boy's angry stare.

"I told you my pa would come for me," Eadwig said.

"I am here, Eadwig," said Leofman, his voice breaking with emotion at seeing his son.

"Now you will let the boy go, and we will leave," said Cynan. "If you follow us, we will kill your lord."

Hunberht took another step closer. He was barely two spear-lengths away now.

"What is to say you will not just kill him when you get away from here."

"Easy now, Hunberht," said Sidrac, in the tone a rider might use for a particularly skittish horse that was hard to control. "We'll just have to trust them."

"Well, I don't trust this Waelisc scum," Hunberht said, spitting into the mud. "The offer to fight you with my left hand still stands."

"There will be no fighting here today," said Sidrac. His tone was still soothing, but carried the hard edge of a command. "Let the boy go."

Raedmund looked from Sidrac and then down at the boy, but did not release him.

"Do as I tell you," snapped Sidrac.

Raedmund stooped to whisper something to the boy. Eadwig listened, his eyes wide. Raedmund nodded and pushed him towards Leofman. Eadwig rushed away, past Cynan and Sidrac and into his father's arms. No sooner had he enveloped his son in his embrace, than both father and son began to sob.

"There is no time for that now," said Cynan. "Start getting the boy to safety."

Nodding, Leofman began leading Eadwig away. Cynan watched the faces of the men who stood before the hall. Their hatred and anger at being humiliated were clear in their expressions. His thoughts were a maelstrom in his mind. Whichever way he turned to look at the situation, he could see no way out of this for Leofman, Sulis and Eadwig while Sidrac yet plotted for their land and the mine. The thegn would not forgive this slight and he had set his mind on the silver he could make from the lead that could be brought from the ground. Leofman would never persuade him to leave his family in peace. Cynan and his men would not be able to stay to protect them for ever. And if they allowed all of Sidrac's men to gather into one warband again, there would be no way that Cynan, Halinard, Brinin and Ingwald could prevail against them.

Cynan surveyed the warriors, wondering if he had already made his decision before this moment; perhaps in the instant when Bumoth had killed Alfwold upon the tree. Or maybe even before then. Mayhap as far ago as when Sulis had come to him for help. For one so heavy with child to make the trip into danger seeking his assistance, the help that she sought could never lead to a peaceful outcome; only to slaughter. Whenever the decision had formed, his mind was now made up.

"Ready?" he asked, hoping his companions would hear the real question behind the word.

"We are ready to follow you, lord," replied Ingwald, his voice flat; obdurate as granite.

Cynan sighed with relief as he released the reins of his fury, unleashing his ire at these men who would torture and kill old men in cold blood, abuse children and threaten to murder pregnant women. With no warning, he dragged his sword across Sidrac's throat, cutting deep and feeling hot blood spurting over his hand. The man's lifeblood pumped in a great arc towards Hunberht, bright and hot in the light of the rising sun.

Chapter 23

Cuthbert rode towards the rear of the column of horsemen. A cool wind blew off the slate-dark sea to his right. The sky was spattered with clouds and dotted with gulls. He watched Beobrand riding at the head of the line of riders and wished he could be by his side. But whatever some of the black-shielded gesithas might think of him, Cuthbert was no fool. Beobrand had made it clear he did not wish to talk to him.

Shortly after leaving the fortress of Bebbanburg, Cuthbert had nudged his mount close to the lord of Ubbanford and asked him when he thought the Black Shields would next ride to war. Cuthbert had felt dejected at having been left behind. Despite having vivid dreams where he relived the bloody clash on the causeway, often awaking drenched in sweat and choking back a scream, he yearned to be in the thick of a true battle.

"Like one of those sung of by the scops," he'd said to Beobrand. "Like Hefenfelth. Or Maserfelth," he went on breathlessly. "Or the great ditch in East Angeln." Their horses had been picking their way down the slope leading from the gates of the fortress. There were rocks and thick foliage tangled at the edges of the ramp; no sign now of the battle that had been fought against Penda's host a few years previously. Bebbanburg had almost burnt and Beobrand had led the Black Shields to a great victory. "I wish I could have fought here at the battle before the gates." He recalled the heat of the flames and the black smoke, the sparks flying on the wind like the screams of the dying. Cuthbert had tried to join the warriors that day, but his father had shoved him back into the hall saying it was no place for a boy.

"You know not what you seek," said Beobrand, sounding just like his father. "You are little more than a child."

Cuthbert felt his face grow hot.

"I am not much younger than your own son," he said, his tone petulant, "and Octa took Oswine's banner at Corebricg, did he not?"

Beobrand had turned in his saddle, the leather creaking beneath his weight. He had fixed Cuthbert in his icy blue gaze.

"You are nothing like Octa," he said after a moment.

"I could be," muttered Cuthbert, but he did not think his lord had heard the words. Beobrand had already touched his heels to his horse and cantered ahead, down the last part of the slope and away on the path that led through the buildings of the settlement that had been rebuilt after Penda's attack. Cuthbert was clever enough not to try to follow Beobrand.

"He can be a grumpy one at times," said Eadgard, disturbing his thoughts. The massive axeman rode a tall gelding from Oswiu's stable. He was not the most talkative of Beobrand's gesithas, but ever since he had carried Cuthbert in the land of East Angeln from the causeway to *Saeslaga*, he seemed to have decided to keep an eye on the young warrior. When the warhost had returned to Bebbanburg, Eadgard had been the first of the Black Shields to find him. Cuthbert had been praying in the cool stillness of the church. It was quiet and serene there, and kneeling before the stark altar and the ornately carved whale-bone casket that rested upon it, Cuthbert found solace from the worries that swarmed in his head.

"But why is he not happy?" Cuthbert asked Eadgard.

Beobrand had been sullen and angry ever since returning from
Corebricg. "You were victorious and his son even captured
Oswine's standard."

"You are cleverer than I if you can unravel what is going
through Beobrand's head," replied Eadgard with a laugh.
"Grindan says it is because he dwells too much on things. And
Grindan should know. He's always thinking, that one."

"But your brother is not as testy as Beobrand," observed
Cuthbert.

Eadgard scratched his head.

"No," he agreed. "Though I don't think I have ever met
anyone who is."

"Careful he does not hear you speaking thus," interjected
Fraomar who rode close by. "You do not need to understand
why Beobrand is the way he is. He has much to concern him. He
is our hlaford, and so must provide us with food and shelter."

"And silver and weapons," added Eadgard, grinning.

"Yes," said Fraomar with a chuckle. "Those things too. What
he shouldn't have to worry about is his men lagging behind and
gossiping about him like two goodwives at their spindles."

With that rebuke, Fraomar kicked his horse on and left
Eadgard and Cuthbert trailing behind the rest of the men.

Cuthbert turned in the saddle, peering back in the direction
they had come. Far off now he could still make out Bebbanburg
atop its rock. To the east lay the island of Lindisfarena. The Holy
Island. Coenred would be there and Cuthbert wondered what
the monk was doing. Would he be praying, or worshipping,
reciting one of the frequent offices that the brethren had to
adhere to? Perhaps he was scratching the symbols of words into
the stretched calf hides the monks used as parchment.

They had talked about all of these things and more in the days
after Beobrand and the others had ridden south to war. Cuthbert
had recovered quickly under the monk's care and he had found
the depth of Coenred's knowledge of healing fascinating. He had

asked him about the poultices and herbs he used, and Coenred seemed happy enough to answer all of his questions.

He had explained to him how swelling could be treated with horehound, silverweed, fine flour, comfrey and a host of other wyrts. Coenred went on to tell him that toothache could be soothed with henbane root, boiled in strong vinegar, and that betony, wormwood and bog myrtle, infused in water, was good for diseases of the lungs. Cuthbert was quick-witted and inquisitive, with a keen memory. It was as though his mind was a bucket and Coenred's words were water. At first they spoke of leechcraft, but they had soon moved on to God and the ways of the monks of Lindisfarena.

"How many times a day do you pray?" he asked on the second morning when he had joined Coenred in the small stone church.

"Hush, Cuthbert," Coenred said. "We will speak later, but for now our words should only be for the Lord."

Cuthbert had bitten his lip and remained silent for the remainder of the time they spent in the shadowed interior of the church. He listened as Coenred intoned his prayers to God, his voice rising and falling in the well-practised liturgy. At times he spoke in a language Cuthbert did not comprehend. In spite of not understanding the words, he liked the music of it. He recognised other parts too, though he had seldom truly listened to the words of the Lord's Prayer, or thought of their meaning before. It was just something the priests demanded that people repeat. Now though, after speaking to Coenred, it seemed as though each word burnt with meaning and resonance.

When they had eventually walked out of the gloomy church and into the watery sunlight of a day that threatened rain, Cuthbert's questions had tumbled from his lips in a torrent. What was the name of the language in which the monks spoke to God? How long did it take to learn? Did Christ listen to prayers in that tongue more than he did Anglisc prayers? Was it God who provided bread for his faithful or a man's hlaford?

Coenred held up his hands and laughed.

"Slow down, young Cuthbert," he said. "When amongst the brethren on the island, we are forbidden from talking most of the time. I have said more in these last days to you than in the previous year or more. You chatter like a magpie."

Cuthbert frowned and looked away from the monk. Why did men always take him for a fool? Coenred reached out and placed a hand on his shoulder, turning him round to face him.

"Do not misunderstand me," he said, smiling. "It is good that you wish to know the answers to these things, but I am but human and need time to gather my thoughts."

Cuthbert said nothing. He still had his doubts about Coenred. He was sure that an angel had come to him aboard the ship. His leg still pained him, but he could walk on it now. He had seen much lesser wounds fester and rot, causing men to lose their limbs or even perish. Surely this must be the work of an angel. He had asked Coenred about this, but the monk had insisted he was merely a man and that God sometimes answered his prayers and worked through him, aiding his skills of healing. When Cuthbert had pressed him, refusing to believe him, Coenred had conceded that perhaps an angel had come to him, but if that was so, nobody else on *Saeslaga* had seen him. Cuthbert's insistence on the matter seemed to unnerve Coenred so he had decided not to mention it again. But he knew what he had seen.

"Why do you not speak when at the minster?" Cuthbert asked.

Coenred smiled and, without answering, he walked towards the palisade of the fortress that overlooked the North Sea. Cuthbert followed him, limping along in his wake. They climbed the ladder and stood side by side gazing out at the rippling sea and the shape of the island of Lindisfarena in the distance. Cuthbert watched the bobbing heads of seals in the dark water following a small fishing boat. Terns, gulls and guillemots flew about the boat, seeking the same fish for which the sailors cast their nets.

"Look at the wonder of the Lord's creation," he said, sweeping his hand to the horizon. "Do you think that speaking brings you closer to God and His creatures?"

Cuthbert watched as a flock of gannets flew to where there must be a teeming shoal of fish beneath the surface of the sea. One by one the birds bent their wings and descended like spears, darting into the waves with barely a splash, to return moments later into the sunlight with flashes of silver in their sharp beaks.

"God does not always speak through words, Cuthbert," Coenred said, watching his face closely.

Cuthbert stared out, the wind making his eyes water as he took in the birds, the boat, the white fretting on the waves that rolled towards the shore. He listened and heard the calls of the terns and the gulls carried on the breeze. If he listened long enough, would he hear the voice of God Himself?

"Does he speak to you?" he asked Coenred.

"Sometimes," he said, scratching at the stubble that grew where the front of his head was shaved in the way of the monks. He raised an eyebrow, amused at something. "When I listen."

"What does he sound like?"

Coenred smiled.

"His voice is not like yours or mine, though some have heard the Lord speak to them directly, like the voice from the angel of the burning bush that spoke to Moses."

Cuthbert frowned. He knew nothing of a bush on fire, but the talk of an angel caught his attention.

"If God does not speak, then how do you hear Him?"

Coenred thought for a moment before replying.

"Sometimes He speaks through the words of His teachings in the Scriptures. That is why we spend so long studying the words of the apostles and the prophets. But God is everywhere and He can speak to you through the cry of a gull or the bark of a seal, or the whistle of the wind through the trees."

Cuthbert started at the monk's words, thinking of the beasts of the sea and air he had been watching and the golden-haired angel that had come to him aboard *Saeslaga*.

"Perhaps the Lord can speak through you," he said, his voice small.

"I pray that is so," said Coenred. "For what greater joy than to be a vessel for the Holy Ghost?"

Over the next days, whenever possible, Cuthbert had sought out Coenred, asking him all of the questions he could think of. Coenred was patient and did his best to explain all that he was able to the young man.

"You remind me of myself when I was your age," Coenred said one afternoon as they walked through the dunes outside of the fortress. "Though I was never as clever as you," he added, laughing.

Cuthbert laughed at the monk's words, sure that he was making fun of him. He had never met any man more learned than Coenred. Angel or not, Cuthbert was in awe of the man's depth and breadth of knowledge.

Coenred had even begun to teach Cuthbert the rudiments of reading and writing.

As they rode, Cuthbert reached back to touch the saddlebag that hung over his horse's loins. He could feel the hard edges of the wax tablet that none other than the queen had gifted him. He blushed to recall how she had entered the church while Coenred and he had been talking. It had been raining and there were few places that were dry and yet not packed with people and chatter.

"You came here with Beobrand, did you not?" Eanflæd asked. She had entered the church alone and it was the first time Cuthbert had been so close to her. His cheeks grew hot at being addressed by such an important person. And one so charming.

The dim watery light spilling in from the open door did nothing to dampen her beauty. She wore a simple woollen dress of blue over a pale linen peplos. The only item that spoke of her position was her gold necklace, adorned with garnets and tiny shaped fragments of blue patterned glass. But there was no escaping her regal bearing, and the intelligence behind her eyes.

Cuthbert swallowed and nodded, unable to force out any words.

Coenred smiled at the queen and appeared relaxed in her presence.

"This is Cuthbert," he said. "He was injured in the fighting in East Angeln. Beobrand left him here under my care."

"And that is the very best care," she said with a radiant smile. "I see Coenred's skills are not diminished, for you seem to be all healed."

"My leg still pains me, my lady," stammered Cuthbert, then, embarrassed at the implication that Coenred was not a good healer, he added, "but if not for Coenred, I believe I would have lost the leg, or worse." He trembled to think of what might have happened and also from the sudden shyness that gripped him under the queen's bright-eyed gaze.

"Well," she said, "I am glad you did not lose it and that you are up and about."

"God is good and answered my prayers," said Coenred, inclining his head.

"This is the best place in Bebbanburg to pray," she said. "You know the head of King Oswald himself rests in that casket?"

Cuthbert glanced over at the finely carved box on the altar. On the sides of the box were engraved the likenesses of men and animals. He had imagined it to be a detailed and skilled depiction of stories from the Scriptures. He could see a bird on one side, perhaps a dove, and in the distance, a tree upon which languished a man. He had thought it must be the figure of Jesu, but now he recalled hearing tales of Oswald's end at Maserfelth.

He shuddered. He had not thought to enquire what was within. He'd thought that perhaps it housed the holy Eucharist that the priests gave to the faithful at Mass. The idea of a powerful king's head in the darkness within the box, staring out with sightless eyes, made him dizzy.

"I had not talked of the saintly relic," replied Coenred. "But we were not praying."

"Oh?"

"I was teaching Cuthbert his letters." Coenred held up his own small wood-rimmed wax tablet that he had lent to the boy to scratch out the letters and words he taught him.

"Oh that is wonderful," Eanflæd replied. "So you plan to join the brethren on Lindisfarena? I think this is a wise choice," she said with a smile. "You have more the aspect of a scribe than a spear-man."

Her words stabbed at Cuthbert.

"I am no monk," he replied stiffly. "I am a gesith in Beobrand's warband. I carry the Black Shield and when I am fully recovered, I will stand with my brothers in the shieldwall."

"I meant no harm by my words," the queen said, reaching out to touch him lightly on the arm. "There is no shame in being a monk, praying for the souls of men and women, and listening to the word of God. But if your path is to fight, then that is also noble. Though I would be saddened to see someone so clearly bright throw away his life lightly."

As he rode now besides Eadgard, watching the line of men walking their mounts up a rise and into the hills that swelled the land to the south of Ubbanford, he again caressed the edges of the wax tablet Eanflæd had given him the day after that first meeting. Beneath it in his saddle bag, wrapped in oiled leather, was the most precious thing he had ever owned. Shortly after that first encounter in the church, the queen had left, but she had evidently thought much about their conversation, for the next day she had found Coenred and Cuthbert once more conversing within the stillness of the stone building. Cuthbert had been distracted by the ornate casket, imagining the severed head of a saintly king within, when he heard the scrape of soft leather on the flagstones.

Startled, he turned. His unease melted away at the sight of the slender shape of the queen sweeping into the shade of the church. He began to babble an apology for his tone the day before, but she silenced him with a raised hand.

"No, Cuthbert," she said, and he thrilled at hearing his name on her lips, "you were quite right. I presumed much. The path of every man's life is his own to discover." She hesitated and he was surprised to see that she appeared embarrassed. "I have a present for you," she said at last, holding out a small parcel wrapped in leather. Cuthbert took it gingerly. It was not a large object, about the size of his two hands placed side by side. Rectangular and solid, he wondered what lay within the wrapping. "Go on, open it," she said.

Carefully, Cuthbert peeled back the leather to uncover what lay within. First there was a wax tablet with its own bone carved stylus.

"So that you can continue to practise your letters," she said, "even when you return to Ubbanford."

His mouth was dry.

"Thank you," he muttered.

"Look beneath," she prompted.

Lifting the tablet and stylus aside, Cuthbert unveiled a small leather-bound book. He had only ever seen one book before: the large Evangelion that rested on a lectern within the church of Saint Peter at Bebbanburg. A gift from Bishop Aidan to King Oswiu, Coenred had said. That Gospel Book was huge, but this tome was a miniature replica, with stiff leather covers enclosed around perfectly cut parchment pages. Gently, he opened it and looked at the first page. It was filled with exquisitely detailed and perfectly formed black letters, penned by a hand with much more skill than he could ever hope to possess. The first letter of the text was over-sized and surrounded by swirling, interlocking patterns and the many-coloured, long-necked image of a bird that seemed to be pecking at the page.

He could not speak for a time. His breath caught in his throat. It was so beautiful. And a thing of incalculable value.

"Cuthbert," said Coenred, gently nudging him in the ribs, "what say you?" Cuthbert's cheeks burnt. He was being told to offer thanks like a small child who forgets itself when one of their kin gives them a straw doll at harvest time.

"Thank you, my lady." His words were filled with awe. "Thank you. I will practise my writing every day with this." He held up the tablet. "But this," he proffered the book to her, "is too much. I cannot accept such a gift. I am not worthy of it."

"Nonsense," she replied with a smile, pushing the book back towards him. "I can think of none worthier. Alas the book is not a complete Psalter, but there is much to be learnt from the Psalms therein. I can see there is a hunger for knowledge within you that must be fed."

"Truly, I cannot take this," he said again, once more trying to return the book to the queen.

She shook her head.

"It is yours until such time as you are able to recite it and copy out all of the words within. Then you can return it to me and I will accept it gladly. Agreed?"

Grudgingly he had accepted, but the thought of it in his bag filled him with worry. And there was something else. Having accepted the gifts from Eanflæd, he fretted that he had somehow become complicit in shifting the course of his life. For what warrior could read and write? As far as he knew, no gesithas in Beobrand's warband, nor the lord of Ubbanford himself, knew how to make the shapes of letters and words on vellum. None of them could decipher the scratched symbols, hearing the words within their mind as he did.

After the queen had left, Coenred had clapped him on the back. "That is a truly royal gift," he said. "Take great care of it."

His words only made Cuthbert more nervous.

"Of course I will," he snapped. "I am not a fool."

"I never took you for one," replied Coenred. "It seems both the queen and I see something special in you. Perhaps you have not yet found the light that we see."

Cuthbert pondered Coenred's words for a long while. He turned the book over in his hands, relishing the touch of the smooth leather. Turning the pages, he marvelled at the markings there. He could barely make out one word in twenty, but his heart soared at the beauty of it; the perfection. He had never felt anything akin to this before. It was as though when he had first watched the seals and the birds, he had begun to hear God's whispering, but now, with the weight of the Psalter in his hands, he began to imagine the Lord of heaven speaking to him in bold, loud words and sentences. Was such a thing possible?

"Is it wrong that I feel this way?" he asked.

"How do you feel?" replied Coenred, his voice gentle.

"I see the beauty in this leather and vellum. The words begin to come to me." Cuthbert paused, struggling to explain his feelings. "I long to learn more, to be able to read as you can."

"You are quick to learn," said Coenred. "Soon enough you will be reading and writing no doubt faster and better than me."

"But I am no monk." Cuthbert let the words hang in the cool air of the church. Outside he could hear the wall wards shouting as they trained with shield and spear. He stood, wishing to go and watch them as he did every day. Soon, he prayed, he would be strong enough to once again join his fellow warriors in practice with weapons and linden boards. "Is it wrong that I yearn to fight?"

Coenred stared at him, frowning.

"Nobody but you can decide what path to follow, Cuthbert.

Some men are destined to fight to protect those weaker than them."

"Like Beobrand."

"Yes," said Coenred with a tinge of sadness in his voice, "like Beobrand." He sighed. "But such a calling is not for all men. Many cannot stomach the taking of another's life. And even for those such as Beobrand to whom killing comes easily, the death of others is a heavy burden."

"You think I am not suited to that life? You think I should join the brethren of Lindisfarena?"

Coenred shook his head.

"We would be lucky to have you. You are intelligent, kind and thoughtful. But you are yet young and only you can decide."

Cuthbert had left him there and gone out into the noisy courtyard to watch the wardens shove each other, shield to shield. The crack of spears against wood and the clang of iron bosses colliding drowned out his thoughts for a time.

Now, Cuthbert noticed that Eadgard had ridden ahead, leaving him to bring up the rear of Beobrand's warband alone. The axeman must have grown tired of his sullen silence, for he now chatted and joked with Fraomar and his brother, Grindan, some way further off.

Cuthbert thought of Coenred's last words to him as he had left the church that day, clutching the queen's gift close to his chest for fear he might let it drop into the mud.

"Do one thing for me," Coenred had said.

"What?"

"Do not ignore the voice of God. He can guide you along the right path, but only if you listen." He had held Cuthbert's gaze for a few heartbeats. "Do not shut Him out. If He speaks to you, Cuthbert, listen."

Cuthbert looked over the land to his right and left. The still of the day had been shattered by the passing of the mounted warriors, but now that most of them were far away, the chaffinches, song thrushes and sparrows began to chirp and trill once more in the hedges. The drone of bees settling on the clover was loud enough to be heard over the clop of his horse's hooves. The wind rustled through the boughs of the beech and hazel that grew near the road. A movement caught his eye and he turned to see a hare, raised up on its haunches, staring at him. Its long ears stretched above its head and it seemed to nod at him as he passed, making no effort to hide itself in the undergrowth.

Cuthbert stared at it, craning his head around until it was lost in the distance. All the while the animal did not blink or take its gaze from Cuthbert's. He wondered at the meaning of that. Was it judging him? What did it see in the face of the young man who rode at the rear of the column of warriors?

Did the animal see another killer of men, a hard-faced gesith, or did he see something softer. Could it be that the hare saw in him what Eanflæd and Coenred had noticed?

Shaking his head, Cuthbert kicked his mount into a canter to catch up with the others. As he rode, he listened to the breeze rushing past and the thump of his horse's hooves on the turf, and listened for the voice of God.

Chapter 24

Sidrac's blood was still pumping from the severed arteries in his neck as Cynan pushed him aside.

Hunberht's eyes widened and a cold smile spread across his face.

"I am going to enjoy killing you," he sneered, assured of his own ability despite his right arm hanging useless in a sling. He leapt forward to meet Cynan, and his agility, sword-skill and courage were all obvious in his actions and lithe movements. His blade flicked out with snake-like speed and Cynan barely managed to parry the blow. As it was, Hunberht's sword scored a long cut down his forearm. Blood welled there, but Cynan did not feel the wound immediately. Cynan was tall, strong and battle-skilled and, without thinking, he rotated his wrist, turning his parry into a counter-strike that pierced Hunberht's left shoulder. The blade buried deep into muscles and sinews and the swordsman's left arm lost its strength. His sword dropped to the earth and for the briefest of moments, Hunberht's eyes were filled with the knowledge of his death. All about them, the other men were fighting and Cynan did not pause. He raised his sword and hammered it into Hunberht's head. The man's skull was smashed and he collapsed instantly.

It was then that the cut on his arm began to burn and Cynan

wondered for a heartbeat how he might have fared against Hunberht if the sneering swordsman had had the use of his right arm. But there was no time to ponder such questions. Halinard was locked in a struggle against a stocky, bandy-legged brute, while Brinin and Ingwald had both dispatched the men who stood before them.

The two of them moved to help the Frank. Together they would make quick work of Halinard's opponent. Cynan fixed his eyes on the last enemy standing. It was the tall youth, Raedmund, the lad who had taken the dogs away to be tethered in the barn. Stepping over Hunberht's still form, Cynan swung his sword in a great arc, testing his hold on the grip and the strength of his wounded arm. Blood flicked from the blade, splattering Raedmund's appalled face. The boy's eyes were wide and terrified. He held a spear before him, pointing it towards the approaching Waelisc warrior. Cynan clenched his jaw against the throbbing pain in his arm and jumped forward. Raedmund gasped and stumbled backwards, raising the spear to ward off the impending attack.

"Please, no," he said. "I do not want to die."

The boy's words were as wind to a fire within Cynan. His rage soared, its flames fanned to a new intensity.

"What about Alfwold?" he spat, recalling the look of horror on the old bondsman's face as he had died hanging on the oak. "Do you think he wanted death? What about Leofman? You were going to kill him," he shouted, as all his anger coalesced on the terrified young man before him. "And what of his wife, and their son?"

Raedmund took another step backward, shaking his head. He tried to speak, perhaps to justify and explain himself, but Cynan did not listen to his words. They were lost in the rush of his blood and the roaring fires of his wrath.

Effortlessly, Cynan batted the ash haft of the spear aside with his left hand and stepped inside the reach of the spear-point.

Raising his sword, he prepared to slam it into this frightened youth when a shout from behind cut through his anger. This was a higher-pitched voice. Like that of a woman.

Or a child.

It took great effort to halt the blade's descent, but at the last possible moment Cynan checked his sword's swing. The steel ended up quivering a mere hand's breadth before Raedmund's wide eyes. The young man dropped his spear and raised his hands, cowering before Cynan, who kicked the spear away and surveyed the scene around him. Everyone from the hall, apart from the terrified Raedmund, who now knelt before him with his head bowed, was dead or dying. With a wave of relief Cynan saw that all of his companions yet stood.

Eadwig ran up to him then, his father limping behind and shouting for the boy to come back. The little boy flung his arms around Raedmund's neck and clung to him, sobbing. Begging Cynan not to kill him. From the barn came the sound of the dogs barking once more.

As Cynan took stock of the situation, faces cautiously peered out of the open door of the hall. Cynan's breathing was ragged from the sprint and the combat. His arm throbbed with each beat of his heart, and looking down he saw the sleeve of his kirtle was stained red. On seeing the figures in the doorway, he raised his gore-slick blade, ready for another attack.

"Show yourselves," he said.

An elderly man, with deep wrinkles on his brow and wisps of white hair on the sides of his head, stepped gingerly into the early morning light, looking about him with wide, sad eyes.

"What have you done?" he asked, though it seemed to Cynan there was no need to answer him. The old man walked towards the slumped corpse of Sidrac with tears in his eyes. "What have you done to the master?"

A younger man followed him outside, looking about warily at the armed men.

"Don't hurt him," he said to Cynan. "Please."

Cynan took in the man's drab attire and noted the music of his voice, so replied in his mother's tongue.

"You are thralls?"

The younger man met his gaze and Cynan liked the defiance he saw there.

"My name is Bleddyn," the man said, "and that is my father, Cadoc." He glanced over at the old man.

Cynan followed Bleddyn's gaze and watched as Cadoc knelt beside Sidrac. Tears tumbled down the old man's cheeks as he muttered to himself or perhaps to Sidrac's still form. Or mayhap he whispered to the man's shade.

"We served that bastard," said Bleddyn.

"Are there more of you?" asked Cynan, moving to one of the fallen men and wiping his sword blade on the dead man's breeches.

"Two more men inside," Bleddyn replied after a brief hesitation. "And eight women. They are too scared to come out."

"You have nothing to fear from us," Cynan said, and Bleddyn looked at him as if he had told him butter was made from gold. "I have not come in search of thralls. Your master is dead. You are free."

Bleddyn still looked unconvinced.

"Four of the women are not thralls. They have children too."

Cynan frowned. Nothing was ever simple.

"They need not fear us either."

Cynan had half-expected the hall to be dirty and slovenly within; a reflection of the character of its owner. But it was a comfortable enough building, with clean rushes on the floor and a small fire on the hearthstone.

As they followed Bleddyn inside, Cynan enquired after the

lady of the hall, feeling a pang of guilt at killing Sidrac. He remembered vividly Eadgyth's grief when she had learnt of Acennan's death. Cynan loathed the idea of being confronted with the effects of his actions. The thought of Eadgyth, too, made him wonder once again what had made him so willing to answer Sulis' call for aid. He could have been safe within his own hall now, not about to confront the wailing widows of men whose blood was still drying on his hands.

But he was spared at least one confrontation that he had feared.

Bleddyn shook his head.

"The lady Herelufu was taken to Our Heavenly Father just after Eostremonath." He had a haunted look about him and he glanced over at his father, who peered at the floor. "She was thrown while riding."

Cynan nodded, glad not to have to answer to Sidrac's wife.

Then, anticipating his next question in the way of the best servants, Bleddyn said, "They had no children."

The other women were too frightened to approach Cynan. They cowered at the rear of the hall with their wide-eyed weeping children. Cynan made no effort to speak with them. What was there to say?

It seemed that since the lady of the hall's death, it had been Cadoc who'd kept a close eye on the running of the household. Once he had recovered from his shock and spoken quietly to his son, he appeared to revert to his usual role of keeping the hall tidy and its inhabitants fed and comfortable. He ordered the women thralls, two of whom were as young as Raedmund, to prepare food for their guests. The women scurried off to do his bidding, looking at Cynan and the others with frightened eyes. They whispered to each other and, once the men had sat down, keeping their swords close, the two girls brought bowls of porridge for each of them. Cadoc poured them ale and they fell to eating and drinking. They had not eaten since the previous day, before riding through the night and then clashing with Sidrac and his men in the morning. They were ravenous and they did not speak until they had emptied their bowls. As they ate, Cynan looked at the men. Their eyes were encircled in shadows.

"We cannot tarry here," said Leofman, when he had finished eating. Eadwig sat close to his side, but did not eat. His face was pale and he stared at Cynan in fear. He had pleaded for Raedmund to be spared and Cynan had complied with the boy's wish, but clearly, seeing so many men hacked down had filled Eadwig with terror at these strangers. He had been through much these last days, but Cynan marvelled at the small boy's bravery. To rush to Raedmund's defence had taken true grit. To run towards men with blooded swords in their hands was something many men several times Eadwig's age would have baulked at. "We must ride now," went on Leofman. "We cannot allow Bumoth and Ludeca to find Sulis." He shuddered at the thought.

Cynan nodded. The man was right, but they could not leave immediately. Halinard was pallid and the bandage they had wrapped about him had already soaked through. The Frank had taken the deepest wound in the fight; a gash to his side. It was deep and painful, and bled profusely, but Cynan had seen enough wounds to know that unless it grew elf-shot and festered, Halinard would live.

"Raedmund," Cynan said, "place one of the seax blades in the embers and see that it is glowing hot." The young man nodded and set about his task.

Cynan clenched his fist, testing the bandage on his forearm. It ached, but the bandage was tight, his grip still strong.

"We will go as soon as we are able," he said. "First we must tend to Halinard. He is in no state to ride until that wound is sealed. Besides," he said, glancing over at the open door, "we wait for Ingwald and Brinin to return with the horses." He had sent them to collect their mounts and they should be back soon.

"How do you fare, Halinard?"

"By Tiw's cock!" hissed Halinard through gritted teeth. "It hurts!" His face was pale and sweat-streaked.

Despite Halinard's obvious pain, Cynan couldn't help but smile. To hear Bassus' favourite expletive spoken with the softness and lilt of the Frank's accent went some way to dispelling the darkness of their situation. They were far from home and there were still enemies to confront. Bumoth, Ludeca and the others were half a day ahead of them and Cynan could not push from his mind the thought of Sidrac's men reaching Sulis before them. And yet he knew he should be pleased with how events had transpired. With only a few bruises and cuts to show for it, they had prevailed.

Halinard growled and cursed again, but this time in his own tongue. He glared at Cynan.

"I see nothing for to smile," he said, which only made Cynan's grin widen.

"Is it hot enough yet?" Cynan asked the gangly youth called Raedmund. The young man knelt beside the hearth fire and blew into the embers upon which he had placed fresh wood. Smoke billowed around him and he coughed. When he had finished spluttering, he turned his soot-stained face to Cynan.

"No, lord," he said. "Not yet." Tears streamed down his cheeks. From the smoke, thought Cynan, but his tear-streaked face gave the young man a pathetic, beaten air. Without awaiting a reply, Raedmund resumed blowing into the fire. The smoke once more clouded about him, hazing the air in the hall.

Cynan looked about the interior of the building and wondered if he had been right to spare Raedmund's life. Time would tell. If the boy gave him any cause to doubt him, he would quickly join Sidrac and the rest of his men in the afterlife. Still, Eadwig had vouched for Raedmund, screaming for Cynan not to slay the tall youth. And if the boy who had been a captive here spoke well of Raedmund, Cynan supposed he deserved a chance to prove himself.

The thralls in the hall did not seem to bear Raedmund a grudge either, which must also bode well for his character.

Cynan beckoned to Cadoc.

The old slave, still nervous of this warrior who had killed his master, bowed.

"Yes, lord."

"I am not your lord," Cynan said to him in his native Waelisc tongue. "You are free, I have told you so."

Cadoc bowed again, lower this time. Then he stepped forward and refilled Cynan's cup from the pitcher of ale he held. He seemed to ignore Cynan's words. Cynan frowned as the old thrall moved along to Leofman and filled his cup too. After that, he poured ale for Halinard and then Raedmund.

Cynan caught Bleddyn's eye from where he stood warily at a distance in the shadows of the hall. He approached and inclined his head, just as Cadoc had done.

"Does the old one understand what I have told you all?" Cynan asked.

The younger thrall had the same dark, deep-set eyes as Cadoc, but his hair was black and thick.

"He understands, lord," he whispered. "But my father has been a thrall for many years. He served Sidrac's father for a long time. Tohrwulf was a good master. My father has always been loyal and this change has been as rapid as it has been unexpected."

Cynan nodded.

He closed his eyes, tightening his grip on the cup of ale and feeling the bandage press on his forearm and the sting of the cut beneath it.

The young thrall spoke the truth of it. Everything had happened very quickly once Cynan had decided on his course of action. He thanked the gods that Ingwald, Halinard and Brinin had all acted without hesitation. If they had been slow to react, things might well have ended very differently.

Cynan drank the rest of his ale and when Cadoc once more

approached with the pitcher, he placed his hand over the cup. He would need a clear head for what was to come.

"Have you got anything stronger?" he asked.

The old thrall barely hesitated.

"Indeed, lord," he said. "We have some fine mead."

"That is not yours to offer, Cadoc," shouted one of the women from the back of the hall.

"Silence!" snapped Cynan, suddenly exhausted. There was no time to waste and he would not spend precious moments on arguing with the women in this hall. "Make no mistake. Everything in this hall is now mine." He fixed her with a cold stare. "Be thankful I let you live."

The woman clutched a small dark-haired girl to her breast and glowered at Cynan.

He sighed.

"I do not seek to make war on women and children. Keep quiet, and we will be gone soon."

She said nothing, but her gaze said much. They must not let their guard down.

"Fetch the mead, Cadoc," Cynan said, "and pour a horn for Halinard. He'll need it."

Cadoc hurried away, seemingly happy to have been given another errand.

"I not drink mead or wine," Halinard said, his words clipped and breathless with the pain.

When they had first found the Frank in Rodomo, he had been drunk, drinking to escape his feelings of helplessness at failing to protect his daughter from the monster, Vulmar. He had found a new purpose, helping Beobrand rescue Ardith from the Frankish nobleman. Since then, he refrained from drinking to excess.

"I know it," replied Cynan, "but for now, think of it as leechcraft."

"Leechcraft?"

"Aye," said Cynan, "like the wyrts or potions Odelyna gives people for the gripe or toothache. This is to dull the pain."

Halinard drew in a sharp intake of breath.

"By Tiw's cock," he said again, repeatedly slamming his left fist into his thigh in frustrated agony, "it does hurt so!"

Cadoc returned with a small jug and a horn. He proffered the drinking vessel to Halinard. Cynan was ready to argue with Halinard, but it seemed the Frank had already made up his mind for he snatched the horn from the old thrall. Cadoc poured from the jug. The horn shook in Halinard's hand. Halinard nodded all the while, willing him to hurry. As soon as the horn was full, he placed it to his lips and drained it. Holding it out, he nodded again.

"More," he said.

Cynan chuckled.

"You didn't take a lot of convincing."

"Nor would you, if it was you who had been stabbed," replied Halinard, before once again drinking deeply.

The heat from the fire was stifling now and Cynan looked over to see Raedmund, sweating and red-faced where before he had been pale. He had backed away from the blaze, but he was still much too close for comfort.

"Raedmund," Cynan said. "That blade must be hot enough now."

The young man wrapped his fist in a cloth and retrieved the long seax from within the fire's hot core. The blade glowed a dull red in the gloom of the hall.

"It is ready, lord," he said.

"Bring it here," said Cynan, "and be careful. If you drop it in the rushes, the whole hall will burn, like as not." For a fleeting moment Cynan wondered at the wisdom of having one of his recent foes hold the heated blade. Ingwald had told him not to split the group up when Cynan had sent him with Brinin to fetch the horses; now Cynan wondered whether the gesith had been right. If Raedmund chose to attack, and the thralls and women joined him, things would get bloody. Halinard was injured and Leofman still not recovered from his wounds. Cynan dropped his hand to his sword pommel, reassuring himself by its touch. He stared Raedmund in the eye as the lanky youth walked towards him. He needn't have been concerned. There was no defiance in the boy's eyes.

"Halinard," Cynan said. "It is time."

The older Frankish warrior emptied his horn of mead for a third time and handed the empty vessel to Cadoc. Nodding to Cynan, he lifted up his bloody kirtle to expose the dark-stained cloth binding beneath.

"Unwind the bandage, Cadoc," said Cynan, taking the hot seax from Raedmund, cloth wrapping and all. Heat emanated from the metal and it was almost unbearably hot to hold, despite the layers of linen protecting his hand. But it had already lost the bright glow as the metal cooled. There was the merest tinge of red on the edge of the blade now. "Hurry," he snapped, moving closer. Cadoc was slowly pulling away the bandage. The cloth was soaked and stuck to Halinard's skin. The Frank winced as the thrall tugged it free. "Out of the way," hissed Cynan.

Cadoc moved aside. Halinard's wound still seeped blood, the flaps of skin peeled apart, exposing the raw flesh beneath. Cynan drew in a deep breath.

"Ready?" he asked.

Halinard nodded.

"Look!" Cynan said, feigning sudden surprise. "What in Woden's name is that?" He looked towards the rear of the hall where the women and children were huddled together, watching them.

Halinard turned to look at whatever it was that had caught Cynan's attention. As he moved, Cynan reached out with his left hand, pinching the lips of the wound together and then, with his right, he immediately slapped the heated seax blade against the closed wound.

The knife blade sizzled and the air was instantly filled with the scent of burning meat and singed hair. Halinard tried to pull away, but Cynan wrapped his left arm around his shoulders and held him close. Trails of fatty smoke drifted around them as Halinard grunted and shook with the pain.

"Hold still," whispered Cynan. "I want to take you home to Gisela in one piece."

After several heartbeats, Cynan let him go and stood back. He handed the seax to Raedmund who had not moved. Absently, Cynan thought that if the boy wished to attack him, now would be the time. He had his back to Raedmund, but the youth made no move against him. Perhaps Eadwig had been right about the lad.

Halinard slumped back to lie on the bench. He was sweating and pallid.

"I understand now," he panted.

"Understand what?" asked Cynan.

"Why you need to heal me."

"Of course I want you healed, Halinard. You are a good man."

"But more than that," said the Frank, grinning through the pain that must surely still have racked his body. "You are frightened of Gisela."

Cynan laughed.

"You have me there. I can stand against a hundred men in a shieldwall, but the thought of facing your goodwife fills me with terror."

Halinard smiled and closed his eyes.

Cynan sighed.

"Let him rest for a while," he said, more to himself than anyone else. "With luck, he should be able to travel soon." He noticed Raedmund still standing with the hot seax in his hand. "Put that down and have something to drink, man. You look ready to drop."

Raedmund seated himself on a bench on the other side of the hall. Cadoc scurried over and filled a cup of ale for him. Cynan sat down again and stared at the young man through the flames of the hearth fire. The stoked blaze now made the hall too hot. Cynan thought about going outside, but then remembered the corpses of the men they had slain and remained where he was.

"What am I to do with you?" he asked Raedmund.

"I do not know, lord," Raedmund replied. His lip quivered and Cynan wondered if he was going to cry.

"Why should I not kill you?" he asked.

"I will serve you."

"As you served Sidrac? Throwing aside your weapon and begging for mercy at the first fight."

"I am no coward," said Raedmund, lifting his chin, at last showing a spark of character.

"No? Well you certainly looked like one out there." Cynan nodded to the daylight spilling in from the open doors. The air of the hall was fogged with smoke and heavy with the stench of burnt meat.

"I did not wish to die for Sidrac. He was not a worthy hlaford."

"Then why follow him?"

Raedmund looked into his cup as if searching for the answer there. When he spoke, his voice was quiet and coloured with emotion.

"I followed Cynehelm here."

Cynan had heard the name before, but could not place it.

"The owner of the dogs?" said Leofman.

Raedmund nodded sadly.

"And what was this Cynehelm to you?" asked Cynan.

"My brother, lord."

At this, Cynan grew silent.

"You have other kin?" he asked.

Raedmund shook his head.

"I am sorry you lost your kin today," said Cynan. "But that is what happens when you ride with men like Sidrac. Men who follow a lord with no honour often die with no honour." Cynan glanced over at Eadwig. The boy was nestled in the crook of his father's meaty arm. "Eadwig, you say Raedmund is a good man? He treated you decently while you were here?"

The boy did not speak, but nodded, his eyes never leaving Cynan's.

"And you, Bleddyn?" Cynan addressed the thrall who was listening intently from a discreet distance. "What say you? Is Raedmund one to be trusted?"

Bleddyn looked from Cynan to Raedmund.

"You would trust the word of a thrall?" he asked.

"I have told you," said Cynan, "you are a thrall no longer. Your master is dead and I free you of your bonds."

Bleddyn stared at him for a long while.

"Raedmund is not like the others," he said at last. "He has ever been good to us. He looked after the boy. And," he flicked a look at the women thralls at the rear of the hall, "he never forced himself on the womenfolk."

Cynan mulled over this.

"It seems you have a second chance to serve a lord, Raedmund. If you can serve the man who had your brother killed."

"Are *you* a worthy lord?" Raedmund asked. "Are you just?"

Cynan smiled, pleased to see the boy's spirit.

"If I were not, would I tell you so? Did Sidrac tell your brother and you of his plans to steal the land from Leofman here?"

Raedmund shook his head, then looked at the rushes on the floor.

"Cynehelm knew what Sidrac was like," he said in a small voice. "He didn't care."

"But you did?"

"Yes."

Cynan stared at him until Raedmund looked up and met his gaze.

"I will let others tell you what manner of man I am," Cynan said after a time. "But know this, if you swear your oath to me, it will bind you till one of us departs middle earth and I will expect from you loyalty in all things, even if that means your death. My men do not violate women, nor harm children. They do not lie, cheat or steal. Those things are for lesser men, and I will not tolerate them. Such is the rule of my lord, too."

"Who do you serve?" Raedmund asked.

"My lord is Beobrand of Ubbanford."

"Beobrand Half-hand?" Raedmund's tone was full of awe.

"Aye," said Cynan, "the same."

Raedmund's eyes widened.

"I see you have heard of my lord's exploits."

The young man nodded. There were tales of Beobrand told throughout Albion. Many were exaggerated, but most had a kernel of truth at their centre.

"If you swear your oath to me, know that you will also follow Beobrand into battle. You will carry a black shield. You will learn to stand strong, or you will fall in the shieldwall, for this is the way of the Black Shields."

Raedmund swallowed and wiped his hand across his face, smearing the soot there.

"What say you, Raedmund," asked Cynan, "will you give me your oath?"

For several heartbeats the tall youth stared at Cynan, perhaps thinking of his future and what alternative paths he might choose. At last he nodded.

"I will swear to you," he said.

"Good. I imagine I will have need of all the men I can get before we leave Rheged."

Cynan had a sudden idea and turned to face Bleddyn.

"What about you?"

"Me, lord?" The Waelisc thrall frowned.

"You seem strong and quick-witted. I could use a man such as you in my warband."

"But I am no warrior. I am a…" His voice trailed off.

"You are no thrall now," said Cynan. "You are free and now you have a choice. You can leave this place and head back to your people, or you can pledge fealty to me."

Bleddyn looked about the hall as if searching for the answer to the question of what he should do with his life. Cadoc stared at him with sad eyes. Sighing, Bleddyn turned back to Cynan.

"I do not know how to fight. What use would I be to you?"

"I was a thrall once, until Beobrand freed me. You can learn, as I did." Cynan held Bleddyn's gaze, staring directly into his eyes. "I believe you are a man of worth. I see it in you."

It took Bleddyn some time to make his decision. He led his father into a shadowed corner of the hall where they talked in tense, hissed whispers.

When Ingwald and Brinin returned with the horses they found young Raedmund and the erstwhile thrall, Bleddyn, kneeling before Cynan, earnestly pledging to be true and faithful, to love all which he loved and shun all which he shunned.

They observed the solemn moment as both men swore never to do anything which would displease their new lord. Then they slapped the men on the back after Cynan had raised them up.

"Halinard," said Cynan, "can you ride? I fear we cannot tarry any longer."

Halinard heaved himself up into a sitting position with a groan and a grimace. He was pale and his face was sheened with sweat.

"I can ride, lord," he said, his words clipped.

"Good man. Brinin, prepare the horses. We leave at once. Ingwald, find Bleddyn a byrnie and weapons. Raedmund, do you have your own heregeat?"

"I have a shield and spear, but I do not own a horse or sword."

"Are there more horses in the stable?" Cynan asked, turning to Bleddyn.

"Yes, lord."

"Take a mount each," Cynan said to his two new gesithas. "And whatever weapons and armour you can find. Anything that is left when we leave," he turned to face Cadoc and the women, "is yours."

With each passing moment, he imagined Bumoth and the others closing on Sulis. By remaining here to fight, had he condemned her to death at the hands of Sidrac's men and her husband's brother?

Clapping his hands together, he shouted, "Come on, there is no time to waste."

His men hurried to do his bidding.

Bleddyn did not rush off with the others, instead, he stepped in close. Cynan was considerably taller and looked down at the man impatiently.

"Yes?"

"Before we leave this place to my father and the others, there is something you should know."

Cynan looked Bleddyn in the eye and saw a sharp intelligence there. He was pleased at his decision to ask this man to join his comitatus, and equally pleased Bleddyn had accepted.

"Tell me," Cynan said in his native tongue.

Chapter 25

Beobrand groaned as Tatwine let out a shout of anger, the shrill sound sending a stab of pain through his skull. Cuthbert had grabbed Udela's son by the collar, pulling him back to slow him down. The two scuffled briefly before Udela shouted at them to keep the noise down. Beobrand nodded his thanks. His head throbbed, as it sometimes did on days when the weather was on the turn. Udela recognised the signs and had brought him a cup of ale where he sat with Bassus beneath the great oak that Beobrand's men referred to as "Sunniva's tree". She had loved to sit in its shadow and watch as the new hall had grown on the hilltop. The hall she had seen built had been destroyed by fire, but the men had built it anew and now it was hard to remember a time before this hall had stood there.

Beobrand took a sip of the ale and forced a smile at Udela, who lingered nearby. He felt a fleeting sense of guilt to be thinking of Sunniva with Udela at his side, but such feelings were foolish. Udela was the mother of his daughter, but no more than that. She tended to his hall and had lain with him once when first he had brought her north from Cantware. She was a good woman. A friend. But no more. Sunniva had lit a fire within him that had never truly gone out. Her body might be ash, but the embers of their passion still warmed his memories. Again, he felt a stab of guilt for his thoughts, wondering how Udela would react if she knew what passed through his mind.

"By Christ's bones," said Bassus, "that boy is not much more than a child."

Beobrand followed his gaze. Tatwine had freed himself and was now sprinting away, with Cuthbert in close pursuit. Both of them were laughing. At thirteen summers, Tatwine was still more boy than man, but Beobrand knew instinctively that his old friend referred to Cuthbert.

"True enough," he said. "Still, better to remain a child as long as possible, I say."

"You do, do you?" Bassus raised an eyebrow. "Well, I'm not so sure. We need men, not boys. Oswine is not defeated and there'll be more battle before the end of the summer, mark my words."

Beobrand frowned.

"You are probably right," he said, wondering if there would ever be peace in the land. Not in his lifetime, it seemed to him. Not while the men who ruled sought ever more power and wealth. Trying to push aside thoughts of war, he watched the two boys run. "There will be time enough for the lad to grow up."

"You say he fought well?" Bassus asked, sounding doubtful.

"He did." Beobrand sipped at his ale. "I am glad to see him running again."

"Aye, it is good to see," replied Bassus. "Though before his wound, Tatwine would never have beaten Cuthbert in a race."

Tatwine was several paces ahead of Cuthbert now, as they rounded a lone oak at the bottom of the slope that led down towards the settlement of Ubbanford. With a shout of defiance, the younger runner began to sprint up the hill with Cuthbert labouring behind him.

"True, but better to be slowed by his wound than killed by it. There was a time when it seemed he would succumb." Beobrand grew silent. He took another swig of ale and rubbed his fingers against the spot on his forehead where a slingshot had hit him years before. Cuthbert had worried him, but now the boy was hale enough to race with Udela's son. One thing Beobrand no longer needed to fret about. The gods knew there were plenty of others.

"Have you decided what to say to her?" Udela's voice cut into his thoughts and he saw she had moved closer.

"To who?" he asked.

Udela nodded down the hill and Beobrand saw Ardith coming up the slope behind the running boys. She held a hand under her distended belly and the climb up the incline was clearly taking her some effort. He considered rising and going down to meet her, then disregarded the idea. They had already spoken on the issue, and he had given his answer. She was furious with him, but none of this was his doing.

"Well, have you?" prodded Udela.

"There is no more to say on the matter. I do not understand how she believes me to blame in this."

Udela sighed.

"You are her father," she said, her tone soft. "You have proven that you are able to save her when she is in trouble. It is a difficult draught to swallow to learn the mighty Beobrand is not able to right every wrong."

Beobrand grunted, her words stirring up mixed emotions within him. He pushed himself up, no longer able to watch impassively as Ardith struggled up the hill. He stalked down the slope towards her, his head aching with each step. The clouds to the north were dark, and there was a coolness in the air. He thought he could smell rain. The summer had been changeable and he wished for the long hot days they had been blessed with in the spring. Glancing back, he saw that neither Bassus nor Udela had made an effort to follow him.

Tatwine and Cuthbert passed him, both panting heavily, but grinning at the thrill of pitting themselves against each other.

Reaching Ardith, Beobrand met her icy blue stare with his own. Her jaw was set and she stiffened at his approach. Gods, but the girl was stubborn. Her eyes narrowed and he could feel the strength of her will in them. Was this how people felt when confronted with his cold gaze?

"I have told you," he said, holding out his arm to assist her on the last stretch of the path. "I cannot ride west in search of Brinin and the others."

"I know, Father," she replied, with a resigned sigh. "Your word is iron and you must await the king's orders."

The mention of the strength of his word dismayed Beobrand. Once his oath had been unbreakable, but now he knew that everything had its limit. Iron could rust. It could bend and break. And yet it was true that he had given his word to Oswiu that he would await his command at Ubbanford. He could not risk breaking this promise. The king was already angry at him for sailing south without his knowledge, and then finding Cynan gone without Beobrand's leave.

Ardith brushed past him, ignoring his proffered arm. He felt his anger suddenly well up within him. By Woden, the girl was infuriating.

"None of this is my doing, girl," he snapped, falling into step beside her. "It was you, was it not, who urged your husband to run off with Cynan?"

She did not reply.

"Cynan has lost his mind," he said, clenching his fists at his side. To think that the woman who had slain Reaghan had somehow managed to convince the Waelisc to follow her filled him with fury. Cynan must have been bewitched to have listened to her. He shuddered. Perhaps that was the answer. Had Sulis used dark powers to bend people to her will? There seemed no other plausible explanation.

Looking up the hill towards the great oak, he saw Udela and Bassus waiting there. Hadn't he once risked everything for

Udela and this young woman who walked beside him? That was different, he told himself. They were family. And yet who could understand the bonds that tied people together. Beobrand remembered the contorted face of the screeching woman who had attacked him by the Wall and he recalled Cynan's impassioned intervention. Surely there had been more than simple compassion there. Had the man loved Sulis even then?

"I do not understand why Cynan would go with Sulis," he said, his exasperation evident in his voice, "but at least he knew the woman. There is history there. But Brinin! And you so close to your time. It is madness!"

"You came to my aid," Ardith said, her voice so quiet he had to strain to hear it. "And you did not know me. Brinin and Halinard merely did what you would do. Cynan too."

"That was different, and you know it."

"How so?" she asked.

"That woman is a murdering bitch!" Beobrand snapped, his anger getting the better of him. "She deserves no help." He sighed. The ache in his head was worse than ever. "You are my child. It was my duty to go after you."

She halted, and turned to stare at him. Tears welled in her eyes. By Woden, what now? Could he not talk to a woman without her weeping? Udela, perhaps sensing the conversation between father and daughter had reached its conclusion, walked towards them.

"Waes hael, Mother," Ardith said, embracing Udela warmly. "Can we go inside, please? This wind is cold."

"Of course," Udela replied, leading Ardith towards the great hall and flicking a disapproving glance at Beobrand.

Beobrand frowned as he watched them walk away. Angrily, he stomped back to where Bassus was sitting beneath the oak. Throwing himself down beside him, he snatched up his cup of ale and drained it.

"Women!" he said. "I will never understand them."

"I wonder if any man ever does," replied Bassus. "Rowena is a mystery to me, that is for certain." The huge warrior stared out at the dark clouds that filled the sky beyond the Tuidi. "She is ill," he said without warning.

"Rowena?"

The huge, one-armed warrior let out a ragged breath.

"She tried to keep it from me, but I knew something was wrong. In the end, I made Odelyna tell me."

Beobrand looked sidelong at his old friend. Bassus' eyes glimmered, brimming with tears.

"How bad is it?" he asked, unable to find any other words.

For a long while Bassus said nothing. He stared at the brooding clouds and cuffed the tears from his eyes.

"Bad," he said at last. He coughed to clear his throat.

Beobrand did not know what to say. He raised his cup and found it empty.

"I'm sorry, my friend."

Bassus offered a grunt of acknowledgement, but did not look at him.

"Women," he said, his voice hoarse and rasping. "They cause us such trouble. They nag and cry and we complain. But who truly wishes to be free of them?"

They fell silent and Beobrand wondered at the pull women had on all men. The wind rustled the leaves above them and he thought of Sunniva again. It was hard to picture her face now; the memory of her only became clear when he looked on the features of their son. Perhaps that was why seeing Octa always saddened him.

"I always thought I would die in battle," said Bassus. "But look at me now." He shrugged and looked down at the stump where his left arm should have been. "I will never fight again. I am old. I will have a straw death, lying in my bed. Once that would have terrified me, to imagine I would not die with a sword in my hand, listening to the crash of the shieldwall. Now the only thing I am afraid of is that Rowena will go before me and I will die alone."

Beobrand reached out and placed his half-hand on Bassus' shoulder.

"You will never be alone, my friend," he said. "Not while I yet live."

Despite his sadness, Bassus chuckled, the sound rumbling deep in his throat.

"I do not mean to offend, Beobrand," he said with a twisted smile, "but I would rather have Rowena warming my bed."

Chapter 26

The pony snorted, scratching at the gravelly floor of the bothy with one of its front hooves.

"Easy, boy," Sulis murmured.

The pony rolled its eyes at her. Its ears were flat against its head. It stared out of the doorway that led to the open land of the hills of Rheged and freedom. The beast longed to be gone from this prison. It was nervous and she could not blame him. She had pushed the poor animal as fast as it could go into the hills. It was sure-footed and strong, and not prone to skittishness. But her own anxieties had seeped into the creature. She'd had a devil of a job to get the pony into the dark interior of the dry-stone hut. Eventually, she had needed to resort to brute force and sharp words, tugging hard on his harness until, the pony's baleful eyes showing white-rimmed in the darkness, the frightened animal had finally relented and made its way into the gloom.

There was little space in the small hut, but Sulis did not wish to leave the pony outside to be spotted by anyone wandering the land. She could scarcely imagine who would be abroad in these hills if it were not someone from Sidrac's steading in search of mischief, but the idea of leaving the animal outside had become something she could not countenance.

At the thought of Sidrac, Sulis shivered. It was cool inside the windowless hut, with damp seeping up from the ground. The rough stones with which the walls had been constructed were green with lichen and moss. Outside, the day was bright, the rain of the night having blown over. Through the doorway, she could see a thin swathe of clover-speckled grass and heather. Bees buzzed over the flowers. But she could not risk going out to warm herself beneath the afternoon glow of the sun. No, she would remain hidden. She pondered the foolishness of her thoughts. There would be nobody up here. If there were, they would be looking for her, and hiding herself inside this hut would not keep her safe from Sidrac's men. And yet, the solid stone walls gave her a sensation of security, even if she knew it to be folly.

Rising, she wrapped her arms about the pony's neck, revelling in the warmth of the animal's body.

"There, there," she cooed. "We are safe in here."

She hoped she was right.

All through that rain-drenched night and the long summer day that followed, her mind had been full of dark thoughts. She had tried to imagine how far Cynan, Leofman and the others had ridden. Were they at Sidrac's hall already? Had they found Eadwig? Was the boy well? *God, let him be safe!* As she had ridden, she had prayed over and over for her son's safe return to her. The Lord would look after him, she told herself. Moments later despair would threaten to engulf her as she remembered Osgar; the brilliant red of his blood, his pleading eyes. Where had God been then? But she had not known the word of the one true God then. Maybe if she had known the true faith, Osgar would yet live. Could that be possible?

She remembered Leofman's gaping wound. He had been lucky to have survived such an injury. But was it truly luck? Was it not divine providence? Perhaps it was Leofman's faith in Christ that had seen him heal from the deep gash in his thigh. Did not Scyldsung say that "the Lord thy God, He it is that doth go with thee; He will not fail thee, nor forsake thee"? But if the Lord protected his own, why had he allowed Swiga to be killed? The mute had travelled with them to Dacor whenever they attended mass. He could not speak, but Scyldsung had allowed him to partake of the Holy Eucharist with the other believers.

"Actions are important to Christ, not words," Scyldsung had said. "As long as the Lord knows you are repentant in your heart, you are one of his flock." Sulis remembered vividly the beaming smile on Swiga's face on hearing the priest's words. The bondsman had always loved that the priest treated him normally, despite his affliction for which others often derided or spurned him.

Sulis felt her eyes brimming as she recalled Swiga's pallid, stiffening corpse; his blood dark and coagulated in the woollen kirtle she had made for him. Then she remembered the broken, tortured form of Alfwold. At the thought of Swiga and Alfwold, she let out a sob and the tears rolled down her cheeks.

Why had Sidrac's men done these things? Did they mean to kill them all? They had taken Eadwig, so they surely believed that having the boy alive was necessary for their plan to work. She had clung to that thought as she now held on tightly to the pony.

How had Sidrac known about the mine? They had told nobody. Beyond the small sample they had processed with the help of Scyldsung, they had not even begun to properly remove the stone from the earth. However Sidrac had learnt of the mine's existence, could it really yield so much that it would be worth murdering everyone in Leofman's household to obtain its riches?

She thought of all the suffering she had witnessed in her life. She knew that men would stoop to any sin in their quest for pleasure, wealth or fame. Why was she shocked that young Sidrac would resort to murder for the promise of precious metal?

Outside, the wind picked up, sighing through the mildewed thatch above her. A thin stream of water trickled from the thatch and ran down her back like the touch of chill fingers; the hand of the dead. She shuddered.

The wind died down and the world was silent again apart from the sound of dripping from the eaves.

What was that? Something had tugged at her senses. A sound she could not place.

She pushed away from the pony and strained to hear anything untoward. Nothing. It was just the wind. Patting the pony's neck again, as much to comfort herself as to calm the animal, she stepped towards the doorway. There she could see nothing but the swaying grass, the clover and the heather, the bees droning about their toil. Perhaps she would lean out of the hut and risk a peek. Before she reached the opening, she heard it again.

The distinct clop of a horse's hoof on stone. Sulis' heart thudded and her hands dropped instinctively to her belly. God, they had found her!

Terror welled within her like a stagnant mere, black and impenetrable, bobbing with the bloated corpses of her fears. If Sidrac's men had come for her, Leofman and Cynan must be dead. Was Eadwig yet alive? Her stomach churned at the thought her beautiful boy might be dead. But surely Sidrac wanted the boy alive...

The sound of another horse's tread reached her, and she pulled the sharp seax from its scabbard. She could easily imagine what would happen to her the moment Sidrac's brutes found her. She had suffered at the hands of their ilk before. Gazing down at the iron blade of the seax, she remembered how easily she had once sliced into her wrists, hoping to end her pain. Perhaps this was the answer after all. Her left hand touched her swollen belly, caressing it anxiously. Could she bring herself to kill her unborn child along with her? And what of Eadwig? If he yet lived, she would leave him an orphan. But better that she slay herself than endure the torments these violent men would inflict on her. So much of her life had been at the mercy of such men. At least now she could choose the manner of her ending.

Outside, close now, a horse whinnied. Another snorted.

The sound of harness creaking. The crunch of men's shoes hitting the earth as they dismounted. Voices spoke in sibilant whispers. Sulis held her breath. There was no denying now that the men had found her. She gripped the seax hilt tightly, preparing to face her wyrd.

She could hear her blood rushing. The silence was suddenly shattered by her pony nickering in welcome to the horses outside. Sulis started, almost dropping the seax in her alarm.

Heavy footfalls approached the bothy.

There was no more time. *Please, Lord, help me decide.* Should she try to defend herself with the knife in her hand, exacting what payment she could for what these men had done to her and her loved ones, or should she plunge the blade into her own flesh, releasing herself and her unborn babe from the miseries of middle earth?

Trembling, Sulis stood there in the gloom, holding the seax before her. Her breath was coming in short gasps now. Her terror was complete. As the bulky shape of the warrior loomed in the doorway, there was no more time to ponder which path to take. Letting out a shriek, she stabbed down with the seax.

Chapter 27

Cuthbert clenched and unclenched his right hand, holding his horse's reins in his left.

"Your hand paining you?" asked Gram. The warrior's scarred and craggy face reminded Cuthbert of the cliffs to the south of Bebbanburg; hard and unyielding. "It was your leg that was wounded, I thought." Gram grinned, spoiling his image of toughness. Cuthbert had seen him fight on the causeway in East Angeln and knew the tall man to be deadly, despite his age. Yet Gram was quick to smile. He often told riddles and jested with the younger gesithas. Cuthbert liked him.

Cuthbert stretched his fingers and closed them again. Shaking his hand in the cool air of the forest shade, he finally took hold of the reins with both hands once more.

"My fingers ache. That is all."

"It is from all that scribbling you have been doing," said Attor, who rode just ahead of them, close beside Beobrand, who led the small group along the tree-lined path to Stagga. "How you can read the marks on the pages of that book and then scratch words onto that wax tablet of yours, I will never understand."

"It is not so hard," said Cuthbert, though he knew that none of the men of Beobrand's comitatus, nor Beobrand himself, truly understood his desire to spend so much time poring over the Psalter that the queen had given him. And yet, in the minds of the warriors, at least the book was a thing of beauty, with illuminated letters and small images in gold and red ink. Why he would wish to scratch symbols into the wax-coated wooden tablet that Eanflæd had gifted him was truly beyond them.

But to Cuthbert it was intoxicating, this magic of being able to form letters and words in silence, that he, or anyone with the right skill, could then see, interpret and speak aloud. With each passing day, he became more adept at reading the text from the vellum pages of the book, and his own writing was quickly growing fluid, and more consistent.

"Well, I know not how you do it," said Attor. "I thought only the Christ monks and priests were able to understand the magic words in their books. I have never heard of a warrior being able to do such a thing."

Cuthbert shrugged.

"Well, I am no monk," he said.

"Perhaps your hand hurts from another use, eh?" said Garr. The slender spear-man rode at the rear of the small band. "We have all been young men," he continued, making an unmistakable, repetitive hand gesture. "Maybe we should find you a willing bed-thrall, to dampen your fires, or you won't be able to hold your sword when battle comes."

Cuthbert felt his face grow hot at Garr's lewd comment.

Gram laughed.

"If he's anything like I was at his age," he said, "Cuthbert will never tire of wielding either of his swords." He paused, and winked. "But I'll wager he'll finish the fights he has with the one in his breeches more quickly than the ones he has with that blade sheathed on his belt."

The others, apart from Beobrand, laughed. But the mention of the sword he had taken from the Mercian in East Angeln brought a sombre mood to Cuthbert. He sometimes dreamt of the man's face. He recalled vividly the thrill and excitement of the fight, and the rush of relief as Beobrand's blade had slain the warrior. And yet, the more he read and wrote, and contemplated the teachings of the Christ that Coenred had shared with him, the more difficult he found it to revel in the act of battle. He glanced about the men he rode with. They were good men all, and he was proud to be accepted as one of them. To be a gesith, or perhaps even, in time, a thegn, such as Beobrand, had ever been his wish. Surely learning his letters and being able to write changed nothing.

His comrades' laughter abated and they rode on in silence for a time. The bright sunshine of the morning streamed through the thick canopy of the oak and beech that almost completely enshrouded the path. Despite the lances of light that speared between the boughs, little of the sun's warmth reached the riders.

Cuthbert shivered. He wished he'd thought to bring a cloak. All of the older men had woollen cloaks wrapped about their shoulders, but he had dismissed the idea of wearing his when they had left. The summer sun was hot and there were only wisps of cloud in the pale blue sky. He felt foolish now, and thought of the misery he would face if the weather turned or if they had to ride back at night.

"How's the leg?" asked Beobrand, disturbing his thoughts.

"It hurts more than my hand, lord," Cuthbert said, with a wan smile.

"It was a bad wound. I imagine you will often feel its hurt over the years. I know I still feel many of the cuts I have picked up since I was your age."

The other warriors nodded in agreement with their hlaford.

"It is much better than it was even just a few days ago," Cuthbert said.

"I saw you racing Tatwine the other day. You might not be as fast as you once were, but Coenred is skilled indeed. We thought we might lose you, or perhaps that you would lose your leg."

"And," interjected Gram with a grin, "as many a woman will tell you, speed isn't everything."

Garr and Attor chuckled. Beobrand sighed and patted his great black stallion's neck thoughtfully.

"Speed is useful in combat," Beobrand said, ignoring his men's teasing of Cuthbert, "but even if your legs are never as fast as they were, you have something much more important."

Cuthbert watched him closely as Beobrand turned in his saddle and tapped his head with his forefinger.

"You are as fast of thought as any man I have known. Your wits will win you more battles than quick feet."

At times it felt to Cuthbert that he thought too much. His head was filled with worries and concerns and he had always found it difficult to concentrate on anything for long. He enjoyed pitting himself against others in feats of skill, speed or endurance, and it was only during races or contests that his mind cleared of the troublesome thoughts that kept him awake at night. It was one of the things that had drawn him to learning the ways of the warrior. For surely battle was the purest contest with the ultimate price to pay for failure.

But recently, he had found the concentrated effort of painstakingly scratching the letters with the stylus helped him to dispel his tiresome fears, losing himself to the shapes and meanings of the words he formed. At such times, he no longer dwelt on petty things that had troubled him in the past, instead he pondered matters of greater import, such as what God had in store for his life. And in the quiet, as he sat in the shade of the hall, or beneath Sunniva's oak, he listened for the elusive voice of the Almighty.

Recalling the pool of shadow beneath the great oak that stood on the hill by Beobrand's hall, Cuthbert's active mind conjured the memory of his hlaford sitting there with his friend, the huge, one-armed warrior, Bassus. When they had arrived at Ubbanford from Bebbanburg, Beobrand had been angry; furious with Cynan and the others for allowing Sulis to escape justice and for abandoning their duty in order to ride westward on some mad scheme. Beobrand's anger was nothing new. He was famed for it. But ever since he had sat beneath the oak with Bassus, Beobrand had become brooding and withdrawn. His nature was often surly and sombre, but there seemed to be a new heaviness to his soul these past days.

"What did Bassus say to you, lord?" Cuthbert said. "To make you so sad?" The instant he had blurted out the words, he regretted them. Beobrand scowled and such was the fury in his expression that for a terrible moment Cuthbert thought he might reach out and tumble him from the saddle.

The moment passed and Beobrand sighed, shaking his head.

"It seems your mouth is often faster than your mind," he said. "If Bassus had meant for his words to be heard by all, he would surely have spoken them to everyone."

They rode on without speaking for a time. Cuthbert, face burning from Beobrand's chastisement, listened to the birdsong, the thump of the horses' hooves on the packed earth of the path, the jangle of the harness and the rustled whispers of the trees.

"Was it about Rowena?" asked Garr, breaking the awkward hush that had descended on the group.

Beobrand gave the tall warrior a sharp look, but then his expression softened.

"He spoke to you too?"

Garr nodded.

"The man is as strong as any I ever knew," he said. "But to lose Rowena..." His voice trailed off, and he puffed out his cheeks, blowing out a long breath.

Beobrand frowned and turned away. His shoulders slumped.

"What is wrong with the lady Rowena?" asked Cuthbert.

"She is ill, lad," replied Gram.

"What ails her?"

"I know not, but Odelyna says there is nothing to be done. Her sickness will take her to her grave."

Cuthbert's mind raced.

"Perhaps Coenred could help her," he said. "And we could pray."

Beobrand wheeled around, his face dark and contorted with rage.

"Pray?" he growled. "Prayers cannot save those whose wyrd it is to die." He ran the fingers of his half-hand over his face. "People die, boy," he said, his tone desolate. "No god can save them when their time is come."

"But—"

"No! Stop your prating," replied Beobrand.

Cuthbert was taken aback by the ferocity in Beobrand's tone.

"Enough of this talk," Beobrand said, touching his heels to Sceadugenga's flanks and galloping away towards Stagga.

Attor patted Cuthbert gently on the shoulder.

"Don't worry, lad," he said, his tone soft. "You are not the only one with a keen mind who worries too much about things beyond your control."

Chapter 28

Bumoth hawked and spat a great gobbet of phlegm over his shoulder. It barely missed Ludeca's foot and the strangely hunchbacked man cursed from where he rode close behind the corpulent leader of the group. By Christ and all his saints, Bumoth thought, how he despised Ludeca. Bumoth half-wished his spittle had hit the man, though he knew that would have caused an argument that would have wasted yet more time, and the last thing he wanted was to have to spend any longer than he had to with Leofman's odious brother. They had already spent long enough travelling Leofman's lands.

They would have been done by now, if not for that ugly whoreson, Ludeca.

Bumoth sighed and gazed up the slope to the shadowed shape of the dry-stone bothy that he could just make out beside the dark clump of swaying trees. Bumoth had never been wholly convinced by the plan that Ludeca had dreamt up with Sidrac, but he was oath-sworn, and would obey his hlaford's command. That didn't mean he had to like it though.

"Is that the place?" He pointed up to the small dip in the land where the turf-roofed hut nestled in the lee of the trees and the shade of a great peak. The sky beyond the mountain was clear and bright, but tinged with the copper-red glow of sunset. It would be night soon. Bumoth had hoped they would have been able to fulfil their task and be back to the hall by nightfall. That would be impossible now, after the time they had wasted.

"Aye, that's it." Ludeca nodded, his tone sullen.

Bumoth did not reply. Ludeca didn't like him either and that was fine with Bumoth.

He scratched at the stubble in the wrinkles on his neck, beneath his short beard. He would have to shave his throat again tomorrow. It always itched when the hair began to grow back, and, as he always did, he toyed with the idea of growing a fuller beard. And yet he knew he would not do so. When he allowed his beard to grow long, he hated the way it made him feel. He fancied it made his face look even fatter than it was. Such vanity was ridiculous, but he could not prevent the thoughts from entering his mind any more than he could avoid plans going wrong or stop young men from doing stupid things.

Bumoth had not been surprised when things went awry as soon as they arrived at Leofman's steading. In his experience, few plans worked the way they were envisaged. This day had proven that once more, as had each twist of events since he had led his men into the ravine where Leofman had been working at the cave entrance with his son and that accursed mute.

What should have been simple, quickly unravelled. Egbalth allowed himself to be killed by that simpleton of a bondsman. Then Hunberht had bungled the job of slaying Leofman, letting the old greybeard slice deep into his arm with a seax. The old man didn't even have a sword! Hunberht was supposed to be a cold killer. His battle-fame and ruthlessness were spoken of in halls all over Rheged and beyond. Sidrac had accepted his oath based on the man's reputation as a skilled and effective swordsman, but from what Bumoth had seen, the man was a hot-headed fool.

After the botched attack on Leofman at the mine, there had followed the disaster at the old oak. What a fool Aescferth had been. Anyone with eyes could see that the Waelisc warrior would take him in a fight. Bumoth supposed Aescferth had hoped to prove himself to Hunberht, whom he idolised.

Bumoth spat again and kicked his tall horse into a trot to scramble up a steep section of scree on the path.

Young men! What fools they were. Aescferth's desire for fame and to impress Hunberht had brought him nothing but a quick death. Truly Sidrac was little better than the young foolhardy gesithas who followed him, but the man had Bumoth's oath and that still counted for something. He would not break his bond easily. Still, if things continued to fall apart as they had of late, he might need to take the difficult decision to ride away from Sidrac's hall for good. It would pain him to forsake the lad, but in the end, he had to do what was best for himself. Perhaps he could ride to Deira. The war with Bernicia bubbled on and men were always looking for warriors. Bumoth might be fat, but he could still fight and had his own battle gear. But he was not ready to break his word just yet. If Sidrac and Ludeca's plan came to pass, Sidrac would become a truly wealthy man, and if there was one thing Bumoth wished for more than a full belly, it was the easy life that came from riches. Perhaps then he would not need to lead such vainglorious young men or witness their stupidity so frequently.

At least the incident with Leofman's old bondsman, Alfwold, had not been completely without value. The old man had told them everything he knew as soon as Aescferth had started cutting him. Hunberht had been furious to hear that Leofman had survived his sword thrust. At first he had denied it was possible, but there had never been any doubt in Bumoth's mind. What would Alfwold gain by lying? No, the truth was that the famed killer Hunberht was fast proving to be less of an asset than Sidrac had hoped. But the most important tidings they had learnt were that Leofman's woman was with child, and that she had disappeared in search of aid. Bumoth assumed they had met the men she had summoned beneath the oak. And that bastard, Cynan, had shown himself to be just as deadly as Hunberht wished he was.

Bumoth reined in his horse, raising his hand for the others to halt. They were still some way from the lone hut on the hill, but they had suffered so many setbacks these last days, he wanted to be certain. He did not wish to go rushing in like these young fools he was surrounded by.

"Fleameld," he said, "you are certain it is just the one rider that came this way?"

Fleameld, a slender man with dark thinning hair that was streaked with frost at the temples, slid from his saddle, leaving his reins trailing and his horse cropping at the tough grass. He walked a few paces ahead of the small group of riders and dropped to his knee. Bumoth waited patiently as Fleameld scanned the earth and pebbles of the track. No youngster, Fleameld was a man Bumoth had ridden with for years. Bumoth liked him. He was serious and quiet, deadly in a fight. Bumoth knew no finer tracker. Perhaps if he should decide to leave Sidrac, he would ask Fleameld to come with him. He could use a man he trusted.

"Come on," sneered Ludeca. "There is no need for all this caution. Look, the hut is there, as I said it would be. There is nowhere else she could have gone." Ludeca rubbed at the back of his twisted neck, as he so often did. Bumoth hoped the man's neck never stopped paining him.

"You have already led us astray once this day," said Bumoth. "I will trust Fleameld's eyes over your memory."

Fleameld had read the signs on the earth in front of Leofman's house that morning and told them the tale of what he saw there. Several men had mounted up and ridden north, while one small pony, with a lighter load, had ridden into the hills. It was then that Ludeca had told them of the bothy and Bumoth had made his mind up that they would finish what they had set out to do. They would follow the woman and kill her. Surely even these fools could manage that. That belief had quickly been put to the test. He had made the mistake of listening to Ludeca, who said he knew the way, and it was only after they had ridden for some time that Bumoth had asked Fleameld to check for their quarry's sign. The tracker found none. Close to Leofman's steading, there had been a fork in the track and Ludeca had been adamant their destination was on the left. Bumoth cursed himself for following the man blindly. Yet more time wasted, as they needed to return to the branch in the path before taking the other route up into the hills.

Since then, Bumoth had Fleameld dismount regularly to scan the ground.

Fleameld looked up now from where he stooped and nodded to Bumoth.

"Just the one pony," he said. "The same one that left the farm."

"No others?" asked Bumoth.

Fleameld shook his head.

"What about the other riders?" Fleameld had asked as they'd stood outside Leofman's empty house. "They might be headed towards Sidrac's hall."

Bumoth had pondered this for a time. They had not encountered anyone on the road, so perhaps Leofman and the other riders had a different destination.

"Sidrac is a big lad," he'd said. "He and the others can look after themselves. We will do at least part of what we came for." He hated having to return with news of failure, something that had become all too common of late. Today he would ride back to the hall with the news that Leofman had no further heirs than Eadwig. Such tidings would bring the plan closer to fruition.

Fleameld swung back into the saddle.

"I don't see the pony," said Inguc, peering up the hill. The young warrior had a thick beard of wavy fair hair and eyes the dark green of holly leaves. He was not as infuriating as some of the other young men in Sidrac's warband, but his luxuriant beard rankled Bumoth.

"Well, it went this way," said Fleameld. "Sometime early last night, I would say."

"Perhaps she rode on after the night," mused Maccus, running his hand through his thick long hair. He was a handsome young man, strong and skilled, but brash and loud; another of the youthful warriors attracted to Sidrac's warband by promises of fame and quick wealth. Bumoth despised him.

"Mayhap she took the pony inside the hut with her," he said. "Look at those slopes." The mountains loomed, steep and ominous behind the bothy. There were no paths there, the only animals that could climb that high would be the hardy goats and sheep that frequented these lands. "There is nowhere for her to have gone. She must still be inside. So let us approach with care."

Ludeca laughed, an ugly, gurgling sound.

"I am going to enjoy killing the bitch," he said, his tone grating on Bumoth's nerves. Ludeca sucked his teeth and licked his lips. "But not before I have my fun with her first."

"I imagine it is not easy for one as ugly as you to find a willing woman," said Maccus. Bumoth found himself siding with Ludeca against this fresh-faced man for whom pretty girls would willingly part their legs.

"You will find, Maccus," he said, keeping his voice low, "that most women become enthusiastic when they have a knife to their throats."

Ludeca offered him a skewed smile of thanks and Bumoth hated himself. By Christ's thorny crown, he should have ridden away to Deira weeks ago.

"I am sure you are right," smiled Maccus. "You and Ludeca must both find it necessary to force your women." He nudged his horse into a trot and grinned. "I have never had to do so."

Angrily, Bumoth kicked his horse forward.

"Slow down," he hissed. "Let us not give ourselves away."

Maccus rolled his eyes and Inguc and Osulf, another young warrior of the same cut as the others, both sniggered. Despite their annoyance, the young gesithas slowed their progress and the six of them walked their mounts up the remaining distance to the bothy. The dense clump of birch shivered and waved. The wind that always gusted so high up in the hills rustled and hissed through the leaves and boughs.

Ludeca's mare let out a whinny, and Bumoth tensed. He held up a hand and pulled his mount to a stop. Without a word, the three younger men dismounted, pulling their blades from their scabbards. Fleameld met Bumoth's eye and he shrugged. There would be no chance of surprising Leofman's wife now. With a grunt at the effort, he swung his leg over his horse's rump and slid down until his feet touched the ground.

Maccus was already close to the hut, stepping forward with the lithe grace of a cat. Bumoth wished the man would trip, but of course, he was sure-footed, and reached the shadowed entrance of the hut without making a sound. Still, if Sulis was yet within the bothy, she could not have missed the noises of the horses' hooves, or the men whispering. As Bumoth thought this, the sound of a pony's nicker emanated from the gloom. So, she had taken the pony inside as he'd suspected.

He shook his head at Maccus's rashness as the young warrior stepped into the entrance. The man showed no fear. It was only a woman inside after all, but even a woman could fight, thought Bumoth. Especially if she is cornered and fearful for her life and that of her children.

Bumoth opened his mouth to call out a warning. But before the sound could leave his lips, Maccus staggered back, arms flailing. The sword dropped from his hand and he reached up to try to stem the bleeding from a slashing cut to his throat. Bumoth knew in that instant that the young man would die. Blood bubbled and spurted through his fingers and was already soaking his kirtle crimson.

Bumoth cursed. The bitch had slain one of them. This would be another disaster to add to the list. By Christ's teeth, he wished he had listened to his intuition and broken his oath with Sidrac before it had come to this.

As Maccus fell to his knees, mouthing silent horror as his lifeblood pumped from the severed arteries in his throat, Bumoth realised things were much worse than he had thought. A figure filled the entrance of the bothy and stepped out into the bright light of the late afternoon. But this was not the slight form of a terrified woman fighting for her life, it was a tall, cool-eyed warrior calmly carrying a blood-smeared sword.

Chapter 29

Sulis hugged Eadwig close to her. She had placed her hand over one of his ears and pressed the other side of his head into her breast in an attempt to stop him hearing the fat man's screams. The boy was trembling in her grasp.

"Hush," she whispered, knowing he would not be able to make out her words, but hoping he would somehow feel the soothing nature of his mother's voice.

The fat man let out another shriek and she gasped. Her own body was shaking violently, responding to the sudden relief of finding her son and husband alive. And at having the terrible decision that had faced her snatched away.

The man at the doorway had not been one of Sidrac's men, but Cynan, and as she had lashed out with her seax, hardly knowing if she meant to strike her attacker or harm herself, he had sprung into the gloom of the bothy and grabbed her wrist. He had gripped her with such force that her bones had ground together painfully and the blade had tumbled from her grasp. For a time she had struggled against his hold, almost blind with panic, until he had pulled her into the daylight and pushed her into

Leofman's embrace. There she had sobbed and shivered until the terror of certain death had subsided. Then she had swept Eadwig into her arms and mumbled her thanks to God and to Cynan, who barely acknowledged her. Instead, he had gazed east and south nervously.

There had been no time for explanations, but she quickly gathered that they had ridden hard along animal tracks across the hills in order to reach her before the men Sidrac had sent to the farm. Cynan's men had led her and the horses away into the stand of birch, where they would be shielded from the track that led to the hut. Cynan had slipped inside the bothy, his face grim. All of the men were severe and sombre, and she noticed that the Frank, Halinard, was unsteady on his feet, his pallid face drenched in sweat. They had hurried down the slope into the small woodland and waited there in tense silence, listening and watching for signs of approach.

"They might not come," she had whispered hopefully to Leofman, but he shook his head.

"They will come," he said, and his hard face scared her anew.

It was not long before Brinin, who was watching the path, hissed for all of them to be still and silent. Six riders were coming up the track towards the bothy.

There was a tense time of breathless waiting, as the riders slowed to check the ground, perhaps suspecting an ambush, before riding on to the hut. There had followed a flurry of vicious violence that made Sulis reel. A man had entered the hut, only to have his throat slit by Cynan, who followed him out into the afternoon sunlight. Without pause, the Waelisc swordsman rushed at a second of Sidrac's men, who stood close to the dying man who was now soaked in the blood gushing from his throat. The second warrior lunged, but Cynan effortlessly parried the attack, hacking his blade into the man's helmeted head.

The wooded area was then filled with motion, as Ingwald, Brinin and two men she had not met before called Bleddyn and Raedmund, rose from where they were hiding in the trees and ran up the incline towards the swathe of open land before the shepherd's hut. They all bore shields and spears, and wore swords at their belts.

Leofman, limping awkwardly, had set off after the warriors.

"Where are you going?" she asked, terrified to be left alone again so soon.

"Halinard will protect you," Leofman replied, stony-faced.

Halinard had pulled himself to his feet with a groan, leaning on his spear to watch the fight. He nodded to Leofman, who turned away from his wife's pleading face and continued up the hill.

For a time, Cynan stood alone against four men outside the hut, while his gesithas lumbered up the slope to his aid. But Sidrac's men did not take advantage of their superior numbers. They were disorganised, dismayed at the sight of two of their number slain so rapidly by the tall warrior who had emerged from the bothy. As she watched, pulling Eadwig's face into her chest so that he would not witness what was to pass, Sulis saw an older warrior close with Cynan. This new attacker was calm and ready for the fight and it took Cynan some time to beat down his defences. The other three dismounted riders watched on in shock for a few heartbeats as the two swordsmen clashed blades, until at last, the fat man, who she recognised as Bumoth, began barking orders.

Leaving the older warrior to his chances with Cynan, the remaining three men took up their shields and prepared to meet the charge of Cynan's gesithas running towards them from the trees. Brinin and Ingwald were the first to reach them, and with the reach of their spears, they drove the defenders back. Raedmund and Bleddyn joined them a heartbeat later and added their spears to the attack.

The men shouted abuse, shoving and spitting over their shields, but none of the spears bit into flesh, and Cynan's men were out of range of Sidrac's warriors' blades.

"Raedmund, you treacherous cur," bellowed Bumoth, but if his words had any effect on the young man, she could not see it.

Raedmund, Ingwald, Brinin and Bleddyn pushed, shouted and probed with the deadly steel-tips of their spears, but the men under Bumoth's command held strong. They had the higher ground, and there were not enough men in either group to easily break the other small shieldwall. Leofman was still some way behind them, struggling up the hill on his injured leg and Sulis wondered at the madness that had driven her husband to join the fight. What use would he be? Surely all he would find was death from the killers before the bothy. She prayed that Cynan's men would defeat them before Leofman reached the fray.

As if in answer to her prayer, Cynan finally dispatched the warrior he had been fighting and without hesitation flew at Bumoth and the two men who flanked him.

Sidrac's men were completely occupied with the men attacking them with their long ash-hafted spears. Cynan gave no indication of his attack, no shouted battle-cry or challenge. Instead, he ran at their rear and hacked his sword into the neck of the nearest enemy. Blood misted the air and the man collapsed without a sound, dead before his body hit the earth.

Cynan turned his attention to Bumoth, who half-swung around to face him, backing away from the spear-bearing men.

The last warrior, a tall man with a strangely twisted neck, fell back, quickly overpowered by Cynan's spear-men. He tried to turn and run, but was tripped. Brinin and Bleddyn loomed over him, piercing him with their spears.

Seeing this, Leofman, almost at the hut now, let out a cry that carried over the clash of the skirmish.

"Don't kill him!" he yelled. "Don't kill Ludeca!"

Ingwald turned to help his lord, but he needn't have worried. Before he could join the fight against Bumoth, Cynan had plunged his sword deep into the man's massive gut. Cynan viciously twisted the blade before tugging it free. Bumoth sagged, losing the strength in his legs as the blood flowed from the wound and pain ripped through him.

Bumoth's screaming had filled the afternoon, drowning out all other sounds. He had not ceased wailing since the fight ended.

Appalled at the violence that had been unleashed, Sulis watched from the shelter of the trees as Cynan and the others gathered around the fat warrior. She could not make out what was happening and was glad of it. The screams from the fat man spoke clearly enough of the pain that was being inflicted on him. She shivered, holding Eadwig tightly, no matter how much he squirmed and begged to be allowed to watch.

Halinard stepped close and placed a hand on the boy's shoulder. Eadwig looked up at him, his eyes wide. Sulis relaxed her grip enough for him to hear what the warrior would say.

"Some things are not for a child's eyes," said the Frank in his strongly accented voice. A pitiful wail emanated from up the hill and the wind moaned through the leaves of the birch trees above them. Eadwig shivered. Halinard reached out and took Sulis' hand in his, placing it once more on the boy's tiny ear. "Or ears," he said, pressing the hand firmly and nodding at Sulis.

Bumoth's howls were weakening now. Sulis drew in a long, ragged breath. She offered up a prayer of thanks to the Almighty for rescuing her boy and her man. Her faith had been repaid and she vowed that when all this was over she would go to Dacor and give a sacrifice to the Lord. The fat warrior on the hill let out a final whimpering cry and then was silent. Sulis shuddered, but part of her was glad that he had suffered. She wanted Sidrac and all of his men to endure such pain before they died. She prayed for forgiveness for such thoughts, but surely God could not expect a mother to feel no desire for vengeance when her family was attacked by such brutes.

She buried her face in Eadwig's hair, relishing the scent and the warmth of him. He was safe now, as safe as the babe that was cocooned in her belly. She would do whatever was needed to keep them so, even if that meant damning her soul.

Halinard touched her gently on the arm, breaking into her thoughts. Looking up, she saw the men were coming down the hill. Quickly, she scanned their faces and her heart leapt. They were all returning. Then she noticed that between Bleddyn and Brinin was the tall man with the bent neck. Every few paces he stumbled and the two warriors half-dragged him on, ignoring his cries for respite.

Reaching the trees, Ingwald, Raedmund and Cynan dropped their shields with a clatter and removed their helms. Ingwald went to the horses and pulled water skins from their saddles. Cynan slapped Raedmund on the back and muttered something to him that she could not make out. The tall young man offered Cynan a thin smile in return. The men were serious and barely acknowledged her.

They were slaking their thirst when Brinin and Bleddyn arrived, pulling the only survivor between them. They threw him down onto the leaf mould. The man cried out in pain as he fell, and she saw that he was wounded. Blood stained his sleeves. His lip was split and bleeding. He pushed himself up onto his knees and stared at her. Something in his gaze made her shiver with disgust.

"You must be Sulis," he said, spitting blood from his mouth.

"Who are you?" she asked. She had heard Leofman shout the name Ludeca, but she knew nobody of that name.

"He says he is my uncle," said Eadwig, his small voice startling her.

"What?"

She looked at the kneeling man in confusion. He appeared a few years younger than Leofman, but he had his height. And could there be a likeness in the mouth and the nose? But this man's neck was bent at a painful, unnatural angle, as if it had once been snapped and repaired, though she had never heard of such a thing.

"It's true, you know," said the stranger with a leer.

"Silence," snapped Cynan, striding over and drawing his seax. "Shut your mouth or I will cut out your tongue." Turning to Sulis he said, "Bumoth told us everything. We know what Sidrac planned. There is another who must face justice for his part in this, but that can wait. Leofman knows where to find him. But your husband stopped me finishing this one."

"Is he truly Leofman's kin?" she asked, her voice barely more than a whisper, but the shape of Ludeca's face and his stature already told her the truth of it.

"I'm his brother, my pretty," sneered Ludeca.

Cynan slapped him across the face with the back of his hand. Dazed, Ludeca slumped to the ground. Cynan grasped his kirtle, hauling him to his knees once more and raising the blade of his seax to his throat.

"I told you to shut your mouth, nithing," hissed Cynan.

"Hold!" shouted Leofman, limping into the shade beneath the swaying birch.

Ludeca spat out a stream of bloody spittle.

"That's right," he chuckled. "He can't bring himself to kill kin, can you, Leofman? You don't want to bear the mark of Cain, do you?"

Leofman hobbled towards Ludeca. His face was thunder.

"You are a fool, Ludeca," he said. "Cynan would kill you in an instant if I asked him to. But you should not die by his hand. I would finish what I once started. I would do it right this time. Bleddyn," he said, turning to the dark-haired warrior. The man was as pale as milk and looked as though he might vomit at any moment.

"Yes," he croaked.

"Fetch me the rope we brought from Sidrac's hall."

Without a word, Bleddyn obeyed, bringing a long coil of strong hemp rope back to where Leofman waited with Ludeca.

"You won't do it," sneered Ludeca. "You don't have the stomach for it. You never did!"

Leofman looked down at his brother and his face was dark with fury and some other emotion she could not make out. Regret perhaps.

"I have never enjoyed killing," said Leofman. "That is where we are different, you and I. But I do not hesitate to kill an animal when it is moonstruck. Or sick."

"We are brothers!" yelled Ludeca, spit and blood flecking his lips and flying from his mouth.

"No," said Leofman, shaking his head sadly, "you ceased being my brother years ago. You are nothing to me."

Ludeca stared up at him. The fire of defiance slowly dimmed in his eyes.

"What are you going to do, husband?" Sulis asked, frightened by the transformation she saw in Leofman.

"I am a man of my word," he said. "I swore a vow to my father long ago. It seems I didn't manage to fulfil that promise, for this murderous craven monster yet lives."

"What was the promise you made?" she asked.

"I vowed I would hang Ludeca from the neck until dead," Leofman said, and began forming a noose with the rope.

Chapter 30

Beobrand sipped the mead that Eadgyth had poured and gazed about him. The hall was clean and ordered, as it always was. Beobrand admired Eadgyth. She was a fine woman, beautiful, kind and strong. She kept an ordered household, with everything just as it should be. Her guests never wanted for anything, and the people of Stagga loved her.

Looking up, he took in the beams of the hall, that were draped with hangings, ornaments and weapons; the trappings and memories from an eventful lifetime. Enough for several lifetimes, he thought, allowing the sweet taste of the mead to carry his memories back to a different time, when a different man had ruled this hall. At the end of the building, above the high table, hung the massive antlered skull of a stag. Acennan had been so proud of slaying the great beast, honouring the animal by naming his hall after it. Beobrand remembered the joy his friend had felt when he had gifted him this land that he might erect a hall, a place fit for him to live with his new bride. Where they could flourish and put down roots. Where their children could be born and grow up safely.

Beobrand had helped Acennan build the hall and now, as ever, to be here filled him with a bitter-sweet melancholy. Each pillar, every wooden joint and trenail, carried a memory of his friend. Nothing had really changed in the hall since Acennan's death. The benches and boards were the same. Fire still warmed the building from the hearthstone at its centre. And Acennan's widow and children yet resided here.

The doors behind him scraped open and Beobrand turned, half-expecting to see the stocky figure of Acennan standing there. But of course, it was not so. The face at the door was Cuthbert's.

There was a new lord of Stagga now. Beobrand had been pleased with how Cynan had settled into his life here. In recent months Beobrand had ignored Udela's comments that perhaps neither the Waelisc warrior nor Acennan's widow were completely at ease with the situation. He had preferred not to think of such things. But now he knew it was his duty as lord of Ubbanford and hlaford of the people of Stagga, to grasp this particular nettle.

"The horses are seen to, lord," Cuthbert said. Beobrand waved him away. When his men had drunk from the cup of welcome he had sent them outside to tend to the horses that he might speak alone with Eadgyth. He was not yet ready for them to fill the hall with their laughter and chatter. They all knew that the lady of the hall would feed them well and the men were looking forward to her hospitality.

The doors closed and the hall was quiet once more. Sighing, Beobrand placed his cup on the board and turned back to face Eadgyth.

"So you do not know what might have caused Cynan to behave so?" he asked. He had posed her the question when they arrived but she had told him to wait for her answer while she hurried off to fetch the Waes Hael cup.

Beobrand had waited for her patiently, knowing it would not do to deny her the rituals of a good hostess.

She sat down, smoothing her skirts delicately and staring at her lap.

"You have bid us all well come and we have drunk of your

good mead," said Beobrand. "I give you thanks. But now you must answer me. What do you know of Cynan's actions?"

For a time, he thought she might refuse to speak, but he should have known better. Beobrand was her lord and she would give him an answer, as was his right.

"Cynan is his own man," she said. "He follows his own will." She hesitated. "And the will of his hlaford, of course."

"He seems to have forgotten his duty to obey me," replied Beobrand, feeling his anger mounting. Cynan was without doubt his finest warrior. He was the best swordsman, the most gifted rider, the fastest runner. But he was certainly not the most obedient. "I left Cynan in command of Ubbanford. He knew better than to leave on some fool's errand."

"Do not women make fools of all men?" Eadgyth said, archly.

Beobrand narrowed his eyes. What was she hinting at? Did she know of what had transpired between him and Eanflæd? Of course she did. His men knew, and they talked to their women. And the gods knew how womenfolk loved to prattle. It was a wonder that the whole of Bernicia didn't know. He grew cold at the thought, despite the warm day and the heat from the embers on the hearth.

"Tell me what happened," he said.

"Lord?" she asked, raising her eyebrows.

Beobrand reached for his cup and held it out to her. Without hesitation, she raised the pitcher and poured more mead. Her hands shook.

"I know Cynan rode to Ubbanford that day to seek counsel," Beobrand said.

Eadgyth placed the jug back on the board. She bit her lower lip. Her teeth were very white.

"You will have to ask Cynan what he wanted when he returns," she said, smoothing her skirts over her thighs.

"I will be seeking answers from him, you can be sure of that," he said. "But I know what he was concerned about."

"You do, lord?" Eadgyth's voice trembled.

"Yes. He spoke to Bassus."

"Oh," she said, "I see." She took a spare cup from the tray on the board and poured mead into it. She drank deeply. "And what is it that Cynan told him?"

"I was hoping you would tell me in your own words."

"I would rather he spoke for himself," she said, her voice not much above a whisper. There was a sharp edge of bitterness in her tone.

"Well, Cynan is not here to speak. All I can think is that he has feelings for…" He hesitated, unable to bring himself to utter her name. "That woman." Unbidden, he remembered Reaghan's pale trembling form. She had died in this hall while he was far to the south. Eadgyth and Cynethryth had tended to her here after Sulis had stabbed her. He'd had Sulis within his reach and Cynan had intervened, damn him. He should have struck the woman down then, when he had the chance.

"Mayhap he does have feelings for her," replied Eadgyth, her tone hollow.

Beobrand stared at her for a long time. Eadgyth's jaw was set, her lips pressed together. Her eyes were bright with unshed tears. He was angry and disappointed with Cynan, but Eadgyth was hurt; slighted, as if what Cynan had done was a direct response to her.

"So it is true then?" Beobrand asked.

"Lord?"

"What Bassus told me of your conversation with Cynan. What had him so upset."

Eadgyth drained her cup of mead and sighed.

"Perhaps I am not wholly free of fault," she whispered.

"How so? Cynan's actions are his own."

"Maybe it was not only Sulis who made Cynan's head spin that day." Having pushed her for an answer, now Beobrand felt guilty for his badgering. The woman had suffered enough.

She had lost Acennan, and now, if what Bassus said was true, Cynan had rejected her.

"You cannot blame yourself for the wrong Cynan has done you," he said.

Tears trickled down Eadgyth's smooth cheeks and Beobrand wished he had not come here. All he had done was cause Eadgyth further pain, and he had already heard from Bassus what had transpired between Cynan and Acennan's widow. What had he hoped to gain from coming? And yet he could not stay away from Stagga just because the place held so many memories of Acennan, and because talking to his widow made him miss his friend more keenly. If Eadgyth could live in this hall, he could at least visit. He owed it to Acennan and to her.

Awkwardly, he reached out to take Eadgyth's hand, but before he could touch her, she rose, cuffing the tears from her face.

"Perhaps it is men who have made a fool of me," she said. Acennan had wooed her, seeking her hand from her wealthy father in Wessex. Did she resent binding herself to him? No, she had been happy here, thought Beobrand. But Acennan had died years ago. When had Eadgyth last been content? "I thought Cynan would have wanted me," she went on in a small voice. "I know he is younger than I, but I could still bear him children should God will it. We talk so much. I thought he was merely slow to make up his mind. Why else has he not married?" Her tone became exasperated. "We already live together. It would not be such a poor match, would it?"

Beobrand swallowed. The woman's distress twisted his gut. He was not suited to deal with such matters. A shieldwall bristling with spears unnerved him less than a weeping woman.

"Hush, Eadgyth." He spoke to her in the soft voice he used to calm nervous horses. "It would be a good match. Cynan could hope for no better wife than you."

He said the words he hoped she wished to hear, but silently he cursed Cynan for putting him in this position. Couldn't the man have married the woman and be done with it?

As if she had heard his thoughts, she said, "Do not blame Cynan." She offered a thin smile. "He is only a man, after all."

The tension dissipated somewhat and Beobrand chuckled at her words, pleased that she seemed to be done weeping.

"Perhaps if I had asked him on any other day..." Eadgyth said. She sniffed and poured herself more mead. "But I chose the day that Sulis came back, and it seems clear to me now."

"What is clear?" asked Beobrand. "None of this makes sense to me. But then," he grinned and shrugged, "I am only a man."

Eadgyth smiled sadly.

"The reason he has not sought a wife all these years. It is obvious now, isn't it? He has been in love with Sulis all this time."

Beobrand did not know how to respond. He would never forgive Cynan for this. He opened his mouth to say as much when the doors to the hall scraped open. He turned angrily, ready to tell his impatient men that this was not the time to be disturbed. If they were not careful, he would have them sleep in the stables with no warm food. By Woden, he had told them to wait. Could none of his gesithas follow the simplest of commands?

Attor was silhouetted in the doorway against the afternoon sunlight. Instantly Beobrand could tell from the stiffness of his stance that the wiry warrior was ready for combat.

"What is it?" he snapped.

"A rider," Attor said. "He is coming in fast."

"One of ours?"

"No, lord."

Beobrand stood and made his way towards Attor, who stood aside. Blinking as he stepped into the bright daylight, Beobrand watched as a small man on a fast, long-legged mare galloped into the open ground before Stagga. Even before the horse had come to a halt, the rider had slid from the saddle and rushed towards the hall.

Gram and Garr intercepted him, pushing him back.

"I have a message for the lord of Ubbanford," said the man breathlessly.

Beobrand did not recognise him, but he thought he remembered the horse from the stables at Bebbanburg.

"I am Beobrand of Ubbanford," he called out.

The man peered past Garr and Gram, trying to push his way towards Beobrand. They shoved him roughly away.

"I have a message for you, lord," said the horseman. "From Oswiu King."

"Check him for weapons and let him through."

His men quickly and efficiently searched the messenger, removing a seax and an eating knife from his person. He scowled as they let him walk between them. Beobrand towered over the newcomer. The rider's clothes were grimy, his face streaked with sweat and dust. His eyes were dark-rimmed.

"You have ridden from Bebbanburg without rest?"

"Aye, lord. I rode first to Ubbanford, but they told me you were here. The king bade me not tarry. The tidings I bring are urgent."

"What is your name?"

"I am Dryhthelm, son of Nothelm."

"Well, then, Dryhthelm," said Beobrand. "You had better tell me your message. But first, let me get you a cup of mead." He led Dryhthelm towards the open doors of the hall. "Cuthbert," he shouted at the young man who was sitting in the shade of an oak tree, scratching into that tablet of his, "tend to this man's horse."

Inside the hall, Eadgyth reverted to the perfect hostess. There was no sign of her tears and her demeanour was calm and welcoming. Beobrand offered up a silent prayer of thanks to Woden for the arrival of the messenger, no matter how grave his news might be. It would at least provide a distraction from the weeping widow and the talk of marriage.

Eadgyth handed a cup of mead to the new guest and offered him a seat.

"Thank you, my lady," said Dryhthelm, draining the cup and smacking his lips with pleasure. Eadgyth grinned and he blushed, reminding Beobrand of Eadgyth's beauty and the effect she had on men. "But before I can rest, lord," Dryhthelm went on, remembering his duty, "I must impart my message."

Chapter 31

They were subdued as they rode down the track towards Leofman's farm. Dusk was drawing in by the time they left the bothy. It would be full dark soon. They were all exhausted, and riding at night down the steep slope would be perilous. But there was no room for all of them to remain in the hut, even if they had wanted to. And none of them could imagine staying up in the hills. Not after what they had witnessed.

Cynan glanced at where Sulis rode just behind him. She was on one of the larger horses they had taken from Bumoth's band, and Eadwig was nuzzled up to his mother, dozing, his head resting on her breast. Her eyes glimmered in the gloaming. She met Cynan's gaze briefly, then looked away.

Behind her rode Leofman, his face in shadow. Cynan could sense the man was looking at him, and he turned back in the direction they were travelling. The sun was behind the mountains at their back and the land before them was dark.

Sulis had barely spoken to Leofman since he had hanged Ludeca. Cynan had seen many men die in his time. Some had met their wyrd with bravado, facing their end with a roar of defiance. Others cried and whimpered, unmanned by the knowledge they approached the afterlife. Many men were silent when death came for them, looking into themselves perhaps, thinking of what they had achieved with their time on middle earth.

Ludeca had died screaming spite and abuse at his brother. Sulis had led Eadwig away to the bothy, but such was the volume of the torrent of insults from Ludeca's lips that she and the boy must have heard every word. All the while, Leofman, stern-faced and silent, refused to be drawn in. No matter the invective Ludeca hurled at him, Leofman simply continued fashioning the noose. As Ludeca accused him of swiving sheep, Leofman spat and threw the rope over a sturdy bough. It took him three attempts, and with each miss, Ludeca laughed, a horrible, sickly, gurgling sound that made Cynan's skin crawl.

Eventually, unable to stand the sound of the man's cackling insults, Cynan had stepped forward and punched Ludeca in the mouth.

"No," snapped Leofman. "Don't."

Cynan was unsure why he should refrain from hurting the man who had plotted to kill Leofman and his wife, but he stepped back, allowing Leofman to finish his work.

They had bound Ludeca's hands behind his back, but when Leofman placed the noose about his neck, his brother had tried to bite him, spitting and snarling like a rabid dog. Cynan stepped in to hold him still, and he gladly helped Bleddyn and Ingwald to pull on the rope.

Ludeca was hoisted into the air, leaves and dirt flying from his kicking feet. He was no longer laughing, and as the rope constricted around his throat, his insults were silenced at last. Glad of the sudden hush, Cynan had watched in disgust as the foul man twitched and swung at the end of the rope.

Leofman hobbled directly beneath his brother and for a fleeting instant Cynan wondered if he regretted his decision to hang him. But jumping up, Leofman grasped Ludeca's ankles. Then, pulling down sharply, he lifted his own feet from the earth, adding his weight to his brother's. He remained that way for several heartbeats, and when he finally stepped away, Ludeca no longer trembled and kicked. His body hung lifeless, swinging in the dappled shade beneath the birch trees.

"That was a good thing you did," Brinin said to Leofman.

Leofman was staring up at the swinging corpse. For a time it seemed as though he had not heard Brinin, but then he turned to him, bemused like someone waking from a deep sleep. Or a nightmare.

"What?" he asked, blinking stupidly.

"You sent him on his way quickly," said Brinin. "You could not let him live, not after what he had done. But he was still your brother."

Leofman looked confused, as if Brinin had spoken in a tongue foreign to him.

"That," he indicated the swaying corpse, "is not my brother." Ludeca's tongue jutted from his lips and his face was dark, blotchy and bloated. "And I did not do that to show mercy." He turned and started limping up the hill towards the hut, where Sulis and Eadwig waited. "I did it to make sure he was dead this time."

None of them knew what it was that Ludeca had done in the past to deserve such a punishment. It seemed that Leofman, believing Ludeca long dead, had never told Sulis he had ever had a brother. While they readied themselves to leave the shepherd hut, Cynan had seen Sulis staring at her husband, as if she looked on a stranger. Perhaps Leofman would tell them in time of the past between the brothers, but for now he was lost to dark memories and the shock of what had transpired.

And he was surely still reeling from what Bumoth had told them.

The shroud of night was wrapping about the land quickly now that the sun had dropped behind the mountains. Cynan glanced back towards the bothy and fancied he could see the pale shape of the naked men they had left there for the wolves and the crows to feast upon. They had briefly considered burying, or burning them, but both courses of action would have required them all to stay another night on the mountainside. So they had ridden away, leaving Ludeca swaying from the hemp rope, and Bumoth and his men, stripped of all of value, lying in a neat row of pallid flesh not far from where they had died.

Their horses were laden with their gear and what Cynan had taken from Sidrac's hall.

"What do you think?" Cynan said in a soft voice meant only for Ingwald who rode nearby. He pointed with his chin at the shadowy shape of Sidrac's former thrall, though he wasn't sure Ingwald would be able to make out the movement in the gloom.

"Hmmm?" Ingwald grunted a reply, and Cynan realised that the man had drifted into a doze in the saddle. The man may be no great horseman, but he was as tired as the rest of them.

"Bleddyn," Cynan murmured. "What do you think of him."

Ingwald scratched his head and yawned.

"I thought he was going to shit his breeches when we attacked," he said. "But he stood and he fought, as well as any man would in his first fight."

Cynan grunted. He had seen how pale Bleddyn had been after the clash. But he agreed with Ingwald's assessment.

"Only a fool would not be scared to face men with swords and shields," he said.

"A fool. Or Beobrand. Or you," replied Ingwald.

"You think we are not afraid when we fight?" asked Cynan.

"You never appear frightened," said Ingwald. "It is why men follow you both."

Cynan mused on this.

"I cannot speak for Beobrand, but my fear is as real as the earth beneath our feet. I just choose not to show it."

"I think that is what is called bravery."

Cynan thought of Beobrand and other great warriors he had

seen. They all had an air of abandon when they fought; a seeming recklessness backed up by strength and skill. He was certain they all felt their bowels turn to water as the enemy charged towards them, but they would never allow their fear to show. Was that courage?

"Perhaps we win our fights because we are too stubborn to admit we are scared," he said, with a shrug. "What did you make of Raedmund?" The lanky youth was riding at the rear of the group, helping Bleddyn and Brinin lead the extra horses.

"He did well," said Ingwald. "I was concerned that he might not fight against men he knew. That is a difficult thing for any man, but he did not baulk and he did his part. I think the two of them are worthy additions to your warband."

Ingwald's horse stumbled in the darkness. Pebbles and gravel scraped as the animal's hooves scrambled for purchase, but after a moment, the beast righted itself and they continued plodding down the hill into the dark.

"My horse is as tired as me," Ingwald complained. "It will be a miracle if we reach Leofman's farm without one of the horses falling or pulling up lame."

Cynan thought of how they had pushed the horses, riding along narrow animal tracks that Bleddyn had known. Without his knowledge of the hills, they would never have reached the bothy before Bumoth. The paths they had traversed were used by the goats and sheep. They were often steep and rocky and the gods must have been smiling on them that none of the horses had slipped on the rough terrain or broken a leg in the frequent gullies they had crossed. But there had been no time to worry about such things. They had ridden the animals hard, trusting to their strength and agility to take them safely across the mountain routes. Thinking back to their careening ride over the crags, Cynan could scarcely believe they had all made it intact. Now, even Mierawin was tiring.

"We will rest when we reach the steading," he promised.

"And then we will be heading home?" asked Ingwald, his tone hopeful.

Home.

Cynan thought of Stagga, roof gleaming gold in the setting sun. Eadgyth smiling as he entered, holding out a cup of mead for him. He would have to face her soon enough. Beobrand too. Ingwald thought him brave? The man did not know how he feared confronting the lady of his hall and his hlaford. But there could be no avoiding it, Cynan knew. He had crossed Beobrand once before and lived to speak of it. He was not certain what his lord's response would be this time. Beobrand would be within his rights to turn Cynan away, to strip him of his land and position. After all, he had broken his oath. The thought of being sent away filled Cynan with dread. With a sudden jolt, a realisation came to him: one of the things that really frightened him was the thought of not being able to spend more time with Eadgyth. Beobrand could exile him, or Eadgyth could reject him. Either way, he would lose her and the thought of it gnawed at his innards. What a fool he had been. He had ridden westward to help Sulis, half-imagining a passion he had once felt for her rekindling within him, but now he knew the truth. She had long since found happiness with Leofman. Eadgyth had offered him happiness at Stagga. With a shock, he understood he had been truly content these past years, and much of his contentment had been due to the warmth of his friendship with Eadgyth.

Cynan pulled on Mierawin's reins almost imperceptibly, easing her around a patch of light-coloured rocks on the path that would give treacherous footing.

"Yes," he said, "we will return home." He recalled Bumoth's pleading screams, as the fat man told them of Sidrac and Ludeca's plan. Two of the plotters were dead, but there was still another who must face justice. "We will head back to Stagga," Cynan said, "just as soon as we have seen this through to the end."

Chapter 32

Beobrand kicked his heels into Sceadugenga's flanks and the black stallion quickened his gait from a canter into his effortless gallop. The horse might not be quite as fast as he had been in his prime, but he was still faster than most steeds. Beobrand chuckled. He supposed he was not as quick as he had been when young either. But neither he nor the black horse were quite done yet. The wind pulled back Beobrand's hair from his face, his cloak streamed out behind him.

Attor, on a grey gelding, caught up with him.

"Pleased to be riding to war?" he asked.

Beobrand realised he had been laughing. Glancing back, he took in the column of men who rode behind him. Most of his Black Shields followed him southward. All except for the half dozen he had left under Bassus' command, and of course, Cynan and the men he had taken with him into Rheged. Beobrand's expression grew sombre, though he still revelled in Sceadugenga's speed.

"I am not happy to be heading for battle," he shouted over the rush of the wind and the thunder of the horses' hooves.

Attor gave him a sidelong look.

"But happy to be gone from Ubbanford."

It was more an assertion than a question and Beobrand could

not deny it. He had welcomed the message that Dryhthelm had brought from Oswiu. Not because it meant war was upon them once more, though he could not escape the feeling that life was simpler while standing in the shieldwall, seax and linden board in hand, but because it meant he could leave the troubles of the womenfolk for a time.

Leading his warband towards Corebricg, he could be free of Eadgyth's tearful beauty, Udela's reproachful glances and Ardith's stony disapproval. And, though it pained him to admit it, he did not have to face Bassus and his grief over Rowena's sickness.

He could leave all of that behind without feeling like a coward for running away. He had been ordered to ride by the king himself. It was his duty, and so he had gathered up his men and left the day after Dryhthelm's arrival.

Dryhthelm's message had been simple and direct. The travel-stained messenger had set aside his empty cup in Stagga and composed himself before speaking.

"Lord Beobrand of Ubbanford," he'd said in a formal voice, clearly reciting words he had memorised, "you are called with your warband to the field of battle. King Oswine of Deira has been reinforced by a host of Mercians led by Peada, son of Penda. There is no time to waste. The fyrd has been summoned once more. You are to ride to Corebricg with all haste where you will assemble with Oswiu King and the fyrd."

Beobrand liked Dryhthelm's direct earnestness, so they had brought him with them. He had no further messages to deliver, and, as a young man, was keen not to miss the battle. He rode with the main group of the black-shielded warriors behind Beobrand and Attor.

They had left at first light and were making good time. Rain had rolled over the land in the night, but the sky was clear now and the puddles on the cracked cobbles of the road were quickly drying in the summer sun. They reached a stream that in winter time often burst its banks and flooded the road. But now, in the height of summer, even after the recent rains, the water was shallow and Sceadugenga and Attor's gelding splashed through the ford without slowing. The cold spray was welcome. The sun was not yet at its zenith, but already the day was hot.

"We can stop and water the horses at the Til," called out Attor. "They'll need a rest."

Beobrand nodded and reined in Sceadugenga. Much as he would have liked to continue at a gallop, eating up the distance and relishing the cooling wind on his face, he did not wish to exhaust the beast or any of the other horses. Attor matched his speed, slowing first to a canter and then to a fast trot. Beobrand patted his steed's neck.

"Feels good to gallop," said Attor.

"Aye, it does," said Beobrand with a grin.

His warband, having urged their mounts to keep up with their hlaford, were now catching up. Beobrand rode on in silence for a time, allowing his men to fall into pace behind him.

Soon they reached the Til and the men dismounted beside the river, stamping their feet and stretching their backs after the morning's hard ride.

"Don't let the horses drink too much," shouted Attor to the riders. "We still have a ways to ride before nightfall and a full belly of this cold water will make a horse sick."

Beobrand offered Attor a nod of thanks. It was usually Cynan who made sure to protect the horseflesh. It was the Waelisc man who would ensure that the mounts were brushed down at the end of the day. And it was he who would notice the first sign that one of the horses was lame. Attor was a good horseman too, and without prompting he had fallen into the role Cynan would have filled.

When he deemed that Sceadugenga had drunk enough, he led the stallion away from the stream. Taking a strip of salted beef that Udela had packed in his bag, he chewed on it absently as he stared down Deira Stræt, calculating how long it would take them to reach Corebricg. Sceadugenga nickered a welcome and Beobrand turned to see Cuthbert approaching, leading his chestnut mare.

"Thank you," the young man said.

"For what?"

Cuthbert hesitated before saying, "For bringing me with you."

Beobrand wanted to snap at him that he was foolish to be thankful, but he swallowed the words. Cuthbert was young and words would not make him grow wiser any more quickly.

"The king has ordered me to bring my warband to battle," Beobrand said. "You are one of my men, so you come. How is your leg?" he asked, wishing to change the subject.

"Strong enough for battle, lord." To demonstrate the limb's strength, Cuthbert lifted his right foot off the ground and hopped on his injured leg.

Beobrand could not help laughing.

"You will not be needing to fight like that," he said.

Cuthbert blushed and lowered his right leg.

"Do you think Penda will be there?" he asked, following Beobrand's gaze southward along the straight line of the old Roman road.

Beobrand shrugged.

"Perhaps, but we are far from East Angeln. He is probably still busy there."

"But he has allied himself to Oswine."

"So it would seem. Or at least, his son Peada has. But this is no surprise. The enemy of your foe is your friend. And Mercia has been the enemy of Bernicia for as long as anyone can remember." Beobrand frowned, wondering how many Mercians he had sent to an early grave. And how many of his friends had died from the stab of Mercian blades.

Cuthbert fell silent for a time. Beobrand glanced at him, surprised by the young man's sudden quiet. The boy was biting his lip.

"What is it?" Beobrand asked.

"I was just wondering..." Cuthbert's voice faltered.

"Yes?"

Cuthbert cleared his throat, but did not speak. Beobrand tired of the boy's uncertainty. He could feel the pressure of war building like a storm cloud in the south. Now was the time to ride, not for talking.

"You want to say something?" he snapped. "So say it."

Cuthbert bit his lip.

"I was wondering whether you might not have caused this alliance."

"What?" asked Beobrand. "How so?" Sceadugenga shook his great head at his master's harsh tone.

"Well," said Cuthbert, clenching his fists at his side, as if readying himself for a fight, "for many months Oswine and Oswiu have fought and Penda and his kin have kept out of it."

"And what makes you think that I am responsible for Peada's change of heart?" asked Beobrand, shaking his head at Cuthbert's audacity. "Peada is a young man, hungry for battle-fame, just like you. But, unlike you, he has his own hearth-warriors. And his father and the people of Mercia will be watching how he fares. He must feel that he had to join the fight in order not to lose face."

Cuthbert nodded slowly, but Beobrand could see that the young warrior was not convinced.

"It seems to me that this change happened after you sailed into East Angeln," Cuthbert said.

"That is true," said Beobrand. "But—"

"There you slaughtered Mercians," Cuthbert interrupted, "and rescued King Anna."

"What else could I have done?" spat Beobrand, not liking where this conversation was going. He had been glad to have been rid of the recriminations of his daughter and the women of Ubbanford and now this youth was questioning him. "Would you have had me leave King Anna to be killed?"

"No, of course not," said Cuthbert, holding up his hands to appease his hlaford. "I did not mean to blame you for what has happened."

"Well, praise the gods," said Beobrand. "I will be able to rest easy tonight."

"I just think that with Oswiu King being forced to offer protection to Anna, whom Penda sought to capture or kill, would not the king of Mercia see it as necessary to show his displeasure with Bernicia somehow? And what better way to do that than to send his son to aid Oswiu's enemy?"

For a time Beobrand was silent. Down by the stream, the last of the men were leading their horses away from the muddy water.

"Mount up!" Beobrand bellowed in his battle-voice, making Sceadugenga snort. Cuthbert flinched, which gave Beobrand a perverse sense of satisfaction. "We have a long way yet to ride."

Ignoring Cuthbert, he swung himself back into the saddle and kicked the stallion into a canter. He did not want to listen to more of the boy's foolish ramblings. And yet, as he rode, he could not prevent his mind turning over what Cuthbert had said, as a ploughshare turns over the soil, exposing wriggling worms. He did not care for the worms he found in Cuthbert's words. And yet he had to admit they held the ring of truth. Much of the cause for the war between Deira and Bernicia could be placed on his shoulders. The assassins who had attacked in the night had been sent for his blood, not Oswiu's. And if he had done as Oswiu had commanded, slaying Wulfstan at Ediscum, would the king have been appeased enough to avoid open conflict with his cousin, Oswine? Beobrand would never know what might have been if he had not broken his oath that day to spare his friend. He tried not to dwell on the past, but he could not avoid wondering if he was at least partly responsible for each man who had died in the war between the Northumbrian kingdoms since that fateful day. Was Cuthbert right that this was another way in which his rash decisions would go on to cause further bloodshed?

By the gods, how much needless death had he caused in his life? He rode towards another battle now, perhaps of his making, and his mind was clouded by the sense that such was ever his wyrd; to ride towards death and to lead good men with him.

Oswald had liked to refer to him as an instrument of his Christ, but Beobrand felt sure that it was Woden, not Oswald's nailed god, who welcomed into his great corpse hall the many men he had slain and caused to be killed. And surely Beobrand must have been blessed by the All-father, such was the slaughter he had witnessed and brought about.

But if the thread of Beobrand's wyrd was to provide blood and enjoyment for the gods, was there any way for him to do otherwise? Could he veer from the path set before him? He saw no way from this course. He was Oswiu's man, for good or ill. He would not break his oath again, no matter what it might cost him. Losing the certainty of the bond of his word, always so important to him, had cost him dearly, diminishing him in ways he could hardly begin to fathom. He would allow his doubts to hinder him no further.

Setting his jaw, Beobrand gripped Sceadugenga's reins tightly and stared towards the horizon. Battle awaited there, calling to him with its promise of bloody freedom. He had been summoned by his king and he would answer the call.

The column of black-shielded gesithas followed in the thegn of Ubbanford's wake, their horses' hooves like thunder in the still summer air.

Chapter 33

Cynan took the reins that Ingwald handed him. Mierawin snorted and scraped a hoof in the soft earth before Leofman's house. The bay mare was eager to leave. Cynan patted her neck.

"Don't worry, girl," he whispered. "We'll be gone soon."

They had reached the farm shortly before dawn the previous day. Several of them had been asleep in the saddles and it was only Bleddyn's sharp eyes that had kept them on the correct path. The riders had tumbled from their mounts, barely able to keep their eyes open.

Cynan hadn't expected trouble, but had set guards nonetheless, starting with Bleddyn, who, along with Raedmund had suffered one fewer sleepless night than the rest of them. They all slept through most of the day. The warriors needed the rest, and were pleased to have Sulis prepare them food. And yet the house was too small to house them all comfortably and as the day drew to a close, Cynan was already sensing that they had outstayed their welcome. Nothing was said, but Leofman was surly and uncommunicative and Cynan had caught Sulis looking at him under her lashes more than once while she stirred the pottage in the large pot over the fire.

They could have done with resting for longer, particularly Halinard, who was still in a lot of pain from the deep cut in his side, but with each passing moment, Cynan felt the pressure mounting, like water rising behind a dam in a stream. He could not put off for much longer returning to Stagga to face the consequences of his actions. He missed Eadgyth, and Athulf and Aelfwyn, and, if he was honest with himself, he missed Beobrand and the other warriors of his warband. This mountainous region, beautiful as it was, was not his land. It vaguely reminded him of the home he had known as a boy, but he was a Bernician now. Stagga was his home. Cynan did not regret coming to Rheged, but his quest here was done.

Almost.

Bumoth had told them much, as he'd writhed in agony on the mountainside. But it was not until the second night at the steading that Cynan had learnt of the dark past between Leofman and Ludeca.

It was Cynan's turn on guard and he stood with his back to the farmhouse wall. The sun had long since disappeared behind the mountains. Stars glimmered in the darkening sky, but a smudge of light still shone behind the dark peaks, the memory of the setting sun.

The night was still, the only sounds the talking of the people within the house, and the distant stamp and snort of the horses from where they had been corralled. The door creaked loudly, and Cynan listened to the uneven footsteps as someone walked around the building to where he stood.

A tall form loomed in the darkness.

"Leofman," said Cynan with a nod he was uncertain the older man would see.

Leofman cleared his throat.

"Here," he said, and Cynan could just make out in the gloom that he was proffering a cup. Taking it, Cynan sniffed the contents. "Mead," said Leofman. "I'd been saving it. Thought now was as good a time as any to drink it."

"My thanks."

Cynan took a sip. The liquid was sweet and warming.

For a time, the two men stood in silence, each holding their cup of mead, and staring into the gloaming. One of the horses nickered. A man laughed from inside the house. Cynan thought it was Brinin.

"I owe you my gratitude," said Leofman, without warning. His words were clipped, as if his throat was constricted.

"There is no need to say anything," replied Cynan.

"Perhaps. But when I think what might have been..." Leofman's voice trailed off.

"Your family is safe now. That is all that matters."

The silence grew between them again.

"When I saw him outside Sidrac's hall," said Leofman, "I thought it must be a shade, a phantom."

Cynan shivered, recalling Ludeca's twisted neck and gurgling laugh. Thoughts of his brother had clearly consumed Leofman ever since they had first spied Ludeca at the midden.

"I have never before met a man who needed to be hanged twice," said Cynan.

"He was dead, wasn't he?" asked Leofman, panic rising in his voice. "When we left him?"

"He was dead."

Leofman sighed and drank.

"I should have known he'd survived," he said after a long while. "He always had the luck of the Devil."

"It seems his luck has run out now."

"I worry it is an evil thing I have done. Slaying one's own brother is a terrible sin."

Cynan thought of what Bumoth had told them of the plot against Leofman and his family.

"It is surely no sin to kill one such as Ludeca. He seemed more animal than man at the end."

"No," said Leofman, "he was no animal." For a heartbeat, Cynan worried that he had offended the man by speaking about his brother so. But as Leofman continued, all thoughts of offending him fled. "An animal takes no pleasure in killing," said Leofman, his tone filled with sorrow and regret. "Ludeca was a monster. We were still boys when I first began to suspect what he was. He would always offer to kill the pigs at Blotmonath, and I saw the gleam in his eyes as he plunged the knife into the beasts' throats. He seemed to enjoy the sensation of their squirming as their blood pumped out.

"Then, one day, I found him with the kittens." Leofman stared into the darkness. He sipped from his cup, his hand trembling. Cynan did not speak, worried that if he interjected, the spell would be broken and Leofman would fall silent once more.

"He was cutting the poor creatures," Leofman said, and in his desolate tone, Cynan could hear the anguish in the memory. "He skinned one alive. I will never forget its pitiful mewling. And all the while Ludeca laughed. He believed he was alone, but I saw him. Our mother had died only weeks before and I was too scared to tell our father what I had seen. Later, I wished I had spoken up. Perhaps things would have been different."

Leofman drew in a long breath of the cool night air.

"A few years later, a young shepherdess vanished." He paused, as if anticipating a question. Cynan did not speak and Leofman continued. "Everybody went out on the hills searching for her. Ludeca too. But she was never found. Some of the people believed she had been taken by wolves, though it was strange that no sheep from her flock had been slain and the girl's body was not found. Not then, anyway." Leofman drank. "Others wondered if she might have been snatched by passing brigands, for the land was dangerous, with many armed men seen on the roads and paths. But I looked at Ludeca's eyes whenever the girl was mentioned, and I had my own thoughts about what had happened to her. But he was my brother, and I buried my suspicions.

"That was before I had this land. Before Hefenfelth. When I returned from the war, all I wanted was to work the land that Oswald had gifted me. My father was very old by then. Too old to help with all the work that was needed. But Ludeca was strong and able. He helped me to build this house." He reached out and caressed the timbers of the eaves above their heads, perhaps recalling lifting the beams into place. "It had been years since I had found him torturing those poor kittens. I rarely thought of it any longer, and when I did, I told myself he had been a troubled boy whose mother had just died. He was a man now. That was all in the past.

"When a girl went missing from a nearby steading, the memories came flooding back. I did not join the search, but rode to the place where I had seen Ludeca with the kittens all those years before. It was not too far from my lands, but I had never gone back, frightened at what I might find." Leofman hawked and spat into the darkness. "I had been right to be scared. She was there. In the shallowest of graves. I uncovered her face in moments of scratching at the earth. Ludeca had barely made any effort to hide her." Leofman made a sound somewhere between a sigh and a sob. "Or the others. Nearby were more graves, so shallow that animals had strewn the bones over the ground. I will never rid my thought-cage of what I saw there. The skulls of his victims stared at me, condemning me. I had known about Ludeca and done nothing."

Leofman passed a hand over his face, rubbing at his eyes as if he could erase what he had witnessed.

"Our father was already very ill, but I think it was finding out about Ludeca that broke his spirit. I will never forget his expression when I told him what I had found. We were both horrified, but I saw in his face the same feeling that had gripped me: knowing acceptance of a suspicion proved, rather than the shock of a revelation. Our father had known, just as I had, and the realisation that our silence had cost the lives of at least two girls destroyed him. He made me swear that I would put an end to it. Like a moonstruck dog, he said. Until we saw him again at Sidrac's hall, I believed I had fulfilled that vow."

"How did he survive?" Cynan asked.

"I know not, but his neck bore the reminder of the day I hanged him. Perhaps he managed to free himself, or someone cut him down. Mayhap the rope parted, for I did not tarry long after the deed. I had overpowered him in his bed, then taken him deep into the woods at night, bound and gagged. Before I left him swinging there, I cut away the ropes from his wrists and ankles and removed the cloth from his mouth. If he was found, better that he be thought cursed for taking his own life, than for me to be thought of as his murderer." He let out a slow breath. "Though of course, the Almighty sees all. He knows the truth of what I did, even if I have kept it secret for all these years."

"You did what you had to do, as any good man would."

Leofman snorted.

"A good man?"

"Aye," replied Cynan, nodding in the dark. "A good man. A good husband. And a good father."

Leofman sighed.

"I'm not so sure. I am glad he is dead. The thought of him with Eadwig makes me sick to the stomach."

"I am certain that slaying Ludeca was not an act of evil." Cynan drank the last of his mead. Far off, in the darkness, an owl hooted, a plaintive sound. "How do you think Ludeca came to be with Sidrac after all these years?"

Leofman shrugged.

"I have thought much on this," he said. He drained his cup and sniffed. "Perhaps it was mere chance. Ludeca must have wandered far in the years since. God alone knows where he has been and what he might have done. Maybe he joined Sidrac's warband and they later found the connection between us that would help Sidrac steal my land, and the mine. Who can say?"

They fell silent again, each lost in his own thoughts.

"I have never spoken of this to anyone," said Leofman. "Not

even Sulis. I was ashamed of what I had done. I thought by not speaking of Ludeca, the memory of him would disappear."

"Did that work?"

Leofman chuckled. There was no mirth in the sound.

"No, it did not."

Cynan handed him back his empty cup. "Thank you for telling me the tale, dark as it is."

"I did not do it for you," said Leofman, his tone bitter. "After holding the secret within me for so long, I hoped that if I spoke of what had happened all those years ago, I might be done with the nightmares. The shame."

"Do you think it worked?"

Leofman said nothing, but limped away into the darkness where he could be alone with his memories.

In the wolf-grey light before dawn, Cynan had roused his men and told them to prepare for travel. On hearing them moving about in the dark, Sulis had awoken. She had wrapped a leg of ham in a linen cloth. The day before, she had baked bread and she put the loaves that remained into a sack and handed them to Brinin, despite Cynan's protestations.

"You have done so much for us," she whispered in the smoky darkness of the house, her breath warm on his cheek. "It is the least I can do. You must eat."

It had not taken them long to ready themselves. Now they were all gathered outside the house, the smell of woodsmoke thick in the air from the newly rekindled fire. Bleddyn, Brinin and Raedmund led an extra horse apiece; the rest of the animals that they had taken from Sidrac's men Cynan left for Leofman and his family.

The sun rose over the hills in the east, painting the land with golden light. The sky was sharp and clear. Cynan's breath steamed in the chill air and he was glad of his woollen cloak, but the day would soon be warm.

The rest of the men had said their farewells and were now

waiting, astride their horses. The last to mount had been Raedmund who had knelt beside Eadwig. Leofman had tensed, taking a step forward, but Sulis placed a hand on his arm and they all watched as the boy wrapped his arms around the tall youth. Raedmund whispered something to the child and his cheeks were wet with tears when he clambered up onto his horse and took the lead rope for Bumoth's tall horse.

The time to leave had arrived and Cynan stepped toward Leofman, holding out his right hand. After a heartbeat's hesitation, the tall, older man, grasped his forearm firmly in the warrior grip.

"You are sure you do not wish me to travel with you?" Leofman asked. "You do not know these lands."

Cynan shook his head.

"It is better this way, Leofman. Better that you are no part of it. Rest, mend. Tend to your animals and land. Put this behind you. Look after your family."

Leofman's face clouded, as if Cynan had insulted him.

"You are a good man," Cynan went on, holding his gaze. "What you need now is time. Time to heal." He glanced at Sulis and Eadwig. "All of you. I will see to it that nobody else questions your claim to this land."

Leofman nodded.

"May God bless you and guide you," he said.

Cynan turned to Mierawin, but Sulis stepped forward, halting him. For the merest of instants, he longed to pull her into an embrace, to hold her tight against him and bury his face in her hair. But Leofman was frowning at him in the dawn light, and the man's son clung to her hand.

"Thank you for coming," Sulis said, her voice small.

He stared into her eyes and wondered what thoughts lived behind them. He found all women difficult to understand, but Sulis was like one of the deep mountain lakes of Rheged to him. He could see all of the surface clearly, but it merely reflected himself back. He could never hope to make out what was lurking in the cold depths far below, where the light of the sun never reached.

"I am glad I came," he said, realising with a start that it was true. He had long wondered what might have been if he had left Beobrand all those years before and travelled into the west with this woman. He could at last close the door on that yearning. He smiled, truly pleased that Sulis had found happiness. And by coming here, his feelings for Eadgyth had become clearer than they might have been had he remained at Stagga.

"You ride for Ubbanford now?" she asked, shattering the silence that had fallen between them.

Cynan shook his head.

"Soon," he said, swinging up onto Mierawin's back. "But there is something I must do first."

With a final nod to the sullen Leofman, and a last lingering look at Sulis' beauty, glowing in the bright dawn, Cynan pulled his mare's head around, touched his heels to Mierawin's flanks and cantered away from the farm. His men followed behind.

Chapter 34

It took them the best part of a day to reach Dacor. Cynan had pushed them hard. He was done with Rheged and wanted nothing more than to return to Ubbanford and Stagga.

The sun was low in the sky when they rode down towards the settlement that nestled on the tree-choked banks of a winding beck. It had been a hot day and the men were dusty and tired, their throats parched. There was some shade here, beneath the ivy-tangled trees that lined the path, and the riders welcomed it after the heat of the sun as they'd crossed the bleak high land.

Cynan's mouth was dry as he looked at the busy settlement through gaps in the trees. As he watched, two riders galloped away from the great hall that towered over the other buildings. The riders, on fast horses, sped up the slope towards Cynan and his gesithas.

"Do you think they are riding to intercept us?" asked Brinin.

"No, lad," said Ingwald. "Those men wear no armour. And there are only two of them. What could they hope to achieve against the six of us?"

"They look like messengers to me," said Bleddyn.

Cynan agreed and he reined in, waiting for the riders to reach them. They were lost from view for a time, but soon enough they were speeding towards them along the tree-lined track. As they approached, the two horsemen shouted at them to make way. Cynan did not move, nor did any of his men. Their horses filled the path and at the last possible moment, the galloping horsemen were forced to rein in their mounts, in a clatter and scrape of hooves.

"Are you deaf?" shouted the older of the two, a man of about thirty with short brown hair and a long moustache. "Allow us to pass." When still nobody moved, he shouted, "I carry a message for Lord Tohrwulf's youngest son."

"Sidrac?" asked Cynan.

"The same," said the rider. "Now stand aside, man." With a glance, he took in Cynan's sword and the shield that was strapped to Mierawin's saddle; the armed, hard-faced men who rode behind him. "You have heard the tidings already, it seems, but Sidrac must hear the king's message."

"Sidrac will hear nothing," said Cynan, his tone final.

"Come now," said the other rider, attempting a conciliatory tone where his comrade had tried bluster. "We must carry the news that Oswiu has called up the fyrd once more. There is no time to waste."

"Do you ride together?" Cynan asked. "To Sidrac?"

The young rider shook his head.

"No, I am to take the message to old Wistan. He has a dozen good men."

"Then you should ride on," said Cynan. He nudged Mierawin, making way on the path. The two riders spurred their horses forward, but Cynan held up a hand. "Not you," he said to the first horseman.

"What do you mean, man?" the messenger said. "The sun will be down soon and I need to cross yonder peak before dusk."

Cynan shook his head.

"I would spare you a wasted journey. Now, if you would lead me to Lord Tohrwulf, I must inform him that his son is dead."

*

The hall was filled with men and noise as Cynan stepped through the portal. The moustached messenger, who he had found was called Thurferth, walked beside him. Thurferth had not believed Cynan at first, but the Waelisc warrior's severe expression and the stern faces of his men soon changed that. Thurferth was clearly nervous of how the news of Sidrac's death would be received, and he shuffled beside Cynan, all of his swagger gone.

Cynan felt naked and exposed, surrounded by so many men he did not know. Taking a deep breath, he straightened his shoulders, pulling himself up to his full height. He thought of Ingwald's words to him. It did not matter what he felt inside, he must show no fear. He had ordered Ingwald and the others to remain outside with the horses. They watched over his weapons, but his finely tooled leather scabbard, golden belt buckle and the iron-knit shirt he wore spoke of his worth. The rings that glimmered on his arms told of his battle-fame and prowess.

A hush slowly rippled over the gathered men, emanating from Cynan and Thurferth as if they were pebbles dropped into a pond of sound. Faces, pale in the shadows of the hall, turned towards them. Cynan swallowed against the dryness of his throat. He cast a glance longingly at the jugs and cups of ale on the boards, but, even if these men did not slit his throat, it would be some time before he would be able to slake his thirst.

After a moment of whispered interest in the newcomers to the hall, a tall man of about Cynan's age stepped through the throng from the high table. Men parted for him with deference, watching him closely. The man had a full beard, and a thick mane of dark hair. He was broad of shoulder, with long, strong arms. Beneath his heavy brow shone dark, clever eyes. He moved with the smooth grace of a warrior. Stepping in front of them, he took in Cynan with an appraising eye, before turning his attention to the man beside him.

"Thurferth," he said, "what is the meaning of this? You should have been over Dun Mallocht and halfway to my brother's hall by now."

"I know, Lord Sigehelm," Thurferth said, his tone obsequious. "But I met this man on the path."

Sigehelm raised an eyebrow.

"And who is this?" He stared at Cynan for a time before asking him, "Have we met before?"

"Perhaps," Cynan said. "I believe I met your father at Caer Luel. After Maserfelth."

Sigehelm frowned, clearly trying to place him.

"You rode with Beobrand's men."

Cynan nodded.

"I still do. I am Cynan, of the Black Shields. Perhaps your father remembers our meeting too?" Cynan cast his gaze towards the high table where he could make out a high-backed chair.

"Who is it, Sidrac?" called the old man who sat there.

Sigehelm stiffened.

"I am Sigehelm, Father," he said.

"What? Speak up," gnarred the grey-bearded man in the ornate chair.

Sigehelm sighed.

"Sigehelm," he shouted, a strained expression on his handsome face. "Your firstborn son."

Tohrwulf either did not hear Sigehelm's answer, or chose to ignore it.

"Who is that man, Sidrac?" he asked again. "Did he ride with Urien? He looks like one of Urien's warriors. Fearsome bunch. Wonderful horsemen."

"No, Father. This man rides with Beobrand of Ubbanford."

"Who? Never heard of the man." The old lord of the hall

drifted into silence. Cynan could not be sure if he remained awake or had lapsed into sleep.

"Alas," said Sigehelm in a quiet tone, "my father remembers little these days. His body is yet strong, but his mind slips away."

"I am sorry," Cynan replied. "It is sad when a great man loses the fight against old age."

"Nobody wins that battle, my friend," said Sigehelm with a shrug. Cynan flinched at the use of the term of endearment. He instinctively liked this son of Tohrwulf, just as he had instantly loathed his younger brother. He sensed that Sigehelm was warming to him, but he could not imagine the feeling would last much longer.

"Now, what brings you here, Cynan? You are far from home. Do you bring further tidings from Oswiu King perhaps?"

"I do not. I had hoped to speak with your father about a matter of grave importance."

Hearing the sombreness of his tone, Sigehelm held his gaze.

"Whatever was meant for my father's ears, you can say to me."

Cynan looked about the hall at the expectant faces. He swallowed.

"You would rather speak alone?" asked Sigehelm.

"No, lord. My words are heavy, but can be heard by all men."

"Then speak them, that we can continue with readying the men of Rheged for war."

Cynan took a deep breath. The commonplace smells of the hall were comforting. Sour ale, sweat, smoke, the lingering scent of bubbling pottage. He wondered for how much longer he would be allowed to breathe in the familiar aromas of the hall once he had given his news.

"I stopped your man here from riding to Sidrac's hall," he said, hesitating for a heartbeat. "For your brother is dead."

Gasps and a murmur of unease and whispered outrage passed through the hall, like wind rustling a field of barley.

"How do you know this?" asked Sigehelm, his tone flat, his features unreadable.

Cynan met his hard gaze.

"It was I who slew him," he said.

Sigehelm held up his hand to quell the cacophony of outraged voices that surged in the hall.

"You are as bold as your master, the lord of Ubbanford," he said, "to ride here with the admission of my brother's murder." Whatever warmth there had been in Sigehelm's tone was gone.

"It was no murder," replied Cynan, keeping his tone level.

"So you say," snapped Sigehelm.

"It is so."

Sigehelm glowered at him, his eyes burning beneath shadowed brows. The hall had grown silent again now and everyone there hung on the two men's words.

"Tell me then, Cynan of the Black Shields," said Sigehelm, his tone clipped and as sharp as shards of flint. "Tell me what happened between my brother and you."

"I will tell you everything. That is why I came here. It would have been easier for me to ride for my home and yet I did not. Think on that as I tell the tale of your brother's death."

"Speak then," Sigehelm said, "for I would hear the story."

"It is simple enough," said Cynan, hoping his words would not carry the hollowness of lies. He had thought long about what he would say, discussing it with Ingwald as they rode. Simple was best, they had concluded. He had thought of fleeing north, but had dismissed the idea immediately. When Sidrac's hall was found abandoned, along with his bloody body and the corpses of his men, doubt would fall on the men who lived thereabouts. By admitting to the killing, Cynan could turn people's suspicion away from Leofman and his family. Now he just hoped he could convince Sigehelm of his sincerity and that the man would see sense.

Sigehelm did not move, giving no indication of his thoughts as he listened.

"I was travelling through Sidrac's lands," said Cynan. "We sought shelter for the night and happened upon his hall."

"Why were you travelling through Rheged?"

"That is my affair," replied Cynan smoothly, having anticipated the question. "I cannot speak of it without breaking my oath, which I will not do."

Sigehelm met his stare. After a brief hesitation, he nodded.

"But know this," continued Cynan, "my errand in these lands had no bearing on what took place between your brother and me."

"And what did take place?"

"Your brother had the rash tongue and quick anger of youth," Cynan said, peering into Sigehelm's eyes for any sign that his words did not ring true.

"You say you have killed my brother and now you would insult him in his father's hall?"

Cynan shook his head, sighing.

"I did not know Sidrac, I only shared his board for one evening, but are you willing to tell me that he was not at times foolhardy, allowing his tongue to run away with him? Particularly when he had drunk too much mead."

Sigehelm fixed him with a hard glare.

"Go on," he said at last.

"There is little to tell but that your brother chose the wrong man to insult that night. I offered him several chances to take back his words, but he would not do so, instead taunting me further. When he drew his sword, things happened very fast, as they tend to do when steel is freed from leather."

There was silence in the hall. Somewhere a man coughed.

A hound gnawed and crunched at a bone beneath one of the tables.

"Was it a good death?" Sigehelm asked.

Cynan remembered the hot blood gushing from Sidrac's throat.

"It was quick."

"And what of his men?"

Cynan lifted his chin proudly. He must not show on his face the turmoil of emotions that roiled within him.

"Sidrac's ruffians were not a match for my gesithas."

"You mean…" Sigehelm's voice trailed off. "You… you killed them all?"

Cynan gave the slightest of shrugs.

"If a man does not seek death, he should not raise his sword against a warrior."

"So," said Sigehelm, stroking his beard, "there are no witnesses to these acts?"

Cynan squared his shoulders.

"I am a witness," he said. "As are my men, who stand without the hall. They will vouch for my words."

"I have no doubt they will," replied Sigehelm. "But with no witnesses save your own oath-sworn men, you could have ridden from these lands. Why did you come here, and," he said, raising a finger as if a sudden idea had occurred to him, "how did you know to come to this place?"

"Both of those questions are easy to answer," replied Cynan. "First, I am a man of honour. I have come here to pay the weregild for your brother and his comitatus. I want no bloodfeud between our families." He paused, trying to gauge what effect his words were having on Sigehelm, but Sidrac's brother gave nothing away. "As to how I knew of this place," Cynan went on, "why, Sidrac himself told me his father's name, and it was not difficult to find where Lord Tohrwulf had his hall."

Sigehelm listened, nodding slowly.

"I thank you for coming here," he said. "As is customary, we will give you time to bring to us the weregild, as laid out in the dooms of the land. Our priest, Scyldsung, will know the blood-price. There will be no feud unless you do not bring to us the agreed amount by, shall we say, Blotmonath? Even with war upon us, that should give you plenty of time to find sufficient silver."

"That is indeed a generous amount of time, but I have come ready to pay the price now."

Sigehelm looked at him in disbelief.

"You must be a wealthy man indeed to travel with such a hoard."

Cynan turned to the open doors of the hall. Outside, the day was the crimson hue of sunset, as if the land was viewed through a film of blood. "Brinin, Ingwald," Cynan called, "bring in the silver."

There was a pause, while the door wards checked the men and the sacks they carried for weapons. Those gathered inside the hall began to discuss what they had heard. The hubbub of voices quietened as Cynan's men entered the building, each laden with a large heavy sack. At a nod from Cynan they dropped the bags at Sigehelm's feet with a clanging crash. Brinin and Ingwald allowed their gleaming contents to spill forth. Small discs of silver, each stamped with the face of some long-forgotten king, poured from a dented silver chalice. A fine platter, engraved with symbols and pictures, tumbled from the second sack.

Sigehelm raised his eyebrows.

"All of this as weregild?" he said, his tone filled with awe.

"I will not haggle with you over the price of your kin's life," answered Cynan, offering up a silent prayer of thanks to Bleddyn for telling him where Sidrac had buried his wealth. Cynan had tried to give several pieces of silver to Leofman, but the old man had refused, saying the Lord and the land would provide.

Sigehelm stooped, retrieving a fine-looking belt buckle, gold with intricate whorls and swirling patterns. It was studded with garnets. One of the blood-red stones was missing and Sigehelm ran his finger over the indentation where the square of garnet should have been.

"This is a fine hoard indeed," he said, standing and offering his hand to Cynan. They grasped forearms in the warrior grip and Sigehelm said loudly, for all to hear, "there will be no bloodfeud between our families, Cynan. I accept this weregild from you as payment for my kin's blood that you shed."

The hall erupted in chatter as the men crowded forward to get a glimpse of the treasure that glinted and glistened red in the light of the setting sun that spilt through the hall's doorway.

Sigehelm did not let go of Cynan's arm, instead pulling him forward and leaning in close.

"I recognise this buckle," he whispered. "It belonged to my brother."

Cynan did not move. His breath caught in his throat. So this was the moment when Sigehelm would denounce him, calling for his death.

He remembered how they had dug beneath the apple tree that Bleddyn had led them to some hundred paces from Sidrac's hall. Most of the treasure in the sacks had come from that deep hole in the earth. But the buckle was from the belt worn by Sidrac. Cynan had stripped it from the man's corpse, cutting the buckle free from the leather and tossing it into the sack. He should never have added the thing to what he offered as weregild. Gods, with so much treasure and to think that this buckle would be his undoing.

Sigehelm held his arm in a tight grip, staring into his eyes without blinking.

Cynan met his glare. He could not decipher Sigehelm's expression.

"Well," Cynan said at last in a low voice that only Sigehelm would hear, "now it is yours."

Chapter 35

"You took your sweet time coming, Beobrand," said Oswiu, looking up from where he sat on a stool in the centre of the leather tent. He was surrounded by men, who turned towards Beobrand as he stepped beneath the flap that hung over the tent's entrance. "I was beginning to wonder if you had run off into the west like that Waelisc man of yours."

It was warm in the tent and Beobrand shrugged off his cloak. The wool was still damp from the rain that had fallen that morning, but since then the sun had shone and when Beobrand and his men had ridden into the Bernician encampment to the south of Corebricg, they had found men lounging in the afternoon sun. The faces of the fyrd-men were sombre. Their frowns and dark eyes spoke of hardship; too many battles fought this season. These were men ready to return to their fields for the harvest. They had answered Oswiu's call once more, but Beobrand sensed a growing unrest in the gathered spear-men of Bernicia that Oswiu would be wise to heed.

"I came as soon as I received your message, lord," Beobrand replied, keeping his tone flat.

"Then perhaps I should have the messenger flogged," said Oswiu. "He must have stopped along the way to swive every shepherdess he saw, eh?"

A couple of the men near the king chuckled.

Beobrand sighed. He knew Dryhthelm was a man of worth who had not tarried in performing his duty.

"Well, I am here now," he said.

"God be praised," said Oswiu. He stood, and quickly strode over to where Beobrand awaited at the doorway of the tent.

"I am pleased to see you have recovered from your illness," said Beobrand, noting that the king displayed no signs of the limp that had plagued him when last they had met.

"I told you it would not last," said Oswiu. "It never does. Damned painful though. Perhaps it is God reminding me of all of my sins, eh, Utta?"

The priest glowered from the far side of the enclosure.

"I can hear your confession, lord king," he said in a weary tone, "if you would care to unburden yourself."

"The only unburdening I need is to be free of this troublesome cousin of mine." Oswiu picked up a cup from a small table and a young freckle-faced boy lifted a jug and filled it slowly, careful not to spill any of the liquid. Oswiu handed the cup to Beobrand with a smile. "It is good to see you," he said, with what seemed genuine warmth. His friendly tone unnerved Beobrand more than any goading or insults. "Has that damned Waelisc cur returned?"

"No, lord," said Beobrand, strangely settled by Oswiu's more caustic tone. He took a sip from the cup in an effort to hide his annoyance at Oswiu's words. Beobrand hated that the king insulted Cynan, and he loathed to be reminded of his man's wayward actions and his clear dereliction of duty.

Beobrand started at the taste of the liquid on his tongue. He had expected mead, or perhaps ale, but this was the warm, rich, fruit-filled tartness of wine, imported from the distant and sunny lands of Frankia. Beobrand relished the taste and scent of the wine, washing away the dust in his throat and the stench from so many gathered warriors surrounding the king's tent.

The wine was good, the flavour incongruous, transporting him to different times and places. He looked about him, taking in the wooden framed bed, the table, chests and chairs in the tent. All of these things would be loaded into carts that would slow down the warhost, Beobrand knew. Oswiu was a fine warrior, when the steel-storm began, but he did so enjoy his comforts that he travelled with as many as his servants were able to carry.

"Pity," said Oswiu. "Despite his Waelisc blood, that man of yours is a good scrapper, I'll give him that. How many men did you bring?"

"More than two dozen Black Shields ride with me."

"Good, good." Oswiu nodded, returning to his seat. "Ethelwin, we should move south now, don't you think?"

"We are still waiting for some warbands from the west and north, but we have the numbers now, I believe," Ethelwin said. Beobrand turned in the direction of his voice. The warmaster was standing to one side of the tent's entrance. He nodded at Beobrand, his scarred face serious. Beside him stood Wynhelm, who offered Beobrand a tense smile of welcome.

"Indeed," said Oswiu, "there is no time to waste. The longer we tarry here, waiting for stragglers and dawdlers, the more men flock to Oswine's banner."

Beobrand clenched his fist tightly around the wooden cup. He took another sip of the fine wine. He would not give Oswiu the satisfaction of seeing that his jibe at Beobrand's supposed lack of haste had succeeded in angering him.

He glanced about the tent. Apart from the men he had already acknowledged, he spied a couple more servants. The men around Oswiu's chair were ealdormen and thegns. Each nodded in sombre greeting to Beobrand. They all knew he was no longer in such good favour as he had once been with Oswiu's brother, but Beobrand was still a formidable warrior, who led a powerful warband, and so they showed him respect. Beobrand was certain they spoke ill of him when he was not present, but what did he care of such things? He cared not for the buzzing words of the men who flocked around the throne like flies on a carcass. Just as long as they did not involve him in their intrigues.

He recognised the faces of all the thegns and ealdormen gathered in the king's tent and he recalled seeing their banners and standards raised over their camped warbands as he had led his black-shielded gesithas through the host, looking for a place to light cooking fires and set up camp. He had seen Ethelwin's raven, and the red wyrm of Wynhelm. But, he realised, as he drained his cup of wine, there was one banner he had not seen.

"Where is Alhfrith?" he asked, and the murmuring conversation ceased.

Outside, a horse whinnied and a man cursed. Laughter wafted to them, carried on the wind redolent of the stink of hundreds of Bernician warriors.

Ethelwin frowned.

"The atheling will be with us when he is needed," he said. The warmaster shot a glance at Oswiu, who nodded.

"If you are worrying about your son," said the king, "do not fret. He is with Alhfrith, and they can both take care of themselves. They have long since ceased to need their fathers' protection, it seems to me."

Beobrand wondered at Oswiu's words and the look that had passed between the king and the warmaster.

"I was not worried, lord," replied Beobrand. It was true, he thought, though now that the seed had been sown by the king, Beobrand could sense the roots of the bitter plant of anxiety for his son's safety burrowing into his mind. "I merely wondered where the atheling and Octa were. We are riding to war and we would not wish to meet the enemy without some of our most valiant warriors." He held out his cup to the thrall boy for more wine. "Perhaps," he added, "we should await their arrival." He raised his cup to his lips, savouring the wine. "Even though they are tardy."

"That will not be necessary," said Ethelwin, and once again, Beobrand noted the silent communication between the warmaster and Oswiu. "We will march at dawn."

"Octa is like a son to me," said Oswiu with a smile. "It pleases me greatly that he is so devoted to Alhfrith. He has his father's sense of honour and duty. He would do anything to protect the atheling. I feel blessed that he is part of my household."

Oswiu met Beobrand's gaze with a grin that did not reach his eyes. Beobrand smiled back through gritted teeth, unwilling to allow the king to see the effect his words had on him. He could not be certain, but he sensed that Oswiu knew exactly how his words would stab at Beobrand. Oswiu was much too cunning to be oblivious of the power he held over Beobrand by means of Octa's proximity to Alhfrith.

Ever since the conversation with Cuthbert on the ride south, Beobrand's mood had soured. He tried not to dwell on what the young man had said, but no matter how hard he tried, he felt the weight of the war pressing down on him. So many dead. How many more to be killed? Could he truly be the cause of such pointless slaughter? Staring into Oswiu's dark, intelligent eyes, he told himself this war had been orchestrated not by him, but by the son of Æthelfrith. Oswiu's father had been known as Flesaur, the Twister, by his enemies, due to his cunning. No man could be truly free of his father. Beobrand had struggled with that knowledge. And no matter how much Octa might hate it, his son was like him in many ways. Even a king could not escape his nature, passed down to him in the blood of his father. Oswiu's ambition and guile were overbearing. His desire for more power had led to war and death.

Beobrand wished he could see a way out of the impending battle. But no path to peace was clear to him. Oswiu's eyes shone in the gloom of the tent and again the king smiled. Like his father, the Twister, Oswiu's ambition could not be contained. He would never rest until he had secured Deira and united Northumbria once more as his uncle, Edwin, and his brother, Oswald, had done before him.

And it was Beobrand's wyrd to help achieve his goals. For Oswiu had his oath. And, as he was keen to remind Beobrand, Octa was a member of the king's household.

"I am glad to hear that Octa pleases you, lord. And that he fulfils his oath to you and the atheling. Alas, I have seen little of him of late. I had hoped to find him here, gathered with the fyrd and your warhost."

"Well, you will see him soon, never fear."

"You know where he is then?"

"Of course I know where he is, man," snapped Oswiu. "I am king of all Bernicians, including my son and yours."

"Lord," said Ethelwin, raising a hand in warning.

Oswiu took a deep breath, controlling his building ire.

"I know where the members of my household are," he said. "You would do better to worry about your own people." Beobrand met his glower without flinching.

Was that the meaning of Oswiu's words? Was the king giving him a warning? Or was he threatening him? For the briefest of moments Beobrand recalled the touch of Eanflæd's lips, the warm softness of her body against him. He wondered if Oswiu knew where each of his household was at every moment.

"After all," the king went on, "you do not know where your man Cynan is, do you?"

"You are right, of course, lord king," Beobrand said. He drank deeply from his cup of wine, swilling the liquid around his mouth to rid himself of the foul taste of his subservience. "So," he said, changing the subject, "tomorrow we march south to face Oswine and Peada?"

"Yes," replied Oswiu, a broad smile on his face. If any of the other men gathered in the tent found his expression strange, none made mention of it. Beobrand recalled the resigned features of the reluctant and tired warriors outside. Was Oswiu so detached from the mood of his men that he was joyful in the face of their approaching despair?

"The men of Deira and Peada's Mercians are amassing at Wilfaresdun," said Ethelwin. Beobrand knew the place. It was a hill close to the joining of the old Roman roads of Burh Stræt and Deira Stræt, near Catrice.

"If they await us on that hill, they will be hard to dislodge," he said.

"That is your problem, Beobrand," said Oswiu, clearly enjoying himself. "You have no faith. But God is on our side, and I will not lead you to a defeat."

Beobrand thought of Oswiu's brother, Oswald, and how his body had been hacked apart, his head and limbs placed on waelstengs at Maserfelth. He recalled the blood-soaked shift of Sigeberht, the holy king of the East Angelfolc, who had also been slain by Penda of Mercia. The idea of facing Penda's son armed with faith in the Christ God did not fill Beobrand with confidence. But he bit back the words he wished to say. Instead, he handed his empty cup to the thrall and said, "I have faith in doughty men with sharp spears and strong shields. And I place my trust in kings who lead their warhosts to victory."

Oswiu's smile slipped, as if he suspected a veiled insult in Beobrand's words.

"Well, I am your king and I will lead you to victory when we face Oswine and Peada."

Beobrand nodded.

"You have never led me to defeat before, lord. Now, if you have no further need for me, I would see to my men."

Oswiu met his gaze for a long while, before finally waving a hand, dismissing Beobrand.

As Beobrand turned and left the tent, the sound of conversation within swelled. The breeze picked up, slapping the leather walls like a ship's sail, pulling the ropes tight. Beobrand breathed deep of the air outside. Despite the stink of so many men, the breeze was heavy with woodsmoke and the scent of cooking. In the distance, he could see his Black Shields setting up camp on a slight rise in the lee of a stand of beech. He strode towards them, leaving the sound of Oswiu and his retinue behind. But even when he had gone some way and he could no longer hear the men inside the tent, Beobrand could not get the taste of the king's wine from his mouth and, along with the sour tang, the unshakeable feeling that a riddle had been told that he alone was unable to solve.

Chapter 36

The church of Saint Trynnian was just as Leofman had described it. The sun had gone down now, but there was no mistaking the timber building with the cross on its roof that was silhouetted against the darkening sky. In the distance, the sound of many people thronging Tohrwulf's hall reached Cynan and Ingwald as they approached the church.

After the commotion caused by Cynan's arrival, and the subsequent payment of the weregild for Sidrac's killing, the boards were being set for a meal. There would be feasting soon, a chance for the people of Dacor to send their men off to war with their bellies full and memories of their kin's faces in their minds. Nobody seemed unduly upset about Sidrac's death. And, after the brief moment of worry when Sigehelm recognised the buckle from his brother's belt, Cynan and his men had been accepted. They were known as warriors who followed Beobrand of Ubbanford, and his battle-fame carried much weight.

"You will join me at the high table this night," Sigehelm had said. "In that way we will show clearly there is no enmity between us. Then, in the morning, you will ride with us to answer Oswiu's call."

"I would be honoured," Cynan had replied. He had hoped to be able to return directly to Stagga, so that he could speak with

Eadgyth, but when he had heard of the calling of the fyrd, he knew his duty was to respond. "But there is something I would do before we eat."

Sigehelm raised his eyebrows enquiringly.

"I am unshriven," Cynan said, using the unfamiliar term that he had heard from Coenred's lips. "When we rode up to your hall, I spied a church and I would cleanse my soul before riding to battle. I have paid the weregild for your brother's death, but I would still wash clean my immortal soul for the sins I have committed."

"Of course," replied Sigehelm sombrely. "But I would hurry. As soon as Scyldsung hears the sounds of merriment and smells ale and meat on the breeze, he will be at the hall faster than a hawk strikes a vole."

Sigehelm was correct. As Cynan and Ingwald reached the thatched church, a slender man in a simple robe stepped out into the dusk. He was hurrying and almost collided with the two warriors.

Cynan placed a hand on the man's chest and pushed him back. "Are you Scyldsung?" he asked.

The man blinked, peering at the two strangers.

"I am," he said. "What is it you require?" He looked longingly past Cynan at the warm light spilling from the open doors of the hall. "I was just heading to the hall. Perhaps you could tell me what it was you wanted as we walk that way."

Cynan did not remove his hand from Scyldsung's chest.

"Alas," he said, "what I have to say to you cannot be overheard. Tomorrow we ride to war, and I would have a priest hear my confession before we leave."

Scyldsung hesitated. He looked first at the tall Waelisc warrior and then the older, shorter man at his side. Both men were unsmiling, hard-faced and serious. Neither man moved and at last, with a sigh, Scyldsung turned back to his church.

"Come then," he said. "But let us hurry. I can smell pork being roasted."

"Surely my soul is more important than your belly," said Cynan, following the priest inside. "When a man has sinned, there can be nothing of more import than hearing his confession and giving God's forgiveness and grace to unburden his soul."

With a nod to Ingwald, who took up guard at the entrance of the church, Cynan pulled the door closed behind him.

There was a candle burning within a pot resting on a silver platter at the far end of the small building. The candle's warm light illuminated a carved figure attached to the far wall, above the altar. It was of a man splayed on a cross. The flickering flame made the shadows on the wooden face of the Christ dance, so that it seemed he was alive, writhing with the agony of being nailed to a tree.

At the sound of the door being closed, Scyldsung turned with a frown.

"There is no need to shut the door," he said, his tone betraying a quiver of fear. "This is the house of God and it is always open to His flock." He made his way to the plain altar, where the single candle burnt beneath the statue of Jesu's anguish. "I keep this candle lit at all times as a symbol of God's undying love for us all."

Cynan took a deep breath to calm his anger. The candle smell was sweet. It was made of beeswax, not the foul-smelling tallow he had expected. He was not surprised. He noted the gold ring on the priest's left hand, and the silver chain that adorned his neck. This was a man of expensive tastes.

He followed him to the puddle of light around the altar.

"Would you kneel with me?" asked Scyldsung.

"I would rather stand."

Scyldsung frowned.

"It is customary to kneel before God when confessing one's sins."

Without warning, Cynan slapped the priest across the cheek. Hard. The sharp sound was loud in the enclosed church.

Scyldsung let out a small cry and staggered backward. Cynan lashed out and grabbed hold of his robe.

"Then perhaps it is you who should kneel, priest," he said, pulling Scyldsung towards him savagely. It was all he could do to refrain from smashing his forehead into the man's nose. He had talked to Ingwald as they had walked over to the church and his gesith had told him not to mark the man's face.

"Such a thing will be too much to explain away," Ingwald had said. "You have managed to make paying the weregild work, which I was uncertain of. But if the priest comes into the hall with a broken nose and bruised eyes, I think Sigehelm may not be convinced of your good intentions."

Ingwald was right, but at the sight of the priest, Cynan's rage threatened to overcome him. He thought of all the pain and suffering this man's actions had caused. The blood that had been spilt. The fear in Eadwig's eyes. Sulis trembling in the darkness, begging for his help. Gods, this priest had made him break his word to Beobrand and ride away from Eadgyth.

"What is the meaning of this?" said Scyldsung, outrage colouring his tone. "Who are you?"

"I am a friend of Leofman's," Cynan replied, and the realisation and fear on Scyldsung's face as he heard the name breathed air on the flames of Cynan's ire. "And a friend of his goodwife, Sulis."

Still grasping the priest's robe in his left hand, he hammered his right fist into the man's stomach. With a groan, the strength left Scyldsung's legs and he fell to his knees. Cynan raised his right hand again and the man shied away. Cynan spat and stepped back, unsure if he would be able to curb his fury if he remained so close.

"I know Leofman," Scyldsung whimpered, "and his goodwife. They are good Christ-following folk."

"And is it not your duty to protect the followers of Christ?"

Scyldsung was regaining his composure now. He looked up at Cynan with a sincere expression on his face.

"I do not know what it is you think that I have done," he said, "but I assure you, I want no harm to come to any of my flock."

With a growl, Cynan drew his seax from its sheath. Its blade glimmered in the candlelight. He moved closer and Scyldsung cowered.

"Do not lie to me, priest," Cynan said. "If you do, I will gut you here."

"You would not dare," spluttered Scyldsung.

"Do not test my patience. Sidrac and Ludeca are both dead. They told me everything before their end. Now I would hear you say the words."

Scyldsung's face was a mask of terror now.

"Then you will kill me too." Tears brimmed in his eyes.

"I would like nothing more," Cynan said. "And I swear to you on this blade, that if you do not tell me the truth of your actions without delay, I will spray your blood across that carving of the Christ on his cross." Scyldsung looked up at the face of his god and trembled. "But I give you my word," continued Cynan, "that if you confess your sins here, before God and me, I will let you live."

Cynan stared unblinking at the terrified priest. He could not recall wanting to kill a man more, but Ingwald was right, slaying the priest would place them all in jeopardy.

The grating sound of the door being pushed open made both men turn.

Ingwald's face was shadowed, but recognisable enough.

"Lord," he said, "make haste. We will be missed soon."

"You heard the man," said Cynan. He stepped forward, grasping the priest's robe in his hand and pressing the sharp, cold steel of the seax blade against the man's throat. "Tell me everything." Tears trickled freely down the priest's face now, but Cynan felt no pity. "Now," he said, shaking the man viciously. "My patience, such as it is, is wearing thin."

Scyldsung swallowed and sniffed.

"What would you have me tell you?" he asked, his voice shaking and pathetic.

"Did you speak to Sidrac or Ludeca first?"

Scyldsung sighed.

"Ludeca came here. He wished to confess and to pray. As he spoke to me, I learnt that he was Leofman's brother. Forgive me." He quickly made the sign of the cross over himself. "For I allowed avarice to tempt me to strike a bargain with such an evil man. The Devil is strong indeed to have caused me to stray. But now I see the error of my ways."

"Do not look to me for forgiveness," said Cynan, pressing the edge of his seax blade hard into Scyldsung's throat, making him gasp. "It is easy to admit to your errors when there is a knife at your throat. But the promise of silver was louder than your fear of sin. Isn't that so?"

"Yes," sniffed Scyldsung. "Yes, it is true. It was after Ludeca had left. The Devil began to whisper to me."

"And what did the Devil tell you?"

"I thought of..." Scyldsung's voice trailed off. "The serpent told me that if Leofman had kin that he believed to be dead, his land could be passed to another."

"Through his heir, Eadwig."

"That's right. I had read the land deeds and written the will for Leofman. On his death, his land passes to his heirs."

"But if the heir was only a child..."

"A kinsman, an uncle of his blood, could seek custody."

"And did you not think that for this to occur, Leofman would need to die?" Scyldsung hung his head. Cynan shook him. "Do not look away. There is blood on your hands, priest. And there is more you did not know. Sulis is with child."

Realisation dawned on Scyldsung's face.

"Did they kill the woman?" he asked in a small voice.

"If they did it would be just more murders to add to your tally."

"I never wanted anyone to be slain," cried Scyldsung.

"Perhaps that is so," replied Cynan, "but you chose not to think of what would occur, didn't you? And you agreed to help Sidrac to extract the metal from the earth, just as you had helped Leofman, didn't you?"

Something in the priest's face told Cynan he had struck at the core of the matter, the way a man's pick might unearth a rich seam of ore.

"And so it comes to that," Cynan said. "Greed, nothing more. How much did Sidrac promise you for your help?"

Scyldsung's face contorted with rage. This was the true man behind the mask of the kindly holy man.

"If Leofman had been generous, none of this would have happened," whined Scyldsung, and it was all Cynan could do to prevent his hand from plunging the seax into the odious priest's throat. "It was I who found the writings at Caer Luel that explained the process. And it was I who then experimented with Leofman to bring forth the lead from the galena ore. And what did he offer in return? Nothing! Just his thanks!"

"You are a priest, not a merchant, trading for wealth," spat Cynan.

"Even Christ's shepherds need to eat."

"What did Sidrac offer you?" asked Cynan, his voice quiet and cold, like a knife in the darkness.

"A tithe of all the silver he made from the mine."

Cynan shook his head in disbelief at the man's greed and stupidity.

"And you thought you could trust men such as Sidrac and Ludeca?"

"Even if they gave me less, it would have been more than nothing."

Cynan stared at the man for a long time. His face was tear-streaked and snot ran from his nose. Cynan imagined drawing the blade of his seax across Scyldsung's throat. He could picture the dark glut of blood spurting in the gloom of the church, hear it splattering across the oaken features of the Christ on his rood. With a great effort, he removed the seax from the man's neck.

Scyldsung let out a long ragged breath of relief.

"After a confession, what does a priest do?" Cynan asked.

Scyldsung wiped a shaking hand across his face.

"He absolves the confessor's sins."

"That is not in my power," said Cynan. "It seems to me that some sins need punishing."

Scyldsung tried to scrabble away.

"But you said you would not kill me if I told you what happened," he said, terror in his voice.

Cynan sprang forward, heaving Scyldsung to his feet and wrapping a heavily muscled arm about his neck.

"I am not going to kill you, priest," he hissed, pulling him towards the altar. "But I am not going to forgive you. Your penance for your sins will be to live in the knowledge that if ill ever comes to Leofman or his family, I, Cynan of Stagga, will hear of it. And I will ride here, and I will kill you. Do you doubt it is so?"

"No," snivelled Scyldsung. "No, I believe you."

Cynan grabbed the priest's wrist, pushing the man's hand over the flickering flame of the beeswax candle. Scyldsung fought against him, bucking and thrashing, but he was no match for Cynan's strength.

The church darkened as the priest's hand partially covered the opening of the pot that held the candle. Scyldsung howled in pain and the stink of burning flesh stung Cynan's nostrils. He held Scyldsung as he wailed and trembled and fought for his freedom. After a time, the man became limp in his grasp.

Stepping back, Cynan let the priest collapse to the floor. He was weeping and whimpering in pain and fear as he gazed up at Cynan's impassive face.

"That hand will help you to remember what we have spoken

MATTHEW HARFFY

about here today," Cynan said, making his way to the door. Tugging it open, he welcomed the fresh air from outside. "Do not tarry here too long, priest," he called over his shoulder. "Sigehelm expects you at the high table." He sniffed the air. "And I think I can smell roasting pork."

Chapter 37

Cuthbert shielded his eyes with his hand and stared up at the hill of Wilfaresdun. The sun was high and the day was already hot. Atop the rise, the Deirans were amassed in a great host. Their spears were as thick as a forest, and in the hazy summer distance, Cuthbert could not keep a count of the numerous banners and standards that hung limp in the still warm air.

The Bernicians had left Corebricg two days before and marched south along Deira Stræt. They had overnighted among the tumbled ruins of the old Roman fort just north of the River Tes. Setting out in the wolf-grey light of the pre-dawn, they had crossed the rickety timber bridge over the dark swirling waters of the Tes, arriving at Wilfaresdun when the day was yet cool.

As they had ridden southward along the cracked Roman road, Cuthbert had looked back to watch the line of the fyrd-men trailing behind them. Beobrand had kept his face stern, but Cuthbert could tell he was distracted, anxious even.

"Why is our lord so nervous?" he had asked Eadgard in a low voice.

Eadgard glanced over his shoulder to where Beobrand had cantered back to converse with Wynhelm at the rear of the column.

"Beobrand is a good hlaford," he said, wiping sweat from his forehead with the back of his meaty hand. "He does not like to lead us into the unknown."

"But all battle is unknown," replied Cuthbert. "Nobody can predict the outcome when two hosts meet."

"True enough," replied Grindan, who rode close to his brother, "but many things can shift the balance in one warhost's favour. Beobrand leads the best warriors, no doubt," he said with a grin, "but it would do us well to meet the enemy on a ground of our choosing. When we are on the march, we are vulnerable to ambush. Oswine knows we are coming, and this is his land."

"But Oswiu sent out riders to scout ahead," replied Cuthbert. The wiry Attor had been among those scouts.

"He did." Grindan nodded. "But even the best outrider can make a mistake. Beobrand doesn't like that we are walking through Deira as if we have already won the war, when we know full well that Oswine and Peada are out there waiting for us."

They had been riding between two wooded hills, and at Grindan's words Cuthbert glanced up at the slopes, expecting to see a horde of riders descending upon them at any moment.

Now, peering up at the thicket of spears and standards on the hill, it was clear to Cuthbert that Beobrand had worried needlessly. They had not been attacked as they marched and the Deirans were amassed just where Oswiu had said they would be.

And yet, Beobrand still seemed on edge.

The hill had been visible for a long way as they had trudged down the Roman road. Attor and the other scouts had ridden south into the gloom of the dark morning before the sun rose, returning with the dawn to guide the host to its current position in a field of barley to the north of Wilfaresdun.

Without delay, the Bernicians had followed the orders of Oswiu's thegns and ealdormen, trampling the crops in the field and forming up into a solid mass of warriors. Beobrand's Black Shields were at the centre, where they were conspicuous for their lack of a standard under which to rally. To the left of their position was Oswiu himself, standing beneath the purple banner of Bernicia. He was surrounded by his comitatus, the hearth-warriors of the king, commanded by Lord Ethelwin. To the right of the Black Shields stood Wynhelm and his small warband of stalwart warriors.

Cuthbert glanced at Beobrand. The tall thegn of Ubbanford held his hand up to shade his eyes, just as Cuthbert had been doing moments before.

"By Woden," Beobrand spat, "I cannot make anything out in this light. What do your young eyes see, Cuthbert?"

Cuthbert said nothing about Beobrand's eyesight, though they all knew he struggled to pick out details at a distance.

"There are many men on the hill," he said.

"Is that so?" replied Beobrand, his tone dripping with sarcasm. "I thought we had gathered here to glean barley from some poor ceorl." He spat into the crushed debris of barley kernels, husks and stalks. "What banners do you see? What standards? How many men?"

Cuthbert, his cheeks hot, focused on the distant hill.

"There is a wolf, I think, and a twisted white serpent on a black cloth." He scrunched up his eyes, trying to make out more details. "I see a boar the colour of blood, and the golden cross and lions of Oswine."

Beobrand shook his head, looking left and then right along their own line. He said nothing.

"It seems to me the Deirans outnumber us," said Cuthbert. "And they are standing on higher ground. That will make it harder for us to attack, won't it?"

"Quiet, lad," Beobrand said. "We all have eyes."

"Though some are sharper than others," quipped Attor.

"I may not see as well as you or the boy," Beobrand said, "but my sword is sharp enough." He patted Nægling's pommel to accentuate his point.

To the left of their position, a figure stepped out from the ranks of Bernicians. It was Utta, the priest, and he made his way out into the barley, before turning to face the Bernician host. At his movement, a multitude of pigeons flapped into the sky from the crop. The summer air was filled with the whirring of their wings and Utta, startled, spun around to see what had made the commotion. He watched the birds wheel in the sky and fly over the hill that held the Deirans. Making the sign of the cross, he turned again to face the warriors.

Cuthbert continued to watch the flock of pigeons, as small as insects now against the egg-shell bright blue of the sky. He wondered what their sudden flight meant? Was this as Coenred had said? Was God speaking through the movement of the birds to His faithful? Cuthbert concentrated, trying to make sense of it, but all he could hear were the murmurs of the warhost as they settled down to listen to what Utta would say to them.

"Kneel and pray with me," said the priest.

Utta's voice was thin, and someone far along the Bernician line shouted, "Speak up!"

Nervous laughter rippled across the men.

"Kneel," Utta shouted. "And let us pray for victory this day."

Nobody moved. Utta scanned the line of fighting men before him, his eyes moving quickly. He wiped sweat from his brow. Cuthbert felt pity for the man. He was a holy priest who could surely hear the voice of the Almighty. If he wished for the men to kneel, they should do that which he asked.

Cuthbert knelt. The broken stalks of the barley prickled his knees. Attor clapped him on the shoulder, and joined him on the ground. Then, like a wave rolling across the sands of Lindisfarena, the rest of the men knelt. Even King Oswiu and the standard bearers dropped to their knees, leaving the banners swaying high over the host and Utta standing alone, up to his thighs in the sea of ripe barley. The priest met Cuthbert's gaze with a small nod of thanks.

Holding up his hands over the gathered men, he began to intone the words of the prayer to the Lord that all men knew.

"*Fæder ure þu þe eart on heofonum; Si þin nama gehalgod...*"

Despite his moment of uncertainty, Utta's voice was strong now, and after he had uttered the first familiar words, he was accompanied by the men of the fyrd, the prayer taking on a mesmeric weight, a power of its own, when voiced from hundreds of mouths.

"... *gewurþe ðin willa on eorðan swa swa on heofonum*," said Cuthbert, lending his voice to the communal prayer. He glanced over to where Beobrand knelt and was not surprised to see his hlaford's mouth firmly shut. Beobrand did not worship the Christ and, unlike some men, made no pretence to do so. His left half-hand gripped the Thunor's hammer amulet he wore on a leather thong around his neck.

"... *urne gedæghwamlican hlaf syle us todæg...*"

Cuthbert thought of the meaning of the words they spoke, of how the prayer to the Holy Father asked for bread and protection from temptations. He understood why Beobrand was anxious as they stood before their amassed enemies. He may worship the old gods, but Beobrand was a good lord, providing for his people food and protection, just as the followers of the Christ beseeched daily of the Almighty.

"... *swa swa we forgyfað urum gyltendum and ne gelæd þu us on costnunge...*"

The prayer was reaching its conclusion now, and the volume of the throng rose. Cuthbert looked beyond Utta. Something had caught his attention. In the distance he saw movement on the hill. The pigeons had disappeared into the haze, but the standards of the Deirans jostled, as if in a great wind, yet the day was still.

The prayer was over now and Utta, perhaps emboldened by the reception from the men, launched into a blessing of his own, exhorting God to watch over His faithful as they marched into battle in His name. The men remained silent, many with heads lowered, but Cuthbert did not take his gaze from the hill. He listened to Utta's words, wondering how many others of Oswiu's force thought it strange that the priest should speak of the Lord watching over the Bernicians, when it was well known that Oswine of Deira was as pious a king as any that lived. Surely God could not bring victory to all those who followed Him, when both warhosts marched for a Christ-following king. Both Oswine and Oswiu looked to Bishop Aidan for their spiritual guidance, so how could God choose between them?

Utta finished his blessing and the men of the fyrd stood once more. Many of them made the sign of the cross as they rose. The expressions on the men's faces were less sombre now. The promise of God's protection had lifted their spirits and Cuthbert wondered at the power of something as simple as a prayer and a blessing. It was as if the words carried their own magic.

"What is happening on the hill?" asked Beobrand, cutting into Cuthbert's thoughts. Beobrand's tone was curt; the sound of a hlaford concerned for his people. "Those banners are moving."

Cuthbert gave the hill his full attention. For a time, even with his sharp eyes he could not be sure what was happening there. And then, all at once, it became clear. Next to him, he heard Attor draw in a sharp intake of breath and he knew the slim scout had seen it too.

"There are more warriors joining the ranks on the hill," Cuthbert said, keeping his voice low so that only Beobrand and those close by would hear.

"It is Peada," said Attor. "I see his eagle standard. And..." He paused, narrowing his eyes, wanting to be certain before he spoke. At last he nodded to himself. "He comes with many men of Mercia. There are at least five new warbands to add to those of Deira." He looked over at their lord. Beobrand frowned, but there was no need to say the words. They had been outnumbered before and had believed it to be the full host arrayed before them. Now, with the addition of Peada's force to Oswine's, there could be little hope of victory.

Perhaps this was God's way of showing which side he wished to vanquish in the upcoming battle, thought Cuthbert, with a sidelong glance at Beobrand. Could the presence of pagans in their midst be sufficient for God to forsake the Bernicians?

Beobrand stared for a long while at the hill in the distance. Cuthbert followed his gaze and tried to count the number of warriors they faced there. It was impossible, but it seemed to him that with Peada's arrival, their enemy might well number twice the Bernician strength.

Without warning, Beobrand strode out from the line of men, and made his way along the ranks towards Oswiu. After a moment's hesitation, Cuthbert, keen to hear what would be said, followed behind. Beobrand ignored him.

"Lord Beobrand, are your men ready for a fight?" asked Oswiu, stepping forward to meet the thegn of Ubbanford. Beside the king, Lord Ethelwin, squinting in the bright sunlight, swiped sweat from his scarred forehead.

"The Black Shields are always ready for battle," replied Beobrand gruffly. "But lord," he continued in a hushed tone.

"What is it?"

Beobrand nodded towards the hill.

"Should we ride out under the bough of peace?"

"Peace?" said the king, his tone disdainful. "There can be no peace while Oswine yet rules the land of Deira."

"But lord king," said Beobrand, "should we not attempt to parley?"

"Have you gone soft, Beobrand? I can scarcely believe it is you who would have me parley when we are here to fight? I know you are no longer the young man who fought the Pictish warrior beneath the gates of Din Eidyn, but surely you are no craven."

Beobrand spat.

"You know me well enough not to doubt my courage, lord," he said, his voice as sharp as a seax beneath a shieldwall. "I am ready to fight, if that is your command, as are my men. But look," he hissed, his voice an urgent whisper, "we are sorely outnumbered. If we stand, I can see no way that we will prevail against such odds."

"We have faced bad odds before, Beobrand. Remember Cair Chaladain?"

Beobrand's features clouded and Cuthbert, who had heard songs of the battle in the land of the Picts, wondered why its name would anger his lord so.

"Yes, lord," Beobrand said, his words clipped. "I remember."

"We were outnumbered there too, I recall," sneered Oswiu. "And in the end, what slaughter we made. And to the victor the spoils, eh?" He smiled.

Beobrand clenched his fists at his side and Cuthbert thought he looked as if he might strike the king.

Oswiu did not seem to notice, or at least he paid Beobrand's rage no heed.

"You need to have more faith, Beobrand," he said.

"Faith, lord?" asked Beobrand, his tone flat.

"Faith in your king and the good Lord above. Besides," said Oswiu with a wink, "with your good fortune, how could we lose?"

"I am not lucky," Beobrand said.

"So you always say," said Oswiu, "and yet you still stand before me when so many greater men than you are dead."

Beobrand scowled, but did not speak.

"Enough of this," said Oswiu. "Go back to your men and await Ethelwin's command."

Beobrand fixed the king with a stern glare before turning and striding back towards his gesithas.

"And Beobrand," Oswiu called after him, making him halt. "Remember. Have some faith."

Beobrand growled, and without another word, returned to where his black-shielded warriors awaited him. One look at his face silenced the questions on the lips of his men. Beobrand, jaw muscles bunching beneath his beard, stared grimly forward.

Cuthbert rejoined his place in the line, biting his lip, and watching the forest of spears and standards on Wilfaresdun.

The day dragged on and still neither side made a move to attack. Men passed around skins of water and chewed on whatever food they could get their hands on. Cuthbert's stomach felt hollow and empty, but he could not imagine eating anything.

The sun was well past its zenith now. A light wind had picked up, fluttering the spear pennants and banners. But despite the breeze, the afternoon was painfully hot.

Cuthbert accepted a half-full skin from Attor, and took a deep draught. The water tasted of the leather and was as warm as blood. Still, it was wet and he welcomed the feeling of the liquid trickling down his parched throat. When he had slaked his thirst, he offered the skin to Beobrand. Absently, his hlaford reached for the water, and raised the skin to his lips.

"Will there be battle?" Cuthbert asked.

Beobrand hesitated, with the water skin just beneath his mouth.

"Well," he snarled, "we have not come to pick turnips, boy."

"Then what are we waiting for?" asked Eadgard. "If we are going to be called upon to fight up that slope, I would rather do it in daylight."

Beobrand said nothing, but several of the men who had heard the axe-man's comment, nodded, muttering their support.

As if in answer to Eadgard, though he was much too far away to have heard the man's words, Oswiu shouted over the murmured conversations of the host.

"You see, Lord Beobrand? I told you to have more faith!"

Everyone turned to look at the king.

"See? The Lord provides!"

Oswiu was pointing off into the distance. Cuthbert followed the direction of Oswiu's finger. When he saw what the king was signalling, Cuthbert gasped.

Beside him, Beobrand was shielding his eyes against the bright sun.

"By Woden," he said, "can it be true?"

Chapter 38

Cynan spurred Mierawin into a gallop. Glancing over his shoulder, he let out his pent-up breath. Thank the gods he was not being followed. Mierawin effortlessly leapt over a deep gully where the old Roman road of Burh Stræt had been washed away in some long-forgotten storm. He was glad he had not allowed Ingwald to ride with him, despite the man's protestations. There was no way the older warrior could have kept up.

"I need you to keep an eye on the men," he had told Ingwald, drawing him aside as the fyrd trudged along Burh Stræt. "The men of Rheged are numerous, and I do not believe the flame of vengeance has been put out in Sigehelm's heart quite as easily as he would have me believe. With Halinard injured, I need you to watch over them."

Reluctantly, Ingwald had agreed. He too had noticed the dark looks some of the men gave them. Sigehelm had shown no sign of wishing them harm and yet there was a coldness in his eyes that spoke of a secret hatred brewing within. And who could blame the man for hating the warriors who had slain his brother? Still, he had accepted the weregild, perhaps allowing his greed and ambition to smother his desire for revenge, so now, in accordance with the law, there could be no bloodfeud between them.

And yet Cynan had been concerned for what might occur on the days' long march into Deira. Men could easily have accidents on such a journey, travelling fast through the barren hills and the pass that cut between the ridge of mountains to the north and the lands of the Pecsætna in the south.

Cynan was not oblivious to how Sigehelm had positioned his hearth-warriors around his black-shielded gesithas. The lord of Dacor was ready to turn on them if needed. Or perhaps he feared they planned to attack him. He clearly did not trust them, and that lack of trust had been heightened when Cynan had contested the route they should follow to answer Oswiu's call.

The messenger had told them to make their way to Corebricg, from which point the gathered fyrd would travel south to engage Oswine and Peada's forces. Sigehelm planned to lead the warriors of Rheged north along Weatende Stræt to Caer Luel and then follow the road that ran beside the great Wall.

They had discussed the route in the hall the evening before they left. Cynan had felt a rush of relief at having convinced the Rheged lord to take the weregild that he had dug from the earth outside Sidrac's hall. He was also pleased to have confronted the priest who had been instrumental in Sulis and Leofman's misery. He wished he could have inflicted a great punishment on the man. There was no doubt he deserved it. But if he had killed the priest, he could see no way he would have been allowed to leave Dacor. No, Scyldsung had been terrified and reminded of what would occur to him if he attempted anything against Cynan's friends. That would have to be enough.

Cynan could scarcely believe that things had worked out so well. Sulis and her family were saved, and he was clear now on his course of action with Eadgyth. And so it was, flush from drinking too much of Sigehelm's mead and with his successes fresh in his mind, that Cynan had disputed the route they should take to battle.

"The path you have described, Sigehelm, will get us to the gathering place in three or four days," Cynan said. "But we know Oswiu plans to march south. And his messenger left two days ago."

"Those are the orders of the king," Sigehelm said with a scowl, his eyes blazing. It was not until the light of the morning, with a clear head after the fog of drink had lifted, that Cynan thought back to Sigehelm's tone and expression and began to wonder at the man's true feelings towards him.

At the high table sat Scyldsung, beside the lord. The priest, pale-faced and with his hand bandaged, had entered the hall after the boards had been set. Sigehelm, noting the priest's cloth-wrapped hand, had enquired what ailed him. Scyldsung had mumbled something about an accident and cutting an apple clumsily.

Had Sigehelm believed him, or had he seen the man's dark glowers at Cynan? Mayhap the priest had whispered something of what had passed between them in the church, but truly Cynan doubted the snivelling Scyldsung would be so bold with him sitting close and the memory of his pain and Cynan's threats so recent. It was impossible to say whether the priest had indicated what had truly happened to him, but one thing was certain: Sigehelm did not take well to having his decisions questioned.

"What would you propose, Cynan?" Sidrac's brother asked, his words cutting and hard.

"I say that rather than following his orders blindly, Oswiu would prefer us to arrive in time to fight. We are on the other side of Albion, so we cannot enquire more of the king's will. But I believe, as leaders of men, we should use what wisdom and knowledge we have to better aid our king."

He thought the words were well-said, and he took a sip of mead to moisten his throat. Sigehelm frowned at him.

"And how do you think we can better use our wisdom than riding directly to meeting Oswiu at the place he has commanded?"

Cynan recalled the headlong rush across the animal tracks to the bothy. If they had ridden first to Leofman's steading and then followed the path into the hills, they would have arrived too late to save Sulis. Despite the feeling of satisfaction that enveloped him in the knowledge of that victory, he shuddered at the thought of what Bumoth, Ludeca and the others would have done to her if they had tarried.

"I say that we take the road south of here that is known as Burh Stræt."

"But that leads directly into Deira."

"Indeed it does. And we know that the men of Deira will be called to amass at Wilfar's Hill. It has ever been so with the Deirans. They will either be there, or marching north to meet Oswiu by the time we reach them. If we cross the ridge of mountains that runs like a spine to north and south, we will halve the time of our journey. This might well make the difference between defeat and victory."

Sigehelm scratched at his chin.

"And if we meet Peada's force on the road? Or if Oswine's warhost is not where you say they will be and we come across them and have to engage…" His voice trailed off. He reached for his drinking horn and, finding it empty, he clicked his fingers for more mead. A servant rushed to fill his horn. Sigehelm drank deeply. "The men of Rheged are brave and doughty in battle, Cynan," he said, "but we are but men. We cannot face the might of Deira and Mercia alone."

"There is risk in such a course, it is true," said Cynan. "But do not fear. You will not be alone, for Cynan and his gesithas ride with you." Cynan let out a bark of laughter and Sigehelm grimaced at his bravado.

Cynan held up a hand before Sigehelm could respond. Serious now, Cynan held his gaze.

"We ride towards battle," he said, "and no man ever gained battle-fame by being cautious. If we follow the course I propose,

I say we will likely arrive sooner to lend our steel to our king's cause. And," he added, with a grin, "a king rewards richly those men who turn the tide of a battle in his favour. Not those who travel the safer path and arrive late."

In the end, Sigehelm had grudgingly agreed with him.

As Cynan galloped back towards the men of Rheged, Ingwald and the rest of his gesithas, he smiled at the memory of how the lord of Dacor had told the thegns and fyrd-men of Rheged that the change in plan had been Cynan's. If all went well now, and they were able to help bring victory to Oswiu, he was sure that Sigehelm would choose to downplay or omit Cynan's urging for them to ride the southern path.

Still, they had to get to the battle first and there was still some way to go. And Cynan cared not who gained renown from this. He just hoped they arrived in time. Then they could return to Ubbanford and Stagga. And he could finally ask Eadgyth to forgive him. As long as Beobrand forgave him first. The lord of Ubbanford was not a merciful man, and without his hlaford's agreement, Cynan would not be able to return.

He pushed that thought away and kicked Mierawin on to greater speed. The Rheged fyrd should be just over the next rise.

As he crested the hill and gazed down into the valley below, Cynan felt a stab of concern. Where were they? He had left before the dawn, riding hard. Many of the fyrd were on foot and so they could not travel as fast as those who were mounted, but surely they should have reached this vale by now. As he had ridden west, he had enjoyed the sensation of Mierawin's power, her muscular, graceful speed, and the control he exerted over her with a soft touch on the reins, or the pressure of his heels on her flanks. And he had revelled in the knowledge that he had been right. Sigehelm might never be his friend after what Cynan had done to Sidrac, but at least the thegn of Dacor would not have this decision to rebuke him with.

But when he began to descend the slope into the valley, Mierawin's hooves clattering on the cracked stones of Burh Stræt, he was suddenly filled with the fear that perhaps the Rheged men had been waylaid, ambushed by some hitherto unseen force. Or, he thought with terrible clarity, maybe the fyrd had halted for a time, so that Sigehelm might exact his revenge on Cynan's men. Images came to him then, clear as memory. Pictures of Ingwald, Halinard, Brinin, Bleddyn and Raedmund, covered in blood, their skin pallid in death, as Sigehelm and his men stood around their corpses. He should never have left their side to scout ahead.

Panic rose within him like bile. He kicked hard at Mierawin's sides, though he knew the mare was already close to exhaustion and could go no faster.

They sped down the hill, Cynan scouring the land for any sign of his men and the fyrd. A heartbeat later, a wave of relief washed over him. His own tiredness must be greater than he knew for how else had he not seen them before? Off to one side of the road, in the shadows of a stand of elm and hazel, the men of Rheged were resting. They must have set a fast pace to reach there in time to rest their weary bodies, but he was glad of it. They would need all their strength if they were to arrive in time and then fight.

He slowed Mierawin's gallop to a fast canter and veered off the stones of the road. Two riders were approaching to intercept him. As they neared, he recognised Ingwald and Brinin. He sighed with relief, cursing himself for allowing his imagination to stampede like a herd of wild horses.

The two men reined in, expecting him to halt too, but he carried on past them without stopping.

"There is no time to waste," he called to them. "I have spied the enemy."

They wheeled their mounts around and caught up with him quickly.

"How do you fare?" Cynan asked. "Is Halinard well?"

"We are well enough, lord," said Ingwald. "Halinard is still in pain, but he is no worse." The Frank had not once complained, but they could all see the strain on his face as they rode. Cynan prayed that his luck would hold and the wound would not grow elf-shot. What Halinard really needed was rest, but such was not possible.

"And Sigehelm?"

"Anxious, I would say," replied Ingwald. "He pushed the men hard as soon as you left this morning. He will be glad to hear your tidings."

Cynan hoped his man was right. The path he had led them on had brought them to battle, but no man could be certain what lay on the other side of the clash of shields when foe-men met in the steel-storm. But what else had they travelled for, if not war?

Sigehelm stepped forward as Cynan rode up. Slipping from the saddle, Cynan threw his reins to Raedmund, who stood nearby.

"Brush her down," Cynan said. "Give her some oats, and water her. But not too much, or she'll sicken." Raedmund nodded sombrely, turning to lead the tired horse away. "And Raedmund," Cynan called, halting the slender warrior. "After you have done that, change my saddle with Halinard's. I will need a fresher mount than Mierawin before this day is through." Raedmund nodded again and hurried off with the horse.

"Well?" snapped Sigehelm.

Cynan could not help grinning.

"Oswine and Peada are at Wilfaresdun."

"And Oswiu? Any sign of him?"

"The king has led the Bernician fyrd to the foot of the hill. If we had ridden to the north, we would yet be three days away. Three days late for the battle."

Sigehelm grunted.

"Well it is a good thing we travelled south then, is it not?" he said, with a raised eyebrow.

"Aye, it is that. But there is yet some way to go. Oswiu's force is outnumbered and it looked to me that the time of battle was upon them."

"Will we reach them in time?"

"Not if we stand here talking," replied Cynan, accepting a waterskin from Ingwald and drinking. "I say those of us who are mounted ride ahead and the rest of the warriors push on as fast as they are able. There is no time to tarry now."

Sigehelm nodded and called for his horse, a fine animal with a dappled grey coat. Swinging himself into the saddle, he rode out in front of the men who slouched in the shade of the trees.

"You have shown great heart these last days, men," Sigehelm shouted in a clear voice. Cynan nodded, impressed by the lord's tone and his command of the fyrd-men. "But now the moment for true heroes is upon us. The future of our king and the lands of Northumbria rest on a sword's edge. And it is we men of Rheged who will win this war once and for all. Rise, brave warriors of the west. Take up your weapons and your linden boards and carry them to the enemy who awaits us on Wilfar's Hill. It will be a long hot march and we will face blades and blood when we reach our destination, but is that not why we have come here? To answer the call of our king? And to fulfil our oaths to him? Oswiu already stands to the east of here before his enemies. And are not the king's enemies also our enemies?"

There was a murmur of assent from the resting men.

"I asked if the king's enemies are not also our enemies!" shouted Sigehelm.

"Yes!" the men of Rheged roared with one voice.

"And the king now stands before his foe-men, so rouse yourselves. For battle and glory await us!"

Sigehelm turned to Cynan.

"See that your horse is saddled promptly," he said. "I do not think you wish to be left behind when the shields crash, and," he went on with a grin that once more made Cynan rethink his opinion of the man, "I will not wait for you."

Chapter 39

"You see, Lord Beobrand," said Oswiu with a broad smile, "I told you Oswine would come to speak with me."

Beobrand scowled, peering to make out who was approaching with the king of Deira. There were several mounted figures riding down the slope of Wilfaresdun, but they were yet too distant for him to make out any faces. The riders' shadows were long and dark, the sun low in the western sky. The day had been hot, and filled with tension and surprises. And it was not over yet.

"But why so glum?" asked Oswiu. "This is just what you wanted, is it not?"

The king was right. Beobrand had been calling for a parley with their enemy, and it was certainly a better outcome than any he could have expected for most of that long day as the men awaited battle. He shook his head, and glanced over at Cynan who sat astride a short-legged dun horse that Beobrand recognised as Halinard's.

"I think it wise to talk before more Northumbrian blood is spilt, lord," Beobrand said. "There has been enough killing between our two kingdoms these past years."

Oswiu scratched behind his ear

"You really are getting old, aren't you?" he said with a chuckle. "At least your Waelisc man still has blood in his veins. I

have seldom seen a more beautiful sight than that of Cynan and
Sigehelm galloping from the west at the head of scores of riders
of Rheged. I shall have to reward you both, when this is done."
Oswiu nodded at both Cynan and the thegn he had ridden with.
Beobrand did not know this Sigehelm, but the man looked every
bit the warlord. He sat straight on a tall, dappled horse. His
arms were ringed in silver and gold and a finely wrought sword
hung at his belt in a scabbard that was decorated with patterns
and carved plates of silver.

"You had better wait to reward Cynan," snarled Beobrand.
"He has much explaining to do first."

"Lord—" Cynan said, but Beobrand cut him off.

"Now is not the time," he snapped. "We will speak when this
is over."

"Come now, Beobrand," said Oswiu. "I understand your ire
at not being obeyed, but even a king has to get accustomed to
his more headstrong warriors disobeying his commands. I have
learnt it is a price you sometimes have to pay." He looked sidelong
at Beobrand. "Better to keep a strong man's oath and his sword
for a future battle than to chastise him for every infraction and
failure to do his duty, eh?"

Beobrand looked into Oswiu's eyes and wondered if the king
was speaking of him and past events. Was this about what had
occurred at Ediscum?

"Surely you of all men," continued the king, "know that such
warriors as Cynan can alter the course of a battle. We need
men who do not always sing to the same tune as everyone else.
Sigehelm here tells me it was your man's idea to ride south and
not to take the longer route to Corebricg."

Beobrand noted how Cynan glanced at Sigehelm in surprise.

"It seems that Cynan is good at riding off in directions he has
not been ordered to ride," said Beobrand, fixing Cynan with a
hard glare.

"Well," replied Oswiu, removing the circlet of gold he wore

about his head, so that he could scratch behind his ear again, "if they had ridden north, they would not have arrived here in time to add their numbers to my host." He brushed his hair away from his face and replaced the gold band. It glimmered and gleamed in the hot sunlight. "Perhaps," he continued, "it was God's will, in His infinite wisdom, that sent your man into Rheged on some errand. Cynan should not be punished for answering the Lord's call."

"But mayhap he should be punished for disobeying his hlaford's command," said Beobrand. "And it seems to me that it was the change of heart of the Mercians that shifted the course of what might have happened here today, not the arrival of the men of Rheged."

Oswiu smoothed his moustache with forefinger and thumb.

"Maybe you are right," he replied, "but the coming of the riders from the west, followed by the fyrd of Rheged, certainly helped our cause."

Beobrand looked over to where the men of Rheged were still arriving from Burh Stræt. There could be no doubt that their numbers would give the Bernicians the edge if, after all, it came to combat. But he doubted now that would happen. For, shortly after Cynan and Sigehelm had led the galloping horsemen into the barley field, Peada's eagle, along with the standards of the Mercians who followed him, had disappeared from the hill. Cuthbert had been the first to see what was happening. At first, the Bernician warriors had watched nervously as the Mercians moved down the far side of the hill. They had thought perhaps Peada prepared to attack from a different direction, now that he had seen the horsemen arrive from the west.

But the newly arrived Cynan had ridden westward a way, returning shortly after with news that the Mercians appeared to be retreating.

Not long after that, the fyrd-men of Rheged, sweat-streaked and bone-weary from their forced march, had begun arriving.

They formed up further in the east, and in a short space of time, with the arrival of those reinforcements from Rheged, along with the Mercian retreat, the Bernicians outnumbered the Deirans.

Oswiu had sent one of his men to cut a leafy branch from an elm that grew beside the ditch running alongside the Roman road. Then, with his man holding the bough aloft as a sign of peace, the king had commanded his leaders to mount up and join him in the field beneath the hill of Wilfaresdun. They numbered some two dozen riders, all still bedecked for war. Beobrand yet wore his heavy byrnie, and the iron strips around his forearm and shins. Nægling was scabbarded and hung from a baldric slung over his shoulder. Like the rest of the king's retinue, he removed his battle helm, tying it to his saddle, allowing his sweat-soaked hair to dry in the afternoon sun.

They had halted with the barley bristling about their horses' knees. Some two hundred paces back, the largest part of the Bernician host was still arrayed in a line ready for the shieldwall. Off to the east were the men of Rheged. The warriors of the fyrd were close enough to remind Oswine of his predicament, yet still too far away to overhear what was said by their lords.

Oswiu had been in a jovial mood ever since Peada's retreat and he was smiling now as they all fell silent to watch Oswine and his retinue approach through the barley.

There were about a score of Deiran riders, and Beobrand recognised many of them. The king, handsome and broad-shouldered, rode at the head of the group. At either side of Oswine was Wulfstan and Hunwald. Just behind them came a man Beobrand did not know, who lifted a fresh birch bough high above his king's head. The branch's leaves rattled and sighed in the light breeze that had picked up as the day grew old. There was a dejected air about the party of riders. Their expressions were sombre, their shoulders slumped. They looked like men who had been defeated in battle, yet no blow had been struck.

Wulfstan caught Beobrand's eye and gave a curt nod of recognition. It seemed to Beobrand that Hunwald did the same to Ethelwin and he remembered that the Deiran lord was married to the warmaster's sister.

"Waes hael, cousin," said Oswiu in a cheery tone.

"I would say you are well come to my lands, cousin," Oswine said, his voice clear and melodious, "but such a thing would make a liar of me." He cast his gaze over the gathered riders and then at the shieldwall beyond. "What would you say to me? I have ridden under the bough of peace to this parley, but the day has been long and I would rest a while before we fight."

Oswiu grinned.

"Fight, is it? It seems to me that your new ally has had second thoughts about crossing me."

Oswine sighed.

"Have you called me here to tell me that which I already know? If so, I will return to my camp. My men are eager to fight and I have held them on the leash for too long."

Oswiu laughed at his cousin's words.

"Is that so, Oswine? I would think that with Peada and his men gone, and with my reinforcements from Rheged, your men would see as well as any with eyes that they are outmatched and outnumbered. If we fight here, it will be a bloody affair, but with the likes of Beobrand and his Black Shields on my side, and our superior numbers, my host will prevail."

Oswine shook his head, his expression one of sadness. His horse snorted and stamped. He patted the animal's neck absently.

"You know I never wished to fight you, Oswiu," he said. "But you have pushed me too far. Too many Deirans have died for me to turn away now. You know me. I am no craven to flee from a fight. You must pay for what you have done. If that is with your blood and that of your men, then so be it. God is on my side, and Deira will be victorious."

Oswiu seemed to enjoy the king of Deira's words and smiled broadly.

"And yet," he said, "Utta here has told us that the Lord is on the side of Bernicia and we will vanquish you." Oswiu looked up at the pale sky. Wisps of cloud scudded high above them. "The Christ looks down from heaven and sees that we both keep His faith. Who can say which of us is more deserving of triumph in His eyes?"

"I know not how to unravel that riddle," said Oswine with a shrug. "But I am sure that the Almighty can do so."

"Indeed," Oswiu said. "Praise the Lord." Oswiu made the sign of the cross over his chest. Men in both parties did the same. Beobrand brushed his fingers against the hammer amulet he wore. "What if I told you," continued Oswiu, leaning in close to his cousin, "that there was a way for us all to ride from this place with no bloodshed?"

"I would say I cannot see how that could be, without one of us fleeing, and that will not be me. For this is my kingdom and I am no coward king."

Oswiu, serious now, met Oswine's gaze.

"If we let it be known that we have both agreed to disband our warhosts, we can bring about peace."

"You truly want peace?" asked Oswine, his disbelief clear. "You have constantly harried my people on the northern marches and now, when your host outnumbers mine, you wish to send your warbands away. Do not take me for a fool."

Oswiu was sombre, his dark eyes downcast.

"I have prayed much on what manner of king I have become, cousin," he said. "What manner of man." He looked away wistfully into the distance. "And husband." He let out a sigh.

"It is true that I led my men here to put an end to this conflict between our kingdoms on the edge of a blade, but last night I had a dream that made me question everything."

"A dream?" asked Oswine, his tone incredulous.

Oswiu nodded.

"Yes. My most holy brother, and your cousin, Oswald, came to me while I slept."

A murmur ran through the men, both Bernicians and Deirans. Oswald had been a great king, lord of both Deira and Bernicia. His remains were revered by the Christ followers, and the earth that soaked up his blood at Maserfelth was used in healing potions and remedies. Beobrand clutched his Thunor's hammer at the talk of spirits talking from the afterlife. Frowning, he wondered why Oswiu had chosen now to mention this dream of his.

"Oswald appeared to you in a dream?" Oswine's voice was doubtful still, but tinged with a sense of awe. Perhaps Oswiu's holy brother could help from beyond the grave to solve this quarrel between the two kingdoms he had ruled in life.

"He did," Oswiu said, once again crossing himself. "And my brother spoke to me."

Oswine and most of the other men made the symbol of the holy rood over themselves.

"What did he say?" asked Oswine.

"He told me that, as followers of the Christ, we should not fight, rather turning to the Lord for guidance."

"But how? I am not sure how prayer can fix that which you have sought so hard to break."

Oswiu held up his hands.

"It is true that I have caused you and your people much harm. I do not deny it. But Deirans have shed Bernician blood in return."

Oswine opened his mouth to object, but Oswiu held up a hand.

"But you are right," he said. "Prayer alone will not solve this, and we will not so easily agree a path forward. No, we must rely on one who is even more holy and blessed by the Lord than my brother. Someone who can act as arbiter between us."

Beobrand could see that Oswine listened intently, pondering the idea, seeing a possible route away from this madness that had gripped Northumbria these last years.

"Who do you speak of?" Oswine scanned the faces of Oswiu's retinue. "Surely you do not mean Utta?"

"Of course not," replied Oswiu, with a laugh. "Sorry, Utta," he said, appearing to remember that Utta was amongst the men who had ridden to the parley. "You are, of course, a very holy soul, but we need somebody wholly beyond reproach. Someone who is admired as much in Deira as he is in Bernicia."

The small priest looked as though he had been punched in the stomach. His strained expression was enough to bring a smile to Beobrand's lips.

"If not Utta," said Oswine, "who would you have act as mediator between us and our kingdoms."

"Why, the father of the church in Northumbria, of course," said Oswiu. "Bishop Aidan."

Oswine rubbed his fingers over his chin.

"There is no man I admire more," he said at last. "Yes, I would trust Aidan to speak true and honestly for both our kingdoms, for there is no man more holy or closer to God."

A commotion interrupted the conversation between the kings as one of the Deiran lords pushed his way forward. It was Brunwine, the champion of Deira.

"My lord king," Brunwine shouted, his voice as loud as the roar of a waterfall. "You cannot truly be contemplating what Oswiu says." He glowered at Oswiu, his contempt clear. "The man is a snake! He should be crushed beneath your boot, not spoken to as an equal."

Brunwine was red in the face and spittle flecked his beard,

such was his fury. Beobrand thought he might mean to attack Oswiu, so he nudged Sceadugenga forward to block the man's path.

"Easy there, Brunwine," he said, keeping his voice low.

"Do not crowd me, Beobrand Half-hand," Brunwine spat. "I will tumble you from your saddle and beat some sense into that thick Cantware skull of yours, if you are not careful."

"I would like to see you try," said Beobrand, his hand grasping Nægling's grip. "You would find it hard without your hands."

Brunwine growled and made to draw his own blade.

"Enough!" Oswine's bellow silenced both men. "We ride under the branch of truce, Brunwine. There will be no fighting here."

The broad-shouldered thegn loured at his king.

"Oswiu is trying to trick you, lord," he said, keeping his anger in check with obvious difficulty.

"Silence!" snapped Oswine. "You forget yourself. Apologise to my cousin king."

Brunwine scowled. Beobrand and Sceadugenga still blocked his path to the king of Bernicia.

"I..." Brunwine said, but no more words came. Pulling his horse's head away, he turned the animal, and spurred it on, shoving Deirans out of his path. "Mark my words," he shouted over his shoulder. "This man no more wants peace than a serpent wants to suckle from a sow."

Kicking his heels to his horse's flanks, Brunwine galloped back across the barley towards the hill.

For a time, they all watched him riding away.

Beobrand moved his stallion back, so that he was beside Oswiu once more.

"I apologise for my man," said Oswine. "Tempers run hot. There has been much killing and it is not so easy to forget that."

"I understand," said Oswiu. "We need such hot-blooded men to stand before our enemies, but they are not always best-suited to diplomacy. And Brunwine is wrong. We have fought, but now is the time to be speaking of peace, not more war. I do not mean to trick you in this. You have my word."

Both kings stared at each other for a long time, weighing the other up like warriors before a duel.

"Do we have an agreement then?" asked Oswiu at last. "We shall disband our warhosts and leave the field of battle?"

"And when will we meet with Aidan, and where?"

"Such a meeting should take place on a holy day. So I say we should meet on the feast of Matthaeus the Apostle. What say you?"

"That is still several weeks hence." Oswine glanced at his closest ealdormen and advisors. They nodded in agreement. "And where would you have us meet?"

"Aidan is old and it seems wrong to make him travel far, so I say we should both journey to him and meet in his sanctuary on the innermost of the Farena Isles."

Wulfstan moved forward and whispered something to his king. Oswine nodded.

"Brunwine is hot-tempered, but he is no fool. How do I know I can trust you not to raise arms against me before we meet?"

"I have given you my word, is that not enough?" They stared into each other's eyes for a long while. Oswiu's face crumpled and he looked aggrieved. "I see it is not. Very well, I give you more. I swear on the saintly bones of my brother, Oswald, that I will disband my forces and ride north to Bernicia."

Oswine held Oswiu's gaze for several heartbeats. Eventually he nodded, seemingly satisfied with what he saw there.

"So be it then," he said, reaching out to clutch his cousin's arm in the warrior grip. "I also give you my word that I will disband the Deiran fyrd forthwith. We will meet at the innermost Farena Isle on Saint Matthaeus's day."

PART THREE

THE DARK PATH

Chapter 40

Oswiu's tent was crowded and stuffy as his closest thegns and ealdormen gathered to celebrate the outcome of the parley. The evening was warm, so the tent's entrance had been left open. Cynan knew all of the men in the tent, but he was not comfortable among them. These were the wealthiest men of the kingdom; many, like Beobrand, had fought their way to riches and land, and such men could be good company, with their boasting, riddles and drinking games. But even though Cynan was a warrior too, as able as any man with a sword and shield, and better than most, he did not belong there. He had been born to poor parents in the distant kingdom of Powys. Taken as a thrall when still just a child, Cynan had been beaten and abused by his Mercian masters. His past set him apart from the other men in Oswiu's tent. But above all, there was one difference that his skill and battle-prowess could never hope to wash away: he was Waelisc.

A stranger, despite having lived in Bernicia for close to fifteen years. A foreigner, in spite of wielding a sword to protect his lord and land.

He didn't want to be there, surrounded by the leaders of the fyrd, but Oswiu had insisted that Sigehelm and he attend, and Cynan knew enough about men of power to know he could not refuse a king. He would much prefer to have remained with the rest of Beobrand's Black Shields, sitting around their fire, laughing and recounting tales of their adventures. To those men, he was a shield-brother, a man who had bled with them in the shieldwall. With the men of Ubbanford, he could truly relax. Not here. Besides, he thought, taking a sip from the cup of mead he had been given by a freckled servant boy, Beobrand was here too and his lord's anger at him was all too evident.

They had barely spoken since Cynan's arrival, but whenever he looked up, Beobrand was scowling in his direction. Cynan had thought it best to avoid him, and now, deeming that enough mead and ale had flowed for the king not to notice if he slipped away, he stepped out of the cloying heat of the tent and into the darkness. A few others had done the same already and stood conversing in small groups on the trampled earth before the tent.

A great guffawing laugh came from inside. Cynan recognised the sound as emanating from Oswiu. The king had been in fine spirits ever since Oswine's agreement to his terms. Cynan was doubtful of the story Oswiu had told of the visitation from his brother's shade, but who could say it was not so? Nobody could disagree with the king and it was impossible to prove or disprove such a thing. Besides, all men had heard tales of spirits offering words of advice in dreams. Surely the brother of one so holy as Oswald could expect good counsel from his brother.

It mattered not whether the dream was truth or a clever way of twisting the devout Oswine's will. If the outcome was peace between the two kingdoms, nobody could complain. Peace would be good, thought Cynan. He could return to Stagga with his new warriors and put them to working the land, and training with the Black Shields. The thought of seeing Eadgyth again filled him with a warm expectation, tempered with anxiety at her reaction to him. Still, he had truly done nothing wrong. When he had left, his mind had been in turmoil. It was made up now.

"Going somewhere, Cynan?"

He halted at the sound of the familiar voice. Sighing, he turned to face Beobrand, who had been standing outside of the puddle of light that spilt from the candles and the rushlights within the tent.

"Lord," Cynan said.

"Don't call me that," snapped Beobrand. "If you thought of me as your lord, you would obey me."

"Can a man not disagree with his oath-sworn lord?" asked Cynan.

From within the tent, Oswiu laughed loudly once more. Beobrand tensed. Other voices joined the king, the laughter swelling.

"A man's lord cannot control what a man thinks, Cynan. But a man's actions speak of what he believes. If he does not follow the commands of his lord, what value has his oath?"

Sudden anger flared within Cynan at those words.

"Do not doubt my oath to you, Beobrand. Do not say such a thing. You know I am your man. I have stood by your side when facing death and uncertainty. I have killed for you," his voice cracked with emotion. "I would die for you. I have even turned away from love for you."

"You love her then?" asked Beobrand. "Is that why you left? For love?"

"Perhaps I thought so." Cynan shook his head. "I don't know. I could not turn away from her. She was terrified and needed my help."

Beobrand's face was in shadow, but Cynan could sense his anger.

"Reaghan was terrified too, I don't doubt," said Beobrand, his voice cold. "Before she died."

"Beobrand—" Cynan meant to ask for forgiveness for his actions. He was sorry for the hurt he had caused, but he knew that if he were confronted by the same situation again, he would act no differently. Before he could continue, another voice, strident and demanding, came like an echo from within the leather tent.

"Beobrand!" shouted the voice. "Where is Beobrand Half-hand?"

It was Oswiu.

With a sigh, Beobrand said, "We will finish this later." Then, without waiting for Cynan to reply, the tall lord of Ubbanford stepped back into the heat and raucous noise of the tent.

Cynan blew out a long breath. He would be happy to leave Beobrand to face the king and his cronies alone, to join the Black Shields, to spend the night with his brothers. But Beobrand was also his shield-brother. And more than that, whatever Beobrand might think, he was his lord. Cynan felt a stab of guilt at not having been by his side for so long. Draining his cup of mead, he followed Beobrand into the tent.

"Ah, there you are!" said Oswiu as he spied Beobrand in the doorway. "I thought you had slunk off, just as your Waelisc man did!" The king's words were slurred. In his hand he held a large drinking horn decorated with cunning silverwork at the tip and around the rim. The blood-red wine he favoured sloshed over his hand as he raised the horn to his lips and drank deeply. As he lowered the horn, his eyes met Cynan's and Oswiu let out a cry of joy. "Oh, your disappearing Waelisc man is here too. Splendid. Don't take your eye off him, or he might vanish again."

"I plan on keeping him close from now on," said Beobrand, with a dark look at Cynan. "Like an errant child."

"Very good," said Oswiu. He drank again and let out a huge belch. "Talking of children, you wanted to know where your son was."

"Yes, lord king."

"All in good time. First, let us all drink to my success. See that none of you has an empty cup." The king stood and waved his arm around to encompass all those gathered in the tent. The movement caused him to lose his balance, and he toppled back into his chair.

Ethelwin raised an eyebrow at Beobrand, and gave a lopsided grin.

"Perhaps you have celebrated your success enough already, my lord," he said.

"Nonsense, man!" said the king, pushing himself to his feet once again. "Fill everyone's cup," he yelled at the servant boy, who promptly hurried about the place, pouring mead into proffered cups and horns.

Cynan held out his cup when the boy bustled past. He needed the blurring that came with drink if he was to face more of Beobrand's wrath. He noted that Beobrand put his hand over his own cup when the boy tried to fill it.

"Come on then, Ethelwin," said Oswiu, nudging the burly warmaster with his elbow. "What are you waiting for?"

It took Ethelwin a moment to understand what the king meant, but after a few heartbeats of confusion, he raised his cup high.

"To the peace that King Oswiu has brokered."

"To peace!" cried a few of the men in response. Cynan drank. That was something worth celebrating.

"To peace?" said Oswiu. "We should be praising the peace-maker!"

"To the king," Ethelwin said dutifully, lifting his cup again to the gathered throng.

"Not me," laughed Oswiu. "To the peace-weaver with long hair. Just like her mother's."

Men murmured, unsure of Oswiu's meaning.

"Do not look so confused," the king said. "It is quite simple and has ever been thus. A pretty wench to warm the bed can avert many a war! I have to say I much prefer to swive my alliances than to fight for them."

Ethelwin fidgeted uncomfortably. Beobrand frowned.

"You speak of a woman, lord king," said Beobrand. "And yet no lady is here. Who is this peace-weaver?"

"Ah, Beobrand! It is well that you ask. It may have been my guile that turned this battle, but it was your son and mine who carried the message that convinced Peada to leave."

"What message, lord?"

"Why, an offer of marriage and power, of course. Such as he could not refuse." Oswiu grinned broadly. "You asked who is the peace-weaver I speak of. It is none other than my daughter, Alhflaed. She is of the line of the Idings of Bernicia and the great Urien of Rheged himself." Oswiu raised his horn to Sigehelm at the mention of that kingdom. "She is a beauty, like her mother, Rhieinmelth. She resides with her at Magilros, but she is of age and has spent long enough with nuns and monks. It is time I put her comely form to good use for the kingdom. Not that Peada would have refused, even if Alhflaed were as ugly as an ox's arse." He laughed and drank from his ornately decorated horn. "An alliance with me and a promise of power when Deira is mine once more, was offer enough. That Alhflaed is pleasing to the eye is the rich cream on the cup of milk. Peada will be doubly thankful when he sees her."

"You speak of Deira being yours once more, lord," said Beobrand. "I hope the peace between our kingdoms will hold, for it seems to me there has been too much killing between men who were once friends. But do you truly believe that Bishop Aidan will be able to negotiate such a peace that you might become king of Deira, as your brother once was?"

"A pox on Aidan!" shouted Oswiu, spilling his drink again. "It will be my cunning and the sharpness of Bernician blades that will bring peace, not God and certainly not that old Hibernian!"

He lowered himself into his chair and drank from the horn, eyeing Beobrand over the vessel's silver rim.

"Oswine will never come to the parley at the Farena Isles,"

he said, his words so quiet that Cynan was not sure he had heard them correctly. Some of the men in the tent had been speaking softly, but now, sensing a shift in the mood, they fell silent, edging closer to the king to better hear what he would say.

"What do you mean, lord?" asked Ethelwin, a frown furrowing his scarred brow.

Oswiu looked about him as if only now noticing the number of men who could overhear him. He grinned, showing his teeth. He was drunk, but he was not a man to be taken lightly. There was a deadly cunning behind his slurred words.

"It can do no harm to speak of it now, I suppose," Oswiu said, as if to himself. "The dice have already been thrown and when they stop rolling, there can be no changing the numbers that are up."

"What dice, lord?" asked Ethelwin. "What has been set in motion?"

Oswiu smiled smugly.

"Your sister's husband, Hunwald, has his hall near these parts." It was not a question.

"Yes, lord," said Ethelwin. "What of it?"

"It seems that Hunwald, like Peada, is a man who can sense the way the wind is blowing in Northumbria."

Ethelwin grew still.

"What has he done?"

"Done? Nothing really. He is leading Oswine to his hall at Ingetlingum so that the king can rest before he returns to Eoferwic. Better than sleeping in a tent or under the stars, eh?" He looked about him, perhaps expecting laughter. None came. The men all stared at the king, intent on the story he was recounting. "And if I say so myself, your sister does keep a table fit for a king," Oswiu went on, taking a sip of his wine. "But I fear that Oswine will find more than Frythegith's fine cooking when he arrives at Ingetlingum."

There was absolute silence within the tent now as all of the men held their breath so as not to miss a word.

"What will Oswine find there?" asked Beobrand.

Oswiu turned to stare at the lord of Ubbanford.

"He will find his end, Beobrand." He drank from the horn. When he grinned, his lips were stained purple from the wine. "I yet have some thegns who will do their king's bidding without question."

"You speak of murder," whispered Beobrand. "Who will do such a thing?" But from the hollowness of his tone, Cynan thought his lord had come to the same conclusion as he about who the king had sent to kill Oswine.

"It sometimes takes young men to carry out a king's wishes, it seems," said Oswiu. "Once I might have sent you, Beobrand. But it seems you are getting old now, soft and filled with the worries of a father." Oswiu held out his arms as if he might embrace Beobrand. "I understand," he said. "I too am older than I used to be, but I have a kingdom to think of, not just my kin. Octa is filled with ambition. And to those who stand before him in battle, he is as deadly as a plague. He is so like you when you were young."

"And he is as foolhardy!" shouted Beobrand, throwing down his cup in rage. "You would make a murderer of my son!"

Oswiu shrugged.

"Octa is a great warrior," he said. "He has already sent many men to the afterlife."

Beobrand took a step forward. His fists were clenched and Cynan feared he would leap at the king and strike him. Stepping close, Cynan placed a hand on Beobrand's shoulder. Beobrand shook it off without turning.

"To kill in battle brings a man reputation, glory and battle-fame," he said, the words cutting through the silence in the tent like a sharp sword through skin and sinew. "There is honour in facing a man in battle and vanquishing him. You know this! But a blade in the dark, stabbing in a hall an unarmoured man like a thief in the night…" Beobrand growled. Cynan could feel his ire rolling off him like the heat from a hearth. He prepared to haul Beobrand back should he decide to throw himself at Oswiu. But Beobrand did not attack. With a great effort, he held himself in check.

"There is no honour in such a thing," he said. "It is murder and a man who commits such an act will be known as a craven. A nithing! He will have to live with that stain on his name for the rest of his life."

"What have you done, lord?" said Ethelwin. The colour had drained from his face, making the jagged scar on his forehead stand out.

"I have used the men of my household to rid me of the troublesome king of Deira," said Oswiu. "The man should never have been named king by the Witena Ġemōt. The throne is mine by right."

"Perhaps that is so, lord," said Ethelwin, "but this is not the way. Have you not thought of Alhfrith?"

"The atheling is strong and he did not travel alone. He took Octa and some of his hearth-warriors with him. My son will succeed."

The warmaster sighed, shaking his head.

"I do not doubt the atheling will be able to fulfil your wish, Oswiu. But Beobrand is right. No man who performs such an act can hope not to be forever tainted by the treachery. Do you not want Alhfrith to reign when you are gone?" Ethelwin held the king in an icy stare. "Who will follow a man without honour?"

Oswiu looked aghast. With shaking hand, he emptied the horn of wine and wiped the back of his hand across his mouth.

"When is this to occur?" asked Ethelwin.

"Now. Tonight. They rode away at dusk."

The warmaster rubbed his gnarled hand over his face and turned to Beobrand.

"There may yet be time to stop this thing," he said. "If we ride like the wind."

"Then why are we yet here?"

Without waiting for a response, Beobrand spun on his heel and ran out into the night.

Cynan and Ethelwin sped after him. Behind them, as they were swallowed by the darkness, Cynan fancied he heard laughter from the tent.

Chapter 41

U nseen, a branch sliced out of the darkness, scratching and scraping its leaves and twigs across Beobrand's forehead and face. Instinctively he closed his eyes and ducked. He thought about calling over his shoulder to warn the others of the low bough, but before he could, he heard a muffled curse from behind. Too late for a warning. Each rider was alone in his own dark world. The darkness was so deep and their speed was such that each rider had to trust to his god or to wyrd that he would reach their destination safely. Beobrand would count them lucky if none of them was thrown from their horse. It was madness to gallop on such a night, but there was nothing else for it. They were riding to stop a madness and it was all Beobrand could do not to scream out his frustration and anger as they hurried through the gloom.

The path to Hunwald's hall was not short, but as they had mounted up, Cynan had given Beobrand a sliver of hope.

"Hunwald does not believe he will be followed," he said, swinging up into the saddle effortlessly. "They will not be riding fast. If luck is on our side, we will reach them on the road, or arrive in time to halt this."

Beobrand had been furious with Cynan, but now he felt his anger dying away, pushed aside by his greater fear that his son would become a murderer, or that he might be slain by Oswine and his comitatus.

What had Oswiu been thinking?

He had uttered the question to Ethelwin as they prepared to ride.

"The king has thought of nothing but defeating Oswine these past years," said the grizzled warmaster. "I fear his desire for victory has clouded his judgement."

"You did not know of this insanity?"

Ethelwin glared at Beobrand, his face red in the flame-glow from the nearest fire that the black-shielded warriors had been sitting around.

"I knew of the message to Peada," he said. "I may be the king's warmaster, but what I desire most is peace. I do not seek more blood when it could be spared. You know this, Beobrand. The offer of this alliance with the atheling of Mercia seemed like the best way to end this infernal war." He heaved himself up into his saddle with the help of Reodstan, who had joined the small group preparing to ride out. "But I knew nothing of this trap that Oswiu and Hunwald have planned. I would have spoken against it if I had. Not only is it cowardly and beneath the lord of Bernicia, but I fear Oswine's death may well bring about more fighting, more bloodshed."

They entered a length of Deira Stræt that was devoid of trees now, and for a time Beobrand could just make out the silver-licked stones of the road by the pale light of the sliver of moon.

Beobrand kicked Sceadugenga on to greater speed, praying silently to Woden that the stallion would not place a hoof into one of the numerous fissures or clefts in the road where countless winters had cracked the stones or washed them away completely. The wind was cool on his face, but there was no thrill and excitement from the sense of speed and freedom. He was not free. His stomach churned with worry and his head throbbed.

He wondered at Ethelwin's words. Were they right to doubt

the king's judgement? If the king of Deira was killed, Oswiu would surely have a much better chance of securing the kingdom and uniting Northumbria once more. It seemed to Beobrand that the only mistake Oswiu had made was allowing his son, the atheling, to be involved in the treachery. Much as he loathed to admit it, Oswiu should have sought to distance himself from any involvement in the plot. By sending Alhfrith, the king's reputation would suffer by association, just as much as the atheling's. Ultimately, men followed power, but honourable men wished to follow men of honour. And no man would look upon regicide by assassination as a virtuous act.

Sceadugenga's easy gallop had carried him close to Cynan, who led the party. Attor, as the second truly gifted horseman of the group, rode at the rear of the small column. Beobrand had ordered Attor to take up that position after they had realised that Cuthbert had ridden with them.

They had saddled their mounts and left the Bernician encampment in haste. Beobrand and Ethelwin agreed that they should take only a handful of their best men. This was not a mission for a warband. It was all about speed and then being able to deal with whatever confronted them when they arrived at Hunwald's hall or caught up with Oswine on the road. None of them had noticed young Cuthbert following them out onto the road and they had not realised he was with them until they had been riding for some time.

It was Attor who spied the boy. Noticing that there was a rider trailing them, the scout had fallen back to intercept whoever it was.

"We should send him back to Elmer and the rest of the Black Shields," Attor had said when he had discovered who followed them.

Beobrand had spat into the darkness. He had enough to occupy his mind without having to worry about the boy too.

"No," he shouted over the rumble of their horses' hooves.

"We are too far from Wilfaresdun now. I would not trust the lad to find his way back, and I cannot spare you to lead him. He has chosen his path, now he will have to follow it where it leads."

"As you wish," said Attor.

Beobrand did not wish for any of them to be there, especially not Cuthbert. But there was nothing for it now.

"Ride at the rear, Attor," he said. "And see that Cuthbert does not slow us down."

That had been some time ago and they had made good progress since then, despite the darkness. Now, Beobrand noticed Cynan slowing as he caught up to the Waelisc horseman.

"How far now?" he called to Cynan.

He saw the pale blur of Cynan's face turn towards him in the gloom.

"Soon we will reach the path to Hunwald's hall. I think then we will need to rein in the horses."

Beobrand pictured Octa stepping from the shadows of the hall and plunging a knife into Oswine's back. He had failed the boy at every turn. He should never have allowed Octa to be fostered in Oswiu's household. And yet, how could he have refused? He shook his head to clear it of such maudlin thoughts. None of that mattered. The past was gone, but he could yet do this thing for his son. He must avert the treachery that was brewing out there in the night.

He must, for Octa's sake.

"We cannot slow now," he said. "We are so close."

"Lord," said Cynan. "If we do not slow when we reach that path, we will not all reach the hall. That path will be as dark as a cave. Men will be thrown, or the horses will snap their legs. Besides, the animals are close to collapse, if we keep pushing them so hard, some won't make it and others will be useful for nothing more than meat."

Beobrand thought back to the last time he had ridden down that path. Oak grew thick along its length, overhanging the track like a tunnel. It was just earth, not covered in slabs of stone like the old Roman road they now rode on. Beobrand's head pounded with each jarring pace of his horse beneath him. He wanted nothing more than to reach Oswine before he was killed, avoiding what would be a disaster for Octa and Alhfrith. Every instinct screamed at him to urge Sceadugenga on, to gallop as fast as possible into the night. His son was out there and needed his help, whether he understood that or not. And yet, Beobrand knew Cynan was right. The man was the best rider in all his warband, and if he said the horses needed to slow down in order not to be winded or to pull up lame, Beobrand trusted him.

They rode on without speaking for some time, each man lost to his thoughts. None of them knew what awaited them when they reached Hunwald's hall. But Beobrand was sure they all sensed what he felt. They were heading towards a difficult fork in the road of their lives, just as much as they were approaching a shift in direction from the straight Roman road and onto the uneven, treacherous ground of the dark path towards Hunwald's hall.

Cynan slowed his horse and patted its neck. Beobrand reined in Sceadugenga beside him, marvelling at the Waelisc warrior's unerring sense of direction. To the left of the road yawned the dark mouth of the track that led to Ingetlingum. At the speed they had been travelling, Beobrand was sure he would never have spotted the path, even though he had been looking for it.

The other riders halted and congregated around the turning. There was no sign now of the stakes that had been placed beside the road here at Oswiu's order, or the grisly totems they had held. Beobrand had overseen skewering the corpses of the men who had been sent to kill him. It was here where Oswiu had declared war on his cousin, using the night-time attack as his excuse for going to war. Beobrand had told Oswiu of his error, that the assassins were sent by Vulmar, the Frankish lord, to kill him and not the king, but Oswiu refused to listen.

It was perhaps fitting, thought Beobrand, that Oswiu now sought to end the war as it began, and in the same place, with treachery in the dark and an assassin's blade at Ingetlingum. Though the truth of it was that this time, the orders actually came from a king of Northumbria. The gods must be enjoying the mayhem wrought at the hands of prideful and ambitious men.

"If you need to piss," Beobrand said, "now is the time. Once we go down that path, we will not halt until we reach the hall. After that, who knows what awaits us?" He slid from Sceadugenga's back, grunting as old wounds ached. He stepped into the weeds that grew beside the road, remembering the pallid, contorted faces of the corpses on their sharpened stakes. He shuddered at the memory, wondering whether the spirits of the dead haunted this place. Lifting up the hem of his byrnie, he loosened his breeches and pissed into the darkness, hearing the splatter of the liquid on the leaves and the mud.

Reodstan stood beside him.

"I wouldn't have drunk as much of Oswiu's wine if I had known we would be riding tonight."

Beobrand grunted.

"I hear you. My head feels as if Sceadugenga has stamped on it." He gave the stocky warrior a sidelong glance in the gloom. "Thank you for riding with me."

Reodstan, finished now, patted Beobrand gently on the shoulder as they returned to the horses.

"What are friends for?" he asked.

Beobrand said nothing as he climbed back into the saddle.

"You think we will arrive in time to stop them?" came Cuthbert's voice from the darkness.

"Who can say, Cuthbert?" said Grindan, before Beobrand could answer. "But now is not the time for chatter."

Beobrand nodded to himself in the dark. Grindan was a good man, as was Fraomar, who was the last member of their small band. Both gesithas were young, brave and quick-witted. He could have brought more men along, but they had needed to ride quickly and the more men that came, the slower they would have travelled.

"Grindan is right," Beobrand said. "We know not what we will find at the hall, but remember what it is we are about. We are to stop Oswine's murder." He did not say that they were to save his son from committing a terrible act. "Keep your eyes open, use your wits and listen to Ethelwin and me. If the gods smile on us, we might be able to prevent a tragedy before the sun rises." He tugged on his reins, pulling Sceadugenga's head around to face the seemingly impenetrable darkness of the tree-lined path. "Stay close and stay quiet. We will ride with caution from now on. Cynan, lead on."

Without a word, Cynan touched his heels to his horse's flanks and rode into the darkness. Beobrand followed and the thud of hooves, and creak and jangle of harness were suddenly loud, echoing from the trees.

Chapter 42

Beobrand grew increasingly frustrated at the pace Cynan set as they rode through the darkness beneath the oaks. He knew Cynan was right. They could not gallop along the dark corridor. Low branches brushed against them, snagging twig fingers in the riders' hair and cloaks. Every now and then one of the horses would stumble, the echoing sound of the regular gait interrupted as the beast placed a hoof in an unseen depression. But with each slow step forward, Beobrand's conviction that they would be too late built within him.

When muffled sounds of fighting reached them, he knew his worst fears had been proven true. His wyrd was ever thus. No matter how hard he tried, he failed to protect those he loved.

A roaring shout echoed somewhere in the night ahead of them. The ring of blade against blade, jagged and harsh, cut through the stillness.

"We are too late," yelled Beobrand, unable to hold back his anxiety any longer. "Ride, Cynan! Ride!"

Cynan did not need to be given the order a second time. They could all hear the sounds of fighting now. The Waelisc horseman discarded his own caution for the horses and kicked his mount into a run. Beobrand dug his heels into Sceadugenga's flanks and the stallion, tired after the night ride, but still brave and anxious to do his master's bidding, sprang forward. The black horse staggered, perhaps tripping on a root, and for a terrible moment Beobrand thought the animal would fall, throwing him into the darkness. There was no time to react. Beobrand clung on to his reins and hoped. Sceadugenga found his footing and picked up speed, lumbering into the gloom. Beobrand let out his breath with relief. The clatter of horses' hooves on the track drowned out the noises of combat for a time, as the band of riders sped through the darkness.

Moments later, they rushed out into the open and the relative light of the night. The eastern sky was tinged with grey. It was still summer and the nights were not long. Beobrand could make out the shadowed shape of the hall before them. The building's doors were open and a thin light tumbled out onto the clear earth before it. After the blackness of the path, the flickering from hearth and rushlights was bright, illuminating the area in front of the hall in a golden glow and stark shadows.

There were several horses there. And men. The sound of fighting came from inside the hall. The light that spilt from the doorway shifted and danced with the movement of those inside.

Beobrand did not slow Sceadugenga until the last moment. Cynan and he both pulled back on their reins at the same instant, causing their mounts to dig in their hooves and slide to a halt. Beobrand did not wait for the stallion to fully stop. Slipping from the saddle, he hit the ground at a run. Frightened faces of the men congregated around the hall's entrance turned to him. He saw no steel or iron in the pale flame light. No gold or silver from warrior rings or adorned weapons. These men were bondsmen and servants. The sounds of battle from within intensified. Through the open doors, Beobrand could see shapes and shadows as men fought.

"Out of my way," he roared, rushing towards the entrance.

Behind him, the rest of his men were reining in and leaping from their horses.

Dragging Nægling from its scabbard, Beobrand pushed past a couple of milling horses. Shrugging his shield from where it was strapped to his back, he scooped it up by its boss handle, not bothering to wriggle his forearm into the straps he normally used to keep it secure. There was no time and he could feel the pressure of that lack of time growing within him.

"Out of my way!" he yelled again. A short man, holding a horse's reins, stared at him stupidly, but did not move. He was between Beobrand and the door to the hall. Beobrand did not slow down. With a vicious punch of the shield boss, he felled the servant. The man crumpled, letting the reins slip from his grasp as he collapsed. Beobrand slapped the flat of his sword against the horse's rump, sending it leaping away with a whinny of fear.

Behind him he heard the confusion of the rest of the Bernician warriors dismounting and beginning to force their way through the crowd of horses and servants that clogged the doorway. Beobrand did not pause. This was not the time for a shieldwall. For all he knew, the king already lay dead within, or perhaps Octa might be lying in a pool of his lifeblood, staring up at the soot-shrouded beams of the thatched roof. No, now was not the time for hesitation.

With Cynan beside him, Beobrand stepped into the hall.

Inside, all was chaos. Boards and benches had been overturned. Men fought in small groups. There was movement everywhere, and Beobrand was forced to slow his advance to take stock of who the fighting men were, rather than leaping into the fray swinging his sword.

A few paces from where he stood lay a corpse. Blood still pumped slowly from a huge gash in the man's throat. It was a tall, broad-shouldered man with fair hair. The byrnie he wore was polished and gleamed by the light from the fire. The blood that puddled around his inert form was slick, shining in the light of the flames. For a time, Beobrand could not pull his gaze from the dead man. The blood was staining the corpse's long mane of hair. Hair that was so like Beobrand's own. The dead man's face was turned away from him, not looking up at the roof as he had imagined, and yet there could be no doubt. It was Octa.

Beobrand staggered. He could not breathe. His son. His beautiful son was dead.

"Look there, lord," shouted Cynan. "It is Octa."

Beobrand did not need Cynan to tell him that his son lay on the floor of the hall, his lifeblood soaking into the rushes. But something in the Waelisc man's tone made him look. Following Cynan's pointing sword, Beobrand gasped.

Octa was standing tall, his sword flicking this way and that, parrying, lunging, thrusting. Alive!

Beobrand glanced back at the corpse and the relief he felt made him giddy. How had he thought that body was his son? There was little resemblance now. For once, the gods smiled on him. Beobrand had arrived in time to save Octa from this madness.

He quickly scanned the rest of the hall. There were other bodies lying in the rushes, but none that he recognised. Searching for Oswine, he finally spotted the tall king of Deira at the far end of the hall. There he was, standing back-to-back with Wulfstan. A man that Beobrand recognised as Hunwald was sprawled at the Deiran thegn's feet. The king and the thegn were battling against two warriors. They were fighting valiantly, but were unarmoured and did not bear shields. They would not be able to hold out for long.

"Put up your weapons!" bellowed Beobrand in his battle-voice. His words carried about the hall, over the clamour and crash of the fighting, but none of the men faltered in their fighting. "Stop this!" Beobrand yelled. Again, there was no reaction from any of the men in the hall.

Without warning, a huge warrior near them spun to face Beobrand and Cynan. He had dealt a mortal blow to the man he had been fighting, and even before his opponent had fallen to the floor, he had rounded on them. His face was blood-spattered, his thick beard glistening with gore.

It was Brunwine the Blessed, champion of Deira.

"I should have known you would be at the heart of this treachery, Half-hand," he screamed, advancing on them. "You will pay for this with your life."

"I have no part in this," said Beobrand, but he could see that Brunwine was beyond listening to reason. With a growl, the champion surged forward. Cynan stepped to meet him, taking the sting from Brunwine's attack on his black shield.

Behind him, Beobrand sensed movement. With a glance, he saw that Ethelwin, Reodstan and the others were crowding the doorway. They came with blades drawn, faces grim. They would bring yet more chaos to this battle-rent hall, but Beobrand could see no way to avert further bloodshed now. His only hope would be to protect his son and prevent the king of Deira from being killed.

Cynan, strong and fast, pushed Brunwine back, making space before the doors.

Across the hall, Beobrand looked over to where Oswine and Wulfstan were still battling against their assailants. They were holding their own, but they would not be able to resist the onslaught from their more heavily armoured foes for long.

Beobrand was momentarily torn as to the best course of action, but then the decision was taken for him as he saw Octa, fair hair bright in the gloomy hall, trip and fall back. The atheling, Alhfrith, was near, but could not free himself from his own burly opponent to help Octa, who tumbled to the rush-strewn floor. The Deiran warrior he faced sprang forward to loom over him.

"Protect Oswine!" Beobrand screamed at his men, and ran forward to his son's aid. He had not come all this way just to watch Octa be slain before his eyes. Beobrand hoped Ethelwin would be able to lead his gesithas to the defence of the king of Deira, but he saw nothing else now apart from the man standing over his son with a gleaming raised sword that caught the light from the flames of hearth and candle.

Chapter 43

Cynan regretted stepping in to meet Brunwine the instant he lifted his shield to intercept the champion's scything blow. The man's sword clattered against the black hide and Cynan felt the enormous strength behind the swing. Cynan quickly stepped forward, to allow the others to enter the already crowded hall. Another hacking blow came, even faster and harder than the first, and Cynan again took it on his shield.

Beobrand shouted something about protecting Oswine. At the edge of his vision, Cynan saw his hlaford dash into the hall, but he could not look to see where he was heading. It was all he could do to stay on his feet and to avoid being gutted by the hugely muscled man before him.

Cynan had faced strong men before, and he had fought against fast men. Few warriors were both. Cynan was stronger than most men, and as fast as the best of them. He had expected Brunwine to be slow. The man was old. He must be closer to fifty than forty, with silver in his beard and hair. And yet he was not only as strong as an ox, he was as fast as a viper. Worse still, he had the cunning and battle-skill that came from decades of fighting.

Cynan did not think he had ever faced a better opponent. Beobrand was as fast, and even had a longer reach, but the sword blows that rained down on Cynan's linden board from Brunwine were as heavy as boulders striking a cliff. The man's strength was as prodigious as his sword-skill, and his great booming voice.

"You think you can stand against me, Waelisc cur?" Brunwine roared, his voice as loud as thunder.

"I do not want to fight you," shouted Cynan, parrying another attack on the rim of his shield and skipping backwards out of range.

Brunwine pressed forward, grinning a maniacal grin.

"Too late for that now!" he shouted, aiming a kick at Cynan's knee that, if it had landed, would have crippled him.

"Hold, man," shouted Cynan. "We are not enemies."

Brunwine spat.

"You seek to murder my king and yet you say you are not my enemy!"

The Deiran champion feinted at Cynan's head. Cynan raised his shield, and with uncanny speed and agility for one so large, Brunwine flicked his sword's blade beneath the shield's rim, opening a cut on Cynan's thigh. Only Cynan's own impressive reflexes prevented Brunwine's blade from opening the artery there. Cynan had seen many men die from such a wound, the blood gushing in spouts. He was lucky he was fast and Brunwine's sword had not sliced more deeply. Even so, hot blood pumped from the wound, soaking Cynan's breeches in moments.

Cynan took a quick step back. The rest of the room was mayhem. Shouts, the clash of blades, curses and screams, all echoed in the flame-licked darkness. But Cynan could not spare a moment to look at how the other fights went, or indeed who was fighting. He was battling for his very life.

Catching another blow on his shield, Cynan twisted the board, allowing the blade to skitter away from him. It was time to attack now. There would be no reasoning with Brunwine, it seemed. Hoping he had not left it too late, Cynan lunged with his sword.

With a bark of laughter, Brunwine sidestepped and parried, then, quick as a cat, sliced a backhand blow towards Cynan's face. Cynan stepped away, allowing the blade to sing through the air a finger's breadth away from his eyes.

Cynan again turned Brunwine's sword away with his shield, and attempted a feint at the champion's midriff, but the man was wise to it, and didn't take the bait. Instead, he stepped quickly back out of reach. Now was the time to press home the attack and Cynan rushed him, leading with his shield and probing with the tip of his blade.

Brunwine held his ground, swaying out of reach of the shield and parrying the sword on his own blade. But he was not the only warrior with guile and speed. Cynan turned his wrist, cutting across and down into the huge warrior's left forearm.

Brunwine grunted and shoved hard against Cynan's shield, pushing him off balance.

"So the Waelisc pup has teeth," Brunwine gnarred, and charged forward.

Cynan had no time to brace himself for the sudden rushing attack and Brunwine's bulk drove him backwards. An eye-blink later Cynan felt his shoulders crash into the hall's daubed wall. Dry daub and soot dusted down on the two men as the timbers of the wall shook under the impact of the heavy warriors.

The wind was driven from Cynan's lungs and he struggled for breath. The advantages he had over Brunwine were his height and his shield. By crushing him against the wall, those advantages had been removed and Cynan felt real terror welling up within him. Brunwine was so close he could smell the man's breath and sweat. Cynan tried to swing his sword over his shield, but Brunwine lashed out with his left hand and grasped Cynan's wrist, pinning it against the wall.

Breathless, and full of sudden fear that he might never see Eadgyth again, Cynan heaved and fought desperately against Brunwine's brawn. But the champion was heavier and stronger, and no matter how he tried, Cynan could not free himself from between his shield and the wall.

"Now you die!" snarled Brunwine, battle lust burning in his dark eyes.

Cynan stared into those eyes and saw nothing but death.

Chapter 44

Cuthbert blinked at the brightness of the light within the hall after the soot-dark night outside. The noise of fighting was deafening. He stumbled to a halt just within the threshold, trying to make sense of what he saw. The metal tang of blood was in the air, hard and sharp, intermingled with smoke, sour ale, sweat and the stink of bowels that had been spilt into the rushes as men died. A dead man lay close by in an expanding pool of blood. Bile stung the back of Cuthbert's throat.

He offered up a silent prayer. Why had he come here? He should never have followed Beobrand and the others into the night when they had mounted up and ridden from Wilfaresdun. But he was so intent on being a worthy warrior and he had so wanted to be in a great battle. The whispered commands and the urgency he had seen on Beobrand's face and the other grim men who had picked up weapons and shields, quickly preparing to ride, had spoken of an adventure such as would be sung of in halls throughout the land. He was not certain what was afoot, but he heard whispers mentioning Oswine, King of Deira. Cuthbert could not bear the thought of missing such an important mission. And so he had saddled his horse and followed them. He had not spoken, knowing that Beobrand would never have let him ride with such experienced men as Ethelwin, Reodstan and Cynan.

But if there was to be fighting and excitement, Cuthbert did not wish to be left behind.

By the time Attor had spotted him at the rear of the column, it had been too late to send him back. Cuthbert had been pleased with himself as they had continued to ride through the darkness. But now, as the cacophony and stench rolled over him, he wished he had never sought to follow the warriors. He was strong, quick and able in combat, but this was not the glory he looked for. In his hand he held the sword that had belonged to the man he had fought in East Angeln. He had been proud of the weapon he had taken from his first battle. Now, the blade felt heavy and unwieldy in his grip.

"Make room," said Fraomar, pushing Cuthbert further into the hall and snapping him out of his momentary shock at being faced with such chaos.

Beside them, Cynan jumped into the path of a huge, bearded warrior that Cuthbert recognised as Brunwine the Blessed. The massive champion hammered blows down on Cynan's linden board and the two combatants moved away.

"Protect Oswine," shouted Beobrand and rushed into the hall.

Where was the king? And where was Beobrand going? For a time, Cuthbert could not make out who any of the men fighting were. Then he understood Beobrand's hurry and saw where he was heading. The atheling fought a warrior at the far end of the hall and near them, another man stood over a prostrate warrior. The warrior on the ground had long fair hair.

Octa! The man on the floor was Beobrand's son.

"Out of the way, boy," shouted Reodstan, giving Cuthbert a shove.

Cuthbert staggered forward. What should he do? In all the confusion, he could not decide. As he watched, Beobrand leapt at the warrior looming above Octa. Surely Cuthbert's place should be at his lord's side. He had chosen to follow these men of battle here, now he would have to stare death in the face and confront the fear that gripped him. Taking a deep breath, he raised his sword and ran after Beobrand.

Behind him, he heard Ethelwin screaming orders for the men to follow him. Cuthbert ignored the warmaster. Beobrand had told them all to use their heads and Beobrand was alone, with nobody to guard his back in a hall that was filled with foes.

Before Cuthbert could reach him, Beobrand hacked his sword down onto the skull of Octa's attacker. Bone splintered, and blood and brains sprayed the air. Something warm splattered Cuthbert's cheek. He flinched.

Beobrand was screaming.

"Death! Death!"

Cuthbert, unsure again, hesitated. In that instant, Alhfrith, still exchanging blows with his assailant, parried an attack and stepped into Cuthbert's path. Cuthbert jumped to the side, to avoid the atheling and the stabbing sword of the Deiran he faced. Stumbling backwards, a bright light, sudden and blinding, filled his vision. A heartbeat later a searing pain followed. The two men continued fighting, moving away from him, oblivious of Cuthbert's presence.

Cuthbert shook his head in an effort to clear his vision. His face was wet and he cuffed at his eyes with the back of his sword arm. His forearm came away slick with blood. Through the haze of blood, Cuthbert could just make out Beobrand locking in combat with another warrior.

He was confused; unsure what had happened. Why could he not see clearly? His ears rang and his head began to throb with each rapid beat of his heart. Slowly, his senses began to return to normal. His mind was less dazed. Wiping again at his face, he smeared more blood from his eyes.

The blood streamed from a gash to his forehead. He must have taken a sword blow from either the atheling or his opponent while the two fought near him. He doubted the blade had been meant for him, the wielder was probably not even aware of what had occurred. He shook his head again, blinking the blood out of his eyes. It did not feel like a mortal wound, but it had stunned him for a time and where the sounds of the hall had been muffled and distant, now they rushed back like a torrent.

Quickly, Cuthbert looked about him. Where was Beobrand? He had come to help his lord and all he had managed so far was to get injured. There was a man standing near where Beobrand had been, and for the briefest of instants, Cuthbert thought it was the thegn of Ubbanford. But no, this warrior was shorter, with a dark beard. It was not Beobrand, but Wulfstan, lord of Ediscum. At his feet, lying on his back, defenceless, was Beobrand. His lips were moving, but Cuthbert could not make out the words. Wulfstan replied, but again, the sound was lost in the tumult of the fighting and the ringing in his ears. Cuthbert knew the two men had been friends once, but now the Deiran thegn stood menacingly over his lord. Wulfstan raised his sword high above him and Cuthbert fancied he heard Beobrand shouting, "No!"

Was this how Beobrand, the famed leader of the Black Shields, would die? Not in some battle clash of shieldwalls, but in a confused brawl in a hall cluttered with overturned benches, noisome with the stink of long-forgotten feasts and recent death. Cuthbert expected Beobrand to spring up, to slay the man who stood over him. But Beobrand did not move. Instead, he shook his head.

On seeing this, Cuthbert felt a surge of emotion so hot it burnt away the pain in his forehead. He was Beobrand's oath-sworn man. He had vowed to protect his lord even with his own life. And what was he doing? Watching as a Deiran slew his hlaford, the man who had trained him and treated him like a son.

No.

Cuthbert could not allow such a thing. He was suddenly certain that this had been why he had followed the riders here. Coenred might say he had listened to the voice of God in the night. This was the moment that would define him; the moment he would save his lord's life, fulfilling his oath and his duty, even if that meant laying down his own life.

With an animal roar so loud that it ripped his throat, Cuthbert sprang forward.

Wulfstan, perhaps hearing Cuthbert's battle-cry, or seeing the movement, hesitated, turning towards his approach. His eyes widened and he tried to bring his sword round to ward off this new attack. But he had been so intent on the Bernician prey at his feet that Wulfstan was too slow to defend himself against the young warrior who rushed to his lord's defence.

With all of his strength behind it, Cuthbert swung the sword that had belonged to a Mercian and cut deeply into Wulfstan's neck. Such was the force of the blow that it carried on down into the thegn's chest, smashing collar bone and ribs, and lodging in the sternum. Wulfstan stared at Cuthbert, his eyes wide. Looking down at the steel protruding from his body, he shuddered.

"You have killed me," he whispered, then fell back. The sword, held firm in Wulfstan's bones and sinews, was tugged from Cuthbert's grasp.

Unmoving, Cuthbert looked down at the dying man.

"What have you done?" screamed Beobrand, clambering over to kneel beside Wulfstan. The Deiran gave a final jerking tremor and was still. Beobrand looked up at Cuthbert. "What have you done?" he repeated.

A sudden movement caught Cuthbert's attention. A figure, having seen Wulfstan fall, rushed forward, leaping over tumbled chairs and tables to avenge the Deiran thegn. In his hand, the man held a bloody sword. Cuthbert looked into the warrior's face and saw his death there. The blade rose and Cuthbert found that he could not move. He had forgotten all that Beobrand and the other Black Shields had taught him. He merely stood, awaiting his death as meekly as a lamb awaits the butcher's knife. He had protected his lord, and now it was his time to pay with his life. Perhaps, he thought, when he reached heaven, he might see the angel who had once saved him.

Cuthbert was ready for death.

But death did not arrive.

Beobrand sprang up from where he was crouched beside Wulfstan and plunged his long blade into Cuthbert's attacker. Nægling pierced the man's side and burst from his chest. The sword fell harmlessly from the man's hand and he crashed into Cuthbert, carried on by his momentum. He was a large man and Cuthbert tumbled over backwards, unable to hold him. As they fell, Cuthbert stared into his attacker's eyes, seeing the light of life dimming. They hit the floor hard and lay there, like lovers in an embrace. The attacker atop him, his face kissing-close, blinked and tried to speak through the choking blood that bubbled in his throat. Through his daze, Cuthbert felt an acute stab of horror, as he recognised the handsome features of the man who even now was dying on top of him.

It was Oswine, son of Osric, lord king of Deira.

Oswine's wise eyes held Cuthbert's gaze. He blinked slowly, as if it took a great effort, and then, with a gurgling sigh, he was still.

With a moan, Cuthbert pushed the king's body off and scrambled away on his heels. He bumped against one of the carved timber pillars of the hall and there halted. Appalled, he gazed at Oswine's face. The king's head had flopped to the side and the staring eyes seemed to follow him, seeing into Cuthbert's very soul. Behind Oswine's corpse lay Wulfstan's body, Cuthbert's sword still jutting from his chest. The blade was surprisingly clean of blood and the iron glimmered in the light of the flames from the hearth.

Cuthbert's head was pounding, and blood trickled into his eyes, stinging them. He blinked the blood away, but seemed to have lost all his strength. Beobrand loomed over him, shouting something, but Cuthbert could not understand the words. After a time, his lord moved away and Cuthbert became dimly aware of continued fighting going on in the hall around him.

He knew not now how the fighting went. The sounds of combat were muted and fuzzy, as if Cuthbert was under water. His mind felt blurred and confused. It was all he could do to keep himself awake as the battle in the hall raged and echoed distantly about him like a far-off storm.

He dragged his gaze away from the shining sword in Wulfstan's chest and once more found himself staring into the king's dead eyes. Cuthbert hoped the storm would pass soon.

Chapter 45

Beobrand righted a stool that had been lying near the hearth. With a sigh, he slumped down onto it and looked about the hall. He had overseen the collection of the bodies of the fallen, and now waves of exhaustion rolled over him. He had barked orders to wrap the corpses in sheets, giving the servants and thralls little time to think. Some of the men who had been with the horses outside had fled into the night. They would raise the alarm soon and there would be little time for rest. Those who remained had been put to work.

The shrouded bodies of the dead had been lain along the western wall. There were sixteen corpses in all, and the hall stank of death. The womenfolk of Ingetlingum, and those servants and thralls who had not run off, were doing their best to return the hall to normality. The benches and boards had been set up once more, logs had been added to the embers, the most soiled rushes had been gathered up and taken outside. Through the open doors of the hall, Beobrand could see that the sun had risen, and the sound of birds singing gilded the golden warmth of the summer dawn.

Beobrand watched as Frythegith, the lady of the hall, bustled past. Her expression was sombre, but she shed no tears. Perhaps she would cry when she was alone, he thought. For now, the hall was thronged with men and her husband, Hunwald, lay dead beside the king he had betrayed.

Shortly after the last of the Deirans had been killed, Ethelwin had found his sister cowering with the other women and servants behind the partition at the rear of the hall. He had called her out. His face had been dark and he shook with fury.

"See what your husband has done," he said, sweeping his hand to encompass the jumble of dead strewn about the hall.

Frythegith did not reply. She could not meet her brother's gaze.

"Take a good look," he said, "for this will no longer be your home."

She had looked at his red scarred face then. She opened her mouth, perhaps to speak out against Ethelwin's words, but his glare silenced her.

"Deira is no longer safe for you, and your husband is dead," he said viciously. "Now, collect what you wish to take with you, and find us some food."

"Can we take the waggon?" she asked, her voice small and pitiful as she saw her life and all she had worked for destroyed in a single night of treachery and violence.

"No," snapped Ethelwin. "There will be no time for that. Take only what you can carry. We will ride soon and you will not return."

The woman had looked as though she might collapse under the weight of her brother's words, but she straightened her shoulders and shuffled off. Shortly afterwards, Beobrand heard the lady of the hall giving commands, and he had no doubt that they would soon be offered a meal to break their fast. The gods knew the men needed sustenance. They had ridden hard and then fought. But no matter the semblance of the familiar running of a household around them, Beobrand wondered how many of the men gathered in Hunwald's hall would have any appetite.

Glancing over at the linen-and-wool-wrapped corpses,

Beobrand grimaced. Good men lay there. Men he had called friends. And what had they died for? Greed and power. Oswiu's ambition and young men's pride.

Beobrand clenched his hands in his lap. They shook, just as they always did after battle. It had been some time since the fighting and yet they still trembled. He wondered if they would ever stop. He had killed many men, but he had never slain a king before. He rubbed his hands over his face. His head throbbed and he longed for sleep, but he knew Ethelwin was right; there would be no time to rest that morning.

Pushing himself to his feet with a groan, Beobrand walked over to where young Cuthbert sat. The boy had not moved since the fight. He seemed more asleep than awake, his eyes unfocused and glazed.

Beobrand rubbed at the pain in his back from where he had fallen onto one of the toppled benches. By Woden, he thought, if he felt keenly the weight of the events in the hall that night, he could barely imagine the impact on the sensitive young gesith. He had been furious with the lad at first. Cuthbert should never have ridden after them. If he had not been there, perhaps Oswine and Wulfstan might yet live. Maybe the others who had died would not have fought on.

But such thoughts were meaningless. The past could not be altered. It was Cuthbert's wyrd to be here, and wyrd was inexorable. Beobrand smiled grimly. Wondering at the gods and the way they played with men. To allow them to arrive in time to see Oswine alive, to believe the plot against him might be thwarted, and then, not only to have the king be killed, but at the very hands of those who sought to save him. Woden must surely have enjoyed the acute torture of such a thing. Blood and anguish were most exquisite sacrifices.

"How is your head?" Beobrand asked.

Cuthbert's brow was covered in a strip of cloth that Fraomar had bound about his head. Fraomar said it did not seem to be a serious injury, unless it became elf-shot. Cuthbert had barely acknowledged the gesith as he had attended to his wound, but Fraomar was quiet and understanding of the young man's shock. He did not voice the concern that both Beobrand and he had, that the blow might have caused more damage than could be seen. Beobrand remembered all too well the days that Fraomar had lain on the verge of death, his own head bandaged.

"Cuthbert?" prompted Beobrand, his anxiety adding a sharpness to his tone. The boy's eyes were open. Surely he would not succumb to this injury, losing his senses, as Fraomar had.

Cuthbert had been staring at a dark stain on the rough-hewn boards of the floor. The servants had not brought fresh rushes yet, and Wulfstan and Oswine's intermingled blood was still vividly visible. Beobrand noticed that Cuthbert's sword lay at his feet, unsheathed and still smeared with drying blood.

Beobrand stooped, picking up the blade. Taking the cloth he had used to free Nægling of gore, he wiped Cuthbert's sword clean.

"You should not leave a blade dirty," he said, hoping for a response. "The metal-rot will set in, weakening it."

He inspected his handiwork and offered the weapon hilt-first to Cuthbert. The young man looked up at him, his eyes dark-rimmed and reddened from crying. He made no effort to take the sword.

Sighing, Beobrand placed it on the table nearest to Cuthbert.

"I killed your friend," replied Cuthbert, his tone desolate. But at the sound, Beobrand smiled, feeling a surge of relief to hear the boy talking.

"You did what you thought right," he said in a soft voice. "No man can be asked to do more."

"I should be dead," said Cuthbert, "not Wulfstan."

Beobrand winced. He remembered Wulfstan's last words to him. Beobrand had been attempting to pull Octa to his feet, but his son, like Cuthbert, had taken a blow to the skull and was stunned. Battle raged all around him in the hall, and Beobrand knew better than to take his attention from a fight. He had often scolded his gesithas about allowing themselves to be distracted. And yet Octa was his son, and the memory of the terror he had felt when he'd believed him dead was still fresh in Beobrand's mind. Wulfstan, having defeated the member of Alhfrith's comitatus he had been fighting, could have stepped up behind Beobrand and slain him in that moment of carelessness. Instead, the Deiran thegn had chosen to trip Beobrand, pushing him to the ground, where he would be at a disadvantage. Beobrand had clattered into an oak bench, bruising his ribs and back. Rolling over in order to see his assailant, and bring his shield and sword to bear, Beobrand had been glad to see Wulfstan's face. The man was pragmatic and clever.

"We have come to halt this!" Beobrand had shouted, looking up at the lord of Ediscum.

That was when Wulfstan had uttered the last words he would ever say to Beobrand on this side of the afterlife.

"Can you stop this madness?" he'd asked, his voice barely carrying over the sounds of battle.

"No," Beobrand had replied. "But you can, if you can get your men to lay down their weapons." They had stared into each other's eyes for a few heartbeats, each weighing up the other's motives. Finally, Wulfstan had nodded, raising his sword. Beobrand thought perhaps he had meant to hold his weapon aloft in a signal to his men, as he addressed them. But he would never know Wulfstan's purpose.

For that was the moment when Cuthbert, believing him about to strike Beobrand a killing blow, had rushed at Wulfstan, halting his movement and silencing whatever he had been about to say.

The following moments had been a blur. Beobrand had rushed to Wulfstan's side, but he knew instantly that the blow was mortal. Then, in a flash of motion, another warrior had come rushing forward, sword upraised. Cuthbert had stood there, unable to react.

Beobrand asked himself if he had known Cuthbert's attacker was the king? He could not truly be certain. It had all happened so quickly. He was almost sure he had reacted instinctively, without thought, but a small voice whispered that perhaps he'd had time to recognise Oswine before slaying him. And yet did it matter? If he had known the identity of the man coming to kill Cuthbert, would he have stayed his hand.

He looked down now at the lad, his face pallid beneath the blood spatter that was streaked with tears. There was nothing to be gained from thinking of what might have been. One of his gesithas had been in danger and it was his duty, as Cuthbert's lord, to protect him. King or no king, Beobrand believed he would do the same again, if the situation was repeated.

He crouched down beside Cuthbert so that he could look him in the eye.

"You fulfilled your oath," he said. "As I fulfilled mine to you. There is little time to think in a battle. A warrior must live with his decisions, for good or for ill." He thought of his nightmares, at the screaming faces of those he had killed that came to him in the darkest reaches of the night. "To do otherwise is folly." Beobrand patted the boy on the shoulder. He noticed that his hands had stopped shaking.

"I am sorry," Cuthbert said, tears brimming again in his eyes.

"What is done is done. It cannot be changed. But I know your heart is true." He gave the boy's shoulder a squeeze and raised himself to his full height in an attempt to stretch the aches out of his back.

Glancing over to the hearth, where flames now licked at the fresh logs that had been placed there, he saw Octa glowering at him. His son was sitting beside Alhfrith, with a couple of the atheling's closest hearth-warriors nearby. Three of the sixteen corpses that lay to one side of the hall belonged to members of Alhfrith's comitatus.

Octa did not take his eyes from Beobrand. They had not spoken since the fight. First, Octa had been groggy from where he had been struck on the temple, and then Beobrand had needed to attend to the dead and his gesithas. As he had moved about the hall, he had felt Octa's gaze, resentful and angry, upon him.

They would need to leave soon and they might face further danger on the road. That would be no time for the confrontation he knew was coming. He could put it off no longer.

Stepping past the hearth, Beobrand positioned himself with his back to the fire, allowing the heat to soak through his kirtle. Like most of the men, he had removed his byrnie after the fight, glad to be free of the bulk of it, even if just for a while. When they rode north, they would need to be armoured. They would not be safe until they were back on Bernician land. Rubbing his half-hand into the small of his back, he acknowledged Alhfrith with a nod.

"How's the head?" he asked Octa.

"It aches," his son replied. His voice was deep and gruff, but Beobrand could not help smiling as he heard in the words the childlike petulance of the boy Octa had been until what seemed to him very recently. Where had the years gone?

"I am glad you find it amusing," Octa said. "I see you did not laugh at Cuthbert's wound."

Beobrand shook his head.

"You are stronger than Cuthbert, son." Beobrand did not mention that Cuthbert's wound had smothered him in blood, whereas Octa merely had a lump on his forehead from banging it into a table. "You are already a seasoned warrior. I meant no offence to you. I was just thinking that it seems like yesterday that you were but a boy."

"Well, I am a boy no longer."

"Clearly," Beobrand said, suddenly angered by Octa's tone. Cuthbert was distraught at what had occurred, but it was Octa and Alhfrith who were to blame. Beobrand looked about the hall, taking in the carnage. "A boy's mistakes do not have such dire consequences."

"You think this a mistake? If so, I am confused." Octa reached for a cup of mead he had got from somewhere. He drained it, slamming it back onto the board. "Why would the mighty Beobrand come here and snatch away his son's chance at glory? Perhaps you feel the mistake was that you did not think to come here sooner. Or that the king did not trust you with such a mission."

Beobrand felt the beast of his anger swelling inside him. He took a firm hold of its leash, forcing himself to remain calm. Now was not the time to quarrel, but he would not remain silent.

"The mistake was seeking to kill Oswine," he said, his tone flat.

"And yet who was it who slew the king of Deira?" spat Octa. "Was it a mistake that you stabbed Nægling through Oswine's flesh?"

Beobrand winced. He did not wish to fight with Octa, but surely his son must see what a fool he had been.

"I wish that Oswine yet lived. But I am glad that neither of you," he took in Alhfrith with his gaze, "held the sword that killed him."

"Oh no," said Octa, "that hand had to belong to the famous half-handed thegn of Ubbanford."

Beobrand shook his head, appalled at Octa's words. Did he truly think so poorly of his father?

"I did not wish to see my son made a murderer," he said. "A killer who lies in wait for his prey and strikes from the shadows like a nithing. For that is how you would have been seen by all men of worth, if you had slain Oswine."

"Oswiu King wanted this," Octa said. "He commanded us to come here."

"He should never have done so." Beobrand let out a long breath. "Even kings make mistakes. No man is perfect."

"You think you are better than the king?" scoffed Octa. "Does Oswiu even know you are here?"

"Even if he did not, I would have come." Beobrand shrugged. "You do not understand, Octa. If you had done this thing, your name, your reputation, would have been sullied. You would be beholden to the king forever by such a dark deed." Beobrand thought of how Oswiu's hand had been in so many despicable acts. How the king had sent him to murder Wulfstan. Fleetingly, Beobrand recalled Wybert, whispering to him moments before his death. He remembered Halga, the giant Mercian and how he had goaded Beobrand before the Wall with tales of how he had been invited into Bernicia. The men who became embroiled in Oswiu's plots died violently, or lived with the shame of their actions. "You would never be free of the stain of it, Octa," he said. "I do not want that for you."

"I care not what you want!" shouted Octa. Men looked up to see what was causing the raised voices. A servant, startled and still frightened after what had happened, dropped a tray of cups and a flask of mead. The earthenware flask shattered, spilling the sweet drink to mingle with the gore that stained the floor. Octa had stood and now he faced his father. Both men had their hands clenched into fists at their side, their chins jutting forward pugnaciously. "You merely wanted the glory of this death for yourself," Octa raged. "Who are you to take this thing from me? Perhaps I would like to be known as the 'King Slayer'. You have your battle-fame, Father. Your name is known throughout Albion. But what of me? I would prove myself too. Do you think it easy having you for a father?"

His words stung Beobrand as though he had been slapped. The man he had believed to be his own father had cast a long shadow that darkened much of Beobrand's life. Grimgundi had beaten him and his brother and sisters, and Beobrand had striven not to be like him. He knew that he had failed. His son hated him, just as he had loathed Grimgundi. Perhaps it was always so, with each generation resenting the one that had gone before.

Alhfrith stood and placed a hand on Octa's shoulder.

"Easy now, friend," the atheling said. "You are not the only one whose life is overshadowed by his father."

"You are both pups," growled a new voice, "whining about the unfairness of life and how your fathers do not allow you to fulfil your wyrd." Beobrand turned to see that Ethelwin had come at the sound of the commotion.

Alhfrith glowered at the newcomer.

"You may well frown at me, Alhfrith," said Ethelwin. "You are the atheling and perhaps I am unwise to anger you, but I have vowed to serve your father and, God willing, I might serve you too one day."

"I do not think I will want such an old man in my comitatus," snarled Alhfrith. "But you are right, I am the atheling and you would be wise to remember that."

Ethelwin snorted.

"It will take more than jibes about my years to wound me," he said. "And it is because you are the atheling that I rode here this night. Beobrand is right in what he said to Octa. The thing you planned here would forever follow your name. You wish to be remembered, but not like this. Yes, Beobrand has battle-fame. For his part in battles, not murdering men in the dark." The warmaster raised his hand to stop the retort he could tell was coming. "You are both brave warriors, of that there is no doubt. But this was beneath you. Perhaps one day you will understand why we sought to prevent you. But think on this: when your father is gone, you might be king. You do not want your people to think of you as a man of dishonour."

Alhfrith stared at Ethelwin. He had looked to calm Octa, but now his cheeks were flushed, his eyes blazing.

"Is that how they will think of my father, Ethelwin?" he asked. "For it was the king who sent us here? We were merely obeying our lord. Fulfilling our oaths to the king."

"It is not for me to say what man has honour. But your father regretted his decision to send you here, and I am glad that we arrived in time to stop you." He looked about the hall, his eyes flicking to the row of bodies against the wall.

"Oswine is dead anyway," said Alhfrith, his tone scathing. "You coming here has changed nothing."

"You are wrong, young atheling. We may not have stopped the king's death, but much has changed, and I am glad of it."

"What has changed? Tell me."

Ethelwin shook his head slightly, as if bemused by the question.

"Oswine might be dead," he said at last, "but he did not die by your hand."

The warmaster turned then, signalling an end to the conversation. Placing a hand on Beobrand's shoulder, he pulled him away. Beobrand could feel the two young men glaring at them.

When they could no longer be overheard, Ethelwin let out a sigh.

"By God, Beobrand, do you remember what it was to be so sure of your decisions?"

Beobrand looked about the shadowed hall. Despite the Bernician victory here, there was no joy. The men were subdued, dismayed at what they had done. He knew how they felt. He glanced over at Octa, who was now seated again, talking in hushed tones to Alhfrith.

"I can scarcely believe that I was ever as young as Octa."

Ethelwin chuckled.

"You seem young to me," he said. "Imagine how *I* feel."

Beobrand rubbed at his bruised side. His eyes were gritty from lack of sleep.

"I do not feel young. I long for sleep, but I fear that will need to wait."

Ethelwin nodded.

"Aye. We will eat, and then we ride. We cannot remain here."

The light from the opened doorway and the sounds of birdsong beckoned to Beobrand. If he could not sleep, he could refresh himself with the crisp morning air, away from the morose stink within the hall. But there was one thing he needed to do first.

He made his way to the far side of the hall, where his gesithas sat apart from the others. He was surprised to find one of Alhfrith's warriors, a slender, rat-faced man, with them.

"Pusa, isn't it?" he asked.

"Yes, lord," replied the man, glancing up at his arrival. "We were just saying how strange wyrd is."

Beobrand took in the faces of the others. There was Attor, Fraomar, Grindan, and there, with his leg bandaged and stretched out on the bench, was Cynan. None of his gesithas had been killed. For the first time that morning, Beobrand allowed himself a moment of contentment. Of the sixteen dead, three were from the atheling's comitatus. Of the men who had ridden with Beobrand and Ethelwin, only Reodstan had met his end in Hunwald's hall. Reodstan was a good man, and Beobrand mourned his loss, but it could have been much worse.

"A man's wyrd is as difficult to fathom as a woman's mind," said Beobrand with a sad smile.

"Then it is impenetrable indeed," replied Pusa. "Would you care for ale?"

The men had a jug on the table and cups in their hands.

"Aye, my throat is as dry as dust," Beobrand said, taking the offered cup. The ale was good and he realised how thirsty he had been as the liquid washed away some of his exhaustion. He held out his cup for more.

"How is your leg?" he asked Cynan. He was still angry at the man's disobedience, but when, at the end of the fight, he had seen the Waelisc man sprawled in the rushes, his face pale and Attor fussing over him, Beobrand had been struck by a deep sense of dread that Cynan might die.

"I was lucky," Cynan said. "If Brunwine's blade had bit any deeper, I doubt I would be speaking to you now. And if not for Pusa's aid, Brunwine would have done for me in the end. The man was a formidable warrior. It was like wrestling a bear. To think that such a weasel as Pusa should be the one to slay the champion!"

The men erupted in laughter and Beobrand was pleased to see that Pusa laughed with them.

"It seems I owe you my thanks, Pusa," he said.

"You owe me nothing, lord," Pusa said. "I merely did my duty. After all, we are on the same side. This is what we were speaking of just now. How wyrd can choose a man's friends, and his enemies."

Beobrand thought of Wulfstan and Reodstan, lying dead beneath blankets. He recalled some unpleasantness between Cynan and Pusa in the past. It appeared their differences had been forgotten, or perhaps burnt away in the fire of combat. Wyrd had chosen for them to be friends in the end, it seemed.

"Well, I am glad that you were there when Cynan needed you," Beobrand said. "Despite what people say of him, he is a good man."

The men laughed again, but Cynan could not meet Beobrand's gaze, sensing the lingering anger behind the jest.

"Yes, lord," said Pusa. "He doesn't fight badly... for a Waelisc."

Cynan's features clouded for a heartbeat, but his frown was quickly replaced with a smile, and he raised his cup.

"To the weasel who slew the bear," he shouted. They laughed and Beobrand found himself laughing with them. It felt good after such a dark night. He emptied his cup and placed it back on the board.

"Do not drink too much," he said. "I know you are all thirsty and tired, but we cannot tarry here. We will ride soon." The men groaned. "Fraomar," he went on, "see that Cuthbert eats and drinks something. He has been alone for long enough."

Fraomar nodded and pushed himself to his feet.

Beobrand turned away. He wanted a moment free of the noise and smell of the hall. Free from the corpses and the reminder that he had slain the rightful king of Deira. He stepped, blinking, into the early morning sunshine, closing his eyes and revelling in the cool freshness of the day and the joyous singing of the birds who cared nothing for the machinations and tribulations of men.

Chapter 46

Cuthbert took a deep breath of the cool air blowing in from the North Sea. The sun was setting over the land, the long shadows of Bebbanburg turning the waters dark beneath his position on the ramparts. It would be night soon, and the people of the fortress would gather in the great hall to feast. Beobrand and the Black Shields would be there. He enjoyed the company of the gesithas, but he knew they would tell tales of what had happened in the hall at Ingetlingum, for warriors found it impossible not to boast. Beobrand would not crow about killing the king of Deira though. The lord of Ubbanford had been even more withdrawn and sullen as they'd ridden north out of Deira, leading a train of horses bearing the womenfolk, servants and thralls from Hunwald's hall. They'd also borne the swaddled corpses of the Bernicians who had fallen in the fray. Ethelwin and Beobrand had debated what to do with the Deiran dead for some time. In the end, they'd ordered the warriors to be left behind in the hall where they could be found. Each man lay with his sword and battle gear, so that he could be identified. The only Deiran bodies they carried north were those of Hunwald, as his widow refused to leave without him, and, the most important corpse of all: the king of Deira himself.

The news of Oswine's death had been on everybody's lips since they had returned to Bebbanburg and it would be the same at the feast tonight. The fight in the hall and the killing of the king and his closest retinue was all people wanted to speak about, but with every mention of it, Cuthbert relived the moment of the king's death, and his part in it. He saw again the blood smearing Beobrand's sword; felt anew the weight of Oswine's body lying atop him, the light of life slowly ebbing from his terrified eyes.

Cuthbert reached down to touch the small leather bag he wore over his shoulder. Within rested the Psalter the queen had given him along with the small writing tablet with its carved stylus. Whenever they had halted on the ride north, Cuthbert had taken the things out and painstakingly worked at practising his writing, copying out lines from the precious book in as perfect a hand as he could manage. He would lose himself then, for a time forgetting the events at Hunwald's hall and the grisly cargo they bore with them tied over the backs of the horses.

Sometimes a sound would distract him as he wrote – the caw of a crow, a gust of wind through the trees beside the road, the distant call of a vixen as the sun went down – and Cuthbert would wonder whether he was hearing the voice of God.

When they had ridden into the courtyard of Bebbanburg, Cuthbert had seen Eanflæd watching the riders, scanning their faces. When she had seen him, she had offered him a thin smile and a nod. Cuthbert had averted his eyes, ashamed of who he had become and what he had done. He was not worthy of the gifts the beautiful queen had bestowed upon him.

At night, his mind filled with the images of the flame-flickered chaos in the hall. He witnessed anew his sword hacking into Wulfstan, the blood gushing, the shock on the thegn's face.

He had had nightmares ever since battling the Mercian warrior on the causeway. Back in Ubbanford, Cuthbert had asked Attor about his dreams.

"Bad dreams are not unusual for a young warrior," Attor had said. "Killing your first foe-man is the hardest. You'll never forget his face. But with each fresh kill, you will find you are less troubled by it. And don't forget," he'd said with a grin, "your enemies would do the same to you if they could. You just need to be faster and stronger than them. This is the way of the gesith. The life you have chosen."

Cuthbert stared out at the great rippled expanse of the Whale Road and wondered at Attor's words. He had slain a man now, and the memory of it haunted him. When he was awake he longed for the respite of sleep, but when he lay down at night, his head filled with the tumbling images of battle, Wulfstan's horror-stricken features and the pale face of the king of Deira, as he had lain dying. When sleep finally came, Cuthbert would often awaken drenched in sweat and horrified at what he had done.

In the distance he could see the hazy shapes of the Farena Islands. Closer, in the darkening waters, swam several seals, their heads bobbing like floating boulders on the sea's surface before they slipped under the waves to fish and swim in the deep.

"They are serene, are they not?" asked a voice.

Cuthbert had been so intent on the creatures and his own thoughts, that he had not heard anyone approach. Startled, he turned to see Coenred, the monk who had healed him.

"They are peaceful, yes," Cuthbert replied, feeling foolish in the presence of the wise monk. Coenred always seemed so at ease and sure of himself. "I wonder if they hear the voice of God," he mused.

"Surely if the Almighty wishes to speak to them, they must hear Him," replied Coenred.

"Perhaps God has nothing to say to them."

Coenred shrugged.

"Does He speak to you, Cuthbert?"

Cuthbert hesitated. He thought of the last, rattling hot breath of the king on his cheek, the clang of blades, the shouts of warriors fighting, the salty tang of blood in the air.

"I worry that there is too much noise for me to hear Him," he whispered.

Coenred placed a hand on his shoulder.

"It is always easier to hear when one is truly listening."

Cuthbert thought of how he peered at his wax-covered tablet in the dying light after a long day's riding, his hand cramping around the stylus. He recalled the sounds of the birds on the wind, the creak of the trees, the cries of animals in the woods beside the road.

"I think I hear Him sometimes," he said, "but I do not understand what He says to me."

Coenred shook his head.

"Listening is the first thing. Then hearing. To understand the word of God requires more dedication than a young gesith can give, I fear."

Something in the monk's voice made Cuthbert turn to face him. Coenred's eyes were red, and tears streamed down his face.

"What is wrong?" asked Cuthbert, suddenly frightened at what the monk might say.

Coenred cuffed the tears from his cheeks.

"These are tears of joy and sorrow combined," he said.

Unsure of his meaning, Cuthbert said nothing.

"Bishop Aidan has gone to sit with Our Heavenly Father," said Coenred, his voice shaking with emotion. "This is a joyful event, for there has never been a holier man than Aidan." His voice cracked, and he cleared his throat. "But I am also saddened by his passing, for he was a good and wise friend. I knew I could go to him with any problem I might have, and his counsel was always welcome."

Cuthbert's mind reeled.

"The bishop is dead?" he asked. "How can that be?" He

instantly thought of men creeping into the abbot's cell and murdering him, their blades blood-soaked and gory.

"He was old and has been very ill," said Coenred.

"He was not killed?"

Coenred frowned.

"No, Cuthbert. Nobody killed Aidan. The Lord took his soul to be with Him. I have been tending to the bishop down in the settlement." He nodded towards the setting sun. There, beneath the fortress on its crag of rock, lay a cluster of buildings. "He wanted to go back to the Farena Isles," Coenred went on, "but he was too weak to travel. He drifted away peacefully while he was sitting in the afternoon sun outside the church." Coenred let out a long, tremulous breath.

Cuthbert stared out at the sea once more. The seals had gone and the sky seemed unnaturally devoid of birds. Was God even now speaking to him? What was He saying?

"Do you think God is displeased with the kingdom for what—" he faltered. Swallowing his shame, he continued. "For what happened at Ingetlingum? Do you think that is why he has taken Abbot Aidan from us?"

Coenred was silent for a while. He stared out over the North Sea and now it seemed to Cuthbert that the sky was teeming with birds as normal.

"I am sure many will see this as a bad omen for the land," said Coenred. "And I am also certain that God does not like to see His children killing one another. Aidan loved King Oswine. When he heard the tidings of his death, he cried as if a child of his had died, which in a way is what happened, I suppose." Coenred sniffed and wiped his woollen sleeve across his face. "But I do not think the Lord snatched Aidan from us as punishment for Oswine's death. If a servant of the Christ were to be taken to heaven each time a king of these lands performed a treacherous act, I fear there would be no priests or monks left on middle earth." He sighed. "I just hope that some good might come of Oswine's death."

They stood in silence for a time. The sun touched the land behind them, and the sky turned the colour of hot iron.

"They are gathering in the hall, Cuthbert," said Coenred. "If you wish to find a place at the benches, you should hurry."

"I have no appetite."

Coenred nodded.

"I am not hungry either," he said. "But more, I do not wish for the company of so many this evening of all evenings."

"But you came to speak with me."

"I enjoy speaking to you, Cuthbert. You listen, and you ask good questions."

Cuthbert was glad of the praise, in spite of his sadness.

"Do you wish to pray with me?" asked Coenred. "In the church of Saint Peter's?"

Cuthbert pondered before answering. Perhaps the reciting of prayers with Coenred would allow him to drown out the memories and dark thoughts that assailed him.

"Can we pray for Oswine's soul?" He remembered Wulfstan's dying face. "And for the souls of his men?"

"Of course," replied Coenred. "We will pray for all those who died, and we can pray for the souls of those who survived too. For I imagine they are sorely troubled by what they saw, and their part in it."

"Yes," Cuthbert said. "I would like that."

"Good," said Coenred. "Let us make our way there now then."

He turned and began to descend the ladder to the shadowed courtyard below. Cuthbert looked once more out to the sea. The sky was full once again of wheeling gulls, terns, gannets and guillemots. And there, on the swell, were the bobbing heads of the seals.

Smiling, Cuthbert followed Coenred.

Chapter 47

Beobrand took a deep breath and watched as Eanflæd screamed at her husband. Even in her fury she was beautiful. The night before, as they had celebrated the return of the atheling and the news of Oswine's death, Beobrand had sat quietly, drinking sparingly. He had been seated at the high table, beside Ethelwin, which meant that to see the queen, he needed to turn and lean forward. Even so, he had dared risk a few glances at her, but she had not once looked in his direction, and the sorrow he felt at the death of Wulfstan, Oswine, Reodstan and the others in Hunwald's hall, had hardened, compounded by Eanflæd's obvious displeasure.

Before the people of Bebbanburg and the gathered thegns and ealdormen of Bernicia, who had returned triumphant from Wilfaresdun, Eanflæd had maintained the impression of the dutiful queen at her husband's side. Whenever Beobrand had looked in her direction during the feast, her eyes had been downcast, as she picked at her food and sipped from the green glass beaker of wine before her.

Now the throngs had left, many returning to their halls with promises of gifts from their joyous king. The hall was no longer filled with smoke, heat and the cacophony of voices raised in boasts, riddles and song. The light of the mid-morning sun lanced through the open doors and unshuttered windows. Motes of dust and ash from the cold hearth danced in the shafts of light. The hall was quiet and echoing, empty of the usual servants and thralls. Eanflæd had sent them all away, so that the only other people in the hall were Oswiu, Beobrand and Ethelwin. The atheling, Alhfrith, had tried to remain there too, perhaps feeling that he had the right to be included as the son of the king, who had carried back the body of the Deiran king. But the queen had pointed at the door and snapped, "What I have to say here is not for your ears, Alhfrith. Begone."

The young man had stared at the pouting queen for a long while, perhaps trying to think of a suitable retort, but her hard, cold eyes did not blink, and in the end, stamping his feet like a rebuked child, Alhfrith stomped from the hall. Beobrand had almost felt sorry for him. Until Eanflæd unleashed her ire, and then he wished that he had followed the atheling. He had so often longed to spend time with the queen, but not like this, watching her berate her husband and certain that she would turn her attention on him next.

"I can scarcely believe that you would do such a thing!" Eanflæd shrieked at Oswiu, her voice rasping with rage.

Oswiu sought to placate her with a smile.

"My lady, I did nothing—"

"Do not lie to me!" she shouted, cutting off his words. "I had thought you a strong leader. A warrior lord. Now I wonder if I am not married to a coward."

Oswiu's face darkened.

"Hold your tongue, Eanflæd," he said, his tone lowering and the smile slipping from his face.

"I will do no such thing," she replied. "Oswine was a good man. He was gōd cyning." She drew in a long breath. "He was my cousin. I loved him as a brother. What is worse is that you knew this and still acted thus. Bad enough that you had set yourself against him in this concocted war, but you are the king of Bernicia, and such is your right." Eanflæd shook her head, holding Oswiu in a withering gaze. "I never believed you would stoop so low."

Oswiu bunched his hands into fists. He rose to his feet in a rush, and Beobrand thought he might strike the queen. If he did, Beobrand knew he would not be able to stand by and do nothing. Perhaps if he threw himself forward to defend her, Eanflæd would feel less disdain for him. To know that she despised him and what he had done filled him with such deep sorrow he could barely breathe. If he had a chance to redeem himself in her eyes, even if that meant his death, he felt sure he would take it.

But the king did not strike his wife. With an effort, he calmed himself and walked over to a table where cups and a jug had been laid out. Pouring himself some wine, he turned back.

"I fear all of this has been a terrible misunderstanding," he said, taking a sip from his cup.

"You expect me to believe you had nothing to do with Oswine's murder?"

Oswiu sighed.

"No, I cannot say such is true. But it was never my intention to have him killed. It seems though that my hot-tempered warriors took their mission too far."

"So you did not send them to slay my cousin?"

"Of course not," said Oswiu, his tone shocked at the suggestion. "I wanted them to bring him to Bebbanburg where we could discuss terms for peace. Ask anyone who was at the parley at Wilfaresdun. This was ever my intention, from the moment I dreamt of Oswald. My brother showed me the way. But I fear the Devil twisted the meaning of my words and Beobrand and Ethelwin here decided that a better course of action would be to kill the king of Deira."

On hearing these words, Beobrand clenched his fists. Oswiu was a snake. He would say anything to avoid his wife's anger, it seemed. Eanflæd looked first at Ethelwin and then at Beobrand, her gaze lingering a moment. Her face was contorted with such sadness that he felt as though his heart twisted in his chest.

"We did what we could to prevent Oswine being killed," said Ethelwin, his voice strangely calm. Beobrand wanted to scream out that Oswiu lied, but he clamped his mouth shut. Octa was yet part of the king's household. Beobrand might not care for his own life, but he had not gone to Hunwald's hall and slain Oswine, only to put his son in danger now. Ethelwin was wise not to gainsay the king, but the warmaster did still attempt to tell the truth of what happened.

"You didn't do enough," snapped the king, siding with the queen against them.

"There was much confusion," said Ethelwin. "You know as well as I, my lord king, that when fighting commences, there is no way to predict the outcome. We did our best, but Oswine fell, despite our efforts."

"I am sure you did your best," said Oswiu in a placatory tone. "I know you both to be honourable men who have served me well over the years. And nothing can now change the past. Oswine is dead." He made the sign of the Christ rood. "It is regrettable, but we must grab the good that comes from a bad thing. The war between Deira and Bernicia will now be over. We can move on to a time of peace. Is that not what we all want? Even Oswine, God rest his soul, would be pleased if his passing led to peace between our two kingdoms."

Beobrand thought it unlikely that peace would reign following Oswine's death, but he kept his mouth shut.

"You speak of my cousin's soul," said Eanflæd. "You should be just as concerned with your own." Oswiu frowned at her words. "You say that this was all a misunderstanding, my lord," the queen continued. "That you did not send these men to slay Oswine."

"That is so," Oswiu said.

"What do you say, Lord Beobrand?" asked Eanflæd, turning her tear-filled eyes on him.

Beobrand swallowed. The queen looked more beautiful than ever to him, and his breath caught in his throat.

"It is as both lord Ethelwin and the king say." He had decided there was no point in muddying the waters further. What was done was done. At least he could keep Octa's name out of the sorry incident. "We rode on Oswiu King's behest to convey the king of Deira north." He saw Oswiu nodding in agreement and wanted to punch him. Looking away from the king, he went on, "Fighting broke out in the hall. In the confusion, Oswine was slain." Staring into Eanflæd's eyes, he saw the sadness there. Her disappointment stabbed at him like a seax blade beneath a shield rim. "I am sorry, my lady."

She held his gaze for what felt like a long time. Then, without a word, she walked past her husband to the table and filled a cup for herself. Ignoring them all, perhaps composing her thoughts, she sipped her wine. The three men in the hall stared at her, waiting to hear what she would say. Beobrand marvelled at the power she wielded over them. He vaguely recalled her mother, Queen Ethelburga, and how she had stood, statuesque and imposing, beside King Edwin as the men had prepared for war. Eanflæd had inherited much from her parents. By all accounts both king and queen were formidable individuals. Eanflæd had their strength of character and intelligence; her mother's grace, and her father's iron will. She had been born to royalty and as she stood with her back to them, her shoulders straight and the sumptuous silk dress clinging to the curves of her body, she looked every part the queen.

Oswiu fidgeted. Raising his cup to his lips, he found it empty. Moving to the table, he brushed past his wife and refilled his cup.

"More wine, my dear?" he asked, holding up the pitcher.

"I do not want any more wine," she replied, replacing her cup with care on the linen-covered board. "And I will not so easily forget what you have done, Oswiu."

"But, my lady," he said. "I have told you, I meant for none of this to happen—"

"Enough." She held up a slender hand and Oswiu fell silent. "I know what you have told me. But still, are you not the lord of these men? Did they not ride in your name?"

Oswiu nodded, but thought better of speaking.

"Then you will atone for the sin of murder."

"Murder? But I—"

She cut him off with a look.

"You will build a monastery at Ingetlingum." Her tone was final.

"But it is in Deira," he spluttered.

"And you will be king of Deira now, I do not doubt. But even if you are not king there, you will see that a monastery is built and you will pay for a grand funeral for my kinsman. And you will give silver to the church for holy men and women to pray for Oswine's everlasting soul."

Oswiu tensed. Beobrand thought the king was going to protest, but Eanflæd said, "If you do not do this thing, husband, I will be most displeased."

Oswiu contemplated her words for a few heartbeats before eventually nodding his agreement.

"It shall be so," he said.

"And the holy brethren of that monastery will also pray for your soul, husband," Eanflæd said, her voice low. "It will take much prayer to wash away the stain of sin from it, I fear."

Oswiu sighed.

"Very well," he said, drinking deeply from his cup.

Eanflæd turned back to face Ethelwin and Beobrand. Ethelwin looked down at the straw-strewn floor of the hall. Beobrand met her gaze. He was taken aback by what he saw there. The sadness and disappointment had been replaced by a seething anger once more.

"And how will you atone for your sins, Beobrand of Ubbanford?" she asked. "You are a pagan. No amount of praying will save your soul."

Beobrand opened his mouth to reply, but the queen held up a hand once more to silence him.

"I do not wish to hear you speak. There is nothing you can say that can justify the evil you have done in my husband's name."

Her harsh words and tone wounded him. Gods, how he wished he had not ridden to Ingetlingum. Would Oswine yet live, if he had not? Would Eanflæd still have that look of utter disdain and fury on her beautiful features when she looked at him? He would give anything to have her look on him with affection once more.

A small voice whispered deep inside him.

But would you give up the life of your son?

If he had not gone to Hunwald's hall, Octa would surely have been slain. With a shiver, he remembered the anguish he had felt when he had seen the bloody body on the floor and believed it to be Octa. Surely even the love of the queen was not worth such a price.

And yet, Octa was safe, and Beobrand would do anything within his power to have Eanflæd look at him as she once had.

"I will do whatever you command, my lady," he said.

Eanflæd's eyes narrowed.

"There is perhaps one way for you to show you are repentant," she said.

Was there a glimmer of affection in her eyes. Beobrand clung desperately to the possibility of redemption.

"Name it," he said.

439

Chapter 48

Cuthbert hadn't been certain of his plan until he finally saw the cluster of buildings in the great loop of the Tuidi.

He had risen with the dawn the day before, saddled his horse, and set out south-west, following the tree-clogged valley of the river inland. As he had ridden he had prayed. When he had stopped to rest and to eat a few mouthfuls of the bread and cheese he had taken from the great hall at Ubbanford, he had read from the Psalter that the queen had given him. He could understand and copy all of the words with ease now, and the next time he travelled to Bebbanburg, he vowed to return the precious book to her. He had contemplated speaking to the queen when he had seen her there the previous week, but she had been devastated to hear of the death of her kinsman, Oswine. When Cuthbert had seen her stern face and red-rimmed eyes he had changed his mind about approaching her.

Ever since they had returned from Deira, death seemed to have gripped the land in its bony fist. The sun shone in the late summer sky, but a pall of misery and mourning hung over Bernicia like a storm cloud. After the initial celebration of the death of the king of Deira, brought by the hope that the war might now be over, the people of Bebbanburg began to grow sombre. It seemed to Cuthbert that they recalled that they had loved Oswine once. He had been a handsome and just man, and before the conflict with Oswiu, he had visited Bebbanburg often. As word of the nature of his death spread like ripples in a black mere, so the people's mood soured. To be murdered in a darkened hall, not in a glorious battle, was not a fitting death for a beloved king.

The tidings of Abbot Aidan's passing further saddened the men and women of Bernicia. As Cuthbert and Coenred had spoken of on the fortress palisade, many people muttered that this was a sign from God, a bad omen showing His displeasure in their king and those who had murdered Oswine.

For his own part, Cuthbert could still not sleep without waking to the sound of his own screams in his ears. He could still feel the crunch of sinews and bones as his sword smashed into Wulfstan's chest. He could still see Oswine's dying eyes. It had been Cuthbert's actions that had led to the king's death. He wondered whether hearing of Oswine's murder had caused Aidan to give up on this life. The abbot had been old, and all men died, he told himself. But the feeling that he had somehow contributed to the holy man's death had snagged in his mind the way a burr will catch on a woollen cloak. The thought scratched and irritated, digging needling barbs into his soul. The only way that Cuthbert could alleviate his pain was to fill his mind with prayer.

He spent a lot of time with Coenred in those few days at Bebbanburg. The monk taught him liturgies and psalms and, when they were not praying or learning the Scriptures, Coenred had told him tales of Aidan's life and the brethren of Lindisfarena. Cuthbert had enjoyed their time together, away from the noise and bustle of the hall, but he had been pleased to leave Bebbanburg that had become a sombre, sad place.

If he had been hoping to find a happier people at Ubbanford, Cuthbert was disappointed. That summer death had not only claimed high-born men who sat on gift-stools and thrones. The lady Rowena had succumbed to her illness while Beobrand and the Black Shields had been away, and everyone in the settlement was forlorn. Bassus welcomed those men who returned with a feast, but he did not smile, and his usual booming laugh was missing from the meal in the hall. The one-armed giant was grief-stricken, and missed Rowena, but Cuthbert could not help but notice how the man's shoulders slumped too, when he heard the news that his friend and lord would not be returning to Ubbanford. There were few people Bassus confided in, and bereft of Rowena and Beobrand, he would be left to battle his anguish alone.

Many others were saddened by the news that not all of the warriors had come home. Women and children who had been waiting for the return of the men were disappointed, and the feast became a sullen and subdued affair.

Bassus had stared desultorily into the flames of the hearth while those in the hall spoke and ate. He had drunk constantly, staggering off early down the hill to the old hall he had shared with Rowena.

One of the few moments of joy was the reunion between Brinin and Ardith. Beobrand's daughter was heavy with child now, and the lord of Ubbanford had sent the young gesith home to her, rather than have Brinin accompany him south on his mission.

When Beobrand had told his Black Shields what the queen had commanded, and who would accompany him, Cuthbert had seen in his lord's face that he believed Cuthbert would be angered to be left behind. Just a few weeks before he would have been, he knew. But things had changed.

He had changed.

He felt a pang of remorse at leaving without saying farewell to the people of Ubbanford, but he would not be so far from them, and he was sure they would see each other again. Besides, he could not bear the thought of Udela fussing over him. He could imagine how Tatwine's eyes would fill with tears to learn that his playmate was leaving. He loved the boy as a brother and did not wish to see him cry.

As he rode, he thought of his decision to leave silently, without fuss. Was it the sign of a coward? Was that why he had made this decision? Was that the truth of who he was? Was he merely a craven, who was unable to stand strong in battle?

Before leaving Bebbanburg, Cuthbert had asked Coenred what he should do.

"No man can answer the question of who you are, Cuthbert," Coenred had said. "That is between you and God. Pray to Him and ask for guidance. If you listen, you will hear His answer, I am sure."

"I have wanted to be a warrior for so long," replied Cuthbert. "But now that I have what I desired, I doubt it is my wyrd." He sighed, running his fingers absently over the hard scab on his forehead where a sword had wounded and momentarily blinded him as his blood had flowed. "I fear I am a coward," he whispered.

"Doubt is normal, Cuthbert. But it is not cowardly to question the direction you have taken. Such a thing is wise and takes great bravery. For would it not be foolish to blunder along a road, knowing that it was heading the wrong way, but too stubborn to turn back to the fork in the path?"

Perhaps there was some courage in changing one's path, thought Cuthbert. But he did not feel brave, sneaking away from the hall he had called home for the past year, without a word to anyone.

Despite Cuthbert's feelings of inadequacy and cowardice, it did feel good to ride beside the river all that long day. He was alone for the first time in many weeks and the solitude acted like a balm to his troubled soul. He recited the prayers he had learnt from Coenred, allowing his horse's easy gait to lull him into a state of half-slumber. Bees droned in the comfrey and clover. A silvered salmon leapt out of the water, coming down with a splash that made Cuthbert's horse shake its mane and snort. Two otters, sleek and languid, slid down the bank and cut through the water of the river, every now and then dipping beneath the surface in a way that reminded him of the seals along the coast. In each of these things, Cuthbert thought he began to hear the whispered words of the Lord. He recalled the stories of Aidan's life that Coenred had told him. The old Hibernian had walked everywhere, rather than riding, and had even given away to a beggar a fine horse that King Oswine had gifted him. Apparently, he had once taken a great silver dish owned by King Oswald and ordered it cut into pieces and handed out to the poor who sought alms outside the gates of Bebbanburg. Coenred's voice had been filled with love when he spoke of Aidan's piety. Cuthbert wondered what it would be like to throw away worldly desires and property and give oneself over completely to the service of God and His flock.

He rested that night beneath a great ash tree. He lay there, watching the stars flicker through the spreading boughs and listening to the murmured sounds of the night: the creak and rustle of the leaves and branches above him, the soft tread of his horse and the mulchy munching of the grass it chewed. An owl hooted close by, perhaps from the forest on the north side of the Tuidi.

It was cool in the night, but Cuthbert did not feel the need for a fire. He recited the paternoster over and over in his mind, thinking of the meaning of each of the words and listening to the darkened world. For the first time in many days, he did not see in his dreams the faces of the men he had killed. Nor did he feel the oppressive weight of Oswine's dying bulk crushing against his chest. He slept soundly and awoke with the dawn, enveloped in a light mist and surrounded by the chorus of robins, wrens, finches and blackbirds singing to the rising sun.

As he rode on that second day, he pondered what he would say when he reached his destination. He had listened and prayed as Coenred had told him to, but still he did not clearly hear

God's voice. And yet, a peace had come over him as if wrapped in a blanket that had been warmed by a fire. And as he travelled ever further from Ubbanford, distancing himself from the life he had known, an inexplicable thing happened.

Cuthbert did not carry many provisions, knowing that his journey would not be long. On top of his meagre provender, he had packed a couple of kirtles, the Psalter, and the wax-covered tablet and stylus. When he had set out, he had not known what the journey would bring, and so he had strapped his baldric about his shoulders. From the leather strap hung his scabbarded sword. And in his hand, he carried a spear, fearing that he might be attacked on the road by brigands, or perhaps a boar. But as he rode and prayed, his fear of attack dissipated and a newfound calm washed through him. All the while, his spear grew uncomfortable in his palm, the smooth ash haft seeming to rub and chafe against his skin, causing him to switch it regularly between his hands. But no matter how he carried it, he could not seem to find a way of bearing the weapon without discomfort. Besides the spear, his shoulder began to ache from the weight of the sword on its baldric, as if heavy stones had been tied to the blade's scabbard. He had ridden much further in the past with spear and sword and had carried a shield and other things too, but he had never experienced such soreness before.

He had been wondering what was wrong when he saw the monastery of Magilros before him. It was afternoon, and light clouds drifted across the pale sky. Several men and women were in the fields around the monastery buildings. Cuthbert could make out a large church and several other well-appointed structures, most with thatched roofs, and a couple of larger halls with wooden shingles. The life of monks and nuns was austere, eschewing pleasures of the flesh and earthly comforts. And yet this minster was also home to women who had been queens of Bernicia. Oswald's widow, Cyneburg, resided here, along with Rhieinmelth, the princess of Rheged, who had been queen before Eanflæd. Rhieinmelth's daughter, Alhflaed, who had been promised to Peada of Mercia, if the rumours were correct, was also a guest here.

As he gazed down the slope of the path to the buildings, a bell began to sound. It must be calling the faithful to None, the mid-afternoon prayer, he thought. Unbidden, his mind filled with the liturgy he had learnt from Coenred. The words had seemed to take root in his mind, and now they came back to him as easily as his name. He kicked his horse into a trot, hoping to arrive in time to be able to attend the service. With a whinny, the animal sped up. Cuthbert changed his spear from his left to his right hand. On doing so, he realised with a start that the weapon no longer hurt his hands. He shifted his weight in the saddle and was amazed to find that his sword, too, had ceased to be a painful burden to him.

There were several robed monks standing by the minster gates watching his arrival. Cuthbert reined in before them. The monks shuffled nervously, taking in his fine cloak, his sword and spear. Cuthbert thought of how he must look to them, an armed gesith, riding unannounced up to their gates. He wondered whether the royal residents of the minster had warriors guarding them. But if there were guards, he saw none.

The oldest of the tonsured men, his hair greying and his forehead wrinkled, stepped forward.

"I am Boisil," he said, "Prior of Magilros. And who might you be?"

"My name is Cuthbert."

Dismounting, Cuthbert held out his reins. After a moment's confusion, Boisil nodded at a young monk.

"Sigfrith, see to the man's horse," he said.

Cuthbert felt his face grow warm. He had grown overly accustomed to hostlers and servants, it seemed.

Sigfrith took the reins from Cuthbert and made to lead the animal away when Cuthbert called him back.

"Wait, take this too." He handed the young monk his spear and then shrugged off his baldric and sword. "And this," he said, proffering the scabbarded weapon. "I'll not be needing it again."

Sigfrith looked to his prior, who nodded. After fumbling with the reins and both weapons for a moment, Sigfrith eventually managed to get a firm grip on everything and began leading the horse through the open gates.

"You say you will not need your sword or spear again?" enquired Boisil with a raised eyebrow. "Are you planning on staying here at Magilros?"

Cuthbert met his gaze, sure now of his decision.

"If you will have me," he said. "I would join you at None, if I may, and then, perhaps we can speak of my future."

"All followers of Christ are, of course, welcome here, my son," replied Boisil. "But we recite the prayers of the offices in Latin. This is a minster and we are monks. Holy servants of Christ."

"I know the liturgy, good Boisil," Cuthbert replied, to the old monk's evident surprise. "It was taught to me by Coenred of Lindisfarena. And with God's grace and your guidance, I too would take the tonsure and become a servant of the Lord."

Boisil stared into his eyes and a silent communication flowed between them. The bell had stopped tolling, but the men around the gate had not yet moved.

Nodding, and with a welcoming smile, Boisil finally gestured for Cuthbert to make his way through the gates.

"Behold," Boisil said to the other monks, "the servant of the Lord."

Passing through the gates, Cuthbert felt again the warming peace that had enveloped him during his solitary ride while he had prayed and communed with the Almighty and His creation.

"Thank you," he said to Boisil, who led the small group over the vallum and towards the shingle-roofed church.

"You are well come," replied the prior.

As the voices of the faithful drifted out of the open door

of the timber church, the words of the liturgy wafting about them like gossamer threads on a light breeze, Cuthbert felt an overwhelming sense of belonging that he had never before encountered in his short life, and he knew the prior's words to be true.

Chapter 49

Cynan followed Beobrand across the gardens towards the great hall. Without conscious thought, he scanned the hedges, stone columns and statues that dotted the open area, for any sign of danger. But he was not expecting trouble. Surely no harm would befall his hlaford here, surrounded by King Eorcenberht's door wards and hearth-warriors. Here in Cantwareburh they were far from the skirmishes and strife of the frontier lands of Northumbria and Mercia. Besides, in the unlikely event something untoward occurred, Cynan carried no blade. They had left their weapons at the entrance of the royal enclosure, so acting as Beobrand's bodyguard was more for show than anything else. And yet the Waelisc warrior remained close by his lord's shoulder, unspeaking, his face stern, his eyes flicking as he took in their surroundings.

Cynan still resented that the lord of Ubbanford had not allowed him to return to Stagga. He yearned for Eadgyth and now the gods alone knew when he would be able to speak to her again.

Back in Bebbanburg, when he had asked Beobrand for permission to return home, leaving the other warriors to accompany him south, Beobrand had smiled. There had been no humour in his eyes.

"Oh no, Cynan, my friend, I am sorry," he said, shaking his head, mock sorrow on his face. "You are coming with me. You have often told me that it is your duty to protect me." Cynan frowned, thinking of how he had fought off the giant brute Brunwine so that Beobrand could go to Octa's aid. He recalled hacking Halga's head from his shoulders as Beobrand lay defenceless beneath the massive Mercian. Perhaps his expression gave away his thoughts for Beobrand held up a hand to fend off any protests. "And you have saved me more than once, I cannot deny it. But you yourself have said that to properly act as my protector, you must be my shadow. And so, you will go where I go. Besides," he added with a grin and a slap on the back, "if I can see you, Cynan, I know where you are."

Cynan hurried to keep up with Beobrand as he strode towards the doors of the great hall. They had left the other Black Shields in the same small hall they'd occupied when they had last visited Cantware. Cynan knew he could have stayed with them. In truth, he did not need to accompany Beobrand to the king's hall. But if the man said he wanted a shadow, by the gods, he would have one.

The sun was low in the sky and Cynan glanced over at the statues of long-dead men of Roma that lined the edges of the ornately kept gardens. The dark shadows and golden light picked out their features. He marvelled at the exquisite skill that had gone into carving such life-like figures. It seemed like witchcraft to him that stone could be fashioned into smooth skin, locks of tumbling hair and soft folds of silk.

As they had ridden into the city, with its crumbling walls and the towering majesty of the great amphitheatre, the memories of their last visit had flooded back like the waves of the cold Whale Road that had almost claimed their lives more than once.

"We should have ignored Eanflæd's orders and gone to Hithe," Beobrand had said, spitting into the mud as they'd passed in the shadow of the vaulted walls of the old semi-circular amphitheatre that was sometimes used to house markets where all manner of goods, from spices to silks to slaves, could be bought and sold. On such occasions the stone tiers of seating would echo with the hubbub of voices and the air would be heavy with the smell of roasting meat and other, less savoury scents. The amphitheatre was silent today and they rode on. They had paid good silver for the horses at Sandwic. Cynan was not impressed with the quality of the horseflesh, and had been prepared to walk away to find another seller. But Beobrand was in a hurry and had not allowed him to haggle as he should have. And so they rode on beasts he would have thought twice about harnessing to a cart, let alone riding.

Ever since he had met with the queen at Bebbanburg, Beobrand had been in a sour mood and rushed to do any task he set himself to. Cynan thought that Eanflæd would have allowed them to travel first to Ubbanford and their families, but Beobrand seemed almost desperate to be gone from Bernicia. They had given their mounts to Cuthbert and the gesithas lucky enough to return home, and travelled south on a merchant ship headed for Frankia. It was much slower than *Saeslaga* and it wallowed between the waves, making them all feel sick, but they had been fortunate with the weather, and had soon reached the coast of Cantware.

"I did not think you approved of warriors who ignored their hlaford's commands, lord," said Cynan.

Beobrand hawked and spat again.

"This was not my lord's command. Besides, I am here, am I not? But it would have been good to see Alwin again. I would raise a cup with him and Ferenbald."

"Perhaps we will be able to do that yet," Cynan said. "After we are done here."

Beobrand had looked at him askance.

"Perhaps," he'd said.

Cynan was surprised when Beobrand did not halt at the doors

of Eorcenberht's great hall. Instead, he nodded at the door wards in their burnished byrnies and polished helms, and walked past. Cynan had been slowing and now was forced to hurry to catch up.

"Don't worry, Cynan," said Beobrand, "we'll go back to eat and drink soon. But I must deliver this message first." Beobrand was unsmiling and sombre, the muscles of his neck and jaw bunching and relaxing.

They reached another large building. Cynan looked up at the roof and saw the timber cross that was raised there, starkly bright in the golden glow of the lowering sun. Fleetingly, he thought of Scyldsung at Dacor. He hoped the priest they sought was more trustworthy. He knew nothing of the young man they had been sent for and, as Beobrand pushed the doors of the chapel open, Cynan found himself interested to see the object of Eanflæd's order.

It took a moment for his eyes to adjust to the shadows within the building, but Beobrand did not slow down. Now that they were here, he seemed eager to get this thing done and he moved quickly towards the altar, where a bejewelled rood and the golden bindings of a great book glimmered in the light from several candles. The church was redolent of incense and the fine beeswax of the candles.

A slender young man had been kneeling in prayer. On hearing their arrival and the clump of their boots on the floor, he rose, turning to meet them. His features were narrow, his chin angular, with deep, penetrating blue eyes that spoke of a keen intellect. He wore his hair in the unusual fashion of the priests who had come from Frankia across the Narrow Sea. The pate of his head was shaved, leaving a crown of hair all about the bald circle at the centre.

Cynan knew little of the man except that he had found favour with Eanflæd. He had studied at Lindisfarena, clearly showing an aptitude for learning, for when he had asked, the queen had sent him south to learn more from the wise and learned men of the church in Cantware.

"Wilfrid," said Beobrand, halting before the young holy man.

Wilfrid's eyes widened as he took in the two tall men who seemed to fill the church. His expression quickly changed to one of serenity. With careful strokes of his soft hands, Wilfrid smoothed his monkish habit where the fabric had creased from kneeling. Cynan noticed that one of his fingers bore a gold ring.

"Lord Beobrand," he said, his voice displaying none of the surprise he had appeared to register moments before. "What are you doing here?"

Beobrand hesitated, then, seeming to gird himself for what was to come, he replied, "I have been sent to travel with you."

Wilfrid frowned.

"Sent?" he asked. "By whom?"

"Eanflæd," said Beobrand. "Our queen."

Wilfrid gaped, the confusion evidently too much to hide, his facade of calm control shattered. Cynan almost laughed to see the young monk's mouth open and shut like a beached fish.

"Surely..." Wilfrid managed, then faltered. Taking a long, steadying breath, he smoothed his right hand over his robes in a calming gesture, as if telling himself to breathe more slowly. "Surely the queen does not mean to call me back to Northumbria." An edge of whining had entered his tone. It made Cynan think once again of Scyldsung. Wilfrid paused, perhaps hearing how his voice might sound to them. Again he drew in a deep breath. "I still have much to learn here." His voice was now controlled and collected. He picked daintily at an invisible speck of dust on his sleeve. His gold ring glimmered in the candlelight. "I cannot travel north again."

Beobrand sighed.

"I am not here to bear you northward."

Wilfrid rocked back on his heels at these words. Staring up at Beobrand, he met his gaze, his twilight blue eyes fixed on

Beobrand's pallid ice-chip glare. Wilfrid did not blink or look away. Cynan was impressed. There were many warriors who could not hold Beobrand's stare for long.

"Do you mean...?" Wilfrid's words trailed off. Gone now was the whine, replaced by a suppressed excitement.

"Yes, Wilfrid," said Beobrand, nodding ruefully. "Eanflæd has sent me to accompany you south. To Roma."

Historical Note

Some characters keep calling to you long after you close the pages of the book in which they reside. This is the same for readers and writers, but when you have created that character, they just demand to have more of their tale told. Sulis, who first appears in *Warrior of Woden*, was one such character for me. I kept picturing her last moments in the story, as she walks forlornly into the west, and I wondered what happened to her next. As Cynan's role grew in subsequent novels, it became clear that he should be the one to meet Sulis again. Their lives had been intertwined ever since Beobrand first bought her from Fordraed, and, like me, Cynan had pondered her fate in the intervening years.

This was the starting point for a large part of *For Lord and Land*, and whilst Sulis' story, and Cynan's quest to protect her family, is purely fictional, it has a firm grounding in what we know about the period.

Women were frequently bequeathed land and possessions in their husbands' wills. And if a child was the sole heir, another family member would be given custody to oversee the inheritance until they came of age. One can imagine that if Cynan and company had not put an end to the plot to snatch ownership of the land and the mine, Ludeca might well have seen to it that

Eadwig suffer an unfortunate illness or accident in the following years.

The lead mine is based on Odin Mine in Derbyshire, believed to be the oldest lead mine in Britain. While it is not clear if the Anglo-Saxons mined for lead there, the mine was active in Roman times and later in the medieval period, only halting lead production in 1869.

The thread of the novel that follows Beobrand's exploits is, as in previous novels, based on historical events.

Around 645, King Cenwalh of Wessex renounced his wife, who happened to be Penda of Mercia's sister. Penda, unimpressed with his sister's treatment, fought Cenwalh, who fled into exile. King Anna of East Anglia took in Cenwalh, and the King of Wessex remained in Anna's court for a few years, where he converted to Christianity before returning to his own kingdom.

Anna, a devout Christian, had endowed the monastery of Cnobheresburg with buildings and rich artefacts. And when Penda invaded in 651 and attacked the monastery, Anna went to the monks' defence, holding back the Mercians and buying them enough time to flee by boat with their valuable books and relics. By this point Foillan was the abbot after his brother, Fursa (or Fursey), fed up with the frequent attacks on East Anglia, had decided to leave for good.

The exact location of Cnobheresburg is unknown. Some historians have placed it at Burgh Castle, a Roman fort that was part of what is known as the Saxon Shore – a string of coastal defences built in the third century to protect the northern Roman Empire from pirates. I have situated it at Caister Castle, another Saxon Shore fort a few miles to the north. It is important to note that the coastline of Britain was different in the seventh century, especially in the northern part of East Anglia, and Caister Castle would have been on the seashore and not a couple of miles inland.

Following Penda's attack on Cnobheresburg, King Anna was forced into exile. Where he went is unknown, so I have chosen to have him transported north by Beobrand, thus possibly pushing things in Deira's favour in the war with Bernicia when Peada, Penda's son, sides with Oswine.

In Bede's *History of the English Church and People*, he writes of how Oswine had amassed a great host at Wilfaresdun (Wilfar's Hill), but seeing he was outnumbered, he decided to disband his troops and head to the hall of a nobleman he considered to be his closest ally, Hunwald. We don't know the exact location of the hill where Oswine had amassed his force, but a possible location for Wilfaresdun has been postulated by Andrew Breeze as Diddersley Hill. It is near the convergence of two Roman roads, north-west of Catterick, as stipulated by Bede, and close enough to Gilling (Ingetlingum), where Oswine travels and is later assassinated.

I have chosen for there to be multiple reasons for Oswine, who was otherwise in a strong position, to disband his army and head off to Hunwald's hall. First, Oswiu uses the promise of power and alliance, by offering Penda's son his daughter, Alhflaed (they are later married in 653). The second lever applying force on Oswine is the arrival of the men of Rheged, led by Cynan and Sigehelm. And finally, it is King Oswiu, who dangles before the very Christian Oswine the chance of brokering a lasting peace and avoiding bloodshed. All this is supposition, guesswork and artistic licence on my part and differs from Bede's account that says Oswine decided to wait for a more favourable moment to engage in battle with Oswiu.

We will never know what really happened at Hunwald's hall, but Bede talks of a warrior called Tondhere who led him to hide at the hall. The assassin's name is given as Ethelwin, Oswiu's military commander. I have omitted Tondhere from the story, changing him for Wulfstan, who already had a troubled past with Beobrand. And instead of alone, I have Oswine and Wulfstan accompanied by a small band of trusted hearth-warriors, as it seemed unlikely that a king would travel alone.

It is true that after the assassination, Queen Eanflæd was furious with her husband and made him build a monastery at Gilling (the site of the murder) and pay for prayers to be said for both his soul and that of her murdered cousin. It is also the case that the queen was the patron of one young, brilliant and ambitious student of the church, Wilfrid. She sent him south to Cantware (Kent) with a letter of introduction for her cousin, King Eorcenberht. Later, Wilfrid would travel on to the continent, undertaking the first recorded pilgrimage to Rome by any English native.

Taking into consideration Eanflæd's dedication to the church and her enthusiastic assistance for bright young clergymen, I chose to have her also help Cuthbert with a gift of a Psalter (a book of Psalms) and a writing tablet. Cuthbert, of course, is also a real figure from history. He will later become the holiest man in Northumbria and be known posthumously as Saint Cuthbert. He is still venerated to this day, not only for his holiness, but also his love of, and protection of nature.

We don't know much about Cuthbert's early years, but in Bede's *Vita Sancti Cuthberti* (*The Life of Saint Cuthbert*), based on an anonymous text of the same name, he tells of how Cuthbert was an energetic and competitive youth, who was naturally agile and usually won the games he played. There is also the tale of how a stranger, who Cuthbert was certain was an angel, tells him how to create a poultice that will cure his diseased knee. It wasn't too much of a leap to have the leg injured in battle and the "angel" be Coenred with his healing skill.

The account of Cuthbert's arrival at Magilros (Melrose) shortly after Bishop Aidan's death is also based on the *Vita*. Cuthbert is said to have been carrying a spear and riding a horse, which speaks of a noble past, and perhaps even that he was a warrior. This was all I needed for Cuthbert to become one of Beobrand's gesithas. Having been embroiled in the murder of King Oswine, one can easily imagine how the sensitive young man would turn away from a life of violence, and dedicate himself to prayer.

As far as I can tell, there is no known name for the Roman road that Cynan convinced Sigehelm to follow to Wilfaresdun, so I have chosen to call it Burh Stræt after the Roman fortress at Brougham Castle in Cumbria, near where the road originates in the west. The name Burh (an Old English word for stronghold) is reminiscent of the modern Brougham and also of the Roman name for the fort (Brocavum).

At the end of *For Lord and Land*, Beobrand is poised to travel to the continent, sent into a form of exile by Eanflæd. But what will happen in Albion while he is gone, and what new adventures await him and his gesithas across the Narrow Sea? Wherever Beobrand goes there is bound to be intrigue and action, but that is for another day, and another book.

Acknowledgements

Firstly, thanks to you, dear reader. Without you, there would be little point in me writing these stories. I truly appreciate all the people who have bought my books, or borrowed them from their local library. You are the reason I am able to do this wonderful job. Word of mouth is the best marketing out there, so if you have enjoyed this book and the series so far, please spread the word and help more people discover Beobrand's stories. And, if you have a moment, please consider leaving a review on your online store of choice. Reviews really help.

Extra special thanks to Jon McAfee, Anna Bucci, Roger Dyer, Holly Smith, Emma Stone and Mary Faulkner for their generous patronage. To find out more about becoming a patron, and what rewards you can receive for doing so, please go to www.matthewharffy.com.

Thanks to my test readers, Gareth Jones, Simon Blunsdon and Shane Smart. The extra pairs of eyes on the early manuscript are invaluable in giving it an extra polish.

No book reaches readers' hands without a lot of help, so thank you to my editors, Nicolas Cheetham and Holly Domney, and everyone else in the wonderful team at Aries and Head of Zeus. They are all a joy to work with and they create the most beautiful books.

I wrote this book during the difficult year of 2020. There were many things competing for my attention, and it was all too easy to become gloomy. So thank you to the ever-supportive online community of historical fiction authors and readers who connect with me regularly on Facebook, Twitter and Instagram. It is always good to be able to communicate with like-minded people, but I feel that this year in particular you helped me stay positive and sane!

Something else that has helped me maintain some semblance of sanity has been weekly online gaming sessions with Alexander Forbes and Gareth Jones. Thank you both!

Thanks must also go to Greg Stewart, Rhiannan Falshaw-Skelly, Connor H. Thomas, James Faulkner and Jordan Woodley, with whom I have spent many hours on Zoom calls. Perhaps by the time this book is published we will again be able to meet in person!

And finally, my everlasting love and thanks to my wonderful daughters, Elora and Iona, and my amazing wife, Maite (Maria to her work colleagues). However hard things get, you make it all worthwhile.

Matthew Harffy
Wiltshire, January 2021

About the author

M ATTHEW HARFFY grew up in Northumberland where the rugged terrain, ruined castles and rocky coastline had a huge impact on him. He now lives in Wiltshire, England, with his wife and their two daughters.

@MATTHEWHARFFY   MATTHEWHARFFY.COM